The Night before Christmas

Scarlett Bailey

EBURY
PRESS

First publ... ...ed in 201... ...bury Pres... ...an imprint of Ebury ...blishing
A Random House Group Company

Copyright © 2011 Scarlett Bailey

The Random House Group Limited Reg. No. 954009

Addresses for companies within the Random House Group can be found at
www.randomhouse.co.uk

A CIP catalogue record for this book is available from the British Library

The Random House Group Limited supports The Forest Stewardship Council
(FSC®), the leading international forest certification organisation. Our books
carrying the FSC label are printed on FSC® certified paper. FSC is the only
forest certification scheme endorsed by the leading environmental organisations,
including Greenpeace. Our paper procurement policy can be found at
www.randomhouse.co.uk/environment

MIX
Paper from
responsible sources
FSC® C016897

Printed in the UK by CPI Cox & Wyman, Reading, RG1 8EX

ISBN 9780091943387

To buy books by your favourite authors and register for offers visit
www.randomhouse.co.uk

With greatest thanks to Gillian Green at Ebury Press for being such good fun to work with and such an inspiration.

Thank you Lizzy Kremer for all your brilliant work as my agent and a special huge thank you to all my dear friends for their steadfast support and patience, particularly as I made them celebrate Christmas with me all year long!

For Adam,
with love from me

Prologue

Lydia Grant hadn't meant to find the engagement ring intended for her, on that dank and drizzly December morning, but she had. Her boyfriend, Stephen, had got up long before the crack of dawn, leaving Lydia with the luxury of the middle of the bed. A rare treat that she relished by assuming the position of a starfish and tapping the snooze button on the alarm clock four times, dipping in and out of sleep with delicious, dozy abandon until 6.50 a.m., when she had sat bolt upright and remembered who she was.

By night, she was a serial romantic, taking every precious spare second she had to lose herself in the golden age of the Hollywood romances that she'd loved so much since she was a young girl. She could fall in love over and over again with Cary Grant or Trevor Howard; and even occasionally – but not quite so much recently – her own boyfriend.

But by day – a day that should have started at 6.30 sharp – she was Lydia Grant, Junior Barrister, a career-hungry, hard-as-nails crusader for justice. And, in just over an hour, she had to be in court representing a forty-six-year-old surgeon's wife who stood accused of credit card fraud running into tens of thousands of pounds. Having only been handed her client's brief at eight-thirty last night, Lydia needed to get a move on if she were to get to court in time to meet and talk over the case with the accused before the start of proceedings, and reassure Mrs Harris that everything would be all right. After all, if there was ever a barrister who could make a judge see that a woman needed two hundred pairs of designer shoes, it was surely Lydia Grant. Failing that, she'd go for diminished responsibility. Who hadn't gone mad lusting over a pair of shoes they could ill afford at least once in their life?

Running dangerously late, Lydia thanked her lucky stars that Stephen's Holborn flat – hers as well now, she reminded herself, though somehow, despite living together for the last six months, she couldn't stop herself calling it 'Stephen's flat' in her head – was only a fifteen-minute walk away from court. She leaped out of bed and allowed herself five minutes in the shower, before bundling her long, dark, chestnut-brown hair into a neat chignon with practised ease. Slipping into a smart white shirt and an authoritative black trouser suit that she'd set out before going to bed, she gave her lucky Gucci killer-heeled boots a quick polish. Taking a moment for a quick glance in the hall mirror – and pulling a face at her reflection – she told herself out loud that today she needed to be a strong, confident and capable woman; a woman who was never in doubt, not even for one second, that she'd show the judge and jury how ridiculous the charges were, and that her client was the true victim in this case, a victim of a wealthy husband who refused to buy her sufficient shoes.

It didn't help that Lydia couldn't find any black socks in the drawer Stephen had ceremoniously cleared out for her when he'd invited her to move in. 'After all, Lydia,' he'd told her when he'd casually handed her the key to his flat, 'it's about time we moved things along, don't you think?' Perhaps it hadn't been the most romantic moment in Lydia's life, but it was a bench-mark, nevertheless. A step towards commitment that, until quite recently, she would never have thought possible, even if it was commitment that afforded her just one drawer.

She could find training socks, pop socks, a pair of pink glittery socks that her eleven-year-old step-sister, from her father's third marriage, had got her for her birthday, plus a quantity of tights all tangled up in one big bundle, but no suitable socks to go under her lucky boots. Verging precariously on the edge of acceptable lateness, Lydia had done what any strong, capable, confident woman would. She'd decided to borrow a pair of her boyfriend's socks, yanking open his top drawer only to find the shock of her life sitting there, right on top of his neatly paired socks, blatantly out in the open, without even a minimal effort to hide it.

It was a small, square box in unmistakable pale greenish turquoise, with the words *Tiffany & Co* printed in black on the lid.

Without even thinking about what it might mean, Lydia grabbed the box and opened it, like a greedy child ripping open a packet of sweets. And there it was, winking at her in the electric light required on the dark, winter morning.

A one-carat, platinum-set, Tiffany Bezet princess-cut diamond engagement ring. Lydia sucked in a long breath. It was perfect. It was beautiful. And most importantly, it was exactly the ring she'd always dreamed of, chosen by a man who had taken some considerable time and care to discover her taste exactly. A man who knew that she always carried a battered and dog-eared copy of *Breakfast at Tiffany's* in her briefcase, and that since her early teens, her idea of the pinnacle of romance was to receive just such a ring, presented in that wonderfully distinctive box. It was a ring chosen by a man who cared enough about her to get it exactly right. By a man Lydia was now certain must love her very much to get it *so* right, and who knew that proposing to her at this special time of year would make another dream come true for her, because finally Lydia would get to have her own happy Christmas.

Which was why the second thought to pop into Lydia Grant's head that morning, as she stared at the ring, was rather surprising.

Lydia Grant wasn't at all sure that she wanted to get married.

Chapter One

21 December

Lydia glanced sideways at Stephen, who had been finger tapping the steering wheel since the last service station.

'Looks like we're going to beat the worst of the weather, anyway,' she said, briefly squinting out of the car window at the voluminous leaden clouds, hanging low over the horizon, pregnant with the promise of snow. 'The forecast said dangerous driving conditions, snow, snow and more snow – but look, it's only just started to come down.' Lydia nodded at the windscreen, where the first few delicate flakes of snow that had begun to waft down were settling briefly before being brutally wiped away in an instant.

Stephen said nothing in reply.

'So are you going to sulk about this for the whole three hundred miles?' Lydia asked him impatiently. 'God, I said I'd pay the toll on the M6.'

'It's not that and you know it,' Stephen said, keeping his eyes on the road. 'This is our first Christmas.'

'No, it's not.' Lydia sighed. 'It's our second Christmas,

or wasn't that you drunk and wearing a Santa hat at my mum's last year?'

Lydia grimaced as she remembered their actual first Christmas together, her mother, who had started on the Bailey's at breakfast, sitting on her step-father's lap, chewing his face off while the Queen gave a speech in the background and Stephen worked his way through an overcooked turkey and undercooked potatoes.

'It is, it *was*, going to be our first Christmas alone,' Stephen said. 'No family this year, you said. No trekking from Kent to Birmingham in the space of forty-eight hours just to make sure that you see all of your various parents and multitude of step-siblings. This year, I distinctly remember you saying, we're going to do as we please, by which you obviously meant do as you please. Silly me.'

'Various parents?' Lydia complained. 'You make me sound like a Mormon or the child of some sort of hippy commune. It's called a blended family these days, Stephen, which you of all people should know, Mr Family Law.'

'You know what I mean. What was it last year? Your mum and Greg on Christmas Day, practically having sex on your gran's reclining easy-up chair. And then we had to get up first thing on Boxing Day to make it to your dad and Janie's in time for lunch, where you have so many half siblings, and half-half siblings, it's like visiting a crèche. I mean, how old is your dad? How does he have the energy?'

'I don't know, perhaps you should ask him,' Lydia muttered under her breath. 'You know what my family's like.'

Lydia's childhood had been far from perfect, something she'd been at pains to express to Stephen since they'd first started getting serious, knowing that sooner or later he'd have to meet them. And love them as she did – most of the time – they weren't exactly the sort of family a girl looked forward to introducing to her most serious boyfriend ever.

Her parents had had a whirlwind courtship – marrying a month after they'd first met, and only discovering once they'd conceived Lydia that they hated each other's guts. The Christmases of her childhood were far removed from her beloved screen versions, where it always snowed, everyone always loved each other and it always turned out all right in the end. Lydia's childhood Christmases had a nightmare soundtrack of angry words, bitter recriminations and slammed doors, until Lydia was twelve and her father had walked out on her and her mum for good on Christmas Day. It had easily been the worst out of a lifetime of disappointing Christmases, and for the next few years she'd become a bargaining chip in the increasingly spiteful war between her parents, alternating holidays between the two of them and not feeling at home anywhere.

Since then, her mother had remarried, perhaps a little too happily for Lydia's liking, given the incident last Christmas, and her father seemed to be competing in some world record challenge for most-married man.

'Dad's got issues. He's been having a midlife crisis all his life. At least you met him in the Janie phase. I actually quite like her. His second wife was a proper cow. She always used to call me "the girl". Never used my name, just "the girl", with a sort of bad smell expression. I used to dread it when it was their turn to have me for Christmas . . .'

Lydia always did her best not to blame her dad for the Karen years – for leaving her alone in the living room in front of the telly for Christmas lunch, for never remembering to get her a gift, even though he always spent every penny he didn't have on Karen. And for agreeing, as soon as Karen demanded it, that Lydia did not have to come at Christmas at all, or Easter, or at any time, for that matter. Lydia resolved not to blame her dad for letting Karen edge her almost completely out of his life, because after all, he had left the witch before it was too late. And after that, he'd made a token effort to rebuild their relationship. At least he had until he'd taken up with the very buxom, though far more personable, Janie. Either way, Lydia was glad that Karen was gone. Janie made her dad happy, and she always remembered to get her some smellies from Lush, which was something.

Noticing Stephen's expression softening slightly, Lydia reached over and rested her hand on his thigh for a moment. 'Anyway, it's not as if we're doing family, is it? We're not trekking from Broadstairs to Birmingham. We *are* having a proper grown-up Christmas in the stunning surrounds of the Lake District, just the two of us.'

'Just the two of us *and* all of your friends,' Stephen muttered. 'I told my mum we weren't going to hers this year because we were doing our own thing, because . . .' Stephen stopped himself from saying more, and Lydia, hearing alarm bells in the vicinity of her heart, thought it best not to press him further. Having met his mother on a number of occasions now, she could honestly say that she'd rather gouge out her own eyes with a rusty nail than have to endure any more of the those 'you'll-never-be good-enough-for-my-only-son' looks again, something that would be tricky if she married Stephen. Mentally, Lydia added 'Stephen's Mum' to her list of pros and cons for marrying him, slotting it very firmly under 'con'. His dad was nice, though, in that quiet, unassuming, had-all-the-life-and-joy-sucked-out-of-him-by-the-cow-he'd married sort of way, which, all things considered, Lydia didn't think could be counted as a 'pro'.

'Look, I'm sorry I said yes to Christmas at Katy and Jim's without exactly running it past you,' Lydia apologised, not for the first time. 'The thing is, when Katy phoned, she was all over the place. It's been six months since she and Jim and the kids bought the hotel, and . . . well, reading between the lines, I think it's been a bit of a money pit. I don't know what possessed them . . . After all, Jim used to be an investment banker, and the nearest Katy's ever previously come to running a boutique hotel in the middle of nowhere is making us all toast after a big night out when we were students. They've poured every single penny they have into Heron's Pike. If it doesn't work out, they're stuffed. Katy said that they're fully booked for New Year's Eve and she needs to practise on someone. Who better than her three oldest friends and their lovely, handsome, sexy men?'

Stephen said nothing, keeping his eyes on the road as the falling snow began to thicken. Lydia turned to look out of the window, a shiver of anticipation running down her spine as she thought of the photos of the house Katy had sent her. Heron's Pike looked like the setting for a perfect Christmas. 'Besides, think of it, Stephen,' she continued, 'it's the Lake District, and Heron's Pike is a beautiful Victorian manor house, a stone's throw from Derwentwater Lake. It's got its own little boathouse and Katy says the village down the road looks like a picture postcard.' Lydia sighed. 'It will be just like the bit in *Holiday Inn* when Bing sings "White Christmas" and I always cry. And, look – it's going to be a white Christmas, too, a real one with snow, and open fires, and food, and wine, and people that actually like each other, for once. I, for one, can't wait to spend it with you and my best friends. I just wish you loved them as much as I do.'

'It's not that I don't like your friends,' Stephen began, carefully. 'Alex is great, although she is quite possibly the most frightening woman I've ever met, especially now she's pregnant. And David's okay if you don't mind talking about Romans or Normans, or whatever it is he lectures in. I've only met Katy and Jim at Alex's wedding, and I didn't get to talk to them too much because – if you remember – Katy got over-excited by the free champagne, burst into tears and then passed out in her dessert. But I'm sure they are a lovely couple. Just as I'm certain that their kids and their grandparents are charming. But Christmas with Joanna Summers? The queen of TV shopping? I'm sorry, Lydia, that is so low down my Christmas wish list that it comes below being stranded on a desert island and forced to eat my own legs to survive.'

'Harsh!' Lydia chuckled, despite herself. 'I know Joanna is an acquired taste, but the four of us have been friends since we met at university, and she's been a good friend to me, the best.' The four girls had met in the first week of their first term, thrown into the random mix of being on the same corridor in their hall of residence. And sharing a house in their final two years – through boys, exams, assorted family dramas and one very real tragedy – had cemented their friendships for life. 'Besides,' added Lydia now, 'if Joanna hadn't let me live with her rent free while I was studying for the bar, then I'd have been sunk.'

'She's just so up herself, strutting around like she owns the place.'

'That's her TV image, not what she's really like. She's had to be tough.' Of all of them, Joanna had found it easiest to adapt to student life and living away from home for the first time. She might joke about having been raised by wolves but, in truth, she'd been dumped by her parents in various boarding schools from the age of seven. She'd had to cope. 'You need a lot of guts to do her job. All that drama and confidence, that's more about keeping up a front than anything else.'

'She's so superficial,' Stephen snapped back. 'She sells cheap tat to people who can't afford it on a shopping channel, Lydia,' he added. 'How does blathering on incessantly about how you can own a genuine fake diamond ring for forty-nine ninety-nine, in two easy instalments, require guts?'

'God, you are such a snob,' Lydia retorted as the snow began to fall in earnest, and the last motorway sign flashed up a new fifty mile per hour speed limit. 'Not everyone can charge about saving the world like you, you know.'

'No, but *some* people could do a little more to try,' Stephen said, glancing pointedly at Lydia. Lydia bit her lip. She did her best to keep up with him, his charity work, all the legal aid stuff and the weekend volunteering, but it never seemed to be enough to please him. He forgot that, while he was at a comfortable, secure stage in his career, she was really still only starting out in hers. She had to do the work that chambers gave her, when it came in, and that barely left her time to breathe let alone spend every spare minute doing good, in the relentless way Stephen did.

'Besides' – Lydia decided to ignore his jibe – 'I'd like to *you* see present live TV. She has to think on her feet all the time. That's why she's the best at what she does, not just because she's beautiful. Sometimes, if I've got a case I'm particularly nervous about, I think of her, and that gives me courage.'

'Who knew that flogging crap could be so inspiring,' Stephen muttered under his breath, but again Lydia let it pass. While she loved Joanna to the depths of her shallows, and would defend her to the hilt, secretly she was rather glad Stephen hadn't instantly been utterly charmed by her stunning, long-legged, titian-haired friend. A fair few of her past boyfriends had rather let her down in that respect, and although Lydia knew that Joanna would never, ever break the golden rule when it came to pinching a friend's beau, she had not been quite so certain of some of her ex-boyfriends. Lydia did sort of take after her parents when it came to bad romances. In the past, she'd fallen in love at the drop of a hat, and her eternal romantic optimism had seen her disappointed in love more than her fair share. That was until she met sensible, stable, Stephen. After a moment's reflection, Lydia added, 'Did not fall for Joanna' to her mental list of pros.

'What I'm intrigued by is this latest guy Joanna's bringing along,' Lydia went on. 'Alex says she's mad about him, she says he's definitely the one she's going to marry.'

'Definitely the one she's going to marry until after she's collected a big, expensive engagement ring that most certainly hasn't been purchased on BuyIt! TV,' Stephen said, cynically. 'Then I'm sure he'll go the way of her other short-lived fiancés, and she'll simply have another obscenely large diamond to add to her collection.'

Lydia wriggled in her seat, yanking at the seatbelt that, after too many hours sitting in one position, had started to grate on her neck. The conversation was also beginning to sail just a little too close to the wind for her peace of mind. For the last two weeks, Lydia had felt the presence of the engagement ring in Stephen's top drawer like a ticking bomb in a bad B-movie. But Stephen had proven himself an expert at keeping his plans to propose to her a secret. Even when she'd dashed his suggestion of a country cottage hideaway just for the two of them, begging him to let them spend Christmas with her friends instead, he'd hid his disappointment well. Before they'd set off this morning, she'd made an excuse to run back into the flat and check, but the bomb was evidently coming with them. And all this talk of rings seemed loaded with unspoken meaning that she was keen to steer clear of.

'I think it's brave of her not to marry a man just because he asks her or it looks good on paper. It's brave to hold out, pause and take a breath. She always realised that something wasn't right and she changed her mind. I wish my parents had done the same; they would have been a lot happier, a lot sooner.'

'Well, I don't,' Stephen said, taking his eyes off the road for a second to smile at her. 'If they had, I wouldn't have you. I just hope this latest poor sod knows what he's getting himself into with Joanna. Still, I suppose if he survives Christmas with the four of you girls in one piece, then he's pretty much capable of surviving anything.'

'We're not that bad, are we?' Lydia asked him, although she knew that, when she and her friends were all together, they seemed to simultaneously regress about ten years and drown out any other noise within a five-mile vicinity, each one clamouring to be heard above the others, just as it used to be on a daily basis in their overcrowded student house.

'No.' Stephen looked a little chastened. 'No, you are not bad at all, not even Joanna, I suppose. It's just . . . it's just that I thought this year it would be different, no family, no friends, just you and me. That was how I pictured it.'

'I know, and that would have been lovely, it really, truly would,' Lydia said, suddenly consumed by guilt at her deliberate decision to avoid spending anything that could be described as 'potential romantic proposal time' alone with Stephen, just in case he popped the question and she wasn't ready to answer yet.

Here he was, sulking because she'd persuaded him to let them spend Christmas with her friends, but little did he know that she was doing this for him. Far better for her to be able to answer confidently when he finally proposed to her, rather than, 'Um, well . . . the thing is, I'm not sure, can you give me a month or year or two to mull it over?' Most of all, before Stephen produced that beautiful ring, Lydia wanted more than anything to have talked herself into saying yes.

Yes, because Stephen was certainly handsome, with his Nordic good looks, pale blond hair, light blue eyes and square manly jaw, and he would make a splendid contribution to the attractive children Lydia had vaguely pictured herself having one day. Yes, because he was genuinely a nice man, the kind of man who cared about what happened in the world and worked to make it a better place. But, most importantly, yes, because she loved him.

This hesitation wasn't at all like Lydia. When it came to love, she usually rushed in where even fools turned back. After all, she'd met Stephen out of the blue, allowing herself to free fall into a relationship with him without a second thought, and she'd been content enough with their relationship for over a year. So why pull up short now?

Perhaps it was the memory of her mother's face, staring unseeingly at the burnt turkey languishing in the sink on the day her dad had finally left home, that was putting her off making that final commitment to one man. Or the string of boyfriends Mum had brought home, in the years before she'd finally met Greg. It seemed at the time like there was a new one sitting at the head of the table every Christmas, while her mum fawned over him with unseemly gratitude, expecting Lydia to treat him like a member of their tiny, disjointed family. Her mum had always been so sure that the next one was *the one*, that this time she would be happy. In reality, though, it had taken her a great deal of broken eggs to make her omelette, and if her mother never knew when she was making her latest monumental mistake, then how would she?

If she were being strictly honest, though, Lydia knew that it was her more immediate past that was holding her back. Not least of all the fact that, when she'd first met Stephen, she had been horribly, utterly – and very dramatically – on the rebound.

Chapter Two

Lydia had met Stephen on a breast cancer charity fun run. She hadn't wanted to go on a fun run, because as far as Lydia was concerned, the words 'fun' and 'run' never, ever belonged in the same sentence. In fact, on that very day, she had made plans to take herself to Selfridges to spend far too much money on a pair of shoes she would never wear, but which, knowing they were there, even in a box in her cupboard, would made her feel better. It was her usual time-honoured tradition of getting over break-ups. Less fattening than drowning herself in the vat of Ben & Jerry's ice-cream that would otherwise be needed to take her mind off her troubles, and a ploy that had never let her down so far.

Alex, however, had had other plans for her. Good, sensible, tell-it-how-it-is Alex, who even now was also heading up the M6 in her husband David's ancient VW Golf. Back then, Alex had told Lydia that healing and self-worth were not to be found in the bottom of a Jimmy Choo box, and that doing something good for other people was the key to soothing Lydia's bruised, if not quite broken, heart. Besides, David had escaped by going to speak at some ancient history convention in Rome, and she needed someone to thrash. Lydia hadn't been totally sure she agreed with her best friend on this, but one thing she had learned in all the years of knowing Alex was that you never said no to her.

Alex was a good person in every respect. She ate well, and exercised daily, running about thirty miles a week, relentlessly pounding the streets of London in every spare minute. She cooked from scratch – actual vegetables and fruit – not meals that she heated up in a microwave to eat in bed. Since graduation, she'd worked as a corporate fundraiser for a breast cancer research charity, basically frightening rich businessmen into giving her their money, a cause close to her heart as the disease had robbed her of her own mother in their final year at college.

Those had perhaps been Alex's darkest days, when grief had worn her to a mere shadow of herself, and all she'd wanted to do was go home to a father who could barely help himself and had no idea how to comfort his bewildered, angry daughter. In those first awful months, Lydia had sat up with Alex every night, sometimes all night, holding her friend while she cried, talking when she wanted to, not talking when she didn't. Downing cheap wine, matching each other glass for glass, and putting on inches with every shared bar of Galaxy. It wasn't that Joanna and Katy hadn't been there for Alex too, they had, but the severity of her loss seemed to scare them a little; they were afraid they would do or say the wrong thing.

Lydia, though, knew something of what it was like to lose for ever the very person you couldn't imagine living without. Even though she still had both her parents, clinging on to what remnants of family she had left had sometimes felt like a full-scale battle. Alex had lost her mum, and she could never get her back, but Lydia knew exactly what her dear friend had had to do to make sure she didn't lose herself in the process. Together with Joanna and Katy, she had kept Alex together, kept her focused on her studies, told her to remember how happy her mother would be to see her graduate, and to keep going come what may. It had been a difficult final year, but when the four of them finally flung their mortar boards in the air on that July afternoon, Alex had taken Lydia aside and thanked her for never letting her go, for helping her have the guts to make her mother proud. And from that moment, Lydia had watched her friend go from strength to strength.

A six-foot-tall Amazonian of a woman, Alex embodied the term formidable; throwing herself out of planes or charging up mountains was all in a day's work for her, as long as she was being sponsored to do it. And with her wedding day only a few months away, she had gone into exercise overdrive, demanding that Lydia, her chief bridesmaid, join her for at least some of the torture. So when all Lydia had to do was a piddling little 5K, as Alex described it, to help find a cure for the disease that had killed her mother, it was frankly impossible, and would have been fruitless, even to attempt to refuse. Dutifully, Lydia had donned a pink T-shirt and a feather boa, got as many colleagues as she could to sponsor her, and lined up with an assortment of runners, variously wearing fairy wings and cow costumes, for what she anticipated was going to be the worst hour of her life.

And then she had caught Stephen smiling at her. Far too handsome to be straight, was Lydia's first thought, admittedly not helped by fact that he was wearing a neon pink tutu and tiara. His face was friendly and open, though, the kind of face that was hard not to like. He looked, Lydia remembered thinking, uncomplicated.

The starting gun had sounded, and predictably Alex shot off like a rocket into the wild blue yonder, leaving Lydia floundering in her wake, desperately wishing she'd worn her brand new trainers at least once before attempting to run in them. It was a hot day and, as she'd suspected, her training programme of taking the stairs instead of the lift was not quite up to scratch. Just as she was considering ducking out to a Starbucks she'd spotted outside the park, the handsome man in the tutu jogged back and started running alongside her before saying hello.

'You suit pink,' he said, managing a relaxed grin as he easily kept pace with her. Suddenly Lydia was regretting her decision to apply full make-up that morning; she could practically feel her mascara travelling down her cheeks, and probably looked like a drunk transvestite, but perhaps that was why he was talking to her.

'So do you,' she tentatively, nodding at the tutu.

'I know.' Stephen laughed. 'But the guys at work said they'd double their sponsorship money if I wore it, so what I could do? They say that only a real man can wear pink, don't they? Well, I figure that this must make me the manliest man in the world! The tiara's my own, though.'

Lydia laughed too. 'Seriously, it's such an important charity, I'm more than happy to make a fool of myself, if it helps.' He continued, 'Although if I'd known a stunning girl like you was going to be here, I might have thought twice.'

'Oh . . . really? Well, um, yes – it is a very important charity.' Lydia had nodded, supposing that already being the same shade as a post box was, in this instance, a good thing, as he wouldn't be able to tell she was blushing.

'Have you lost someone to breast cancer?' Stephen asked her. 'I lost my aunt, when I was younger. I was devastated. She was the definition of a cool aunt, I could talk to her about anything, she always inspired me – I still miss her every day.'

'No, not me, not personally,' Lydia said. 'But my best

friend, Alex, the one up there at the front, she lost her mum when we were at university. It almost destroyed her. I wouldn't normally . . .' Just in time, Lydia stopped herself from saying 'ever do anything like this, I'm far too lazy', and instead finished with, '. . . let her do anything without me. Skydiving, abseiling – you name it, we've done it. Together. We're a team. A fundraising team of good deeds. Plus, I'm scared of her.' Lydia smiled brightly at Stephen. It was then that she noticed his ice-blue eyes, sparkling with laughter.

'You must be a very good person to have on side,' he said.

'Oh, I am, I'm a barrister. I'm like the Wonder Woman of the legal world, helping the needy, putting away the baddies.' Lydia remembered feeling delighted at how impressed Stephen was by her claim.

'Really? I'm a solicitor, actually. I do divorce, family law, mainly to pay the bills. But I also do as much legal aid as I can, representing asylum seekers, travellers, homeless people – you know, the sort of people who never have anyone on their side. I just think it's so important to stick up for those people who so often don't have a voice, don't you?'

'Oh, yes,' Lydia said. 'Yes, I do too.'

They had jogged on in silence for a few minutes, while the sun rose in the sky, the August heat intensifying as the day wore on. Lydia found herself wondering if Stephen would notice her checking her face in the compact she'd slid into her pocket, desperate to know exactly how bad she looked, with her make-up sliding inexorably south and her thick hair plastered with sweat to her head. None of her usual weapons of seduction were available to her. Alex had insisted she take off her favourite plunge bra and put on a proper sports bra, and not even she had thought about running 5k in the sort of killer heels that made the best of her legs. Which was why she had been surprised and delighted by what Stephen said next.

'Er . . . would you, you know, like to go for a drink afterwards? Doesn't matter if you don't, no worries,' he told her, awkwardly backtracking, which made it all the more charming.

'Oh . . . um.' After the heart-wrenching end to her last entanglement, Lydia had promised herself at least a year without men, to get her head straight. But it was such a nice day, and Stephen seemed so sweet, it would be churlish to refuse. 'I would, thank you. But look at me – I'm all sweaty and bleugh.' Lydia pulled a face.

'You look great to me,' Stephen said, with simple, easy charm. 'But if you'd prefer it, I could meet you somewhere later? After we've both had a chance to spruce up.' As the finishing line finally came into sight, they'd made arrangements to meet at a pub halfway between their respective homes, exchanging casual goodbyes just as Alex thundered across the field, looking as fresh a daisy, to question her.

'Did you just pull on a fun run?' Alex had demanded, half in admiration, half in horror, as if flirting might have somehow undermined the charitable act.

'No! Yes!' Lydia caved in instantly under her scrutiny. 'Did you see him? He's lovely.'

'You are such a tart,' Alex chided her mildly. 'Seriously, Lyds – aren't you supposed to be heartbroken?'

'I am, but what's the point in moping about?' Lydia waved at Stephen as he walked away. 'I could do with a nice, uncomplicated man to take my mind off things, and anyway, you met your soon-to-be-husband on a walk across Siberia!' Lydia reminded her, thinking of sweet, shy David, who didn't seem like enough man for a woman like Alex, but who somehow clearly was, as she had never been happier.

'Well, it was cold, and he had a better sleeping bag than me.' Alex smiled fondly. 'So has this fun run made you feel better than shallow, pointless retail therapy?'

'I would say that, on this one and only occasion, yes, the impossible has been achieved,' Lydia was forced to concur.

'Half marathon in Leeds next week?'

'Not even if you promise me George Clooney at the finish line!'

That evening, Lydia had carefully selected a linen tea-dress printed with tiny pink and yellow roses, and brushed her hair so it waved and rippled its way down to the small of her back. She'd thanked serendipity that she'd decided to have a spray tan the day before in the vain hope it would improve the sight of her thighs in Lycra shorts, and put on just a little bit of make-up, mascara and lip-gloss. The amount of make-up that a virtuous, fun-running, legal aid doing, heart of gold barrister girl would wear, she thought as she slipped on a pair of lemon-yellow mid-heeled pumps and went to meet Stephen.

Spending time with him that evening had been wonderfully soothing, like bathing in cool water after far too much heat. Stephen proved himself to be funny, charming, self-deprecating and gentle. He was, apart from Alex, the first person she had met who seemed positively evangelical about charity work, so much so that his day job was more of an inconvenience than a career. He really seemed to care about the world outside of his own little bubble of existence, and Lydia could tell that the compassion he displayed as he talked about the people he helped was truly genuine. It was humbling, inspiring and, rather unexpectedly, sexy. Sort of like going on a date with a super hero.

At the end of the evening, Lydia had let him escort her home to the flat she was sharing with Joanna, and then she had let him come up for coffee, safe in the knowledge that her 'landlady' would be out all night. The kettle had not even boiled when Stephen kissed her. It was a polite kiss, barely there at first, so tentative that Lydia almost wondered if she was imagining it. Gradually – ever so slowly – a sort of consensus of enthusiasm had built between them, Stephen politely holding her waist with one hand, the other accidentally brushing the side of breast, as they endeavoured to get to know each other's mouths. After quite some minutes of kissing, and uncertain of what to do next, Lydia – as impulsive as ever – had invited Stephen to stay the night. But he had refused her.

'Would you like to see me again?' he asked. Lydia nodded. There was something about Stephen's reserved good manners that soothed and cooled the fiery ache in her bruised heart. 'Then there's no hurry, is there?' Stephen had said, pausing to kiss her once more on the tip of her nose. 'Besides, as far as I can tell, you seem to be my idea of the perfect woman. I'd be crazy to walk away from you. Let's take it slow . . .?'

Those had been exactly the right words, at exactly the right time. Words that Lydia hadn't realised how much she'd needed to hear until Stephen had said them. From that moment on, nearly a year and a half ago, they had officially been together. Everyone said how perfect they were for each other, how Stephen was a keeper, a charm, the kind of steady, loyal man that's hard to find. And with all those plaudits ringing in her ears, Lydia had let herself slip, albeit slowly, into a full-blown, moving-in, sock-drawer-sharing, grown-up relationship with Stephen, the first of that kind she had ever had.

Before finding the ring, she'd always vaguely supposed that the life she had made with Stephen would inevitably culminate one day in marriage. But the ring had made her supposition real, and forced her to focus on the tiny little cracks and fissures that, up until that moment, she'd done such a good job of glossing over.

Like the fact that for the last few months, she and Stephen had barely seen each other for more than two hours a day; that the last time they had made love, or even kissed more than in passing, had been on the long weekend away they had snatched last September, almost three months ago. The worst thing was that the stalling of their sex life didn't seem to bother Stephen at all. He never even mentioned that he missed it.

Also, Lydia worried that the so-called perfect woman Stephen had thought he'd met that first evening after the fun run was only an approximation of the real her, and he was gradually coming to realise that she wasn't quite the angel she'd made herself out to be. Work was a dog-eat-dog world, and while she did as much legal aid work as she could, she could only do it when her clerk allowed. And as her first fun run had also been her last, her near spotless trainers had been languishing in the bottom of her third of their shared wardrobe ever since she'd moved in.

Lydia couldn't help but wonder whether, if Stephen

ever put just a little of the time he devoted to his causes into 'them', gave her just a little of the attention that he gave the people he helped, then perhaps she might feel a little more relaxed about marrying him and a little less worried that, now she was officially his consort, he'd done with romancing her and no further effort was required. It was true, Stephen had made her a better, more mature woman; he'd made her care more about the world outside of her bubble, too, and Lydia loved him for that. But she doubted that he'd love all the vain, silly, paranoid, immature little thoughts that still ran around her head, no matter how grown up and sensible the world around her demanded she be.

She doubted that he'd love her nagging, persistent fantasy that at least some of the passion he had so much of should be directed towards ravishing her every chance he got. By that same token, she wished that the touch of his hand, even in passing, would ignite her with desire. She wanted to share a look between them across a crowded room, a look full of a promise, of longing to be fulfilled as soon as a room with a door that locked could be found. Secretly, Lydia had always expected the man she married to kiss like Rhett Butler, to kiss her like every woman deserved to be kissed. Instead, since she had found the ring, Lydia felt more and more like Holly Golightly in *Breakfast at Tiffany's*, pretending to be the sort of person she simply wasn't. Holly tried to hide the raggle-taggle runaway she really was behind a vacuous veneer of glamour and sophistication. Some-times, Lydia found the struggle to hide her imperfections from her perfect man simply exhausting.

She also couldn't help but feel that, even if every relationship did reach this stage, when its mere existence was enough for both parties to live in easy contentment, it really shouldn't come quite so early on, even before a proposal. She thought of the last time she'd plucked up the courage to initiate sex with Stephen. He'd already been in bed and she'd just watched Harry finally real-ising he was meant to be with Sally, so her heart was full of the conquering power of love to overcome any obstacle, even an exhausted boyfriend. Gingerly, Lydia had crept naked into bed, pressing the length of her body against Stephen's back and running her fingers lightly up his thigh. Before she could explore any further, he'd stopped her hand with his own, patting it firmly and then removing it from his leg entirely, returning it to her own.

'Sorry, darling, do you mind? I'm just desperate for a good night's sleep.'

Lydia remembered how the sting of such a mild, thoughtless rejection had kept her awake for hours, staring into the dark.

No one knew better than her exactly what chasing the fantasy of romance and passion got you: a succes-sion of broken hearts and a life full of chaos and confusion, bouncing from one disappointment to the next. At least with Stephen she knew he would be there at the head of the table every Christmas, always. And for her, more than most, that should be enough.

Yet somehow, it wasn't.

Now, glancing over at Stephen, who, despite the almost totally clear road, was driving a sensible three miles below the speed limit, Lydia sighed inwardly. She was determined that this was going to be her perfect Christmas. The only person that could stop it happening exactly the way she dreamed was her.

'Listen . . .' Lydia breached the silence as Stephen took the slip road off the motorway onto a road that snaked into the mountainous countryside. 'I just want to say thank you for agreeing to come. I can't wait to see all the girls in one place again, that's true. But there isn't anyone I'd rather spend Christmas with than you.'

'I know this means a lot to you,' Stephen smiled in acknowledgement. 'And I know it will be great. It's just . . . I know we seem to have been a bit like ships that pass in the night, recently. My work at the drop-in centre has taken over a bit, and your chambers have been keeping you flat out. I'm always exhausted, you always stay up far too late watching those silly old films of yours. We have been less than intimate. I do notice these things, you know, even if you think I don't. I've been waiting for the opportunity to come up so that I can focus on you. This Christmas I am all yours, even if I don't get you all to myself quite as much as

I hoped. I want to make sure you know how much I love you.'

'Do you?' Lydia asked, feeling unexpectedly touched and hopeful that the early promise of their relationship – the spark of passion they'd once had for each other – might be about to make a spectacular return. 'Well, there'll be plenty of time to get "reacquainted". Katy says our room is one of the nicest, with a view of the lake, a four-poster bed and an open fire.' Lydia glanced coyly at him. 'As soon as it's decent, we'll hide away upstairs and perhaps get . . . um . . . reacquainted?'

'I wonder if it ever gets so cold that the lakes freeze over,' Stephen mused absent-mindedly, ignoring her overture yet again, slowing the car as the road bent sharply. 'I wonder if it'll freeze thick enough to walk on.'

'Hmm.' Lydia tried to hide her disappointed expression by peering out of the window at the scenery just vanishing in the rapidly diminishing light. 'I wonder.'

Chapter Three

'I don't think I've ever been so far away from everywhere before,' Lydia said a little breathlessly as Stephen, guided by the slightly smug-sounding sat nav lady, carefully drove through the narrow, twisting country lanes, snowflakes dancing erratically in the beam of the headlights.

Snow was falling thick and fast by the time Stephen pulled the Prius onto the rather grand gravel drive that led up to Heron's Pike House. The sun had set some hours before, shrouding the hills and lakes in a cloak of darkness, and Lydia had only been able to catch glimpses of the surrounding mountains, looming like shadowy giants against the winter sky. The lakes, which she knew must be there, were completely invisible.

'Everywhere is close to somewhere, Lyds. Location is not always defined by how near you are to Harvey Nichols.' Stephen chuckled, doing that thing he did when he pretended she was just some silly, fluffy-headed girl and not a hard-hitting, highly educated barrister at all. In the beginning, Lydia had quite liked it, finding it funny and sort of sweet, the way he shepherded her around as if she needed protection. Recently, though, it had rather started to grate, just a little. But, determined to be happy for the next four days at least, she ignored his teasing and waited, like a child eager to be the first to see the sea, to catch her first glimpse of Heron's Pike House sparkling in the snow.

When her friends' new home finally came into view, it glowed like a beacon. It was so pretty that Lydia felt almost like she'd been transported into one of those Christmas cards from her childhood, the ones always featuring a snow-laden scene and smothered in glitter. Each newly planted conifer tree that lined the drive had been adorned with glittering lights, creating the perfect runway for Father Christmas to land his sleigh. From their vantage point, the house itself even seemed to pulsate with warmth, bathed in carefully placed floodlights that cast dramatic shadows from its faux gothic towers and ramparts. As a carefully designed finishing touch, the red-painted panelled front door was lit perfectly to show off the handmade wreath tied to it, bristling with holly, shiny tartan ribbons, cinnamon sticks and dried oranges.

'Textbook Katy,' Lydia said fondly, as she gazed up at the house. 'She's been waiting all her life to bake cakes and trim things in gingham. She must be in her element now as lady of the manor. I bet you ten pounds she'll be making the children playsuits from an old pair of curtains by Boxing Day.'

Built from Cumbrian stone, the house was a high

Victorian flight of fancy. Katy had told her that it had previously belonged to the same family for several generations and had gradually fallen into disrepair. Originally designed as a sizable twin pair of houses, Katy and Jim had knocked through to create a double-fronted mansion with long elegant bay windows that Katy told her had cost a fortune to refurbish. The ostentatious and entirely decorative ramparts lining the roof were brought to an extravagant full stop by two delightfully fanciful turrets, majestically rounding off each corner of the house, looking for all the world as if the only thing they lacked was a pair of long-haired princesses to languish in them.

It was clear, even from the outside, how much Katy had revelled in bringing the old place back to such glittering form. It had also been a total steal, according to Katy's husband, Jim. But what they'd saved on buying their Victorian folly, they were obviously spending on turning it into a going concern.

'It is very grand,' Stephen said, leaning over to look out of Lydia's window and kissing her on the ear at the same time, which made her forgive his fluffy-headed girl comment.

'Grand!' She smiled warmly at the classic Stephen understatement. 'It's gorgeous! I want to wrap it up in Christmas paper, pop a bow on it and take it home. This is just the right place to spend a perfect Christmas!'

Stephen smiled, gently drawing her face to meet his.

'I've never known anyone as sweet as you, Lydia Grant,' he said, and at that moment, as Stephen kissed her, all of Lydia's doubts, her entire list of cons, melted away in an instant. Perhaps, Lydia thought, she truly was being silly and fluffy-headed; perhaps, on this one occasion, she was over thinking and analysing too much. Perhaps she was the one with the issues, not Stephen. He thought she was sweetest person he knew, and maybe that was a very good reason to marry a man. Perhaps everything was going to be all right after all.

Suddenly unable to wait any longer, Lydia threw open the door, instantly feeling frozen as a blast of cold Cumbrian air engulfed them. She wrapped her coat around her and practically ran up the white marble steps to the front door, negotiating the impressive wreath to find an old brass knocker in the shape of a lion's head. Lydia sounded it three times, and then, just to be on the safe side, pressed the brand new electronic doorbell too, instigating, somewhere deep in the depths of the house, the sound of a very excitable dog.

'I've got a feeling we might be staying here for a bit longer than four days,' Stephen said, stamping his feet in the several inches of snow that continued to accumulate as he got out of the car. 'The snow is really coming down now. You go in and get warm, I'll grab our bags from the boot.'

Lydia clamped her arms around herself and hopped from one foot to the other as she heard squeals from inside. The sounds should rightfully have come from the children, but she recognised Katy's voice and, sure enough, it was she who flung the door open, enfolding Lydia immediately in an enthusiastic hug. Katy's dog, a motley-looking grey lurcher of indeterminate age, skipped around her knees. With her free hand, Lydia rubbed the soft head of Vincent Van Dog, so called because he'd arrived at the dog's home where Katy had rescued him lacking in one ear, for reasons unknown.

'Lyds!' Katy exclaimed as she grabbed Lydia's face and kissed her on both cold cheeks, drawing her inside the glorious warmth of the house. 'God, it's so good to see you! For a while, there, I was worried *no one* would make it. Alex and David came up this morning, but Mum and Dad are stuck in Perth, Jim's folks are still in Surrey and there's no sign of Joanna yet, although she's en route. Jim reckons in another hour or two the roads around here will be impassable and we'll be snowed in!' Katy squealed again, clapping her hands together like a little girl. 'But at least you're here. I have really missed you, you know.'

Gently, Lydia prised the hem of her coat from between Vincent's teeth, sure that he was only attempting to chew a hole in it by way of a greeting.

'There's no need to sound surprised about it,' Lydia said, rubbing Vincent's muzzle as she looked happily around the impressive hallway. It had been converted into a lobby, complete with shiny leather chairs and a reception desk, the cosy area accessorised with a little brass bell and a Christmas tree, sitting in the crook of the sweeping staircase, that would put the one in Trafalgar Square to shame. 'I shouldn't miss me at all if I lived here,' Lydia breathed, squeezing her friend. 'Oh, Katy, it's *wonderful*! This house was built for Christmas.'

'I know!' Katy exclaimed. 'Brilliant, isn't it?'

The heavy door creaked open behind them, and Stephen staggered in, his hair and shoulders encrusted with snow, his arms weighed down by all of their bags and presents.

'Oh, Stephen, you poor love, come in,' Katy said, taking one of the bags from him.

'Seriously, Lyds, what have you got in these?' Stephen asked her, depositing the bags on the tiled floor with relief. 'Did you feel the need to bring a kitchen sink?'

'Wish she had.' Katy smiled as she kissed Stephen in greeting. 'We actually could do with one.'

'All I brought was, you know, just the essentials.' Lydia grabbed another bag from Stephen, who winced, putting his hands on the small of his back and making what sounded distinctly like an old man noise.

'Although many people might question whether four pairs of high-heeled shoes are strictly essential for a few days in the Lakes,' he said dryly, winking at Katy.

'Only four? Lyds, you are calming down! Is it the recession?' Katy joked, suddenly feeling compelled to hug her friend again, and kiss her once more too, for good measure.

'Goodness, I don't think anyone's ever been so pleased to see me since . . . I don't think anyone has ever been that pleased to see me,' Lydia said. 'So do we just arrive, or are you going to officially check us in like an official lady hotelier?'

'What? Oh yes – yes, right.' Katy gave a mock bow to her guests and bustled efficiently behind the tiny reception desk, where she was rather dwarfed by what must have been fifteen feet of Norwegian spruce. The staircase, Lydia noticed happily, was *exactly* the sort of staircase for sweeping down in a red velvet dress, Scarlett O'Hara style, which was exceptionally fortunate as she had just happened to pack such a garment for Christmas Day. Granted, it was only knee length, and lacked any sort of bustle, but it was quite the statement dress and would go brilliantly with a statement staircase. Lydia resolved to ask Katy to video her on her phone as soon as no one else was looking, especially not Stephen. Or Joanna, who probably would bring a floor-length dress with a bustle and train to boot.

As they waited for Katy to play hotelier and shuffle various bit of headed paper, Lydia felt Stephen find her hand and hold it, squeezing her fingers gently. Lydia smiled at him, Christmas warmth spreading through her as she looked up at the tree. Katy and the children had certainly gone to town on it; not a single needle had been left unadorned. It was garlanded with yard upon yard of tartan ribbons, and every branch was laden with a glittering array of ornaments, ranging from a selection of somewhat macabre robins that looked to be fashioned out of actual feathers, complete with beady eyes, to homemade salt-dough stars, some lacking what might be considered the conventional number of points, and a few with considerably more. She knew Katy could be relied upon to give her children a conventional, old-fashioned Christmas, and Lydia's inner child, who'd never had a real Christmas at all, gave a happy sigh.

Finally, Katy seemed to be ready to greet them officially.

'Welcome to Heron's Pike Hotel,' she recited carefully, treating them to a fixed grin, which she snapped on and off instantly. 'You are in room eight, perhaps the finest of our rooms, with stunning views of the lake and mountains. Breakfast is served between eight and ten, reservations for dinner must be made by four and takeaways in the rooms are not permitted, which to be honest doesn't matter because the nearest Indian is in Keswick and by the time you got it back here it'd be cold anyway, but Jim says we have to be specific.'

Katy re-composed herself. 'You'll find a tourist information pack in your room as well as tea and coffee making facilities, and complimentary biscuits. Only there's no kettle quite yet because the delivery has been delayed by the snow, and quite possibly no biscuits either as the kids were up there earlier and they do love a shortbread.' Katy presented them with a big, heavy looking, old-fashioned metal key. 'Oh, and don't lose it because we can't get another one cut without having to find an actual blacksmith. Apart from that, enjoy your stay!' The smile snapped on again. 'How did I do?'

'Getting there, definitely getting there.' Lydia smiled encouragingly. 'Perhaps try a little less honesty for the actual paying guests. So where are Jim and the kids?'

'Torturing Alex and David,' Joanna said. 'Just to warn you, Alex is a little bit ... um ... testy, probably the long journey. Leave your bags there for now and come and say hello. We're in the family sitting room, it's much cosier than the guest one, hope you don't mind.'

Katy led Lydia and Stephen through what Lydia assumed must be the more formal, guest sitting room. Situated at the front of the house to the left of the staircase, it was a grand, self-important room, with what looked like its original plasterwork intact on the high ceiling, forming an ornate central rose surrounded by swathes and swags of some kind of fanciful plaster foliage. The floor-to-ceiling stripped oak window shutters were open in defiance of the glass-shuddering wind that was whipping the snow into a balletic frenzy outside. Not strictly in keeping with the period, the walls were painted a more Georgian white and duck-egg blue, which Lydia supposed was more fashionable and guest friendly than some heavily patterned wallpaper. There were two pairs of sofas, some mismatched 'shabby chic' armchairs and even one chaise, arranged around an assortment of what looked like lifestyle magazines fanned out on small tables, to create three or four little intimate areas in the imposing grandeur of the room. Trimmed with fresh holly and made of white marble, there was a beautiful, original fireplace, over which hung an integral oval mirror that must have returned the reflection of many a hopeful young woman over the last hundred years. A fire had been set, but not yet lit, giving the room a sense of anticipation, like a sleeping princess on the verge of being awoken with a kiss.

'It's almost impossible to keep this room warm,' Katy said, rubbing her hands together and shuddering as they followed her, Vincent Van Dog padding closely at heel. 'Jim says it's because of the ghost of one of the sisters that used to live in the houses. Nonsense, obviously, and really irritating as the kids believed him and now they arrive in our bed every single night screaming about being dragged into the lake by Mad Molly. I wouldn't mind, but they won't lie still. Tilly's the worst; it's like going to sleep with a hyperactive octopus. It's okay for Jim, he could sleep through an earthquake, but, quite honestly, if I don't get some more sleep soon I'll be chucking myself in the lake!' Katy smiled ruefully, but Lydia noticed she did look a little wan beneath all the Christmas cheer. Hosting Christmas must be taking its strain on her, Lydia decided, resolving to be an extra helpful guest.

'There really aren't any ghosts here, though, just high ceilings and drafty windows, and, given the fact that the ancient central heating didn't make it as far as this room, no radiators either.' Spotting a china shepherdess ornament out of place on the mantelpiece, Katy hopped over a footstall to realign it, turning back to survey the room and all her handy work. 'This room hadn't been used for years, we don't think. When we arrived, it was full of junk and looked like the family had been letting their pets run riot in it. But I did find that old chaise, in surprisingly good nick, under all the rubbish, and a few other bits and bobs that we've put around the place, like Little Bo Peep here, and this old, old photo of the year the lake froze over and people could skate on it.'

Lydia flashed a surprised look at Stephen, but he seemed engrossed in staring at his new surroundings.

'Of course,' Katy continued, 'we'll get the fire going once the real guests arrive, but it took me an age to get this looking right, so for now I just like to come and stare at it sometimes and threaten the children with murder if they touch anything.'

'It is very posh,' Lydia said. 'I feel like I should be taking a turn around the room with Mr Darcy on my arm. Katy, you are so clever, you've turned all this into a spread from *Country Living*.'

'Do you think so?' Katy beamed, all traces of tiredness at least temporarily banished from her round face. 'I am rather proud of it, I must say. Come on, now for the hidden delights of the Heron's Pike servant quarters.' Crossing a dark, narrow, wood-panelled corridor, Katy opened another stripped door to reveal the family sitting room, about half the size of the other one, but even more lovely and infinitely more cosy, almost glowing with the warmth of a roaring fire scented with pine cones. His hosting duties over for now, Vincent curled up on the hearth, falling fast asleep almost immediately, despite the din from a room teeming with excitable children. Lydia knew that, technically, two children could not be considered great enough in number to 'teem', but somehow, despite being aged only six and four respectively, Jake and Tilly usually managed it.

'Do you want to hear a song about a bra?' Jake asked Lydia by way of greeting, the moment she entered the room.

'Did you say a bra?'

'Please God, not again. Jake, if you sing that one more time in my hearing, I will throw you in the lake,' Alex grumbled.

'You won't because I shall just run away and you won't be able to catch me,' Jake scoffed, not in the least bit offended or intimidated by his honorary aunty. 'You're not very fast and you are very fat.'

'Jakey, mate, we all love your song,' Jim said, crossing the room to greet the new arrivals, 'but at least wait for Aunty Lydia to sit down and have a glass of pop in her hand!' Lydia dodged Jake, and hugged Jim, kissing him lightly on the cheek, which took some doing as he was an impressive six foot four and looking rather rugged these days since he'd lost the city suit and let his sensible haircut grow out a bit. The stubble wasn't a bad look either, Lydia mused, wondering if the same look would suit Stephen. Stunning house, strapping husband, cute if unruly kids, a slightly mutilated dog . . . Lydia felt a pang of jealousy; Katy really did seem to have it all.

Obviously a little merry already, Jim's breath was scented with mulled wine, Lydia noticed before he released her to give a rather stunned Stephen one of his trademark bear hugs.

'Glad you two aren't dead in a ditch,' he said, cheerfully. 'Did Katy tell you our folks are all stuck where they are? So, no grandparents for these guys. Shame for them, but we can have another celebration in the New Year. And, you know, any day without an in-law in it is always a bonus in my book.'

'Jim!' Katy chided him gently as she peered into an old dark-wood sideboard and produced a couple of wine glasses, handing them to her guests.

'Don't pretend like you don't feel the same,' Jim chuckled as he filled the glasses with ruby red wine straight from a cut-glass decanter. 'What is it you call my mum? Medusa?'

'The children!' Katy hissed, nodding at Jake, who, after having his song offer rejected, was now scratching Vincent's ear, and Tilly, who was humming away in the corner as she fashioned herself an outfit made purely from tinsel.

'Well, are you going to say hello to me, then, or am I passé now I'm the size of a house?' Alex asked Lydia from the sofa, where she was sort of beached, her long legs resting on a footstall, her bump rising before her like a full moon.

'Hello, love,' Lydia said, slumping down next to her. 'I swear you've gotten even more massive since I saw you last week! Are you sure you're not due for another month?'

'Quite sure,' Alex said, frowning at her bump. 'Although it is starting to feel like I've been pregnant for about a hundred years.'

'Elephants are pregnant for nearly two years,' Jake said, getting up from the fireplace, resting his chin on the bump and peering down his nose at it. 'Perhaps you're an elephant.'

'Nice,' Alex said, pursing her lips. 'Really nice.'

'Hello, Lydia, Stephen,' Alex's husband, David, said as he came back from somewhere that was evidently quite cold, as he still had a scarf on and was rubbing his hands together. 'Good to see you! Awful out there. Lexi, don't, whatever you do, go into labour now, we've got no chance of getting you to a hospital and I very much doubt this house is sterile.'

'Hey, I clean,' Katy protested.

'And I'm not due for five weeks!' Alex snapped. 'Can we all please stop dwelling on my huge, massive stomach and talk about something else for once, *please*!'

'Hormones,' David mouthed silently at Lydia, causing Alex to shoot him a look that would have killed him, if only the laws of the universe would allow it.

'So!' Lydia said, taking a seat besides Alex and holding her hand. 'Isn't this perfect? The four of us together at Christmas. Do you know that, in all the years we've been friends, we've never done this? Even when we were at uni, we always went our separate ways at Christmas. And then there were boyfriends, husbands and in-laws. And look at us now, there's snow, and a fire, and a tree, and countryside and isn't it just a wonderful life?'

'Bloody hell, have you been possessed by the spirit of Judy Garland?' Alex asked irritably. 'I expect it *is* wonderful, if you don't have piles and constant acid reflux. And cankles, just look at my cankles! What if I never get my ankles back? What if I turn into one of those women who can only ever wear elasticated trousers and who constantly have their kids' tea down their top and never get a decent haircut?'

'What are you saying,' Katy said, self-consciously tucking her mass of blonde curls behind her ears, and rubbing at an orange stain on her top. 'And this isn't the kids' tea, it's yours. I made you lasagne, Alex, because it's your favourite. Because I *love* you, you fat cow.'

Alex buried her head in her hands and groaned. 'Oh, God, I'm sorry, I'm sorry. I'm such an awful bitch at the moment, it's the hormones.'

'That's what I said,' David interjected, earning him a reprise of the killer look.

'Cows are pregnant for the same time as human beings,' Jake told her. 'You do look a bit like a cow.'

'And now,' Tilly said, emerging from the corner, a shimmering spectacle of a fire hazard, 'I shall put on a show.'

'Oh, God save me,' Alex wailed, once more burying her head in her hands.

It was at that exact moment the doorbell sounded and Vincent leaped from his slumber like a rather lopsided attack dog.

'Oh, that'll be Joanna,' Katy said delightedly, looking at Lydia.

'And Joanna's new boyfriend!' Lydia exclaimed. 'Come on, let's go and get a look at him!'

Two women, two children and a dog raced for the door, all of them, with perhaps the exception of the dog, keen to get a look at the latest man in Joanna Summer's life.

'Wait for me!' Alex yelled, gesturing frantically for David to pull her to her feet, her voice receding into the background as Lydia and Katy vied for first place. 'Bloody wait for me, you bastards!'

In the end, Katy, who wasn't wearing a stylish but impractical pair of stiletto boots, made it first, flinging the door open and dragging Joanna inside for one of her biggest hugs.

'Jo-Jo!' she yelped happily, as Vincent did his best to maul the latest arrival. 'Look at you!'

Joanna was indeed a vision of loveliness. Wearing a white woollen coat trimmed with faux fur, and a matching hat, her red hair cascading down her back. She looked like she'd just stepped off the set of a remake of *Doctor Zhivago*.

'How do you get out of a car after three hundred miles looking like *that*?' Lydia asked her old flatmate, kissing her on the cheek.

'I don't know, darling, I'm just naturally glamorous, I suppose.' Joanna grinned at her. 'And so are you two. Look at you, Katy, with your country rosy cheeks, and you, Lyds, all city sophistication – you put me to shame, the pair of you.' It was part of Joanna's charm that she always responded to a compliment with one of her own. Now she bent down and graciously kissed Tilly, before ruffling Jake's hair, distastefully but gently edging Vincent out of her way with the toe of her boot.

'We want to know if you are really going to get married this time!' Jake told her.

Katy shrugged. 'I'm not even going to pretend that I haven't coached him to say that. So, are you?'

'And can I be bridesmaid?' Tilly followed up.

'Shhh!' Joanna put her fingers to her lips, glancing over her shoulder into the night. 'It's early days, but the signs are good.' Careful to address the children directly, she added, 'But we don't want to frighten him off, do we, kids? So if you can manage to keep your questions to yourself, then, yes, Tilly, you can be bridesmaid and, no, Jake, you don't have to be pageboy.'

'Aunty Jo,' Tilly said, 'I watch you on telly all the time. I hope you've got me a tiara for Christmas, like the ones on your show made from purest diamonique.'

'Any chance anyone could give me a hand with this trunk?' an American accent enquired from behind an armful of presents. 'I think Joanna's packed London!'

Lydia froze. Something in those few muffled words sounded a chime of recognition within her. No . . . it couldn't be, could it?'

'Here, let me help you,' David offered, arriving with Alex, who waddled a step or two ahead of him, eager to greet Joanna.

'Hello, Jo, you look like a Russian hooker!' Alex greeted her cheerfully.

'And you are glowing!' Joanna informed her serenely.

'What, like radioactive waste?' Lydia dimly heard

Alex retort as, with everything seeming to happen in slow motion, she watched David relieve Joanna's boyfriend of his pile of gifts, one by one. Her heart pounded in her chest as saw his head dip with the effort of dragging a large brass-cornered trunk into the lobby. Hair, light brown, thick and wavy, with that familiar much-kissed hairline. It could not be. Lydia held her breath, hoping that she was delusional or somehow drunk on one sip of wine, but knowing she wasn't.

His heavy cargo finally in place, the mystery man looked up and smiled.

'Hi, everyone, I'm Jack.'

But Lydia knew at once that he wasn't Jack to everyone. To her, he'd been Jackson Blake. Handsome, American and utterly charming. Joanna's new boyfriend was the long-lost love of Lydia's life.

Chapter Four

The day Lydia had first met Jackson Blake had been a boiling hot Thursday in May, about a month and a half before she'd met Stephen. As in recent years, summer had arrived early, and to Lydia, as she left the heat and fug of her chambers in Lincolns Inn, it felt like three months' worth of polite English sunshine was being burned off in a single fever-pitched day.

Lydia's day had not gone well. She had lost a case and her client was about to serve six months for dealing cannabis. Just her luck to get an exceptionally right-wing judge that didn't see that her elderly client had only taken up buying drugs to ease the pain of her husband's arthritis, picking up a few extra ounces for her neighbours in the sheltered housing while she was at it. Grounds for appeal were already in place, even if the process probably wouldn't work fast enough to get her client out of prison before her sentence was up. Lydia was determined to have the conviction quashed, not only for a client's sake, but because she hated to lose. More than that, though, she'd hated seeing the look on Janet Thorne's face as she'd waited to be taken away, sitting quietly in the stifling holding cell, knowing she wouldn't see her disabled husband again for at least three months.

Lydia had slowed down as she approached the tube station. She knew Joanna wouldn't be at home, as she was doing the prime-time shift on BuyIt! TV. And she wasn't looking forward to an empty flat, smelling of last night's Indian food and beer binge that neither one of them had bothered to clear away. The pub over the road was thronging with drinkers, spilling out onto the pavement. Lydia wondered if the inside would be cool by comparison and relatively empty. Not normally one to drink in bars by herself, she had crossed the road without really thinking, and was standing at the bar ordering a long G&T before she knew it.

The inside of the old-fashioned pub, although cool and spacious, was indeed largely empty. Pulling up a stool, Lydia positioned herself at the bar, and was just about to take out some client files to go over when she thought better of it and took out her battered but beloved Penguin Modern Classic edition of *Breakfast at Tiffany's*. Over the years, she supposed the book had become something of a talisman, a sort of lucky charm. To begin with, though, it had simply been her favourite book, one she had read and re-read ever since, at the age of twelve, her English teacher had handed it to her and said, 'Look, I know how hard it must be, stuck in the middle of your mum and dad's divorce. Try getting lost in a good book, I find it helps.' She had lost count of the number of times she had read it since, but it always helped.

Absorbed in the pages of her book, it had taken some time for Lydia to realise someone was watching her. She glanced up to catch the eye of a man across the bar, and looked down instantly, staring at the words in front of her without really reading them. In that fraction of a second, she'd gleaned that the man was rather tall, well built, wearing a pristine white shirt without a tie and had eyes that were blue enough for her to notice them across the room. Waiting for another moment or two, Lydia looked up again. The man was gone.

'Film or book?' a soft American accent asked her, causing Lydia to swivel round on her stool. There he was, leaning against the bar, his thick honey-brown hair a little longer than most men wore it, his open-necked shirt revealing tanned skin. He smelled divine, and those blue eyes . . .

'Book,' Lydia replied instantly, gratified to see he was impressed that she knew what his rather cryptic question meant.

'Really? Really Capote's Holly over Audrey Hepburn's? The misery and bleakness over George Peppard bringing back Cat in the pouring rain? I would have thought most girls would pick the movie ending any time.'

'The movie is wonderful,' Lydia said. 'And I love the

idea of Holly getting a happy ending, but the book came first so it has to be the book . . . and, besides, I am not most girls.' Lydia allowed herself to say the line she knew perfectly well he'd set up for her.

'I can see that.' He glanced down at his drink for a moment, and then back up at her face. He really was very good at this, Lydia remembered thinking. And perhaps that should have been a warning sign for her – the practised flirting – but she was too caught up in the moment.

They had introduced themselves, first names only, and shaken hands. Lydia remembered that, as he clasped her hand briefly but firmly, it sent a bolt of electricity through her.

'Would you let me buy you a drink?' Jackson asked her, and Lydia had hesitated, even though she knew she was going to say yes, playing the game as expertly as he.

'I shouldn't really,' she said, slowly, thoughtfully, nipping her bottom lip between her teeth.

'Please?' Jackson pressed her. 'It's been a long time since I've met anyone to talk about great American literature with, too.'

'Oh, in that case, I'm afraid I will disappoint you, then, as this is really the only American classic I've ever read, well, unless you count *Gone With the Wind*.'

Jackson observed her with a long sideway glance. 'You do have something of Miss O' Hara about you.'

'Why, thank you kindly, I think.' Lydia let her lashes flutter, her chin dipping as she leaned forward a little, improving by just one tantalising fraction the view of her cleavage, quietly pleased that she still remembered how to flirt.

There had been a time when she and Joanna were the menaces of the male world, two finally honed flirting machines on an endless loop of dating and casual romances that never really came to anything. And then, one morning, Lydia had woken up with her mascara spread across the pillow, and a thumping headache, to realise that if she ever wanted to get ahead in chambers, she couldn't try to keep up with Joanna any more. Her beautiful, vivacious flatmate already had it made; she had done ever since a talent scout for a modelling agency had spotted her in the shopping centre when they'd all been at university. From that moment onwards, Joanna had traded on her looks and personality to get ahead, and why shouldn't she? If Lydia looked like Joanna, she'd have done exactly the same.

Joanna had quit uni before she completed her sociology degree – no one, including herself, believed she was going to pass her final exams, in any case. A brief career in underwear and catalogue modelling led to an appearance wearing a Chinese silk dressing gown on a shopping channel, where she had outshone the jaded and slightly drunk presenter and got herself a lucrative new job and a new beau – her director – all in one afternoon. The career had lasted longer than the romance, in fact, but while Joanna was still content to work her way steadily through London's male population, Lydia had begun to tire of the dating scene. The plain truth was, she couldn't keep up with Joanna, especially if she wanted to make a success of her career. Consequently, it had been a long time – almost two years, in fact – since she'd flirted with a stranger in a bar; two years of being professional, keeping her head down, and working her behind off to get where she was today.

Only today was hot and tinged with failure, and looking at a face like Jackson Blake's was exactly what she needed.

'I'll have another G&T, thank you,' Lydia said.

As the sun sank behind the skyline, leaving a trail of stars in its wake, and the heat mercifully ebbed away, Lydia found out more about Jackson. He'd grown up in New Jersey, son of a plumber father and a grade school teacher 'mom'. He'd worked his way through college, pounding the streets of New York as soon as he'd graduated, knocking on the door of every big-name publishing company to try and get a break. Finally, he'd landed a job as an intern at Seinfeld and Sachs, and worked his way up to become publishing director, taking a transfer to London a few months earlier with the remit of getting the floundering London office back on track.

'What no one tells a straight, single guy about

publishing, though, is that it's like throwing a tender little lamb into a pool of man-hungry, stiletto-wearing piranhas,' Jackson joked. 'As soon as you've stepped through the front door, they've got your place of residence, marital status, income, and bonus scheme out of you, and are asking which days you've got free next June.'

'Oh, poor you, are all the ladies in love with you?' Lydia pouted playfully. 'How awful it must be for you.'

'It's terrible,' Jackson confirmed solemnly. 'And worst of all – they all get PMS at the same time! It's the group crying I can't take.'

'Jackson, you chauvinist!' Lydia had half gasped, half giggled, punching him lightly on the shoulder and feeling a frisson of excitement as he caught her hand and held it.

'I know, I'm sorry. It's not like that at all.' He raised a brow. 'Much.'

Lydia had held his gaze as he had used her entrapped hand to pull her closer to him until their lips were millimetres apart.

'You are like a long, cool glass of water,' he said.

Lydia had let their lips meet for a moment and then pulled back, slipping off the bar stool and picking up her briefcase.

'I've got to go,' she said. 'It's been very nice to meet you, Jackson Blake.'

'Would you like to meet me again?' Jackson asked

her. 'I work just round the corner, maybe we could have lunch?'

'I don't really have the sort of job where you get a lunch break.' Lydia shrugged, enjoying pushing her luck for a moment more.

'Then will you meet me here again tomorrow night? I'll make reservations and take you to dinner.' Lydia had hesitated; she was supposed to be having dinner with Alex and the girls to talk about bridesmaids dresses, and the fact that Alex seemed determined to make them all look as hideous as she possibly could, having unexpectedly developed a new-found interest in puffed sleeves. As much as she'd enjoy an evening of looking at this sexy man across a table, a wedding planner dinner with your best friend was not something you could just duck out of, even for a lantern-jawed, prime specimen like Jackson.

'Sorry, I can't. I have plans.' Lydia mentally crossed her fingers, hoping he'd persist just once more.

'Wow, you really are playing hard to get, very unusual for an English girl, you are usually all so easy.'

'Hey!' Lydia scolded him.

'Sorry. Look, I would really like to see you again. How about Saturday?' he asked her apprehensively, cringing as if he expected a slap just for asking.

'Yes, okay, then, I suppose.' Lydia was very careful not to sound too thrilled. 'But not here. I live on the other side of town, and I don't like to come back to where I work on my day off. I'll meet you in The Porcupine on Tottenham Court Road at seven-thirty. Look it up and find somewhere wonderful to take me for dinner.'

'Yes, ma'am.' Jackson saluted. 'Now, please allow me to escort you to the subway station.'

'But why, it's only over the road?' Lydia asked.

'You need to ask why?' Jackson chuckled, shaking his head as he picked up her hand. 'Because I need a good reason to kiss you goodbye, woman, that's why.'

As Lydia let the rattle and rumble of the tube train lull her half to sleep on the way home, she had leaned her back against the seat and, with a slightly tipsy smile, concluded that as good night kisses go, it had been a great deal more than satisfactory.

The following day had been spent entirely fixating on two things. What to wear and would he turn up? In all the heated, sultry promise of last night, she and Jackson had failed to swap phone numbers. He had no way of letting her down gently if he'd decided to back out, and the only way she was going to find out if he'd been real or just a symptom of heat stroke, was to turn up. The thought of being stood up caused Lydia serious alarm, remembering the awful sense of humiliation she'd felt when, at the age of sixteen, she'd gone to meet Tony Bellamy outside the cinema on the high street, in shoes she couldn't really walk in and far too much lipstick. And how she'd had to endure the laughter and taunts of her school mates as she stood there, until one of Tony's friends told her he wasn't coming. He was down the graveyard getting off with Melanie Davies.

Which meant that with every outfit that Lydia now tried on, she found herself imagining not how she'd look in the arms of Jackson Blake, but instead how she'd look standing like a lemon in a silk print dress and strappy-heeled sandals on a Saturday night at the bar of The Porcupine on Tottenham Court Road, waiting for a date who didn't turn up.

For every third minute out of five from then on, Lydia decided she wasn't going to go. And then she remembered that goodnight kiss, and butterflies would leap and whoop and loop the loop in her tummy.

'You may well be an utter idiot, Lydia Grant,' Lydia told her reflection in the full-length mirror, 'but you can't risk missing out on being kissed like that again.'

Just before she was due to depart, Joanna had emerged from her bedroom with her hair all tangled and last night's make-up smeared under her eyes. Yet still she looked beautiful.

'Ouch,' she said as she flopped across the kitchen table. 'I think I might have officially had too much sex. Make me breakfast, darling.'

'Breakfast? It's almost seven in the evening, Joanna. And besides, where did you disappear off to last night after the Great Bridesmaid Debacle? One minute we were all trying to persuade Alex that no one suits puce, and the next you've vanished into the night.'

'Not the night, darling, Cuba,' Joanna said, pouting meaningfully at the kettle, which Lydia filled and switched on in spite of her exasperation. 'There was a salsa party happening on the first floor, so I thought I'd just pop in after I went to the loo, and have a little look. Which was when I bumped into Enrique. I was going to come back and argue about the puffed sleeve thing, but darling . . . the hot Latin rhythm was calling me, so I thought I'd leave it up to you to persuade Alex not to dress us as mutants. You do sort of argue for a living, after all. Enrique taught me all about hip action . . . and we did a bit of dancing too!' Joanna giggled, making Lydia smile despite herself.

'And what about Ted?' Lydia asked, reminding her friend of her fiancé, whose ring she was even now sporting on her left hand.

'I love Ted, I do. But I just needed a little bit of Latin spice to get me through the endless discussions about duchess satin. When Ted and I get married, I'm not going to have any bridesmaids, just . . . swans, with ribbons round their necks.'

'Nice, well, I'll see you later . . .' Lydia had attempted to exit, a little too hastily.

'Hang on, why are you neglecting to lecture me on my alley cat morals, and where are you going looking so lovely?' Joanna asked her, gasping as the realisation of Lydia in a pretty dress on a Saturday night hit her befuddled brain. 'Oh my God, Lydia's got a date! Where's my phone, I need to text everyone.'

'Don't you dare!' Lydia cried, grabbing Joanna's phone before she could. 'It's not a date. It's a business meeting.'

'Do you normally get your knockers half out on display for a business meeting?' Joanna asked her, nodding at Lydia's cleavage, which she had secretly dusted with a little bit of bronzer and just a smidgen of glitter.

'It's the fashion,' Lydia replied.

'In the porn industry!' Joanna pressed her fingers to her forehead, and groaned. 'Oh, God. *Never*, ever drink tequila. Not even with a mixer, it's death. Okay, you may go, but only because I am too poorly to get the details out of you now. But I shall when you return, you mark my words, missy.'

'Fine,' Lydia said, handing Joanna back her phone and giving her a quick peck on the cheek. 'Give my love to Ted, oh, and Enrique.'

Lydia was fairly certain that Joanna had thrown her phone in the general direction of her head, just as she closed the door.

The hours of self-doubt and uncertainty had been wasted because Jackson was waiting for Lydia as she'd arrived, himself looking utterly delicious in a pair of dark chinos and a black T-shirt that was not so form-fitting as to indicate a vain and body-obsessed man, but was tight enough to show that what lay beneath would be worth a lick – a *look*, Lydia corrected her unruly train of thought, stifling a giggle as she went to greet him.

'Wow, you came,' Jackson said, a slow smile spreading over his face.

'Did you doubt me?' Lydia asked him, channelling Lauren Bacall cool to hide the fact that she was a bag of nerves.

'Sure I did, I had to practically beg you to meet me tonight. You are one cool customer.' Lydia smirked, thinking that she so wasn't, but rather liking the perception of her that Jackson had somehow formed. 'It's okay, though, you know us guys. We always want what we can't have.'

'So what you're saying is that, if I want to keep you interested, I'll have to keep turning you down?' Lydia asked him. Jackson's smile was wry as he shook his head, his eyes growing suddenly intense as he looked at her.

'We could do this all night, this banter and flirting, back and forth. And if you want to, I don't mind. I like it. You're smart and funny as well as beautiful. But here's the thing: I like you, Lydia, I like you a lot. Maybe that's not the cool thing to say, but it's how I feel. I don't want to play games with you because, well,

I get the feeling that this could be the start of something . . . So, how about you let me buy you dinner and we just talk? I want to know everything about you. I want to know what makes you smile, and see you laugh, and hold your hand and kiss you some more. Would that be okay with you?'

Lydia paused for a moment, mentally running the scripts of all the romantic movies she had ever seen in her whole life, which was many, just in case Jackson had memorised that impossibly romantic speech.

'I'll have a gin and tonic, please,' she said, sliding into the seat next to him. 'Well, let me see, where shall I start? I was born in Broadstairs to the world's least compatible couple . . .'

It had taken about another hour for Jackson to kiss her again, standing outside an Italian restaurant on Waldorf Street. They had kissed for a long time, such a long time, in fact, that they were a little late for their reservation, which was at the very restaurant they were standing outside of. Eating very little and kissing very much, they hadn't been able to keep their lips apart for more than a few minutes, their kisses growing so fevered that the waiter came over and very politely asked them if they would like their bill, even though they hadn't made it to dessert yet.

Giggling like teenagers, they fell out onto the street, and Jackson kissed her again, in exactly the same spot as where they had been standing on the way in.

'So what now?' Lydia asked him. 'We've only got up to the time I was thrown out of ballet for swearing . . . You're never going to hear my whole life story at this rate.'

'How about we skip to the next instalment?' Jackson grabbed both her hands in his. 'Come home with me, Lydia, I want to make love with you.'

'Bloody hell!' Lydia had giggled.

'Please, please come home and spend the night with me. I don't want this evening to end with having to say goodbye to you.'

Suddenly a little more sober, Lydia had hesitated. Quite what she had been planning when she left Joanna that evening, she wasn't sure, but it wasn't this. She wasn't even entirely certain that she had 'acceptable for sex' knickers on, never mind the fact that it had been a very long time since she had engaged in sexual congress with a man. Self-doubt and anxiety engulfed her once again.

'I've asked too much, haven't I?' Jackson said, abashed. 'You're not the sort of girl who likes to be rushed.'

'No, no . . . you haven't, I am . . . um.' Lydia touched his cheek with the tips of her fingers. 'No, you haven't asked too much, I don't want this evening to end, either. It's just that I'm . . . I don't usually . . . The thing is, I'm not entirely sure I know what to do any more.'

Jackson smiled at her, picking her hand up and kissing it.

'Come home with me and I'll show you,' he said, so softly, so sweetly, that Lydia felt her knees momentarily buckle.

'Okay, then,' she said, flinging what little caution she had so easily to the wind. 'Yes, I will come home with you.'

Jackson had hailed the next black cab and given the driver his West London address. Looking out of the window as the cab drew away from the curb and merged into the traffic, Lydia felt the tips of Jackson's fingers touch hers as they rested on the seat between them, and that is where their hands remained until the taxi pulled up outside an impressively large, rambling old rectory.

'Wow, this is amazing,' Lydia breathed, looking up at the old house. 'All this is yours?'

'Sort of, I'm a custodian tenant,' Jackson told her, as she followed him through the front door and into the hallway. 'It's owned by the diocese, but there's no rector in situ now. So, to keep squatters and vandals at bay until they work out what to do with it, they let it to me on a short-term basis for a fraction of what I'd pay for one room around here. They can throw me out any time, of course, but until they do, I have this whole amazing house. And practically no furniture except for a futon . . .'

'A futon?' Lydia echoed, suddenly feeling very nervous.

Before Lydia could ask any more, Jackson, his hand on her waist, manoeuvred her against the wall and kissed her hard on the lips, his hungry mouth tracking its way down her neck. Pausing for a moment to look at her, he whipped open the knot that held her wrap dress in place, exposing her flesh to his gaze. For a second longer, his eyes devoured her, pinning her to the spot with their desire, and then in one deft and practised move, he unhooked her bra, tearing it from her.

Shy no longer, Lydia pulled at his T-shirt, thrusting it upwards so that she could feel her hot skin pressed against his. In a frenzy, they undressed each other, right there in the hallway, and then in one movement Jackson picked her up in his arms and carried her upstairs.

Afterwards, they had slept for a little while, his arms entwined around her, his lips nestled into the back of her neck. A few minutes or hours later, Lydia didn't know which, she felt his fingers tracing a delicate journey over her breasts, rolling her over to kiss each one, and then every part of her as the whole wonderful experience began again.

Some time just after dawn, Lydia found herself crying a little as she re-told him the plot of one of her favourite films.

'And it's just so sad, because they know this is the last time they are ever going to see each other again.

And they know they are doing the right thing – that she has to stay with her husband and he has to go and do doctor things abroad – but they love each other so much, even though they can't be together. Every time I see it I weep and weep!' Lydia sniffed and giggled simultaneously. 'Look at me, what an idiot.'

'Sounds intense,' Jackson said, wiping her tear away with the ball of one thumb. 'I know, let's rent it.'

'Rent it?' Lydia laughed.

'Yes, there a really good Blockbuster down the road. As soon as it opens, let's get down there and rent it, and we can watch it together.'

'You'd sit and watch all of *Brief Encounter* with me?' Lydia remembered asking, thinking that might have been the very moment she'd fallen in love with him.

'I'd do more than that, I'd make you breakfast to go with it.' Jackson smiled, picking up his watch and peering at it. 'Now, let's see, Blockbuster opens at ten, which give us a whole four hours to kill, what *shall* we do?'

'I could explain the plot of *Casablanca* to you, if you like?' Lydia teased him.

'Maybe not today, maybe not tomorrow, but soon . . . right after I've kissed you again.'

And that was how it started. Six perfect weeks: from the beginning of May to the middle of June. Of course, Lydia hadn't expected it to end so soon, not ever, now she came to think of it, but especially not the way it did. Six wonderful weeks during which she and Jackson had spent every possible minute closeted away together, watching movie after movie, reading to each other and kissing, always kissing, so much so that Joanna reported her missing in action and Alex almost fired her from her job as chief bridesmaid. And then, one evening, she had gone to meet him at the vicarage for dinner as planned, humming the theme music from *Love Story* to herself as she'd skipped up the stone steps and rang the bell. It had come as something of a surprise when a stranger opened the door.

'Oh, hello,' Lydia said, taking in the unkempt-looking old man, who didn't look anything at all like he might be a friend of Jackson's. 'I'm here to see Jackson?'

'Gone, love,' the old man told her, and he would have shut the door in Lydia's face if she hadn't stopped him with her sandaled foot.

'Gone? Where and for how long?'

'I dunno, I'm not his mum,' the man grumbled. 'I work for the diocese. I'm the caretaker. They phoned me this afternoon and said he'd vacated the premises. I've just come to check the old place over before we let it to someone new, are you interested?'

'Gone?' Lydia repeated the world slowly. They'd spent the previous evening apart, for the first time since they'd met. She had an important case to work on, one that would keep her up all night, and now they had become so close, now that she was so certain of how into her he was, she'd almost been looking forward to her first chance to miss him. He'd taken her for dinner and afterwards they'd spent a very long time kissing goodbye before catching separate cabs home. He said he'd see her the next day, at his place at nine, for dinner. How could he be gone?

'What do you mean "gone"? Is he in hospital, or dead?' Lydia asked, aware of how mad she sounded, but at a loss as to how to appear sane.

'I don't know, love,' the old man reiterated irritably, nodding at her door-stopping foot. 'I've got to get on, so if you don't mind . . .'

Uncertain what to do next, Lydia had walked back down the steps and out into the busy street. Trying Jackson's phone, she found it went straight to voicemail, then and for the rest of the night. After no sleep at all, she waited until nine the next morning, and, with her heart in her mouth, called his office.

'Jackson's not here,' an efficient-sounding woman told her. 'He's on leave.'

'What sort of leave? Why?' Lydia pressed her, knowing she sounded desperate. 'I'm sorry, it's just I didn't know he was going on leave.'

'I'm sorry, it's against company policy to give out personal information over the phone,' the woman told her with more than a hint of pleasure. 'I can put you through to his assistant, if it's a professional matter.'

'No, you see . . . you don't understand. I'm his *girlfriend*.'

There was a brief silence on the other end of the phone.

'Join the club, sweetheart,' the woman said tartly, and then she hung up.

Devastated, confused and disbelieving, Lydia had sleep-walked through the next day, grateful that her current case was an easy one she could handle in her sleep; and then, in the middle of a tearful night, during what must have been the only few minutes she had actually slept, her phone had woken her with a text from Jackson.

'Darling, so sorry. Had to go home, family emergency. Will call as soon as I can. xxx'

And that was it. He had never called. He had never texted again, and, hurt and humiliated by being so spectacularly dumped, Lydia had determined to forget him.

It had by no means been the first time in her life that a man had finished with her, but it was the first time ever that he'd moved house and left the country to do it.

After Lydia had cried for a solid week, she gradually started to get in touch with her friends again, explaining to them why she'd been so preoccupied over the six weeks and what exactly had happened with Jackson. Always there for each other when they'd needed to be, they had taken care of her with as much wine and chocolate as she could stomach, and no difficult questions. And Alex, who reinstated her as head bridesmaid, enrolled her in a charity fun run for breast cancer care, to boost her spirits or break them, one or the other.

It had been beautiful and then it had been viciously, brutally over, and feeling utterly battered and totally foolish, Lydia had come to accept that Jackson Blake had seen the wide-eyed romantic in her and taken her for one hell of a ride. Still, Lydia counselled herself, determined not to give in to her aching heart, she'd had a wonderful time for as long as it lasted, and maybe it was just Lydia being Lydia to expect more than that in real life. Romantic heroes as perfect as she had thought Jackson was didn't really exist and, after all, as Bette Davis would say, you can't go expecting the moon when you've got the stars. So she'd locked those six extraordinary weeks away in her heart and got on with the business of living, knowing she was never going to see Jackson Blake again, and doing her very best to pretend she hadn't fallen in love with the bastard.

Which was why it came as something of a surprise to find him standing in Katy's hallway.

Chapter Five

'So, this is Alex.' Lydia watched, frozen to the spot, as Joanna introduced Jackson, Jack, or whatever he was calling himself these days, to all of her friends. 'Alex is pregnant,' Joanna added in her honeyed, TV-friendly tones.

'I'm sure the man's got eyes,' Alex said, smiling and shaking Jack's hand.

'I was just making sure he didn't think you were simply fat,' Joanna teased her, tucking her arm through his as she guided 'Jack' on.

'This is David, Alex's victim, I mean husband. And this is Katy and her husband, Jim, our lovely hosts. This young man is Jakey, and this little delight is Tilly. That smelly article is Vincent Van Dog, because he's only got one ear, although as far as we know he doesn't suffer from any sort of personality disorder. Oh, and this is Stephen and . . .' Lydia felt all of the air sucked out of her lungs in the fraction of a second it took for Joanna to propel 'Jack' towards her. Perhaps he hadn't noticed her when he first came in; after all, Joanna hadn't allowed him to take a breath. This would be the moment, the moment of recognition . . . and then what?

'Lydia, this is Jack, isn't he hot?' Joanna smiled. And Jack nodded at Lydia, extending his hand, the warm, strong hand that had once caressed her, in a formal greeting.

'Very pleased to meet you, Linda,' he said, without even a hint of what they had once been to each other showing on his face. Unable to dissemble so quickly, Lydia just stared at him, her hand lying limply in his, as her brain struggled to process what was happening. Had he forgotten her? Was she one among so many that faces simply became a blur to him? Or was he merely going to pretend not only that he'd never once kissed her naked body from head to toe as she lay sprawled on his staircase, but that they had never even met before?

'Lydia, darling, her name's Lydia.' Joanna laughed. 'Oh dear, I think you've offended her.'

'I beg your pardon.' Jackson held on to her hand. 'Lydia is such a pretty name.'

'Nice to meet you,' Lydia said, recovering a little and pulling her hand out of his, glancing around at her friends, laughing, talking, slapping shoulders, shaking hands. For a moment, she felt like one of the ghosts of Christmas, present but invisible, unable to take part. Or no, not the ghost, like Scrooge, looking in on the life he could never be part of. This was supposed to be her perfect Christmas, the first one ever. Now she couldn't think of any other way that it could be less perfect. The single most humiliating and hurtful moment of her life had been wrapped up in gorgeous packaging and delivered at her feet.

'Right, well . . .' Joanna broke the moment, taking off her coat and flinging it casually over the reception desk. 'We could stand about here all day gawping at my stunning boyfriend like idiots, or we could get on with the business of Christmas cheer. Point me in the direction of the mulled wine, at once!'

Frantically gathering what was left of her wits, Lydia waited for a moment as her little group of cherished friends, plus one, moved from the hallway, following Katy towards the sitting room, Jake already regaling Jackson with some tall tale about monsters in the lake.

After a moment, she felt something tugging her, and looking down she saw Tilly, still decked out in tinsel, her vest peeking out from under her homemade fairy outfit.

'Are you okay, Aunty Lydia?' Tilly asked her. 'You look very surprised.'

'I am very surprised,' Lydia said, shaking her head. 'I am very surprised indeed.'

'Did you see a ghost?' Tilly asked her, wide-eyed, still clinging on to Lydia, gazing into the dark corners under the stairs. 'Was it Mad Molly?'

'I didn't see a ghost, Tilly,' Lydia said, remembering the feel of Jackson's hand in hers. 'No, he very definitely wasn't dead. Not yet anyway.'

By the time Lydia and Tilly caught up with the others, they had moved from the sitting room into the dining room. Lydia was grateful to see that Joanna and Jackson weren't present, at least for the moment. Joanna had probably gone to change into some designer ensemble for dinner: it was one of her foibles. Sometimes she even dressed for dinner when it was a takeaway from the local Chinese. Joanna would rarely be drawn on what little family life she had as a child was like before her parents handed her over to boarding schools. Lydia only knew that it had been exceptionally privileged, if markedly lacking in parental love. The absence of a conventional happy family was one of the main things that bound the two totally different women together, even if they did come from entirely different sides of the tracks. That and the man they had now unwittingly shared. The terrible thing was that Lydia was sure Joanna would be in for the same treatment as her. She had to warn her – but when? Which part of Christmas should she ruin first?

Katy had opened up what would soon be the guest dining room to accommodate them all, arranging the selection of tables in one row and covering it with a long red paper tablecloth, candles and Kirsty Allsopp-inspired, make-your-own crackers. Katy, being Katy, had run up a gingham-themed runner that afternoon, decorating it with appliqué holly leaves and sprinkling little silver stars over the place settings. It looked beautiful, Lydia thought, a small lump forming in her throat; just how she imagined a Dickensian Christmas table would look. (If *A Christmas Carol* had been styled by Disney.)

'Please excuse the paper tablecloth,' Katy said, as she observed the overall effect of her work. 'I thought I'd save my best linen for the big day. I have to take everything to the dry cleaners in Keswick to get the stains off, as the washing machine we've currently got here is literally one step up from a mangle. The industrial one doesn't arrive until the New Year.'

'We helped Mummy make the crackers!' said Tilly proudly.

'I wrote the jokes,' added Jake.

'Are the cracker jokes funny, Jake?' David asked, winking at the boy as he pulled out a chair for his wife.

'Really hilarious,' Jake told him seriously, bagging the seat next to Alex, who looked first at him, grinning up at her, and then longingly at the forbidden wine. Lydia hung back, standing in the doorway as she watched her friends chatting and bustling about, picking chairs around the long table. A natural order soon emerged: all the girls would be seated at one end, with all the boys at the other, the need for a good catch-up far outweighing any boy, girl, boy, girl protocol.

'Excuse me.' Lydia jumped as she heard Jackson's voice in her ear. Hurriedly, she stepped out of his way as he walked into the room followed by Joanna, her friend wearing a chic, backless little black dress that stopped just about mid thigh, to make the most of her long slender legs.

'Chop, chop, Lyds, I'm ravenous,' Joanna said, eyeing Jackson. 'Go and sit with the men, Jack, darling. You boys can bond while we girls catch up.'

'Enjoy it while you can.' Stephen grinned at the newcomer in their midst as he obediently took a seat where he was told. 'Once this lot get together, it becomes impossible to get a word in.'

Jack chuckled, revealing the dimple under his chin, the one Lydia used to kiss and put her finger on as they lay in bed, face to face, talking, laughing. He seemed utterly at ease, taking his banishment to the boys' end of the table in good spirits, sitting, much to Lydia's horror, next to Stephen. Covertly, she watched the two of them as Stephen offered to fill Jackson's glass, and they exchanged a few friendly words.

It wasn't fair to say that Jackson was better-looking than Stephen, he wasn't, not really. If anything, he was maybe a couple of inches shorter, and his cheekbones weren't quite so perfectly cut. Stephen was too busy saving the world to work out, which Jackson had to do in order to maintain the six-pack that Lydia had run her fingers over more than once, although, in the brief time she'd known him, she never saw him go to a gym. Stephen was funny when he wanted to be, and sweet sometimes. And when the moment was right, which it admittedly hadn't been for many months, he could be a thoughtful, careful lover. He was loyal, steadfast, honourable and reliable. He'd never skip the country, or at least pretend to, in order to get rid of her. And yet, as she watched the two of them make polite, manly conversation, she knew it wasn't the sight of her boyfriend that was making her heart thunder in her chest.

'Come on, Lyds, stop hovering,' Katy ordered from the head of the table. 'Jim will be arriving any minute with the food. Come and sit down.'

Of course, there was only one chair left vacant at the table, positioned with Joanna on the right and Jackson on the left.

Jackson smiled at her politely as she took her seat, betraying no flicker of recognition. Had he truly forgotten her? Lydia wondered. Maybe he told all the women he got into bed that they were his one and only. He looked at her now with the same polite interest that a stranger would, before turning to ask David about what sort of history he taught, prompting friendly groans from Stephen. Jim arrived with a large dish of steaming lasagne in his oven-gloved hands, and Lydia's stomach rumbled in spite of its current state of turmoil, as the rich scent of tomato and garlic filled her nostrils.

Now seeming much more relaxed, Katy reminded Tilly that the silver star confetti liberally scattered on the table was not to be inserted into noses, and Jake that he had to wait until he was eighteen before he could try wine, no matter how much he pleaded, as she piled food onto every one's plates. Lydia looked down at the sumptuous – if homely-looking – feast, but didn't know if she could take a bite. How was it possible that Jackson – her Jackson, despite his new diminutive – was here, sitting next to her, pretending he'd never met her, let alone whispered in her ear that he would always love her?

Her mind was reeling: he was *here*, now, at this very minute. Not where she'd always imagined him, in New York, when she'd allowed herself to think of him at all. In New York, taking care of whatever emergency it was that had wrenched him away from her. Gazing wistfully out of some skyscraper window and perhaps missing her and wishing he hadn't accidentally dropped his phone in the Hudson and somehow was unable to contact her through any of the many means of modern communication. Lydia had known it was a foolish fantasy, that, really he'd simply left her, but it was one that just occasionally she had allowed herself to indulge in, until now. Now she could never again imagine him somewhere far away, longing for her, because he was *here*.

Which drew her rattling towards the conclusion that he'd lied about leaving London, and that he'd most probably lied about the family emergency, making her feel all the more foolish for letting herself treasure the memories of the those six short weeks.

Lydia turned to look at Jackson, who was looking interested as David explained his theory on the truth about Dark Age Britain, nodding, inserting little 'uh-huhs' and 'Oh, reallys?' as David talked. It was impossible to take in.

'Wine?' Joanna tapped her on the shoulder, winking at her as she filled her glass with Merlot, whispering in her ear, 'Darling, isn't he wonderful? I know I've never been able to settle down in the past, but I'm telling you, this man . . . this man is something special. It's only been a couple of months, but already it's like we're made for each other. He really knows me, better then I know myself, almost. It's an incredible feeling, isn't it, to be really understood?'

Lydia nodded, watching Joanna's face light up with something she had never seen before, something akin to hope. 'I honestly think, this time, this is the real thing,' Joanna, went on, *sotto voce*. 'I really do. In fact, don't tell the others, but I think, *I hope*, that a proposal over Christmas might be on the cards! Eeek!' She shrieked like a little girl.

With some force of will, Lydia bent her mouth into the approximation of a smile, swallowing the bitter taste that rose in her throat. 'I'm so pleased for you, Joanna.'

Joanna's smile faded as she observed her friend's expression.

'What is it? What's wrong, darling?' Joanna asked

her, concerned. 'Is it Stephen? Aren't things going well for you two? How typical of me to be all gushing and smug, without taking a second to find out how you are?'

'No, not at all,' Lydia heard herself say, as if from a distance. She leaned in close. 'Actually, promise to keep this to yourself, I found an engagement ring in his sock drawer. I'm expecting a proposal any minute too.'

'Oh!' Joanna's cry of delight turned all heads towards her as she hugged Lydia, seeming not to notice her stiff shoulders.

'What?' Katy demanded. 'Share at once, you two!'

'Yes, what are you two brewing up between you?' Alex asked, raising a brow.

'Nothing!' Joanna smiled triumphantly. 'All we're saying is, watch this space, right, Lyds?'

'Right.' Lydia nodded, artificially bright. 'That's all we're saying!'

'Sounds interesting,' Jackson said. It took Lydia a moment or two to realise he was talking directly to her. Slowly, she turned and looked at him.

'Yes,' she said, unable to hide the strain in her voice. 'Things around here are suddenly very interesting indeed.'

'Can we talk?' Jack asked her, his voice pitched low, beneath the chatter around the table.

'I really have nothing to say,' Lydia managed to reply. 'But . . .'

'So, Jack, what sort of work do you do?' Stephen interrupted them. 'Something more interesting than digging up pots?'

'Publishing,' Jackson said. 'I spend all day with demanding, glamorous English women, it's trained me perfectly for life with Joanna.'

Amid the laughter, Lydia abruptly scraped back her chair back and stood up.

'Do you know what, I've suddenly got a really terrible headache. I think I might go and get an early night . . .'

'Are you okay, love?' Stephen asked her, topping up his glass with more wine.

'No, I mean, yes, it's nothing. It's just . . . I think I must be car sick, you know, like, delayed? Delayed car sickness, that'll be it. I get it all the time. I just feel like I really need to go to bed and lie down.' She picked up an unopened bottle of wine and tried to tuck it surreptitiously under her arm. 'I just need a hot bath and an early night.' Everyone groaned.

'Oh, don't go,' Joanna begged. 'We can't have a proper gossip without you.'

'Besides, I'm not sure a bottle of wine is the best medicine . . .' Katy pointed out, her brow furrowing.

'This is what comes of a diet consisting entirely of biscuits and alcohol.' Alex wagged a finger at her, adding wistfully, 'Sounds like bliss.'

'Do you want me to come up with you?' Stephen half-rose from his chair.

'No, don't be silly. I'm fine, really. I've just come over all hot and . . . I'll be as right as rain tomorrow.' Still clasping the wine bottle firmly by the neck, Lydia waited for the two excruciating seconds it took for Jackson to pull his chair in and allow her to exit, and then made her way out of the heat and glare of the dining room. She was grateful for the chill of the hallway, which soothed her fiery cheeks. Glancing around, she twisted the screw cap off the wine and took a long draught before turning to look for her bags underneath Joanna's.

'Are you really all right, darling?' Stephen made her jump as he appeared behind her. 'I know how long you've been waiting to see all the girls. It's not like you to duck out of things early?'

Lydia mustered a smile for him. 'I'm fine, truly. I just suddenly felt a bit . . . sick.'

'Here, let me take that,' Stephen said, picking up another case that belonged to her too. 'You know they're laying odds in there on whether or not you are pregnant.'

'Typical.' Lydia shook her head, suddenly grateful that Stephen had come out to check on her. Although his hands were too full for them to embrace, she took a step forward and rested her forehead on his shoulder, breathing in his safe, familiar scent.

'You're not, are you . . . you know, pregnant?' Stephen asked her. 'Not that it would be a problem, you know, if you were. It's maybe not the best timing, and we'd need to buy a bigger place, and it's not the best time to be getting a mortgage. Still, it would be fine, if you were. We'd work around it.' Lydia lifted her head, staring up at him, speechless. 'But you're not, are you?'

'No, Stephen,' she said, slowly. 'I'm not pregnant . . . apart from anything else, we haven't had sex for weeks. Months, actually. Or hadn't you noticed?'

'It's not months, is it? Is it months?' Stephen frowned. 'I knew it had been a while, and it's not that I haven't noticed, Lydia, or wanted to. It's just our lives very rarely seem to coincide at the right time, do they?' Lydia shook her head. 'Come on,' Stephen said fondly, 'let's get you tucked in, and then maybe we can rectify that particular little oversight.'

'Actually, do you mind?' Lydia took her case back from him, desperate for some space alone to reflect, thinking it was typical that Stephen would choose to make a move when she wasn't in the mood. 'I'm really not feeling that great. Let me have a bit of time first, to have a bath and freshen up. You go back to dinner, have fun. It's the least you deserve after all that driving. I'll be waiting when you come up to bed,' she added as a sop.

Stephen hesitated for a moment, and then, after reaching into his pocket, he handed Lydia the key to their room. 'Katy said it's at the top of the stairs. You're sure you'll be okay?'

'Yes, I'll be fine. Completely fine.'

'Love you,' Stephen said, leaning forward and kissing Lydia on the tip of her nose.

'I love you, too,' Lydia replied, although at that moment she had never felt less sure of it, or indeed anything, in her entire life.

The room Katy had given her and Stephen was indeed lovely, decorated in a cool sage green, complete with a wonderfully romantic four-poster bed swathed in brocade curtains that were tied back with ribbon. Sweetest of all, there was her very own slither of turret, forming a separate little room, with windows on three sides and just enough room for one over-stuffed armchair. Happily, the room was as warm as toast, the ancient radiators pumping out plenty of heat, and in the grate of the charming wrought iron fireplace, a fire was set, waiting to be lit.

After throwing her bag onto the bed, Lydia crossed to the turret room and sat down on the armchair, pressing her hand against the cool glass as she looked out into the night, dense with snow. It was impossible to make out the contours of the landscape through the dark and the storm, or even guess where the shore of the lake might be, although Katy had assured her it was practically at the bottom of the garden. The cars parked out front were now shapeless white humps, entirely covered with snow, and what Lydia could make out of the long driveway had once again been resurfaced in smooth marble white. For half a moment, she considered opening the window and shimmying down the drainpipe to make her escape, but only for half a second. There was no way the Prius was going anywhere in this weather, and, besides, she had neglected to pack any sort of footwear that could resist even a light drizzle, never mind a few feet of snow. Lydia smiled faintly, imagining a search party finding her body, frozen in a snowdrift, only discovered because of her seven-inch Gucci stilettos poking out of the snow.

What on earth was she going to do? Watch Joanna fawn all over Jackson, and pretend, just as he was doing, that the two of them had never met? Make nice, polite love to Stephen tonight when Jackson was sleeping under the same roof? Never, not once, had Lydia been angry with Jackson for disappearing; she had been so wrapped up in the romantic tragedy of her own little *Brief Encounter*. But now there was no hiding from what, deep down, she had always known: that, all along, he'd played her.

Theirs hadn't been a story of star-crossed lovers doomed to a fateful end. He'd used her for his own amusement, until he'd tired of her, and instead of having to deal with tiresome tears and anger and aftermath, he'd run away without so much as a 'It's not you, it's me.' Leaving Lydia to spin a foolish little fairy-tale of love that could never be.

Lydia banged her head gently against the heel of her hand, tears misting her vision, as she remembered, a week or so after he'd left, going to Jackson's house and standing outside like a loon, gazing up at the window, lost in romantic, wistful memories. Now she thought he'd probably just been out or, worse, in bed with his next conquest. Maybe he'd even paid the so-called caretaker who answered the door to fob her off.

Suddenly galvanised, Lydia knew exactly what she had to do. She had to go back downstairs and confront him, at least make him tell the truth to Joanna about what had happened between them. After all, surely it was only a matter of time before one of them slipped up, and it was better that Joanna should hear the story direct. And if Jackson was the type of man who fell in love all too easily, and out of love just the same, then it was also better Joanna found that out now, too. Sometimes you had to be cruel to be kind.

In her fury, Lydia made it all the way to the bedroom door before she changed her mind. There was no way she could tell anybody about what had happened between her and Jackson, no way, not unless she was prepared to ruin Christmas, not just for herself and Joanna, but for everyone, including Katy, who had worked so hard. Also, there were the children to think of – they were so happy and excited. She didn't want anything the grown-ups did to affect what should be a magical time of year for them. The bottom line was, she couldn't ruin Christmas and, thanks to the snow, she couldn't run away, either.

This was even worse than the first Christmas after her dad had left. It had been a long, miserable year, her mother trying to hide the fact that she was always crying, and her dad, who was already secretly seeing Karen at that point, leaving longer and longer gaps between phone calls and visits. Lost and lonely, Lydia hid in her bedroom as much as possible, losing herself in a book or one of the old black and white movies on BBC2 on Saturday afternoons, longing for a world where women were ladies who wore hats and gloves, and everyone was ever so polite about everything, even falling in love. That first year after the divorce had come through, her parents had decided it would be good for her if they all spent Christmas Day together, to show Lydia that, despite everything that had happened, they were still friends.

Even at the age of thirteen, Lydia had known it was a terrible idea, that for her entire life the moments that her mum and dad had actively liked each other could be counted on the fingers of one hand, but it seemed she had no say as to what was good for her. It hadn't taken long for the temporary ceasefire to disintegrate into accusations and recrimination over her mother's lumpy gravy, and Lydia had sloped upstairs, unnoticed, to watch *It's a Wonderful Life* on the little second-hand TV her mum had got her for Christmas. Lydia had pretended to be asleep when, after more shouting and door slamming, her tearful mother finally called her down for dinner. As she concentrated on lying perfectly still, her eyes closed while her mother kissed her on the forehead, Lydia remembered wondering if perhaps a Christmas angel might come and visit her and show her how wonderful her life really was, even if just at the moment she couldn't see it.

Sighing, Lydia returned to the bed, flinging herself back onto its soft mattress, trying to reason with herself. This was not nearly as bad as that long-ago Christmas; then, she had been a lost, lonely child, unable to escape the drama and turmoil created by the adults around her. Now *she* was the adult, even if she didn't feel particularly grown-up at this exact moment. More than that, she was an adult who'd waitressed her way through her law degree, and battled all the sexism and old boy network to gain her hard-won place at the bar. Yes, her overworked heart was a tender and romantic one, but her career depended on her being rational, logical and fearless. If there was ever a woman who could get through this situation, then she, Lydia, was that woman.

Okay, Jackson had more than likely lied to her, and that was a good reason to be hurt and angry, but perhaps, in a way, he'd been trying to protect her. Some people might say that vanishing into thin air was actually preferable to saying I'm bored senseless by you, or similar. And it wasn't as if he'd cheated on her with Joanna. There were more than eighteen months between their affair and now; eighteen months and Stephen. Stephen, who she lived with, whose name appeared alongside hers on the gas bill, something he'd been as efficiently practical at sorting out as he had been about letting her have her own shelf in the fridge, and who, in his one, efficiently packed suitcase, had possession of a Tiffany engagement ring. All facts that should mean seeing Jackson again, even under these torturous circumstances, even if he had forgotten her, shouldn't matter at all.

And just because she clearly hadn't been the one for him, who was to say Joanna wasn't? After all, in the few weeks they had spent together, he'd never wanted to meet her friends or her family. In fact, he'd made a point of only wanting to be alone with her, telling her, when she had once called him to suggest he come out for dinner with the girls instead of spending another night in at his place, that the idea of having to share her, even for a few hours, was simply out of the question. Yet here he was, after little more than a month of being with Joanna, ready and willing to spend Christmas with her friends, which in Joanna's case was like meeting the parents, as strictly speaking she didn't have any family to speak of, none that she was talking to, anyway. And everybody knew that spending Christmas with a girl or boyfriend was akin to accompanying him or her to a wedding. It was tantamount to being engaged already.

Jackson's relationship with Joanna was on record; it was official. When Lydia had been seeing him, she'd virtually moved into Jackson's place, avoided seeing or talking to her friends at all, answering their texts with 'busy at work' and screening their calls, until it got to the point when Alex turned up at her chambers one day and demanded to know there and then whether or not she wanted to be a bridesmaid at all, or if she was being so mean and horrible because she hated David and didn't want Alex to be happy. Even then, Lydia had been reluctant to tell Alex everything about Jackson, somehow sensing that if she did, the enchantment she was living in would be broken, and her much more mundane real life would come crashing back in.

'I'm sorry,' Lydia had apologised, taking Alex outside to talk. 'I know I've been a terrible bridesmaid, it's just that I've met someone, and he seems to have rather swept me off my feet.'

'Really?' Sceptical Alex had seemed uncertain, even though she'd recently become softened by her own love story. 'Tell me all about him, then. What does it look like, shag like, that sort of thing?'

Although the temptation to talk about Jackson had been strong, because even having the excuse to say his name out loud made her happy, Lydia had hedged.

'It's early days yet, but maybe, maybe, you never know, I might just have a plus one to take to your wedding!' Alex had pursed her lips. 'Look, I swear to put my bridesmaiding duties right back on the top of my agenda, and by the way, I love David. I think you two are perfect together.'

The two women had hugged, arranged the next pre-wedding meeting, and Alex had gone on her way. But she never did get to meet Jackson. None of her friends ever did, nor had even seen a photo of him, because there were none, not even on Lydia's phone. As far as she knew, there was no documentary evidence at all that they had ever been together. Not like with Joanna, she thought ruefully. This year's group photo in front of the Christmas tree would probably be next year's Christmas card for her and Jackson, the happy couple.

As painful as it was, Lydia had to admit that, just because Jackson hadn't loved her, it didn't mean he didn't love Joanna. And Joanna obviously adored him; it was as if the missing ingredient she had been searching for, as she'd flitted from man to man, was finally present. Perhaps Jackson loved Joanna, and perhaps Joanna loved Jackson. And as for acting as if he'd never seen her before in his life . . . Well, Lydia supposed bitterly, if he loved Joanna, and he wanted to keep her, then what choice did he have? After all, what girl wants to think that her new boyfriend has slept with her best friend before her?

It was ridiculous, all of it. Snowed in, in the middle of nowhere, with the man she'd thought of as long gone and lost to her about to check into the room next door with her best friend; it was the sort of crazy coincidence that would be too farfetched even for a Rock Hudson and Doris Day film. But sadly, not so crazy in terms of her own life; this was Christmas, after all, the time of year that never seemed to meet up to her persistently idealistic hopes and expectations.

Lydia knew she couldn't go back downstairs and ruin Christmas for everyone. Not only was there no place to run to, she also realised that what wasn't meant for her was perhaps meant for Joanna. And she only wanted her friend to be happy. Besides, there was one other huge, glaring factor Lydia seemed to be overlooking. She had Stephen, Stephen loved her, and he was about to ask her to marry him. Her future was what she should be thinking about now, not the past. And this was *her* Christmas, the one she'd been looking for since she was a little girl who believed in Father Christmas. There was snow outside and the people she loved most in the world were all around her. Resolute, Lydia determined that the only thing she could do was take her cue from Jackson, and say nothing. And in the meantime, she had to concentrate on her future, and, more importantly, concentrate on being in love with Stephen.

Dimly, Lydia became aware of hot breath on her neck and something heavy on her chest. She frowned, muddled by sleep and dreams. Stephen kissed her ear.

'Pyjamas,' he said gleefully, running hands over the cotton. 'I love you in pyjamas.'

Groggily, Lydia forced herself to open her eyes to find Stephen, who was obviously a little worse for wear, smiling down at her.

'What time is it?' she asked him. After a hot bath and a large toothbrush mug of wine, she must have fallen asleep almost as soon as she'd climbed into bed. She'd forgotten that she'd told Stephen she'd be waiting for him. He, evidently, had not.

'Sexy time,' Stephen said, drunkenly, and it was so out of character that Lydia giggled. Honestly, she had never been less in the mood for the polite, affectionate, friendly sort of sex she had with Stephen, but it had been so long since they'd been close in that way that it seemed bad manners to refuse.

'Hope you're feeling better, because I'm going to ravish you, like that Darcy bloke does that Jane Brontë woman.' Raising a rakish brow, he began to unbutton her top.

'Darcy doesn't do any ravishing, as such,' Lydia admonished him fondly, as he fumbled with the third button. 'And it's Elizabeth Bennett and Jane Austen, there isn't a Brontë in sight.'

'Well, I do do ravishing,' Stephen said, his brow furrowed in concentration as he finally undid enough buttons to gain access to her bosom. 'Hmm. Boobs.'

Lydia lay back as she felt his hand slide over her breast, squeezing it, pulling back the material of her top to reveal one pink nipple, which he kissed and nipped at in quick succession. She closed her eyes as, growing bored with all the buttons, Stephen pushed her top up in a bunch under her chin.

'I've always loved that you're stacked,' he said, which was perhaps a little short on romance, but still heartfelt. Lydia felt that she shouldn't be too churlish. It was, after all, the first interest he'd shown in her for months, and a girl could only handle so much rejection before she got the message and gave up. He slid his body down hers, buried his face in her hair as his hand travelled lower, negotiating the drawstring of her pyjama bottoms with one hand, the other still firmly clamped on her bosom. One of her hips was under a little too much pressure from the weight of him, and her back hurt. But Lydia didn't say anything, instead making herself concentrate on his lips against her neck as his left hand pulled down her trousers.

Sex, Lydia thought. I'm about to have sex with the man I love and will probably marry. I should be so excited; I must show him that I am excited. She tried out a little groan to let Stephen know exactly how excited she was, and was disappointed that he didn't respond. Another moment passed and Lydia realised that, although his right hand was still clamped to her breast, he'd stopped moving, his breathing had evened out and then, to cap it all, he let out a snore.

'Stephen?' Lydia prompted him. 'Darling?'

The only response was another snore. Furiously,

Lydia pushed him off her body, pulling her pyjama top down as she climbed out of bed and marched into the bathroom. Running the cold tap, she let the water flow into her cupped hands and doused her heated face with it. After months without any sort of sex, he'd fallen asleep on her! She'd let him drunkenly molest her, like a schoolboy, and then . . . then he'd passed out. Bitterly, Lydia wondered if it was possible to feel any more humiliated or hurt than she did at that moment.

And then she heard it, the dull thud of the door shutting in the next-door bedroom, followed by peels of Joanna's distinctive seductive laughter. Hating herself, even as she did it, Lydia took the remaining tooth mug, pressed it to the wall and listened. Unable to make out words, she could only hear Jackson's deep tones against Joanna's lighter voice, a conversation punctuated by giggles. There were a few moments of silence and then a sort of rhythmical creaking. Realising a little too late exactly what she was listening to, Lydia dropped the glass, which fell unbroken into the sink with a thick thud.

Looking at herself in the mirror, Lydia took in her dark brown eyes staring back her, her long, tangled hair, her flushed cheeks, pyjama top half undone, exposing the curve of her breast. Everything seemed disjointed and out of place, as if the natural order of the universe was entirely out of line. Here she was, pulsating with life, love and lust, burning like a flame, her body and soul aching to be touched by somebody who – what was it Joanna had said? – somebody who understood her. And the possibility of that happening now seemed like a month of Christmases away.

'Your trouble is,' she told her reflection unhappily 'you've spent your life watching old movies in which happy endings always happen.'

But this was real life. This was *her* life. A life where her parents hated each other, and where Christmas – a proper storybook Christmas – had never existed for her. Where past lovers appeared with best friends, and made rampant love to each other while her boyfriend fell asleep on her. Surely now, Lydia thought painfully, as she heard Joanna climax typically dramatically in the next room, surely *now* things couldn't get any worse.

Chapter Six

22 December

Lydia awoke, almost immediately aware of two things: that the room, which looked less chic and infinitely more shabby in the cold light of day, was filled with that particular kind of artificial light that meant the outside world was smothered in snow; and secondly, that she was freezing cold. Dragging what was left of the covers up under her chin, she shivered and huddled against Stephen's indifferent back for some warmth. He had not stirred since passing out last night, except to roll over onto his side and take most of the quilt with him, tucking it between his legs as if he were embracing a lover. It came to something, Lydia thought ruefully, when the bed linen got more action than she did.

Gingerly, she poked a toe out of the covers and then yanked it back, noticing her breath misting in the air as she sat up. Looking around, she spotted a deep, dark crack, the sort of crack that usually harbours spiders, running down the wall opposite the bed, and although the room had been nicely painted and furnished, there was still an aged musty scent to it, as if it had not been lived in for a hundred years. It wasn't quite up to hotel standard yet, Lydia had to admit, wondering if she should mention her impressions to Katy or not.

'Bloody hell,' she whispered as she leaned over and touched the radiator, which looked so old that it should probably be an exhibit in some sort of museum. Last night, it had been boiling and gurgling away to its heart's content, but now it was silent and cold to the touch. Flinging herself back on the pillow, Lydia assessed her chances of going back to sleep and decided that, what with the risk of frostbite, not to mention the fact that one of her best friends was in bed in the next room with her secret ex-lover, the chances were low.

With a brief, scathing glance at Stephen's slumbering form, she braced herself and clambered out of bed, deciding to bypass looking for socks and pulling on her ankle boots as soon as her feet hit the icy cold boards. Stealing one of Stephen's many jumpers off the back of a chair, she tugged it on over her head before finding an official Heron's Pike dressing gown hanging behind the bathroom door and wrapping it tightly around her. True, she did look a bit like a style-starved Michelin man, but she was warm, which at this point was about the only plus in life she could think of.

Going into the little turret room, Lydia leaned against the windowsill and traced the tip of one finger along the lacy film of frost that had formed on the inside of the glass during the night, etching a beautifully symmetrical pattern across the glass. She pulled the towelling sleeve of the dressing gown down over her wrist and rubbed clean a circle of glass with the heel of her hand, then peered through it.

The outside world was silent and still. All signs of life had been muffled under acres of white, but Katy had been right about one thing. This was the perfect location for a hotel. The snowy mountains that bordered the lake looked majestic against the freezing blue sky. They were much bigger and more imposing than Lydia had ever imagined. The lake itself, laced with ice around its shores, stretched into the distance, its dark and calm waters keeping all its secrets under its smooth implacable surface. It was a landscape so raw and untamed that it made Lydia feel tiny – an insignificant scrap of humanity lost in an indifferent wilderness. Well, if you could call it being in a wilderness when you had an en-suite bathroom.

Her watch indicated that it was ten past eight, and yet the house seemed silent. Perhaps everyone had frozen to death in the night, which at least would get her out of any awkwardness over the next few days. More likely, most of them had all consumed at least the same amount of alcohol as her darling boyfriend had last night, and were still sleeping it off. Hugging the dressing gown around her, she set off to find breakfast, intent on keeping herself busy by boiling, poaching or scrambling something. Preferably, the brains of all the men who had ever wronged her, including the two still sleeping upstairs. But if those weren't available, then eggs would have to do.

It took a while to find the kitchen, and she only managed to do so by following the sound of Katy's trademark sanitised swearing that she reverted to whenever the children were around.

'Banana poops!' Katy yelled furiously as Lydia walked into the large but seemingly ill-equipped kitchen. Slate flagstones lined the floor, and the units and tiles looked like they would have been the height of fashion circa 1979. All Lydia could see was Katy's bottom. The rest of her was leaning into the depths of a rather aged-looking Aga.

'Fat, fat, teddies!' Katy growled. 'I knew it. I knew we should have done the kitchen first. Fat, f— f— fat teddies!'

'It's not the teddies' fault they are fat,' Tilly said, somewhat offended, colouring in what Lydia thought at first was a piece of paper and then realised was the table top. 'It's all the honey they have to eat to stay alive.' She looked thoughtful for a moment. 'Mummy, do teddies go to the dentist?'

'Twice a year,' Lydia said calmly, pausing to admire the child's rather spectacular doodle. 'Anything I can do to help?'

Katy looked up at her, her usually serene face wrought with distress. 'Can you install a new boiler? Ours has conked out again, which, judging by the fetching outfit you're wearing, you've already worked out for yourself. I don't know what I'm going to do, Lydia. It's pantsing freezing and of course nobody wants to come out to patch it up a couple of days before Christmas, and in this weather! And to cap it all, I can't pantsing get this pantsing thing working, and if I want to have it hot enough to cook Christmas dinner in, then today is the last chance I have to get it lit. Every time I think I've got it going, it goes out again. I pantsing hate farting Agas!'

'Pants, farts!' Tilly giggled, before adding forlornly. 'I'm awfully starving, Mummy.'

'Excuse me.' Lydia pressed the back of her hand against Katy's creased forehead. 'Who are you and what have you done with my friend Katy, you know the one that was reading *The Aga Cookbook* aloud back when the rest of us were living off Pot Noodle on toast? The one that spent her university years channelling Martha Stewart and owned her first set of homemade ceramic *napkin rings* by the time she was twenty-four?'

'That was then, before I actually had a f— farting Aga,' Katy wailed. 'No one said anything about them being bast . . . bar stewards. Honestly, Lydia, owning an Aga doesn't make me feel nearly as smug as I'd hoped!'

Lydia smiled, hugging Katy tightly; the poor woman was clearly suffering from a serious bout of reality.

'Okay, well . . . It's not the end of the world if it's not working. It probably needs some sort of service, or something. You'll be able to get it up and running before New Year, I bet. And in the meantime, you made a feast last night, how did you do that?'

'That thing,' Katy said sullenly, nodding at a stand-alone electric cooker that was stuffed in the corner. It looked decades old, was dented and slightly rusty around the hob, and Lydia had to admit that, if she hadn't been in the presence of her uncharacteristically highly-strung and stressed-out dear friend, she would have immediately recommended that it be condemned as a health and safety hazard. Still, looks weren't always everything, and Katy had clearly been using it for weeks, judging by the large quantities of what looked like homemade mince pies, mini Yule logs and brandy snaps that were stacked up in Tupperware all around the kitchen.

'Well, that looks perfectly up to the job of cooking a turkey to me,' Lydia lied.

'I know, it's just that I'll have to do everything in shifts, and try and keep stuff warm while I'm waiting for other stuff to cook, and . . . and . . . oh f— fiddle sticks, Lydia. How am I ever going to cook breakfast for twenty people every day on that pile of junk? I told Jim a kitchen was more important than all those flood-lights, I told him!'

'Katy, breathe,' Lydia said firmly, pointing at the seat next to Tilly. 'Sit down. I'll make coffee and breakfast.'

'But you're the guest,' Katy complained. 'I was going to do a great big feast in the dining room, with cinnamon lattes and . . . and gingerbread croissants.'

'Please let Aunty Lydia make breakfast,' Tilly begged her, plaintively. 'So that I can eat again.'

'Sit!' Lydia commanded her. 'Let's sort us, and Tilly, out first, and then I'm sure we can rustle up something for everyone else. Relax. I've got this all under control.'

'Isn't that what you said when you were trying to hail us a taxi back from that night club, and it turned out to be a police car and we all spent hours in a cell?'

'Yes, that's true, but I was eighteen then. I'm a grown-up woman now.'

'Debatable,' Katy said, but she was smiling as she leaned her chin on her hands and watched Lydia fill the kettle and heap spoonfuls of instant coffee into two mugs, and hot chocolate into another. Sensing something food related was afoot, Vincent appeared from somewhere, shuffled in, sniffed the air and then collapsed in an unruly heap under the table to await whatever gastronomic delights might come his way, courtesy of the ever-generous Tilly.

'I wish I had fur like Vincent.' Tilly shivered. 'I'm an icicle!'

'I know, darling, I'm sorry. I'm sure that as soon as

Daddy gets up, he'll sort it. He did last time, remember? Although, to be honest, I think that had more to do with luck than judgement . . .'

'I've got an idea,' Lydia said, clapping her hands together and grinning at Tilly. 'Why don't you take this smelly, hairy dog and your freezing little feet, and go and jump on Daddy until he's up? I promise you I'll have reams of toast and hot chocolate ready by the time you get back.'

'Okay!' Tilly was obligingly excited by the idea, unlike Vincent, who had to be forcibly persuaded to leave his vantage point under the table with a firm prod from Lydia's pointed toe.

'Jim is not going to appreciate that,' Katy said, hugging to her chest the mug of coffee that Lydia handed her, defrosting the tip of her nose in the steam. 'He's not a morning person, he says. It must be a new thing, though, because when he worked in the city he was always up at six a.m. and at his desk by seven. I thought I'd see more of him out here, more of him awake, I mean.'

'Perhaps he's just kicking back, you know, getting into the country pace of life,' Lydia said, as she discovered a large fridge brimming with food, and set about cracking eggs into a bowl before whipping them with a fork.

'Or perhaps he's just a lazy sod who's quite happy to act the lord of the manor while his wife does everything else,' Katy replied, with more than a hint of bitterness.

'Is everything okay with you, Katy?' Lydia asked with concern. 'I thought this was supposed to be your dream? Is life here not as idyllic as you'd hoped?' Lydia asked, handing Katy the first round of toast to come out of the toaster for her to butter.

'Yes, yes it *is*,' Katy said, seemingly cautiously. 'I'm just tired and cold, that's all. I'm not being fair. Jim's worked so hard on this place, getting it ready. And we've spent almost everything we have, already, which is a bit of a worry when the kitchen still needs doing, and the boiler's so ancient . . . Anyway, I suppose it's only fair that he gets a rest before we open for business, officially. It's just that . . .'

'You could do with a rest too?' Lydia prompted her.

Katy nodded. 'It's my own fault. We could have had a quiet Christmas, just the four of us. All this was my idea. I so wanted you all to see what a good job we've done on the place. And I know how much you like the idea of a traditional Christmas . . . I really wanted to be the one to give you that, after all those terrible Christmases you used to tell us about, like the one when your mother had 'flu and couldn't get out of bed and you had to make yourself beans on toast.'

It was just like Katy to be so sweet, but Lydia didn't want her to feel guilty that her perfect Christmas wasn't going to plan. 'I like beans on toast, and anyway it was a wonderful idea, and it *is* going to be a lovely Christmas, and you are going to be brilliant hoteliers, I promise,' Lydia reassured her, mentally crossing her fingers as she poured the eggs into the frying pan. 'You know what it's like, these things always come together brilliantly at the last minute, you'll see.'

'So what do you think of him?' Katy asked her.

'Jim? Bit of a twat, but basically okay.'

Katy giggled, taking no offence. 'No, what do you think of Joanna's new bloke? He is rather handsome, isn't he? And funny? You should have seen Jo-Jo last night after you went to bed, she literally looked like the cat that got the cream.' Lydia's egg scrambling slowed down as the weight of the situation in which she had found herself settled on her shoulders. 'And when you think about it, that's not like her at all to be so keen,' Katy continued. 'I can't think of a single past boyfriend that she hasn't picked on or criticised from the beginning. But with this Jack, it's like the sun shines out of his very pert and muscular arse.'

'So, what do you know about him?' Lydia asked carefully, tipping out steaming eggs onto Katy's toast.

'Not much, just that he's something big in publishing, lived in the UK for a couple of years, is the world's most fantastic lover. Joanna says he's never been serious about anyone, always been a confirmed bachelor . . . until now. I don't think she knows for sure, but she suspects he's been a bit of a player in the past. Well, of course he has, look at him.' Katy stared at her breakfast. 'I wouldn't mind him on toast, sunny side up. Anyway, I think that's partly what she likes about him. All her other men have been totally under the thumb, but he's his own man. Which is why she nearly imploded with excitement when she told us last night that, just before they came up here, he told her he'd never met another woman like her, and that he thought that what they had could be something really important.'

'Really,' Lydia said flatly, sitting opposite Katy, pushing her breakfast away.

'Are you all right, Lyds?' Katy asked her. 'I hope you don't mind me saying, but you seem a bit put out by Joanna and Jack? I know she can be a bit overpower- ingly smug sometimes, but, to be fair to her, I've never seen her like this about a man before. I think she might actually love him.'

'I know, I know it's just . . . Katy, you're not going to believe this, but . . .' Before Lydia could say any more, Jackson appeared in the doorway, his honey- coloured hair all messed up, looking sleepy eyed and very kissable.

'Thank God, at least it's a little warmer in here,' he said. 'It's freezing upstairs. Joanna refuses to get up until I've brought her coffee and got the fire going in our room. Do you have any matches?'

'Kettle's there,' Lydia replied, nodding in its direction,

preventing Katy from offering to do it for him. She studied her toast, sensing his eyes on her as he found some mugs and switched the kettle back on, wondering if he recognised her at all, his play-acting at never having met her so believable that she was almost convinced herself.

'I'm so sorry about the cold,' Katy told him. 'The boiler's ancient, it's given up the ghost again. Do you know anything about boilers?'

'Pot boilers only, I'm afraid,' Jackson said, running his hands through his hair. 'I'm sorry, I'm not really very practical.'

'Oh really? I'd heard you were rather good with your hands,' Katy said, her giggles trailing off as she saw Lydia's stony expression.

Fortunately, before Katy could pick up on any tension between the two of them, a whirling cyclone of children and dog swept into the room.

'Daddy did very bad swearing when I got in bed with him,' Tilly giggled, sliding back into her seat, with Vincent taking his place at her feet, all of them considerably cheered by the appearance of food.

As he sat down, Jake reached over and grabbed a piece of Katy's toast. 'But he is getting up now, even though he says his mouth tastes like a rat's arse,' the boy added.

'Daddy said Vincent had better learn to swim,' Tilly said, as she messily fed Vincent scrambled eggs. 'He said next time that sodding dog gets in his bed he's going to drown him the lake, just like Mad Molly.'

'There is no Mad Molly!' Katy rolled her eyes. 'Daddy is an idiot!'

'Mummy!' Tilly looked appalled. 'How rude!'

Despite her mood, Lydia smiled at Tilly balking at her mum's use of idiot when clearly her dad had just subjected her to worse.

'Daddy is an idiot! Daddy is an idiot!' Jake chanted, more or less in Lydia's ear. Seeing her chance to not be in a room with Jackson Blake, Lydia jumped up with the sort of energetic enthusiasm she usually reserved only for shopping and court, and clapped her hands together.

'I know!' she said, cheerfully. 'Let's put on our coats and scarves and wellies and go and be the first to make footprints in the snow!'

'But we're not dressed,' Tilly said, looking at her mother. 'We can't go outside in our jammies, can we?'

'Who cares?' Lydia clapped her hands. 'It's Christmas, we can do whatever we want . . .' She hesitated. 'We're allowed, right, Katy, as long as we wrap up warm?'

'Well, I suppose so, as long as you . . .' Whatever Katy had been about to say was lost in the deafening cheers.

Amid the chatter and scramble to get dressed in as many layers as possible, Katy smiled at her, silently mouthing thank you, unaware of Lydia's urgent need to be anywhere that Jackson Blake was not.

As the children got togged up in the lean-to attached to the side of the house, Lydia reluctantly slipped off her lovely boots and, still barefoot, borrowed the likeliest looking pair of wellies and a thick woollen coat that was probably Jim's but looked the warmest candidate, and headed outside into the pristine white day.

It was a decision she instantly regretted, particularly as it turned out that the snowdrift she stepped into was considerably deeper than the height of her borrowed footwear. Icy snow leeched inside the rubber and her feet were instantly wet and freezing. Whimpering miserably, Lydia knew she couldn't go back inside now, not until Jackson had made Joanna's breakfast and left the kitchen. Not after she had done such a good job of looking fun and outdoorsy, attributes that, although she was sure Jackson didn't give two hoots about, were nevertheless the best chance she had of clinging on to her dignity right now. Utterly uncomfortable, she waddled determinedly from one frozen foot to the other, supposing that five toes on each foot weren't strictly necessary, anyway. Rigor mortis set in around her frozen face as she watched the children tear around after Vincent, who was bounding through the snow like a puppy reborn, yapping for joy as he buried his snout in the alien stuff and tossed it in the air. Lydia was finding it impossible to smile, even though she wanted to.

Looking around her at the breathtaking landscape that was so silently powerful, she thought that, if she had to die of stubbornness-induced hypothermia, at least Heron's Pike had to rank as one of the world's top ten most beautiful places to do it.

'Snowball fight!' Jake announced with sudden ruthless terror, giving Lydia precisely no seconds to duck out of the way of the freezing, if thankfully soft, snowball that exploded on her nose.

'Oh, you little . . .' Galvanised into action, she kneeled down, desperately attempting and failing to gather up the powdery snow to fashion into a ball, while the children, who had remarkable aim and dexterity for such small people, pelted her with round after round of perfectly formed missiles, most of which hit their mark, despite Vincent's best efforts to catch them mid-flight.

'Not fair!' Lydia complained fruitlessly. 'Give me a chance . . . Haven't you heard of the Geneva Convention?' Apparently they had not, because within minutes her face was red raw, and her hair and layers of clothes were soaked through and clinging to her damp skin. Just as she was about to surrender, and beg for a quick death, reinforcements came out of nowhere. Lydia was still struggling with only her third pathetic snowball, when four or five perfectly formed spheres shot over her head in quick succession, one of them landing squarely on Jake's shoulder, prompting him to yell like a banshee.

'This is war!' he shouted. Lydia spun round to find Jackson re-arming.

'I haven't had this much fun since I was a kid in Central Park. Get behind me, ma'am,' he joked, doing his best GI impression. 'I'll be your personal human shield.'

'Charge!' Jake had scooped a wad of frozen snow off the top of a bench and was running at them with an excited, snappy, yappy Vincent in tow and a screeching Tilly in hot pursuit.

Stepping in front of her, Jackson turned his back on the oncoming assault, just as Vincent hit with the full force of four paws, knocking man onto woman and both of them into the thick snow. From somewhere, buried as she was underneath Jackson's chest, Lydia heard Jake triumphantly shout, 'Subject destroyed, retreat!' and Vincent's barking recede into the distance. Wriggling upwards, she opened her eyes to find Jackson on top of her, his nose millimetres from the frozen tip of hers. For one perfect, happy moment, Lydia forgot everything except that it was so very good to see him.

'Hello, you,' she said, smiling faintly, in spite of everything.

'Lydia Grant,' he whispered. 'It's been a very long time.'

'So you do remember me, then?'

'You are not someone I am likely to forget.'

As they stared at each other, Lydia realised that, even through the many layers of clothes she was wearing, it felt as if there were nothing separating her from her former lover. She could feel the rapid beat of his heart against hers, and was overwhelmed by a sudden ache to touch him, to entwine her fingers in his hair and kiss him, just as she had done hundreds of times before. That would have been tricky, though, considering he was now the property of her best friend, and they weren't supposed to know each other.

Coming to her senses, Lydia struggled to break free, but Jackson had her pinned to the spot, reluctant to let her go.

'What are you doing?' she asked him, desperately. 'Look, if you want to act like we never met, fine, I get it. But don't chase me out here and find an excuse to roll around with me. You're with Joanna now, and whatever we had is over, isn't it?'

'I . . . I know.' Jackson looked embarrassed, and for one triumphant moment Lydia thought she'd gained the moral high ground. 'I only came out here to get my phone. You're . . . er . . . wearing my coat,' Jackson said, still making no move to get up.

'What? What on earth is it doing hanging up on the coat rack? Why didn't you hang it up in your room like a normal person?' Lydia fumed, uncaring that her anger was not precisely rational. 'Oh, get off me! Get off me right now!'

At last Jackson obliged, clambering up and brushing the snow off his body before extending a helping hand to Lydia.

'Just go away,' Lydia instructed him, realising with horror that her bottom appeared to have gone completely numb.

'Don't be so silly, take my hand.' Grudgingly, Lydia accepted, letting him pull her to her feet, but blocking his attempt to brush off some of the caking of snow. Jackson glanced up at the house, lowering his voice. 'Lydia, we need to talk. Get some things straight.'

Lydia pushed her wet hair off her face and sniffed. 'Look, it's fine. I get it. You went off me, you disappeared like the cowardly bullshit artist you clearly are, and I got over you. And now, for some reason that God alone knows, you're going out with Joanna Summer, one of my very best friends. I presume we have to pretend we don't know each other, because otherwise her pretty little nose might be put rather out of joint if she found out that the latest love of her life had once spent several solid weeks screwing her best friend in fifty different ways!'

Jackson's smile was infuriatingly sweet. 'Wow, was it only fifty? Look, I'm so sorry about how I behaved when I saw you last night. You were the very last person I expected to see. Joanna hasn't really talked about her friends that much, so I didn't know how to react. It seemed the best thing to do at the time and, well, with hindsight it was wrong and appalling behaviour, but I've never been in that situation before.' He seemed genuinely apologetic, which made Lydia hate him slightly more.

'Sure about that, are you?' she growled.

'I appreciate it must be difficult for you, but—'

'No!' Lydia cut him off, with a chop of her red-raw hand. 'It's not difficult at all. You see, Jackson, you and I are the very, very distant past. I'm with Stephen now. I met him a couple of weeks after you allegedly "went back to New York", actually, and yes, I am going to marry him. So you and Joanna can do what you like, as loudly as you like, which, by the way, is very loud and frankly rather vulgar. I don't care. Now let's just forget we ever knew each other and try and get through the next few days without ruining it for everyone, okay?'

'Okay, but . . .'

Lydia did not stay to hear what he had to say. She forced her numbed feet to carry her indoors, perhaps not as gracefully as she would have liked, but just as fast as she could manage on her useless stumps of frost-bitten legs.

'Bloody hell, darling, you look like you've been ravished by the abominable snow man,' an immaculate, TV-ready Joanna declared as Lydia entered the kitchen with her hair plastered to her ruddy cheeks, and feet already painfully thawing out. 'I wondered what could possibly be keeping Jackson from delivering my breakfast as promised.'

Joanna pretended to be stern with Jackson, who contritely kissed her on the lips.

'Sorry, sweetheart, I was rescuing this fair maiden from very short bandits.'

As Joanna giggled, Lydia gritted her teeth, relieved even to see that Stephen had finally emerged from his coma, although she was still not talking to him after last night's performance, or rather lack of one.

'Hello, love,' Stephen said a little sheepishly from the doorway. He looked like death warmed up, and was obviously nursing a shocking hangover. 'You okay?'

Ignoring him, Lydia looked at Joanna, with her long red hair cascading down her perfectly white, silk dressing gown, and for one horrible moment she considered pouring the mug of steaming coffee that Katy had handed her over her dear friend's head. And then she remembered that none of this was Joanna's fault. Or Stephen's. None of it was Jackson's fault, possibly. Maybe it was just some cruel joke the universe had decided to play on her, Lydia Grant. Perhaps she'd committed some really terrible crimes against women in a past life, like making hipster jeans eternally fashionable or Pringles addictive, for which she was now being forced to atone.

'I'm going to get dressed,' Lydia said, quite calmly, she thought, considering the circumstances, looking at Katy. 'And if any of my toes fall off once they've defrosted, I'm suing your children.'

It took some time to rub the blood back into her various extremities, and several more minutes thawing herself out with a hair dryer, before Lydia began to feel human again. Once she'd raised her body temperature to acceptable levels, she found a pair of the aforementioned evil hipster jeans, that only a woman with no hips could ever truly look good in, pulled on a contrasting grey and white vest combo, and finished it off with a knee-length off-the-shoulder sweater that was probably a bit loosely knitted to be practical, considering the Artic conditions, but which looked sexy. And Lydia decided that, right now, looking as sexy as a quite short, quite curvy, brunette girl could when standing next to a quite tall and willowy, very beautiful, semi-famous redhead was more important to her than being warm, even if her very best efforts would pale into insignificance next to Joanna's effortless beauty. She brushed out her hair, until it wended its way in long, dark ripples down her back, and smudged a little eyeliner around her chocolate-brown eyes, before applying the mascara she never usually went anywhere without. A few squirts of Coco Chanel and she felt, and more importantly looked, human again, and able to face the farce that her life had somehow descended into.

Returning downstairs, she found everyone – bar Jake, who was industrially building what appeared to be a very female snowwoman outside the window – in the sitting room, with plates of toast on their laps and mugs of steaming coffee balanced on chair arms.

Although Stephen was most certainly not off the hook, Lydia chose to take his toast from him and sit on his lap, wrapping her arms around him and planting a kiss on his cheek, quite amused by the sudden confusion on his face. The room was pleasantly silent for a moment, as everyone munched through bloomer bread, the only noise coming from Jim stoking the fire and Vincent snoring in the corner. Covertly, Lydia examined Jackson through her lashes. He had also changed clothes, and was sitting by the window, with Joanna curled up against him, looking utterly in love and relaxed. Alex had assumed her position in the middle of the sofa, with her feet up on the stool, resting a plate on her bump. David sat next to her, his head buried in a book about childbirth.

'All I'm saying is,' David said, breaking the silence, 'if anything did happen, we wouldn't be able to boil water very efficiently without a working boiler.'

'David,' Alex snapped at him. 'Nothing is going to happen, I'm not due for five weeks, remember? Will you please stop bleating on about boiling water!'

'I'm just saying,' David repeated under his breath.

'And how are you this morning, darling?' Stephen whispered in Lydia's ear, as Alex and David bickered. From experience, she knew he was being particularly affectionate due to the fact that he couldn't exactly remember what happened last night, and wasn't exactly sure how much trouble he was in.

'David has got a point,' Katy said, with a now exhausted Tilly nodding off on her lap. What *are* we going to do about the boiler, Jim? No, heating, no hot water?'

Jim shook his head. 'I tried resetting it, like last time – but there's nothing. It's totally dead, and none of the plumbers I know can make it out before next week.'

'Oh, no.' Katy looked appalled. 'I'm so sorry, everyone.'

'There is this one bloke. I have a drink with him in the pub every now and then. He's some sort of handyman, from what I can gather, and seems to be a bit of a Jack-of-all-trades. I could mosey on down with the lads, here, and see if he's in? He lives in the village, so even if he's not in, he may well be in the pub. I'm sure we could track him down. He might be able to keep the boiler going for a few more days.'

'A drunk, unqualified Jack-of-all-trades is not exactly the sort of person I was hoping to entrust the lives of my children to,' Katy said miserably.

'Mal, in the pub, says he's great. Says we should talk to him about any stuff we need doing up here. Look, he seems decent enough to me, at least we could get him to take a look at it. See if he can doing anything?'

Katy sighed. 'Typical that you getting help involves a trip to the pub.'

'Can I help it if it's the hub of the local community?'

Jim asked her. 'You should come down some time, it would do you good to meet a few people.' In response, Katy kissed her sleeping daughter on the top of the head.

'Okay, but take Jakey and Vincent with you, a good snowy walk might actually mean Jake sleeps for more than five minutes tonight.' At the sound of his name, Vincent lifted his head, sighing heavily and looking as though trudging for a couple of miles through snow was the very last thing he had on his mind.

'Right, lads.' Jim rubbed his hands together. 'Who's coming on a rescue mission to the pub?'

'I think I should stay here,' David said. 'Just in case . . .'

'Go to the bloody pub!' Alex shouted, clapping her hand over her mouth when she remembered dozing Tilly.

'Fine,' David said. 'Only there might not be any mobile service, so . . .'

'Just bloody go!' Alex warned him.

'What about you, Jack? Want to experience a genuine British pub?'

'Oh, go on, darling.' Joanna draped one hand over his shoulder. 'Once you're out of the way, I can brag properly about how wonderful you are.'

'Sure.' Jackson smiled. 'Why not? Sounds like fun.'

'Don't all die in a ditch, will you,' Lydia said churlishly.

'And remember to come back, we're all freezing here!' Katy warned Jim.

'Don't you worry about us,' Joanna got to her feet and, producing her capacious Orla Kiely handbag from the side of the sofa, brought out a bottle of fine single malt whiskey. 'As soon as the sun is over the yard arm, I'm sure we'll be able to keep ourselves amused for a few hours.'

'Speak for yourself,' Alex said, gloomily.

Lydia and Joanna went with the men as they hunted out a sufficient number of boots and coats to protect them on their journey, a very reluctant Vincent refusing to be enthused by the idea of walkies.

'What kind of dog are you, anyway?' Jim asked him, as the dog in question looked dolefully at his lead. 'What normal dog doesn't always want to go out?'

'It's terribly exciting,' Joanna said, cheerfully, as she zipped up Jackson's jacket. 'It's just like Scott of the Antarctic.'

'Hopefully not just like.' David smiled. 'You will keep an eye on Alex, won't you?'

'Hard not to, she does practically eclipse the sun.' Joanna smiled back at her friend's husband. 'Of course, David, Alex will be fine. Her bark is much worse than her bite, you know,' she told him.

'Oh, I know! Her bark is part of the reason I love her. Never scared of anything, my Alex.'

Just as they were about to depart, Stephen pulled Lydia to one side. 'You look beautiful,' he told her. 'It seems like a long time since I've seen you in anything other than a business suit.'

'You had your chance to see me in a lot less last night,' Lydia hissed at him.

'Oh, God.' Stephen looked appalled. 'Did I pass out? Right in the middle?'

Lydia nodded. 'Well, we hadn't really got further than second base, but still it was extremely disappointing.'

'I'm so sorry,' Stephen said. 'I'm just not that used to drinking, I suppose. It's not that I didn't want to, I did, I do. I really do. You look so great today, I'd like to see you wearing that holey jumper and nothing else.' Taking Lydia by surprise, he pulled her into his arms and kissed her passionately. Surrendering into his embrace, she waited for the fire to kick in, in the pit of her belly, and for her own desire to rise to meet his. She waited. And waited. Perhaps her longing was still frozen solid somewhere in her core, because all she felt when Stephen kissed her were his wet lips and irritating stubble.

'Bloody hell, you two,' Jim joked. 'Get a room – oh, you have.'

As they broke apart, Lydia resisted the urge to wipe her mouth with the back of her hand, and did her best sexy, smouldering smile for Stephen, sensing Jackson's eyes on her. 'We'll have to pick up where we left off later,' she purred in a loud whisper, so unlike herself that for a second Stephen looked a little alarmed.

'Must be something in the water,' David said, nodding at Joanna, who'd more or less pinned Jackson against the wall and was quite going to town over the business of a goodbye kiss.

'Honey,' Jackson spluttered, as she finally allowed him to come up for air. 'I'm only going to the pub, not Iraq.'

'I know, it's just that you are so delicious.' Joanna let him go, hooking her arm through Lydia's. 'Oh, Lydia, isn't it lovely when your man is such a hunk?'

'Very,' Lydia agreed, smiling to see Jackson flush red. 'Now, let's go and find some whiskey glasses; in these freezing conditions, it's practically medicinal.'

'All I know is,' Joanna said quietly, a tiny delighted smile on her lips, 'I have never been so happy. I mean really happy, you know? It's not like in the past, with Ted or Sebastian, or any of the others. Even from the beginning with those two I could feel it wasn't quite right. Yes, Ted had a speed boat, and Seb was hung like a racehorse, but since meeting Jack, I've realised that none of those things really matter if you love someone. Not that he doesn't have a massive cock, he totally does.'

Joanna winked at Lydia, who tried her very best not to gag in horror, drowning the impulse with a large sip of whiskey.

'And do you think he feels the same way about you?' Katy asked. 'I mean, do you think he's serious? Will we all be arguing over your choice of bridesmaids dresses in a few months?' Joanna said nothing. 'And can they not be puce?'

'There is nothing wrong with puce,' Alex insisted.

'It sounds like puke, that's all I'm saying,' Katy muttered.

'All I know is that he makes me so happy,' Joanna said. 'And I know it sounds corny, but when I'm with him I feel like my life finally means something. You know, some people might think I live an awfully shallow existence, selling Slankets to pensioners and the unemployed, and I suppose in many ways I do. The funny thing is, up until now, I haven't minded that it's all been about the glamour and the money, the celebrity . . .'

'Celebrity?' Alex raised an eyebrow.

'Suddenly none of that matters, and I find that I'm thinking of things I've never thought of before. Settling down, baking, children . . .'

'Not putting your latest engagement ring on e-Bay,' Alex added.

Joanna was unperturbed, adding wistfully, 'It's like I've found my soulmate.'

Lydia watched as Katy sighed and Alex grinned.

'Wow, Jo-Jo, you really mean it, too, don't you?'

Joanna nodded, smiling. 'I know, it's weird for me to be so serious, right?'

'Do you think he's sincere?' Lydia asked her. 'I'm just saying, you haven't really known him very long, have you? And, you know, some men, they play the game and say all the right things, say anything, in order to get what they want. Some men are even in love with the idea of falling in love, just like some girls. They live for the chase and getting girls to fall for them. Then as soon as they know they've got you, they move on, leaving you stranded and feeling like a fool.'

Alex and Katy exchanged loaded looks, but Joanna seemed immune to any negative vibe, she was so cosseted in love.

'I do know what you mean, Lyds,' she said serenely. 'I've been around the block. It's not like I haven't met some slime balls in my time. But Jack's not like that. It's different with him, I swear. It's like we're meant to be and . . . I hadn't mentioned this before, because I don't want you lot planning a wedding before he's had a chance to buy a ring, but he's taking me back to New York in the New Year, to meet his mum! Imagine, me, meeting a mum. How will I know if I'm any good at it? I haven't met my own mother in the best part of a decade.'

Typical Joanna, Lydia thought, to shrug off the persistent state of estrangement that existed between her and her parents with such marked flippancy, although Lydia knew that their lack of interest in her life cut her friend to the quick. They'd more or less disowned her when she failed to finish her degree, and point blank refused to acknowledge any of the success she'd had as a model or TV presenter. They found the whole thing terribly vulgar, Joanna told her once, which was mainly why she did it. Some years ago, Joanna had decided she simply didn't need the constant disappointment of her family's disapproval, and stropped trying to impress them. What hurt her the most, though, was that they hadn't seemed to notice or care.

'He's taking you to meet his mother?' Katy gasped. 'That sounds serious?'

'Yes, right after my annual New Year party – you are all coming, aren't you?' Joanna beamed. 'This year it's going to be extra special with Jackson on my arm.'

'Well, I'll be working,' Katy said.

'And I'll be pregnant. Still,' Alex said.

'But you will be there, won't you, Lyds?' Joanna asked her. 'I insist that you are there.'

'I wouldn't miss it,' Lydia assured her, taking in a deep breath. 'Well, it really does sound like you have met your perfect man.'

She stared into the amber depths of her whiskey glass, chewing on her bottom lip. Jackson was taking Joanna to meet his mum. And because she knew him, she knew Jackson would only do that if things were serious between him and Joanna, because in the short time she'd known him, she'd learned that his family meant the world to him. So he must really mean all those things when he said them to Joanna. The realisation hurt her all the more. How rock solid were they? she wondered bitterly. Would Joanna still think her 'Jack' was so flawless if she knew about his affair with Lydia? Feeling the whiskey burn the back of her throat, Lydia tried to picture the look on Joanna's face if she told them all her secret, then and there.

'Anyway, enough about me and my sickening happiness.' Joanna grinned. 'Anything you want to share with us, Lyds?' She waggled her eyebrows conspicuously, and Lydia knew exactly what secret she wanted her to spill. She shook her head.

'Me? No, nothing exciting ever happens to me.' Lydia smiled at Alex. 'What about you? Does David really drive you up the wall as much as you make out?'

'No, not really . . . I know he loves me,' Alex said, as she sipped her ginger tea. 'And I love him. It's just that he fusses so much. It's like the only thing I am to him is pregnant, like I'm just a massive great big incubator for his progeny. He doesn't see anything but this bump any more.'

'Oh, don't be silly,' Joanna said, sipping the fiery, golden liquid from her glass. 'That man adores you, of course he's going to be a bit jumpy. It's his first baby. Not everyone can be as calm and as in control as you.'

'Me?' Alex laughed. 'I'm bloody terrified, and I can't even get drunk before lunch to drown out the fear.'

'Not you, Alex,' Katy said, stroking slumbering Tilly's

hair from her forehead. 'Nothing frightens you, it's one of the things I've always envied most about you.'

'That's not true,' Alex said, cradling her bump. 'When my mum died I was terrified then. It was the hardest time of my life, a time when I really didn't know if I could keep going. I don't think I would have, if it hadn't been for you lot.' Lydia reached out, covering Alex's hand with her own. 'And then the thought that something might happen to me, that I might get cancer too and have to leave little this little mite. That keeps me up all night, wondering if I should even have got pregnant. What if I die and he or she grows up not even knowing who I was?'

'Don't be silly,' Joanna said gently. 'Losing your mum so young was awful, but do you think she would have wanted you to have a life half lived? Don't forget, we all knew your mum. Remember that time she came for a surprise visit in the first year, and made us clean the house from top to bottom, standing over us with a litre of disinfectant? She was just as scary and tenacious as you, and she'd be so proud of everything you've done, Alex, and so proud of what a brilliant mum you're going to be. Besides, you get checked out every year, so if, heaven forbid, they ever do spot anything, you will be treated early and everything will be fine. All that good work you've been doing for breast cancer research has started to pay off, you know.'

Lydia smiled, reaching out to hug Alex. That was

the thing about Joanna. Just when you started to believe she was all gloss and surface, she showed her true colours. Deep down, under all the artifice, was a sweet, caring woman, who knew exactly the right thing to say. The woman that all of them had loved as a sister since the moment they'd met her touting for flatmates in Fresher's Week at university.

'Thanks, Jo.' Alex mustered a smile. 'It does help to hear you say it. Now all I have to worry about is that I am going to have a baby! Fuck!'

'Are you scared about the labour?' Lydia asked her, as Joanna topped up her glass with her second large whiskey. The warmth of the alcohol was slowly melting through her body, and had done a lot to take the edge off her secret nightmare. Besides, hopefully the men would be gone for a very long time, and here she was in front of a crackling fire with some good whiskey, a mountain of mince pies and her favourite people. For a few hours at least, life was okay. 'Because my dad's latest wife says it's not as painful as you think it's going to be, and when it does get so painful that you think you might die, that's when you know you've reached the hardest part and it's all downhill from then on! Unless something goes wrong, of course . . .'

'Thanks, Lyds, if it was the labour that I was worried about, then, yes, that would definitely put my mind at rest,' Alex said sarcastically. 'But no, it's not that. It's what comes after.' Alex smiled fondly at Tilly, who was curled up asleep with Vincent on the sofa. 'I'm not like you, Katy. I'm not a natural mother. I do what I want, when I want to. If I want to go for a sponsored trek along the Andes, at a moment's notice, then I go. I don't even ask David, I tell him. But I can't do that with a baby, can I? A baby's going to need me, to feed it, and stuff. And you can't run twenty miles a week with a baby in tow, or work ten-hour days. I was really happy when I fell pregnant, so excited, and then one day I couldn't bend down to lace up my trainers, and it hit me. I'm not really a baby person.'

'Of course you are.' Joanna patted her on the knee. 'I'm sure you are, I don't think God would let you get so royally knocked up unless somewhere deep in there, beneath that tough exterior, beats the heart of a woman made to smell of baby sick and need incontinence pads.'

'Bitch!' Alex smiled despite the insult.

'I don't think you have to worry,' Katy said, stroking Tilly's forehead. 'Nobody's a natural mother; I know I wasn't. For the first three months after Jake was born, I felt like sticking my head in a gas oven every day. Thank God we only had electric . . .'

'So far, none of this is helping,' Alex told her friends ruefully.

'What I mean is, just because you get pregnant, you don't suddenly and automatically have all the maternal wisdom in the world downloaded into your psyche. You have to learn by your mistakes and sort of feel your way. And, yes, it is a pain not being able to do what you want, when you want, any more. But all of that is outweighed by the totally amazing, all-consuming love you will feel for your baby. Even when it throws up on you and you don't notice till you're in the super-market . . .'

'But what if I don't love it?' Alex asked Katy anxiously. 'What if it hates me?'

'Have it adopted!' Joanna suggested, making Lydia giggle. 'By Madonna or Elton John – oh, or Angelina. She likes a baby.'

'I promise you right here and now that you and that the little person in there . . .'

'Massive person,' Joanna interjected, digging Lydia in the ribs.

'. . . will adore each other unreservedly,' Katy finished, shooting Joanna her best chastening look.

'I hope you're right,' Alex said. Katy leaned over and kissed her on the cheek.

'Of course I am. Trust me, becoming a mother is the one thing I know something about.'

Alex looked a little reassured as she balanced her empty mug on her bump. 'I tell you what, though, what I wouldn't do for a good old-fashioned forward-facing fuck!'

Lydia glowed with happiness as she watched her friends dissolve in giggles at the unexpected comment. Despite all of the nasty surprises that life might hold in store for a person, there was always one thing she could count on. Her friends – they would never let her down. And at that moment, she knew with total certainty that nothing and no one would ever make her do anything to hurt any one of them. As long as Jackson Blake could keep their past relationship to himself, then so could she.

Chapter Seven

The sun had long since retreated behind the low and brooding cloud that hung, full of snow, over the peaks of the mountains, when the men returned, plus one. It was no coincidence that by that time all the women – bar Alex – were a little tipsy, and even she had caught the girly, giggly mood, despite her enforced sobriety. The girls could spot the little party, torches flashing, coming round the bend, and went en masse to greet them.

'We have returned bearing expertise!' Jim said, his ruddy cheeks due either to the cold or beer, or most likely both. Jake was slung over one shoulder, clutching a can of fizzy orange in one hand and a packet of Skittles in the other. Lydia could almost see Katy waving goodbye to her easy bedtime and unbroken night.

'A little bit worse for wear,' Stephen told her, kissing her fondly. 'Hey, hey . . . Shall we go and light the fire in the bedroom, know what I mean?'

'So who is this?' Joanna had wound herself around Jackson the moment she'd seen him, practically dragging him inside and out of his coat, and kissing both of his cheeks feverishly. But even in the first throws of love, Joanna was not blind to a new male specimen standing in the hallway.

The handyman stood looking rather awkward, with his hands in his pockets, glancing around at the house, finding a particularly fascinating bit of cornicing to focus on as the women rather obviously studied him. He was a little younger than Stephen, probably more or less Lydia's own age, with longish, dark curly hair and eyes as black and deep as the waters of the lake at the bottom of the garden. A growth of stubble added just the right finishing touch to his windswept look, which, even in his sensible country-person snow wear, had quite an impact on the girls.

'Blimey, you've brought us Heathcliff!' a slightly tipsy Lydia found herself saying out loud, drawing the attention of the handyman from the ceiling to her flushed face. 'Er . . . um. No offence, or anything.'

'None taken,' he said, with a smile, his accent pure Cumbrian. 'But you need to go back down south a hundred miles or so, if you want real Brontë Country.'

Lydia was surprised, and then in turn horrified that she was surprised he'd even heard of *Wuthering Heights*. As if he might be as wild and feral in all respects as he looked, and hadn't bothered going to school as he was too busy out killing deer with his bare hands, which as it happened wasn't such a terrible image.

'Are you sure you're qualified to look at my boiler?'

Katy asked him, the whiskey making her perhaps a tad more confrontational than was polite. Joanna and Alex cracked up, giggling like schoolgirls. 'Because, I have children in this house, and despite their father's insistence on poisoning them with additives, I do not wish them, or any of my friends, to be killed in an explosion.' She finished off her statement with a rather wayward point in the general direction of the boiler, followed by a little hiccup.

'Sorry, mate.' Jim clapped the handyman on the shoulder. 'Wife appears to be a bit rat-arsed.'

Lydia liked the handyman's twisty-mouthed, repressed smile. He was trying very hard not to laugh at them, which oddly enough only added to his allure.

'I'm Corgi registered, for installation and maintenance,' he told her politely. 'My name's Will, Will Dacre. I've got my paperwork, if you want to have a look?'

He rooted about in his tool kit, and produced some papers, which Katy took off him and scrutinised for several seconds before turning them the right way up and reading them again.

'Will's doing us a big favour,' Jim told his wife, depositing Jake unceremoniously on the floor and dropping a heavy arm around Katy's shoulder's, knocking her a little off balance. 'Not only did we have to drag him away from his lunch, it took us about an hour to walk back, and only partly because we are quite drunk.

The snow is mental, plus Will here reckons it's going to chuck it down some more in a minute. So the very least we owe the man is a drink and a hot dinner.'

'Do you understand the weather, Will?' Joanna fluttered her lashes, letting loose her hold of Jackson a little. 'Does your country upbringing mean you are terribly in tune with nature?'

'No, but I do have a weather app on my iPhone,' Will said. That twisty, trying hard not to laugh smile appeared again.

'So anyway, be nice to him, wife!' Jim commanded Katy.

'I suppose he looks qualified,' Katy said, eyeing Will suspiciously. 'And don't call me wife.'

'Right, men, draw your torches, let us commence to the cellar and fix shit!'

'Don't let him touch anything,' Katy warned Will. 'That's how it got broken in the first place. 'I'll make you some coffee.'

'Alcoholic coffee!' Jim shouted, as Stephen blew Lydia a kiss and followed the others towards the cellar door.

'Oh, my God,' Alex said. 'We are all going to die.'

'Still, the handyman's a bit of a shag, isn't he?' Lydia commented, her tongue loosened by whiskey, just at the precise moment Will walked back in to retrieve his tool kit. The girls hooted with laughter, Katy snorting through her nose, Joanna doubled up as Lydia stood there, two bright spots of colour igniting on her cheeks.

'I'll take that a compliment,' Will said, picked up his back and headed back to the cellar.

After Lydia had banged her head several times against the nearest wall, and the others had mostly stopped pointing and laughing at her, they came to the collective conclusion that it was probably a good idea to sober up, at least temporarily, so that they stopped trying to throw themselves at the local hunk and at least tried to appear to be respectable grown-up women.

Katy sent Jake off to colour something with Tilly, and Alex went along to ensure that, this time, they didn't colour in the enormously expensive reproduction wallpaper in the dining room, although she grumbled about always being the one to miss out on all the fun.

'Right, I'll start dinner – and Lydia, would you mind lighting the fires in the bedrooms, just in case Heathcliff down there doesn't get the pilot light going.'

'He can light my fire any time,' Joanna giggled, peering out of the window where a new snowfall was being dashed against the glass by merciless winds. 'With any luck, we'll all be snowed in together and we can devour him whole, starting at his toes.'

'You are doing the veg,' Katy informed Joanna, dumping one pile of potatoes and one of carrots in front of her.

'Doing the veg, you say?' Joanna seemed to find it a difficult concept to grasp. 'You know what you need? You need an EasyPeel Automatic Potato peeler, only fifteen ninety-nine, and with ten pounds worth of attachments absolutely free – yes, free, if you order before four p.m.'

'No, I don't,' Katy said, 'because I've got a peeler. It's you. Get on with it, it will do you good to get your hands dirty, for once.'

'Anyway Jo, why are you letching over Heathcliff? Aren't you supposed to be in love?' Lydia reminded her friend.

'Yes, Lydia, I am totally in love. As are you, aren't you? But how did you so succinctly put it? That Will is a bit of a shag, isn't he?'

Lydia found that there was nothing so effective as several large glasses of very nice whiskey when it came to taking the edge off her situation. Here she was in Joanna and Jackson's room, ignoring the rumpled bedclothes on the bed behind her and the trail of underwear Joanna had left across the carpet, and feeling really rather Zen about it. Perhaps it had been the look on Joanna's face when she'd been talking about Jackson, or the news that he planned to take Joanna back to New York. Either way, no matter how she felt or thought she'd felt about him in the past, that moment in her life was gone now. As Lydia inserted the fire lighters in among the logs, as Katy had shown her, she thought that, perhaps, as long as she remained permanently ever so slightly drunk on very good whiskey from now until the end of all eternity, she'd eventually be fine about it, and would maybe even possibly be a bridesmaid at Jackson and Joanna's highly alliterative wedding.

Lydia sat back on her knees, so engrossed in the tiny lick of fire creeping its way across the wood that she didn't notice the door open and shut behind her.

'It's a long time since I've found you in my bedroom,' Jackson said, making her jump.

'God, you gave me a fright,' Lydia said, beginning a smile before remembering her new whiskey-fuelled resolution. 'Sorry, Katy sent me off to be fire monitor. I'll get out of your way.' The room span a little as Lydia got to her feet, forcing her to take a moment and wait to find her feet.

'Don't rush off,' Jackson said. 'Jo's up to her elbows in potato peelings. Let's talk.'

Lydia sighed, forcing herself to look Jackson in the face – still that same boyish smile, those intense blue eyes, the look that made you feel like you were the only girl in the world, even though there was solid proof to the contrary.

'I just can't believe you're here,' Jackson said, looking her up and down with such close scrutiny that Lydia felt uncomfortable. 'You look exactly the same; you look beautiful. I've missed you, Lydia.'

Lydia raised her eyebrows, wishing her feet would move from this spot to which they seemed rooted.

'I know what you must be thinking, but you're wrong,' Jackson said. 'I didn't just disappear, or hide. That night, the night you insisted on going home to work on a case, I got a call from my mom. Dad had had a massive heart attack; it was touch and go. I had to go to the airport and get on a plane and deal everything else out later. All I could think about was being with my family. I never imagined it would be the end of us. I never meant for that text I sent you to be the last.'

'Really.' Lydia crossed her arms. 'So what happened, then? You suffered temporary amnesia about how to use a phone and your dad made a miraculous recovery?'

Jackson dropped his eyes from hers 'Hardly. It was the worst time of my life. He hung in there for a while, and we got to take him home, but he was very sick. A few weeks later, he was gone . . . I wanted to call you, to speak to you. But my mom needed me, and there's so much to deal with when someone dies. Not just the emotional stuff. I had to arrange my father's funeral, support Mom while his estate was settled, try and get used to the idea that the big, brash bull of a man I'd worshipped wasn't in the world any more. That kind of blotted everything out for a while . . .'

Chastened, Lydia saw the shadow of pain pass across his face as he remembered his father's death. She couldn't help but feel sympathetic, thinking back to

Alex having to deal with the aftermath of her mother's death, emotionally, practically and bureaucratically. 'I'm sorry,' she muttered, feeling her heart melt a little at Jackson's confession. She knew he was telling the truth about his father, at least. Or if he was lying, he deserved an Oscar for his performance. No, it must be true. After all, no one would lie about such a thing. But even now she knew what had happened, there was one thing that bothered her. 'But why didn't you call me . . . after?'

'Well, the days turned into weeks and the weeks into months, and suddenly it felt too late just to call you. After all, I pretty much just left; I know that, even if I did send you a text. Given that, I really thought it was all over for us. In fact, I planned to stay in the US and help my mom, but then I found out that my job was on the line if I didn't come back to the UK, and Mom told me I had to come back. She knew how much I'd loved London. I'd been talking a little bit about you. She persuaded me to come back, and to come and find you.'

'You didn't look very hard, did you?' Lydia said, unsettled by the way he was looking at her.

'I did, I came to your chambers, straight from the airport. I saw you with Stephen. You looked so happy, so over "us". I realised I'd missed my chance and that maybe I didn't deserve a second one anyway.'

Lydia stared at him, unable to speak. 'Is that true?' she said at last.

'Of course it is,' Jackson told her. 'I tried to put losing you behind me. I moved on. I got through a lot of women trying to forget you, Lydia. And then a few months ago, I was at this publisher's bash, a launch for some chat show host's novel, and there was Joanna. Beautiful, funny, sweet Joanna. Exactly the kind of woman I wanted in my life if I couldn't have you. We e-mailed and texted for a while, and then eventually I asked her out on a date. And it turns out that she is pretty great.'

'She is great,' Lydia said, still reeling from what he'd told her. 'She is one of the best people I know. So, let me get this straight, you didn't call, or text, or even send me an e-mail because you saw me with another man? I mean, what if Stephen had been my brother, or my gay best friend?'

'I don't think you'd kiss either of those the way I saw you kissing him,' Jackson said, wincing as if the memory still grated. 'No, it was clear to me you'd moved on. And then, when I met you here . . . Jo's talked about her girlfriends, about how wonderful you all are and how much I'll love you all. She calls you "Lyds". I never made the connection. I never guessed that Lyds was you. Until I saw you, and now . . .' Lydia waited. 'I wasn't prepared for how I felt when I saw you standing there.'

'Jackson,' Lydia warned him.

'The way I felt about you back then, it hasn't gone away . . .'

'No, Jackson, don't do this.'

'Lydia.' It only took a fraction of a second for Jackson to cross the room and kiss her, but Lydia watched it all as if it was taking place in slow motion. Knowing what was about to happen, unable to react, as those deep blue eyes locked on hers, and she was lost. She felt his arms encircle her, his lips crush against hers, and although rigid with shock for a moment, all too soon her body answered his as she remembered the heat of that lost summer.

'Hello?' At the sound of Stephen's voice, they sprang apart, Lydia pressing the back of her hand to her enflamed lips just as Stephen wandered into the room.

'There you are!' He grinned at her. 'That Will fellow's done the trick. Got the old boiler going again, so the house should warm up pretty soon. Looks like he's staying over, too, as the weather's come in something shocking out there. You want to get down there, Jack, and guard your woman. The girls are all of a flutter over him.'

'Right, I will.' Jackson smiled. 'I just need to . . .'

'Oh, sorry, yes, of course, this is your room! Come on, Lydia.' He picked up Lydia's limp hand and led her away to their room. The moment the door was closed behind them, he pressed her up against it, burying his face in her neck, his hands instantly finding their way under her jumper.

'I've been thinking about this all day, Lydia,' he muttered. 'You're so sexy . . .'

'Um.' Lydia pushed herself off the door and slipped out from under Stephen's hands. 'The thing is, I said I'd help Katy with dinner. And, besides, I've been in this old thing all day. Let me make myself a bit more beautiful for you, and then perhaps later . . .?'

'It would be impossible for you to look hotter than you do now,' Stephen said, advancing on her again. 'I don't tell you enough how amazing you are, or how much I love you.' He took her face in his hands. 'But I do love you, Lydia. I love you very much.'

'I love you too,' Lydia replied, the words automatically escaping her lips before she had a moment to think about what they meant or if she were a liar. 'But I promised I'd help Katy with dinner, so I better not let her down.'

Stephen sighed, sitting down on the bed with a sulky pout. 'So this is payback for last night, is it? I thought you were the one who was up for a bit of sex,' he muttered, crossing his arms.

Lydia looked at him, sitting there, slightly drunk and put out by her not putting out. As handsome, as clever and talented as he was, at that moment she could not have been further from loving him, even as a brother or a gay best friend, and the realisation made her feel sick.

'I've got to go and help,' she said, blowing him a kiss. 'I'll see you in a bit.'

Jackson was sitting on top of the stairs when she

came out of the room. Shaking her head, Lydia tried to pass him.

'Did you . . .?'

'Just don't,' Lydia said. 'Don't say anything else to me, Jackson. Nothing. Just leave me alone.'

'That's just it,' Jackson told her as she rushed down the stairs. 'I don't know if I can.'

Chapter Eight

In her bid to stay away from traditional Christmas food until at least Christmas Eve, Katy had used her retro oven to bake a whole salmon in a salt and herb crust, stuffed with homemade black olive pesto, and served it with a selection of roasted root vegetables, murdered by Joanna's own fair hand.

After making her escape from both Jackson and Stephen, Lydia, utterly confused and slightly hungover, had discovered there was nothing very much to do in the kitchen after all, and so she helped Tilly set the table in the grand dining room.

'Sometimes,' Tilly told her, as she lined up the knives perfectly, in the way that only a daughter of Katy would, 'Mad Molly peers in through the window with her hair all dripping, and begs to be let back in. But you mustn't let her come in, because if you do, she will kill you until you are dead.'

Frowning, Lydia polished the glasses as Katy had instructed her, a set for red wine, another set for white and then tumblers for water. Katy liked a lot of glasses. 'Who told you that?'

'Jake,' Tilly said, suddenly rushing to draw the

heavy red velvet curtain against any possible sightings of Mad Molly.

Lydia scooped Tilly up into her arms and pulled out one of the heavy dining chairs to sit down with the little girl on her knee.

'You know Jake is just trying to scare you, because he's your big brother and it's sort of in his job description, don't you?'

Tilly stared at her as if she were an idiot. 'Jake hasn't got a job. He's a *child*.'

'What I mean is, Jake is just making up stories. There is no Mad Molly, Tilly. She's pretend, like Rapunzel or . . . Cinderella.'

'Cinderella is not pretend and neither is Mad Molly,' Tilly said, her blue eyes solemn. 'She's buried in the garden!'

'Nonsense,' Lydia said. 'Honestly, I'm going to talk to your mummy about this . . .'

'About what?' Katy asked, as she came in with a tray of silver-potted, decanted condiments, looking much more relaxed now that the heating was on again.

'Jake's told Tilly that Mad Molly is buried in the garden! No wonder the poor child comes into your room at night! You need to have a word with him, Katy.'

'Ah,' Katy said, setting down the salt and pepper, precisely in the centre of the table. 'The thing is, she *is*. Well, not Mad Molly, there is no Mad Molly. But, well, there is a Margaret Drake, who this half of the hotel was built for, and she is sort of buried in the garden, up the hill behind the house. It was her favourite spot, apparently.' Katy smiled.

'What?' Lydia exclaimed. 'A . . . *what?*'

'See, I told you,' Tilly said. 'And she's a zombie, Jake says.'

'Tilly, sweetheart.' Katy kissed the top of her daughter's head and lifted her from Lydia's lap into a hug. 'Will you go and find everyone and ask them to come to dinner?'

Tilly eyed the shadowy hallway with trepidation.

'Go on, darling, they're all in the sitting room.' Katy went into the hallway with Tilly, switching on all the lights, and watched until the little girl had made it safely to the other adults without being kidnapped by a zombie-ghost. 'You know I told you that the hotel was originally two semi-detached houses that we had knocked into one?' Lydia nodded. 'Well, they were built in 1885 by Morton Drake, a rich local landowner, for his unmarried daughters. They were in their thirties, and I suppose in those days that qualified you as a confirmed spinster.'

'Nothing's changed,' Lydia said, with a wry smile.

'They lived here, side by side, on the shores of the lake, quite happily for a time. It was just when the Lakes were becoming fashionable with the Victorians, and so quite a few tourists used to pass by, and sometimes the sisters would invite them in for tea. And then, one day, Margaret's sister, Elizabeth, got talking with a walker, a gentleman widower from York. The short story is that Elizabeth fell in love, married and moved away, leaving Margaret all alone here. And, trust me, this place can be pretty bleak if you've got no one to turn to. Apparently, one spring morning, they found her body on the shores of the lake, and legend has it that she drowned herself from despair and heartbreak.'

'Nice,' Lydia said, shuddering. 'And so they thought they'd pop her in the garden, did they? Fertilise the roses?'

Katy looked apologetic. 'Well, yes. It was the place she loved, and as a suicide, in those days, in this part of the world, she couldn't be buried on consecrated ground. It's not like there's a gravestone or anything, more like a plinth set into the ground, mostly covered in moss. You wouldn't know it was there, except it's listed as a place of local interest, so we couldn't move it. But there has never, *ever* been any sort of ghost story attached to the place until my stupid husband made one up and guaranteed that I would never sleep again.' Katy bit her lip, hearing the sound of laughter and chatter approaching from the hallway.

'Well, on the bright side,' Lydia said. 'Punters love a ghost story. The newly invented legend of Mad Molly will probably boost your bookings. You should put it on your website.'

'Do you really think so?' Katy asked her.

'Yes, I do, along with a photo of the gravestone. Milk it for all it's worth, I'd say. You could have paranormal weekends, the works.'

'That's actually a really good idea,' Katy said, thoughtfully. 'But what about my petrified children?' Katy said. 'It seems absurd that we tell them and tell them that ghosts don't exist, and then ask them to believe that a strange man in a red suit comes into their bedroom once a year, knowing whether or not they've been naughty or good! I feel like such a hypocrite.'

'You have a point,' Lydia said. 'I'm sure Jake will get bored of it, and Tilly will forget everything sooner or later. In the meantime, just beat your idiot husband over the head with that copper-based pan I saw in the kitchen.'

'Why, what have I done?' Jim asked, as he walked into the room, with Will close behind him. Unwrapped out of his sensible snow gear, Lydia couldn't help but notice that Will looked even better in a red and white checked shirt, worn over a T-shirt, his sleeves rolled up to reveal rather impressive forearms. He smiled at her as he came in, his dark eyes meeting hers briefly before he looked away, no doubt still laughing to himself about the last, mortifying comment she had made about him.

'Telling this young man here' – Lydia put her hand on top of Jake's head as he walked past – 'that there is a ghost in this house. I put it to you, Jim, that you made the ghost up, because you thought it would be funny, didn't you? Admit it!'

'Well . . .' Jim began, but faltered to a stop when he met Lydia's most fearsome barrister's glare. 'No, Miss Grant, there is no ghost. I made it all up. I'm sorry, your honour.'

'See?' Lydia said to Tilly and Jake. 'No ghost.'

'He's just saying that,' Jake told Tilly, 'so that you won't be scared. But it is true. And she's got maggots in her eyes.' Tilly screamed, flinging herself into her mother's arms.

'Jake! Honestly, I despair,' Katy said, leaving the room as the others came in, taking Tilly with her to calm her down a little.

Lydia noticed Stephen, Alex and David laughing over something Jackson had said, and for one sickening moment, she wondered if she was the butt of their shared joked. Then she caught Jackson's eye and remembered what he'd said to her only an hour or so ago, that he missed her and still had feelings for her. That he hadn't just dumped her after all, but had left for a very real family emergency, and then circumstances had kept them apart. It was like the cruel twist in *An Affair to Remember*.

She didn't doubt the truth of what he said had happened, but watching him lean over and kiss Joanna on the ear, Lydia couldn't help but wonder if the way he said he still felt about her was also true. After all, it was pretty clear, even to Joanna, that Jackson had been no angel in his past – at least when it came to women – and she certainly knew from experience that he was adept at saying exactly what a girl wanted to hear, exactly when she needed to hear it. Even after everything he'd said to her in the bedroom, the way he was behaving now towards Joanna, so affectionate, so tender, seemed very genuine too. And his feelings for at least one of them had to be a charade. Or, at the very worst, he seemed to be hedging his bets by keeping both his girlfriend and her best friend happy while he waited to see how the whole stupid mess would play out. Suddenly, it seemed like a very good idea to get ever so drunk. Again.

By the time the bread and butter pudding had come out of the oven, Lydia had almost eaten and drunk herself into a coma, which was, she decided, probably the best state to be in, considering her circumstances. Largely silent through dinner, she had sat watching David lavish love and attention on Alex, who, now a little more relaxed, rested her head on his shoulder, smiling and laughing, as she they talked about how life would be with the baby. Stephen sat next to her, his arm resting on the back of her chair, perhaps being protective, perhaps proprietorial, but never the less making Lydia feel utterly uncomfortable.

Katy looked flustered and tired again, juggling various dishes and culinary demands from the children, but dismissing any attempts on Lydia's behalf to help. She disappeared for half an hour between the salmon and dessert to try and settle the kids into bed, and then got up again halfway through pudding when Tilly came back down to complain that Jake had kidnapped her best bear.

Joanna was in her element – the only one of the girls who had changed for dinner, she looking stunning in a dark teal-green dress that set off her flame hair beautifully. With Jackson on her left and Will on her right, she was charming, vivacious and funny. All of the things Lydia simply did not have the energy to be herself.

'You're very quiet this evening, darling,' Joanna commented, interrupting her reverie. 'You haven't been quite yourself since we arrived. Are you okay?'

'I'm fine,' Lydia said, mustering a smile. 'I shouldn't have got drunk during the day, it always makes me dopey by the evening.'

'And moody,' Stephen said, half to himself.

'Trouble in paradise?' Joanna asked, giggling. 'Tell you what, Lyds, you come over here and sit next to this gorgeous man for a bit, he's perked me up marvellously.'

Will looked uncomfortable, and Joanna leaned close to him, running her palm over his jaw. 'Ooh, stubble.

So rough and ready, and look at those strong hands. I bet you are a very masterful lover, aren't you, Will?'

'Back off, Jo,' Lydia said, before she could stop herself. 'He's not a prize stallion, you know. Not every man alive longs to be molested by you!'

'Lydia!' Stephen admonished her, and Joanna looked stunned but sat back in her chair.

'I'm just messing around,' she said. 'I'm sorry, Jo, Will.'

'No bother,' Will said uncertainly, no doubt wondering how he'd been trapped in a room full of people he didn't know or understand. 'Actually, I might just nip outside for a smoke.'

'I'll join you,' Lydia said, standing up, desperate to be out of the hot, complicated, confusing room.

'You don't smoke!' Stephen exclaimed as she headed out of the door.

'I do now,' Lydia snapped back, as she followed Will down the hall to the kitchen and out into the blissfully cool air of the lean-to. With the rickety half-rotten door propped open by some Tilly-sized wellies, it was as a good as being outside, but slightly less cold.

For a moment or two, Will and Lydia stood there in silence, their breath frosting in the air, saying nothing.

'Is now a good time to tell you I don't smoke, either?' Will said.

Lydia looked at him in surprise, and smiled. 'You poor thing,' she said. 'You get coerced up here to fix a boiler, then snowed in and forced to have dinner with a load of . . . of . . .'

'Offcomers,' Will finished for her, as if that was more than enough of a insult to sum up the horror he'd been forced to endure.

'Offcomers?' Lydia asked him.

'Not from round here.' He nodded, a hint of that intriguing smile playing on his lips. 'Moaning southerners who can't change a plug, let alone fix a boiler.'

'We're not all like that, you know,' Lydia told him, wrapping her arms around herself, against the cold. Thinking she could at least change a plug if absolutely forced to do so. 'Bloody hell, you poor man – you must have thought you'd walked into some nightmare version of a Richard Curtis film.'

'Who? Anyway, I wouldn't know, I avoid going south of Manchester,' Will said, but he was smiling. 'That lot are southern enough for me.' He looked up at the crystal clear sky studded with stars, relaxing against the doorframe and taking a deep breath of cool air. 'I tell you what, though, Jim should have got me to do the renovations on this place. Whatever half-arsed London outfit he got to come up here has made a right hash of it, and I bet they charged him double what I would have.'

'But you're a plumber, aren't you?'

'Yes, and an electrician and a plasterer. My dad made

me qualify in all of them. Helps when you run a building company.'

'Oh, you're a builder,' Lydia said. 'So what do you build?'

'What do you want me to build?' He looked at her, raising one winged eyebrow.

Lydia laughed. 'Well, I never knew it until I came here, but I really, really need a house with a turret or two for me to moon about in while I wait for my prince to come. Maybe even an entire castle, with ramparts and a moat – yes, I'd like to have a drawbridge to pull up – can you do that?'

'Well, I can do it, but I probably wouldn't.' Will laughed. 'For me, a house has got be part of its surroundings, sort of grow out of them, you know, like something organic. If I was going to build from scratch, I'd look at the plot, the landscape and the materials I can source locally. My dream house would look as if it has always been there, even before men needed houses.' Will glanced at her, looking a little embarrassed and perhaps even surprised at saying so much in one go. 'Mostly, these days, I rebuild and renovate. I love old buildings, love the history and care that went into them. So since I took over the business, I've specialised in bringing places like this back to their former glory, but fit for the modern world.' He reached out and caressed the rough wall of the house with his long fingers. 'Take this place, it's a perfect Victorian gothic romance made out of rugged Cumbrian slate. It's unique to this area, to this very spot. It couldn't have been built anywhere else. And that makes it beautiful and rare.' He traced lightly and lovingly over the layer upon layer of greenish-grey stone. 'This slate is so pure, so rough and wild, like the mountains it comes from – and it's been forced into this mad wedding cake of a house. It's brilliant. This is one house where turrets are exactly right!'

'You're more than a builder,' she accused him with a smile. 'You're an artisan.'

'If you say so!' He laughed out loud with sheer delight, and Lydia couldn't help but join in with him, finding his pleasure in the building contagious.

Will smiled as his eyes met hers, and Lydia returned his look with warmth, caught up with his enthusiasm. He had a musical voice, and like a balm, it soothed Lydia and slowed her beating heart as she listened to him talk about something as real as bricks and mortar, finding it utterly refreshing to meet someone who was obsessed and passionate about something other than themselves, or the latest cause.

'Whatever cowboy Jim got in knew nothing about how this house should have been renovated, the layout, the colours, the paper. All of those things are mostly from completely the wrong period, typical London types trying to make everything Georgian because that's what the suits like. It might look pretty enough, but it's totally wrong for this old girl. Still, the money's spent now. Perhaps Jim will let me do the rest and save himself a few bob.' There was perhaps a minute's silence as they both gazed into the now still and silent night, the snow having ceased, for now at least.

'I'm sorry I said you were a bit of a shag,' Lydia said suddenly. 'I was quite drunk and it was very rude.'

Will chuckled. 'It's better than saying I'm a right gowk, I s'pose.'

'I beg your pardon?' Lydia asked him.

'Ugly bloke,' he said, grinning.

'It's practically like another language,' Lydia said, laughing.

'Ah, not so much, these days. You still hear the dialect round and about now and then, among the old folk, but mostly I just trot it out to impress pretty girls or baffle the tourists.'

Lydia was still trying to decide if Will was flirting with her when they were interrupted.

'There you are!' Joanna appeared in the doorway, with a bottle of wine in her hand. 'What are you two doing out here? Sorry, Will, I need a quick word with Lyds, is that okay?'

Will raised his eyebrows at Lydia, in commiseration, and taking a deep breath made his way back into the house.

'Darling, please tell me what's wrong?' Joanna asked her. 'Why did you get so uppity with me before? I was just being me . . . you of all people know what I'm like. I'm just having a bit of fun with Will, that's all.'

'Yes, I do, I know, it's just . . .' Lydia faltered to a stop. 'Jo-Jo, I'm sorry. I don't know what's wrong me.'

'I think I do,' Joanna said, her expression still and serious.

'You do?' Lydia caught her breath, guiltily.

'You're not sure if you want to marry Stephen, are you?' Joanna asked her, more dismayed than Lydia would have expected. 'He's got the ring, and the pressure's on, and now you're not sure about it. I should have spotted it sooner, but I was too busy being all loved up. I'm sorry, Lydia, I got all caught up in my own excitement, I should have seen what was going on with you. You know you don't have to say yes, don't you?'

Lydia didn't speak. After all, Joanna was mostly right. Only, she wasn't just sure that she didn't want to marry Stephen, she was now quite certain that she couldn't stay in a relationship with him at all, no matter how much she cared about him. How could she, after what had happened? After Jackson had kissed her just a few hours earlier and told her he still had feelings for her? It didn't matter that she didn't know if she still had feelings for him, or if he even meant what he'd said. What mattered was that the moment she'd recklessly kissed Jackson back, she knew she didn't feel the way she ought to about Stephen. If you were meant to marry a man, you simply wouldn't kiss another one, no matter who he was.

And yet here they were, right on the brink of Christmas, *Christmas*, the one day of the year Lydia had always longed to be perfect, just as it was for those few precious years before her parents split up. When she was a very little girl and her mum used to read her *The Night Before Christmas* as she tried to settle down to get some sleep, eventually drifting off dreaming of hearing sleigh bells sounding somewhere in the sky. But since her father had moved out and both of her parents had remarried, that perfect time had never come again. All the to-ing and fro-ing, all the back and forth between houses, one incomplete miserable Christmas lunch followed by another, always with something missing.

Lydia had thought that this year she'd cracked it; this year, in the perfect place with the perfect people, she'd feel again the way she had used to about this time of year that meant so much to her. How naïve, she thought bitterly; she should have known that was impossible. Even here, with her very best friends, amid the beautiful snowy landscape and in the house that looked like a wedding cake, there was still something missing.

'So what are you going to do?' Joanna asked her.

'What *can* I do?' Lydia asked desperately. 'It's Christmas in a couple of days, everyone's stuck here because of the snow. I can't say or do anything now, I'd ruin everything.'

'Perhaps you're right, but what if he proposes in front of all of us and you have to say no? Or what if you wait until you are back in London and then you break up? He'll know all this was just you pretending everything was okay when it wasn't.' Joanna shivered, pulling Lydia back into the relative warmth of the kitchen, and sloshing two large slugs of wine into a pair of mugs, before handing one to Lydia. 'Sometimes I think it's better to know the truth, even if it's painful, rather than find out later that you were the last to know, do you know what I mean?'

Lydia looked at her old friend, who was trying so hard to help her. If there was ever a moment to tell her the truth about Jackson, then this was it. She steeled herself for the fallout.

But Joanna interrupted her gathering bravado. 'The thing is, Lyds, I will be there for you, I promise, however you decide to handle things. But please, be nice to Jackson. It's so important to me that he likes my friends and that you like him, because, you know, if you don't like him, I won't be able to marry him.'

'Don't be so silly,' Lydia said. 'If you truly both feel that way about each other, then what we think doesn't matter!'

'But it does, it does,' Joanna told her. 'You know that you and the girls are the nearest thing I have to family.

Oh, I know I swan about acting like I'm the bee's knees, but honestly, Lyds, without knowing that you three are always there, no matter what . . . I'd be lost.'

'And I'd be lost without you, too,' Lydia said.

'Good, come here and hug me, and let's go back in there and see how long it takes to make that handsome Will blush.'

Chapter Nine

Lydia brushed her teeth for a very long time, in the hope that, after the large amount of wine and food Stephen had consumed, he would be asleep by the time she came out of the bathroom. The rest of the evening had passed quite pleasantly. She could see Will sitting quietly in the corner, sipping a whiskey, taking in the conversation, resigning himself to at least one night snowbound with a load of offcomers. Joanna calmed down considerably after her talk with Lydia, contenting herself to curl up on Jackson's lap, like an over-indulged cat, while he stroked her hair, careful not to meet Lydia's eye. Alex and David excused themselves early, for 'back to front' sex, Alex whispered in Lydia's ear as she kissed her goodnight, and the hours slipped gently away until the clock on the mantel chimed eleven and Jim snored in his chair.

Lydia had almost nodded off herself when the sitting-room door creaked slowly open, and a small girl's tousled head appeared around it.

'I'm scared,' Tilly said in a trembling voice.

'I'll go,' Lydia said, before Katy could get up. 'I'm beat, so I'll settle Tilly and then get to bed myself.'

'Thanks, Lyds,' Katy said with a yawn. 'I think this is the first time I've sat down all day.'

'I'll come too, then,' Stephen said. 'You two young ladies should definitely have an escort.' Lydia smiled, as Stephen lifted Tilly into his arms, kissing her on the forehead. He was such good man, so kind and sweet. He could be a little vain sometimes, a little too self-absorbed and worthy, and sometimes a little thoughtless, but no more or less than anyone else, especially herself. Why did she have to fall out of love with him, without even noticing?

Maybe, Lydia thought to herself as she smoothed moisturiser over her neck and face, maybe she never had been in love with him? After all, they'd only met a few weeks after Jackson had returned to New York. Perhaps being with Stephen was just easy, a quick fix to the hurt she was feeling when Jackson left. He was so effortless to be with, loving but undemanding. He understood her work, her hours; he didn't mind coming second to her career, because he felt the same way about his. It was fine that they kept odd hours, barely seeing each other most days, because, Lydia realised, they didn't need to see each other every day. They didn't long for the time when they could be together. If anything, she sometimes got the feeling that Stephen felt he was at a stage in his life when he ought to settle down, and that Lydia was as good a candidate to be his wife as any he was likely to meet. They fitted together so perfectly, everybody said so; a match made in law school. Unhappily, Lydia couldn't help but feel that the easy falling into step alongside another person had far more to do with convenience than it did with love.

After carrying Tilly to the foot of the stairs, Stephen had handed her over to Lydia and gone up to their room. Lydia took Tilly, her warm little body curled up in her arms, through to the back of the house where the family bedrooms could be reached by a separate staircase to the rear of their private living quarters.

'What a lovely room,' Lydia said, as she set Tilly down and looked around her at the floral-papered room illuminated with soft-pink fairy lights. 'It's very pretty and cosy.'

'I don't like it,' Tilly said. 'I keep thinking Mad Molly is going to come and get me.'

Lydia thought for a moment. 'When I was a little girl, I used to be scared of a glove puppet that my dad got me for my birthday. It was a Punch puppet, you know, like Punch and Judy, with a wooden head and pointed chin and nose, and evil little eyes. I hated it, but I didn't want to say anything to Mum and Dad because I didn't want to hurt their feelings. So I buried it at the bottom of all of my toys in the toy cupboard. But I couldn't get to sleep at night, because I thought it would push its way out and come and get me. A glove puppet! Silly old me!' Tilly giggled, drawing her quilt up under her chin. 'The only way I used to feel better was to get all of my soft toys, every single one, and pile them up on my bed, because everybody knows nothing scary can get you if you've got your animals protecting you. Would you like to try it?'

Tilly nodded, chuckling merrily as Lydia set about gathering various teddies, bunnies, puppies, kittens, lambs, chicks and even one rat from the four corners of Tilly's bedroom and covering the little girl's bed in them, until only her heart-shaped face peeped out between the plush.

'There, now all of your friends are looking after you, and you will be totally fine.'

'Promise?' Tilly asked.

'I promise.' Lydia nodded once, bending over to kiss the tip of the child's nose, as Tilly snuggled down into her soft-toy army. 'And if you sleep extra well tonight, then I'm sure that when Father Christmas visits you on Christmas Eve, he'll leave you a little extra gift.'

'Really?' Tilly's eyes widened. 'Like what?'

'Like . . . perhaps a lipstick or slightly used bottle of perfume,' Lydia said, wondering what she had in her bag that she could give away.

'Wow!' Tilly breathed, clearly impressed by the promise of cosmetics. 'I could spray Vincent with it.'

'You could! But you know what you need to do now, don't you, sweetie?'

'Go to sleepy bye-byes,' Tilly told her solemnly, before turning on her side, tucking her best teddy under her arm and inserting her thumb in her mouth. 'Night, night.'

On her way back to her room, she paused outside Jake's door, peering in to see him clutching his bear, arm flung above his head, flat out. Perhaps, at least tonight, the pair of them would let their mother have one rare good night's sleep.

Stephen had been lying on top of the covers wearing his dressing gown when Lydia entered their room, a glass of the brandy Katy had left in a decanter for them cradled in his hand.

'Hello, darling,' he said, holding out his hand to her. Obediently, Lydia had gone to him, letting him pull her into a hug. 'I've been a crap boyfriend, haven't I?' he asked her.

'No,' she said into the thick towelling of his dressing gown.

'I have, I moaned about coming here, even though I knew you really wanted it. I fell asleep on you . . . got all grumpy and stupid. I'm sorry, Lydia.'

He rolled her onto her back and kissed her briefly on the lips, his rather bleary eyes roaming her face. 'Let me make it up to you now.'

Lydia stopped his hand, venturing under the hem of her top, with her own. 'After I've brushed my teeth,' she said, pushing him off her.

'That's not very romantic,' Stephen complained, as she clambered off the bed and headed for the bathroom.

'Yes, but neither is my garlic breath,' Lydia said, shutting the door, wondering if he'd realise they hadn't eaten any garlic that night.

After some more teeth brushing, just to be on the safe side, Lydia peered out of the bathroom door and spied Stephen lying like a starfish in the middle of the bed, snoring gently. Gingerly, she tiptoed across the floor and ever so slowly slid herself under the covers to occupy what tiny slither of bed was left. Reaching out to turn off the lamp, Lydia looked into the darkness. She heard the sound of Joanna's voice next door, the shutting of doors, footfalls on the stairs, the ancient timber creaking and settling as the heating switched off, all the noises of a house going to sleep, and Stephen slumbering next to her. Her mind was spinning as she tried to make sense of everything that had happened to her that day.

Did Jackson really mean what he'd said? Had he really come back from New York and found her with Stephen, or was he just adding his own spin to their story, trying to save face? She knew how all-consuming grief could be, but surely he could have made some effort to get in touch with her after his father's death. And what about now? She wasn't sure how she felt about anything. Did he really have feelings for her still? And if he cared as much about Joanna as he seemed to, what the hell was he doing kissing another woman?

More importantly, what the hell was she doing, letting him?

Perhaps she and Jackson were meant to be together. It was certainly one radical twist of fate bringing them back together this way. If he did still have feelings for her and she for him, then this could be their last chance to work things out. But at what price? Lydia seriously doubted Joanna would be as understanding about her taking Jackson from her as she was about sharing a pair of shoes or some earrings. It was far more likely that Jackson was just a serial romantic, a drama queen, unable to resist complicating a complicated situation just a little more, addicted to making women love him. One thing Lydia knew for sure was that she didn't know anything about the real Jackson Blake at all, and she wasn't sure it would be very sensible to try and find out.

As she laid there, any chance of sleep seeming impossible, Lydia noticed a flickering against the wall opposite the window, like a butterfly of light, coming and going, rising and falling in the darkness. Perplexed and intrigued, she got out of bed, her toes curling on the cold floorboards, and went to look out of the turret-room window, pressing her nose against the glass. She was just able to catch a glimpse of the light disappearing into the boathouse at the bottom of the garden on the shore of the lake. The tiny hairs on the back of her neck stood up, and Lydia gasped as the dirty narrow window of the boathouse was illuminated with the same unearthly glow.

Without thinking, she pulled on her socks and a sweater over her pyjamas and headed downstairs, feeling like the naughty little girl she had once been, long ago, creeping down the stairs in the early hours of Christmas Day, desperate to catch Santa or at least open her presents before the sun was anywhere near up. The smell of the tree brought back memories, kneeling on the patterned carpet, with pine needles scratching between her toes, ripping through the cheap, waxy sort of paper that her mum always used to buy in bulk, the anticipation of what she might find beneath always outweighing the reality.

Lydia felt like she was walking in a dream as she found her coat and, careful to tuck her pyjama bottoms into the boots that she borrowed, advanced into the silent night to look for the light. The moon was huge in the sky, casting an eerie light over the lake that shimmered in a silvery greeting, and gliding over the tops of the mountains with an ethereal glow. If ever there was a night to see the ghost of Mad Molly, Lydia thought, this was it. It was the perfect night for a Christmas ghost story.

The crunch of the frozen snow beneath her wellies seemed to echo around the mountains, seeming loud enough in the hushed landscape to wake the dead. Which, now she came to think of it, wasn't such a good idea. Still, if there were an actual ghost to be found, Lydia thought it was her duty to be the one to find her – for Tilly's sake, at least – and perhaps to ask it, ever so nicely, to go away.

She held her breath as she approached the old run-down boathouse, with its ancient rotting timber, still standing precariously on crooked stilts that somehow held it up above the water. Steeling herself, she put her hand on the rough, mossy door and pushed it open, gasping at what she saw before her.

Will Dacre, artisan builder, was sitting huddled in a leaky-looking rowing boat, drinking from a silver flask, a little Calor gas lamp flickering at his feet, as he gazed up at a broken skylight.

'Fucking hell,' Lydia exclaimed with a laugh, flooded with relief and a sense of stupidity as she realised just how much she'd been caught up in her expectation of meeting Mad Molly. 'You're not a ghost!'

Will looked quizzical. 'A ghost? Don't be a divvy. No such thing.'

'Tell that to the kids, they're sure the lady buried in the back garden's going to get them.'

Will observed her for a moment and then held out his flask to her.

After a moment's hesitation, Lydia took it and sipped from the metallic-tasting neck.

'Just so you know, I'm not an alcoholic,' Will told her. 'I couldn't sleep, for some reason. It's a long time since I've been in this house, and, well, this place used to be quite important to me.'

'The boathouse?' Lydia asked, accepting his hand as she climbed uncertainly into the boat, looking dubiously at the slick of water that covered its bottom.

'Aye, when I were a lad I used to go out with the girl that lived here,' he told her, nodding in the direction of the house. 'I was fifteen, she was a year older.'

'A toy boy!' she teased him. 'How scandalous!'

'Prettiest girl in Aldersbeck, in Keswick, too. All the boys liked her, with her long black hair and skin that shone. And boobs.' Will's boyish grin took Lydia by surprise. 'She had great boobs.'

'You rake,' she said with a smile.

'We went out for a whole summer. Her dad would be working the farm, as it used to be back then, so he'd be out most of the day and her mum was always busy running the B&B next door. They owned both houses but kept them separate. So we'd more or less have the whole place to ourselves.'

'Is this where you . . . became a man?' Lydia was uncharacteristically coy.

That crooked smiled again, and Will shook his head. 'No. I told all the lads we did it all the time, but she wasn't ready and, in truth, neither was I.' He hesitated, his eyes reflecting a treasured memory. 'But she was my first love, and I mean love. I could have just looked at her all day long and that would have been enough.

But she let me kiss her and . . . a bit more. One night, I just couldn't wait for it to be morning so that I could see her again, so I came up to the house from the village and threw pebbles at her window. I don't know how I got away with it, but she came down. And we lay here, maybe even in this very boat, in each other's arms, looking at the stars through that broken skylight. Nothing has changed here; it's like time's stood still. This is still the perfect place to bring the girl you love.'

Lydia followed Will's gaze up and saw the black square in the ceiling, beautifully framing the magnificently starry night.

'How romantic,' she breathed, catching Will smiling at her as she looked back at him. 'Like Romeo and Juliet.'

'It ended badly,' Will said, suddenly serious. 'Really badly.'

'Oh no, what happened?' Lydia asked him, on the edge of her damp little seat. 'Did she die unexpectedly, leaving you heartbroken and never able to love again?'

'Not exactly.' Will raised an eyebrow. 'She found out that I told all the boys we'd done it, when we hadn't. She dumped me and told me she never wanted to see me again. A couple of years later, she married an industrial butcher and went to live in Penrith. Last I heard, she was the size of a house and had five kids.'

Lydia laughed. 'Well, I just hope that you learned your lesson,' she chided him.

'Never kissed and told ever since,' he assured her. 'My mum taught me to be a gentleman, and if there's one woman you never want to get on the wrong side of, it's her.'

Lydia smiled. 'I suppose your family live in the village too?'

Will shook his head. 'Not exactly. A few years back, when Dad's arthritis couldn't stand the cold any more, they went to live in Florida near my sister Becky and her family. I go over when I can, and they always come for a week or two in the summer, to top up on some proper Cumbrian air.'

'You weren't tempted to leave with them?' Lydia asked him. 'Build beach houses in the Keys?'

'No, it would take a hell of lot more than constant sunshine to get me to leave this place,' Will told her. 'I can't imagine anything that would.'

As they looked up at the stars, they were content to be silent for a while, listening to the water lapping against the boat. For some reason, Lydia didn't feel the least bit cold; it must be the whiskey keeping her warm, she told herself, clasping both hands around the hip flask.

'So what are you doing up?' Will asked her. 'Don't tell me you were on a ghost hunt, you don't seem to be the sort of girl to take to that kind of nonsense.'

'Couldn't sleep,' Lydia explained, the words falling out of her mouth before she could stop them. 'My boyfriend, Stephen. I found this diamond ring in his drawer. I know he's going to propose to me at any minute and I . . . I've just realised I don't want to be with him, let alone marry him, and then . . . well, it's complicated. I just don't know what to do. The last thing I want to do is hurt or embarrass him, especially at Christmas time. I'd run away but, well, we're snowed in. And this is where I came *to* run away.'

Will looked thoughtful, taking a sip of from the flask after Lydia handed it back to him.

'Strikes me that Christmas is just another day. Folks get all riled about it, thinking that if they are not happy at this time of the year, then they can't really be happy at all. Strikes me as a bit foolish to get so het up over a single day, same as any other.'

'Well, when you put it like that . . .' Lydia said.

'And Stephen hasn't popped the question yet, has he?' Lydia shook her head. 'So why are you fretting about something that might not happen? A ring in a box is a long way from a ring on a finger, trust me, I know.'

Lydia was silent as she let his words sink in, making sense and somehow soothing her tangled nerves. 'Can I ask you a question?' she said eventually.

'Depends,' Will said. 'What is it?'

'What do you think of Joanna?'

Will looked thoughtful. 'She's very beautiful, puts me in mind of that painting, you know, the one of Ophelia in the water.'

Lydia raised an eyebrow at him and he laughed.

'We do have art and galleries up North, too, you know!'

'I know, but would you go for her?' Lydia asked him.

'You mean rather than you?' Will asked, cutting brutally to the chase. Lydia nodded awkwardly.

'The thing is, Lydia, both of you are spoken for. I'm not the sort of bloke who goes after a girl who's already been taken.' Lydia nodded, feeling rather contrite. 'But if you were free . . . well, put it like this, I prefer a woman who can sit and look at the stars instead of trying to be one. Now, we'd better get inside before we both freeze to death or this boat sinks, whichever comes first.'

Chapter Ten

23 December

Stephen was gone when Lydia opened her eyes. Reaching for her watch on the bedside table, she saw that it had gone ten, and fell back onto her pillow trying to remember the last time she had slept in that late. Not even on the weekends did she get to sleep in with Stephen. He was always up and out, volunteering at the drop-in centre he supported, or attending a demonstration for or against his latest cause. And, even if there wasn't a demo, Stephen always wanted to do something, make the best of the day; living life to the full, he called it. Once she had thought it was charming and impressive, but now, as brilliant and worthy a person as Stephen undoubtedly was, Lydia realised his relentless determination to do good above all else, including spending time with her, was exhausting.

Noticing the chill in the air, Lydia leaned over and touched the radiator. It was deathly cold again. Groaning, she grabbed whatever clothes she could reach from the confines of the bed, and dressed hurriedly under the covers. Allowing herself a minute more to catch her breath, Lydia remembered last night's adventure with a sudden little thrill. It was impossible not to like Will, he was so real and at ease in his own skin. No uncertainty, no hang-ups or neurosis that the rest of them seemed to have in spades. Lydia could tell by the way he talked and carried himself that he was comfortable with who he was, and content with his life, keeping the secret of happiness locked behind that crooked half-smile. It didn't hurt that he was extraordinarily handsome, either, Lydia thought idly, before stopping herself abruptly. She had already broken one of her own rules by kissing another man when she was in a relationship. Getting fantastical thoughts about a super-sexy northern builder who quite obviously only just about tolerated her was simply out of the question.

Before she could allow herself any ill-advised daydreams about anyone else, she had to talk to both Stephen and Jackson; she had to get this whole tangled mess straight again. For goodness' sake, she was a grown woman, a barrister and an independent adult-type person. So why did she feel like staying in bed and hiding under the covers until New Year's Day?

Lydia found the girls in the kitchen, standing at the table, staring down at whatever lay on its surface.

'Morning all, boiler packed in again?' Lydia asked. Alex turned to look at her before standing aside to reveal the biggest turkey Lydia had ever seen, languishing on the bare wood.

'Holy Mother of God,' Lydia said.

'It's not what you think,' Joanna said, mischievously. 'Alex hasn't given birth in the night.'

'If the baby's that big, I'm changing my mind,' Alex said, staring at it.

'Bloody hell, that is *massive*.' Lydia realised she was rather stating the obvious.

'I know.' Katy pressed her palms to her cheeks, transfixed by the corpse. 'Bless him, the farmer just delivered it on the back of his kids' sleigh. I ordered it in October and he said how many for, I said fifteen, and he said he'd sort it. He didn't say anything about feeding it on radioactive waste.'

'Still, you can never have too much turkey!' Lydia told her, patting her on the shoulder.

'Actually,' Alex said, nodding at the humble little electric oven huddled in the corner, 'it turns out that you can.'

'It doesn't fit in the oven?' Lydia asked.

'I don't know,' Katy wailed. 'I'm too scared to try! I thought I'd be cooking on the Aga, not a nineteen seventies relic. Damn that bloody Aga, it's ruined my life. I swear to God, from now on I'm only ever using a microwave.'

'I know,' Alex said, brightly, 'we could burn the turkey to keep warm.'

Katy wailed again, and Alex shrugged. 'It was a joke! What, too soon?'

Lydia repressed a smile. 'Okay, come on, let's just pop it in for a trial run. I know it looks gigantic, but I'm sure it's got a bit of . . . give.'

With Katy taking one cold, clammy leg and wing, and Lydia the other, they approached the oven as Joanna opened its door, taking out all trays and the spare oven shelf – anything that might impede the bird's safe entry to its destiny.

The neck and wings just about eased in, but then as they reached the pinnacle of the breast, it wedged firmly stuck. Wrinkling her nose, Lydia popped her hand inside its bottom and managed to ram it in another centimetre or two, and that was most definitely that.

'Oh nooo,' Katy groaned. 'Christmas is ruined! Again!'

'Hold your horses,' Lydia said, washing her hands in freezing water, as she thought of Will's wise words. 'This isn't over yet. We're going to cook this mother fucker if it kills us.'

'It probably will,' Alex said. 'It's going to take ten days in an industrial oven to cook that bastard through.'

'We can do this,' Lydia rallied them. 'We are smart, capable women. With jobs and banks accounts. We can get this turkey in that oven.'

'Um, in case anyone hasn't noticed, getting it in isn't

our immediate problem,' Joanna said, repressing a giggle with the back of her hand. 'Our immediate problem is getting the bastard out again.'

Katy handed round the rubber gloves, and with sleeves rolled up, they set about dislodging the bird. They tried pulling, they formed a chain and attempted a sort of tug of war with the oven, but it seemed reluctant to give up its prize, and the creature would not budge. Alex came up with the idea of using some sort of crowbar device, and so a variety of spoons and spatulas were used to attempt to lever the poor creature out, succeeding only in making it look all the more forlorn.

'And this is why I know I can never be a lesbian,' Joanna said, causing everybody to stop and stare at her for a second, before they began their epic battle once again.

'Please stop attacking it,' Alex said. 'I feel like I should call the RSPCA, post mortem division.'

'That's it,' Katy said, throwing her gloves on the floor in a gesture of defeat. 'That's it. I'm going to kill myself. Goodbye.'

'I've got it!' Lydia shouted.

'What?' Alex asked her.

'When you moved in, we all bought you house-warming gifts, didn't we? I got you some lovely photo frames, Alex got you that cookery book and Joanna gave you an electric carving knife that was on special offer at work.'

'It was not on special offer,' Joanna protested. 'It was the end of the line. And anyway, since when has an arty farty photo frame saved Christmas?'

'*Anyway*, we'll just cut the fucker up,' Lydia said. 'And then we can cook it in bits for our added convenience. Where's the knife?'

Looking nearly as forlorn as the turkey, Katy dragged a chair from under the kitchen table across the flagstones to the storage cupboard in the corner, opened the door, and climbed up on the chair. She took out a box, passing it down to Lydia. And then another box, followed by an assortment of plastic bags, and then, standing on her very tiptoes to reach right to the back of the highest shelf, she rooted around with her fingertips until she managed to edge out Joanna's electric carving knife, still boxed and shrink wrapped.

'Oh, I see,' Joanna said. 'Thanks very much.'

'What? I was saving it for best,' Katy muttered, handing the knife to Lydia, who expertly de-boxed it with a bread knife.

'You have to plug it in!' she said, unwinding the cord.

'Yeah, that's why it's called electric. It's not magic.'

'You couldn't get them a cordless one?'

'You'd still have to charge it up, whereas this way, it's instant. It's better.' Joanna smiled primly. Fortunately, there was a plug next to the cooker, which looked like it might have been wired shortly after electricity was discovered, but still, taking her life into her own hands,

Lydia plugged it in and put a large soup pan at her feet to catch the offcuts.

'Turn away, Katy, you might not want to see this.'

As Lydia mercilessly lay into the bird, hacking at it with relentless brutality, while Katy buried her face in Joanna's neck and Alex heaved in the sink, it occurred to Lydia that perhaps she was the only person in the entire world, the universe even, who at that precise moment in time was actually finding violently dismembering a turkey a welcome distraction. At last, Lydia dropped the final section into the pan, with a wet thud.

The four women stared at its remains for some time, heads bowed in respect.

'Look at it this way,' Joanna said finally, 'it's perfect for turkey stew.'

Katy started to laugh, a little chuckle at first, but then it soon evolved into hysterical gales of laughter as she bent over double, pointing at the butchered turkey. 'I was going baste it in orange and cranberry,' she half sobbed. 'I was going to present it on my grandmother's carving plate, surrounded by all the trimmings and garnished with holly, and now . . . now it looks like it should be Exhibit A on *Crimewatch*!' They watched in horror as Katy's laughter turned to tears, and she sank onto a chair at the kitchen table, burying her head in her arms, her shoulders heaving as she gasped in ragged breaths.

Lydia, Alex and Joanna exchanged glances.

'Hey,' Alex said, putting an arm around Katy's shaking shoulders, 'at least this has happened with us, your best friends, and not with real guests. We don't care what the turkey looks like as long as it tastes good. And actually we don't even care if it tastes good, as long as there is wine.'

'But I wanted it to be . . . to be . . . *perfect*,' Katy said with a hiccup. 'I wanted just one thing about this hell-hole to be perfect, so that you'd think that . . . that . . . that everything was perfect!'

'Everything *is* perfect, isn't it?' Lydia asked her, pulling up a chair beside her. 'Perfectish, anyway?'

'No!' Katy cried, ticking off each complaint on her trembling fingers. 'Everything's horrible. The house isn't at all how I wanted it, Jim's paid too much to get things done wrong, and not saved enough for the basics like heating and hot water and a . . . a . . . kitchen with a fucking oven that works. We've got no bookings beyond New Year, and we're no way ready for the ones we do have, and . . . and I never see Jim, he's always swanning off doing his own thing, it's like he's on holiday! The kids never sleep, I feel like I never stop and . . . none of the mums at the village school talk to me, and I'm so lonely, I'm so, so lonely.'

'Oh, Katy.' Lydia took her friend's hand, rubbing it briskly between hers. 'I think we could all see you were a bit frazzled, but we had no idea you felt *this* badly.'

'I feel like such a fool,' Katy said, palming away the

tears that wouldn't stop now they had started. 'This was my idea, my dream. I thought I could do it; make a go of it. But it's a nightmare, a nightmare. I want London. I want Thursday evening Pilates and NCT coffee mornings. I *hate* the country!'

'Well, you can't go on like this,' Alex said, grimly. 'Where's Jim? I'll go and beat him up for you.'

'Or, alternatively, you could just talk to him,' Lydia said, carefully. 'I mean, I know Jim can be a bit of a, well, a dick, but he loves you and the children. He's probably just got a bit caught up in the *Boy's Own* adventure of it all, and hasn't noticed how much pressure you're under.'

'It's not like he can't handle pressure,' Joanna said. 'Didn't he used to handle millions at his old job?'

'That's exactly it. As far as he's concerned, he's retired,' Katy said. 'This is supposed to be like a hobby, a bit of fun between trips to the pub and larking about with his new friends. He doesn't understand that we need to make money from it, and soon, and that I need some real help from him.'

'But you haven't actually said any of this to him?' Alex asked her.

'It's almost like I haven't had time,' Katy said, calmer now. 'My feet don't seem to touch the ground. Besides, this was my dream, my idea. I feel like I've failed if I go to him and say I can't cope.'

'Honestly, Katy, I'm sure things aren't as bad as you

think they are,' Lydia told her gently. 'This house is stunning, and perhaps it's not exactly how you want it yet, but what house is after, what, six months? And yes, you've made some mistakes. Perhaps getting a new heating system and kitchen should have come before the full-size billiard table. But, well, at least during his trips to the pub Jim has made friends with a very talented builder, who I'm sure will get it sorted for you at a reasonable price. And as for the kitchen, I know that right now you think that oven over there is your nemesis, but look at all the lovely meals you've cooked us since we've been here.'

'Lyds is right,' Joanna said. 'Your trouble, darling, is that you are a perfectionist. I know because I'm one myself. You put too much pressure on yourself to be right all the time, and take it from me, that's not just possible.'

'Especially not in Jo's case,' Alex said very seriously, eliciting the ghost of a smile from Katy.

'Look,' Lydia said. 'If anyone is guilty of wanting a picture book perfect Christmas, then it's me. Most of my life, I've wanted to walk right onto the set of *Miracle on 34th Street* – you know, the original black and white version, not the sappy re-make – or *It's a Wonderful Life*, and feel the magic that everyone always bangs on about.'

'And I so wanted to be the one to give it to you, but this is more like *Nightmare on Elm Street*!' Katy wailed.

'I know, Katy, and that's really sweet, and when Stephen and I pulled up here, I thought I'd never seen anything more beautiful than this house, all lit up in the snow. But a pretty house and a whole turkey isn't the reason I risked life and limb to get here. I came because if there is one thing I think I'm finally learning in life, it's that Christmas isn't about how the turkey looks, or whether or not you can feel your toes. It's about being with the people you love and who love you best. The sort of people you can murder a dead turkey with and laugh about it afterwards. And we are all here to help you, aren't we, girls?'

Katy looked around as Joanna and Alex nodded.

'Thank you,' she said, sniffing and smiling simultaneously. 'I do feel better just for admitting that everything isn't exactly as I'd hoped. I really do. And I will talk to Jim, you're right. I can't complain about him being insensitive and stupid when the very fact that he *is* insensitive and stupid means he wouldn't notice that he's being insensitive and stupid in the first place.'

'Exactly,' Lydia nodded. 'I think . . .'

'Oh, Lyds, I wish I were together and strong like you. You've always got everything sorted. Great job, great man, no complications. You know exactly what you want and you go for it.'

'Are you sure you are talking about flaky, incurable romantic, always impulsively foolish Lydia there and not another sensible person of the same name?' Alex asked her.

As her friends chuckled fondly at the far more apt description, it came as more of a surprise to Lydia than anyone to find that now she was the one in tears, burying her head in her arms.

'What?' Katy asked her.

'What?' Alex demanded. 'I was only joking!'

'Tell them,' Joanna nodded sagely. 'Get it off your chest.'

'You told *her*?' Alex looked offended. 'What did you tell her that you didn't me?'

'It's Stephen,' Lydia said, the words tumbling out of her before she could stop them. 'He's so nice and good and kind and handsome and I found an engagement ring in his sock drawer.' There were gasps of delight and excitement from her friends. 'But it's no good! I want to *want* to marry him, more than anything, but I just don't. I don't even think I love him any more! I wonder if I ever did . . .'

With her head in her hands Lydia waited for the flood of friendly support and advice to wash over her, as it had done for Katy, but there was only silence.

'Um,' Katy said.

'The thing is . . .' Lydia heard Joanna say.

'Lyds.' Alex tapped her on the shoulder. 'Mate.'

Lydia looked up, fearing what she was going to see even before she took her fingers away from her eyes.

Stephen was standing in the doorway, and the look on his face told he'd heard every single word she'd said.

'The boiler's working again,' Stephen said, the muscles in his jaw taught. 'Will said he'd need to get a part in the New Year to fix it for good, but it will be fine for now. Right. Okay, I'll be off, then.'

Lydia watched in shock as he grabbed his coat and marched out of the back door into the latest flurry of thick snow tumbling erratically from the sky. Then she scrambled to her feet, going after him, leaving her friends staring at each other with horrified expressions as freezing air whipped in through the door that she left gaping open. When she caught up with Stephen, he was scooping inches of snow off the Prius with his bare hands.

'Stephen, wait,' she said. 'Look, look around you. You're not going anywhere in this, especially not in that.'

'Oh,' Stephen said. 'So you secretly hate the Prius too, do you? When were you planning on telling it that it was over between you? Before or after it had made an idiot of itself proposing to you in front of all your friends on Christmas Day?'

'Oh, Stephen.' Lydia grabbed his arms but he shook her off, tears filling his eyes.

'How could you, Lydia? If you knew you felt that way about me, then don't you think it should have been me you told first, not your cronies? Instead I catch you gossiping about me like I'm some sort of joke to you.'

Lydia could think of no defence. She hung her head, letting snowflakes garland her hair, glistening for a moment before melting away. 'I didn't know I felt that way, not until I found the ring, back at home. And it started me thinking about you and me and if we'd be happy together, if we really fitted. And the thing is, I don't think I should be thinking those things, do you? I should just be happy and excited . . . but I'm not.'

Stephen shook his head. 'I don't know what to say . . . I love you, Lydia. I didn't have to think about it; all I know is that I want to marry you. I *want* to be with you.'

'Look, we can't talk here, let's go inside, please,' she begged him.

Everyone was in the kitchen when they walked in. Stephen stormed past them, his head down as Lydia hurried after him, trying hard not to notice Jackson's expression. By now he must know what had happened, and if she saw his face then she'd know if this was what he'd wanted, if everything he'd said to her last night was real, or just part of a game he'd been playing to amuse himself while he waited for the snow to thaw and life to begin again. And Lydia was only ready to deal with one disaster at a time.

Following Stephen's rapidly thawing footprints into the guest sitting room, Lydia found him standing in the huge bay window, staring out at the fierce peaks of the mountain, which intermittently pierced the snow and mist. When she saw him, her heart contracted with guilt, shame and loss. Stephen was right, she shouldn't have told everybody else about how she was feeling until she'd told him herself; he didn't deserve that. He did, however, deserve the truth, and Lydia was certain that the truth was that the way she felt about him had nothing to do with Jackson turning up, or the things he said or did. The truth had been there for some time now, long before she'd even found the ring. It was just that she'd been trying her very best not to notice that, even though she had feelings for him, she had never loved him enough to marry him.

Taking a deep breath Lydia went over to the window to join him, the bright white light reflecting off the snow outside, seeming to wash all the colour out of the room, making it seem to Lydia as if she was suddenly starring in her own black and white movie.

'I'm a horrible person,' she said, looking up at Stephen, whose gaze remained on the horizon.

'If only that were true,' Stephen said. 'But you're not horrible. You're the most lovely, loyal, clever, sexy and beautiful person I have ever met, and I was foolish enough to think I'd done enough to make you mine.' He shook his head, dropping his chin. 'I let things slide, thinking there'd always be enough time to make it up to you. And now I'm out of time.'

'It's not just you who let things slide, Stephen, I did too. We both put work first; we both knew that was how it was when we got together. And . . . and, well, a lot of the time I feel like now you've crossed off getting a "plus one" from your "To Do" list, you feel like you don't need to give me any of your attention. I so admire everything you do, it's really inspired me. But it's every spare minute, Stephen; there was never any time for us.'

'You never said you felt that way,' Stephen said. 'I didn't know.'

'Maybe I should have, but I thought that if you cared, perhaps you'd notice.' Lydia shook her head. 'Look, it's not your fault, I really wanted to be the sort of person I let you think I was, and I think because of you I am a little, but I need more from a relationship than you can give me. I need to feel loved, and wanted . . . and desired. Maybe it's my fault, maybe you would want me more if I'd lived up to your expectations.'

'What on earth do you mean?' Stephen asked her.

'When we first met on that fun run, I more or less made out that I did a sponsored marathon a week. It can't have escaped your notice that it was the first and last time you've seen me run anywhere.'

'Well, you've been busy,' Stephen said uneasily. 'We both have. I never expected you to become Mother Teresa for me. I like you exactly how you are. You are a great person, Lydia. You don't make a song and dance about it, like I do. But I know the cases you work on, the people you help. People who are at their wits end with only you left between them and disaster. And you are kind, and funny and very beautiful. You are exactly the kind of woman I want to marry.'

'But I'm not exactly *the* woman you want to marry, am I?' Lydia asked. 'If I were the exact one, I'd know it. I'd feel it, but I don't. And neither do you.'

'Please, give me the chance to make you feel that way, *please*,' Stephen said, turning to look at her, his expression achingly hopeful. 'Perhaps I could just put the ring away for a bit and we can have a nice Christmas together, and go back home and then start again. Perhaps now I know where I've been going wrong, if I try really hard to make this work, it will this time. Because I swear, Lydia, if you stay with me, I'll do better. I will never let you down again.'

Lydia turned her face away. It would be so easy to say yes, and for all this pain and awkwardness to be neatly hidden away, wrapped up in Christmas paper and tied with a glittery bow, at least until the New Year had been rung in. But then what? There would be the cold indifference of inevitable January; the great grinding wheel of work rolling once again into unstoppable action, and the truth would still be the truth.

'I'm sorry, Stephen. I'm sorry this is so horrible, and that you are stuck here with me. The trouble is, I think we both fell into this because it was so easy, so *nice*, and it seemed to make so much sense. But both of us deserve more than just settling for the convenient option. And the truth is that I'm just not right for you and you're not right for me.' Hesitantly, Lydia stood on her tiptoes and kissed him on the cheek. 'I'll ask Katy if there is another room I can stay in.'

'No.' Stephen shook his head. 'I'll move. Look, I know how important this time of year is to you, so you don't have to worry. I'll do my best not to spoil it. Just answer me one thing, the ring – was it right? Was it the perfect ring?'

Tears sprung into Lydia eyes and she nodded. 'Yes, it was the perfect ring.'

Chapter Eleven

A quiet, persistent knock at the door woke Lydia. She must have drifted off while reading the same line on the same page of the same book over and over again, and then instantly forgetting it. She was surprised to find that the room, now devoid of any sign of Stephen except for his faint scent on the pillow, was in darkness, and checking her watch she realised that it was almost six.

Pushing her tangled hair out of her eyes, Lydia opened the door and found Joanna on the other side with a bottle of wine and two glasses.

'How are you holding up?' she asked.

'I don't know, really,' Lydia said, stepping back to let her in. 'It feels like a bad dream. I mean, did that happen? Did Stephen and I split up?'

'Judging by the male bonding session that's going on over a bottle of brandy in the billiard room, I say that's a definite yes. None of us girls have been allowed in there all afternoon.'

'I mean, how did that happen?' Lydia sat down on the edge of the bed, her arms flopping at her sides. 'A couple of days ago, I really thought I was going to talk myself into marrying him and then . . .' She stopped herself just in time from mentioning Jackson's name. 'And then it all just falls apart? I don't get it.'

'I do,' Joanna said, sitting next to her and screwing the cap off the bottle of Shiraz she'd pilfered from the bar. 'It's Christmas. T'is the season for the shit to hit the fan. Tra la fucking la. We're all so stressed about how we all have to be happy that suddenly we examine our lives and all we can see is everything that's wrong with it. It's horrible that you and Stephen have broken up now. But if not now then it probably still would have happened, maybe in a month, just before the wedding, maybe after you'd been married ten or twenty years and you're ancient and wrinkly with saggy tits and no hope of ever getting a man again. Think of it that way and you'll see that, actually, this is the best possible outcome.'

Lydia looked at Joanna.

'I'm not helping, am I?' Joanna said, handing Lydia a glass of wine and watching as she knocked it back. 'Look, I've broken up with more men than you've had hot dinners, and I get a lot of stick for it, mainly from you. But the truth is that I want to believe in love, with my whole heart, so I always jump right in up to my neck in the stuff in the hope that this time it will be the right time. Oh, I know I'm beautiful and I've got a glamorous job and lots of money, but my life has been pretty short of real love. Boarding school from the age of four, so my parents could lounge about on yachts in the Caribbean, and a mother who hired a housekeeper to look after me during the holidays, spending "family" Christmases with great aunts and second cousins I didn't know from Adam.

'The first people ever to teach me anything about what it meant to feel love and to be loved are you and the girls. And finally I think I am learning by your example. Finally I think I've worked out what love means, with Jackson. So don't you feel bad about learning from my extremely excellent example; it doesn't matter how lovely the ring is, if it isn't right, it isn't right.' Joanna took a swig from the bottle. 'Just a shame you didn't get your hands on the bling before you did the dirty deed.'

'Joanna!' Lydia couldn't help but chuckle.

'There, a smile. Now, are you going to come down for dinner?'

'How can I?' Lydia flopped back onto to bed. 'Everyone hates me for ruining Christmas. Stephen will be there, it will be awful.'

'Yes, it will be awful, but it's better to get the awfulness out of the way tonight so that tomorrow is a bit less awful and Christmas Day is tolerable. Come on, think of poor Katy. We all need to be putting on our best, bravest faces for her. Now go and have a shower and I'll find you something to wear.'

'Don't make me look like a slut,' Lydia grumbled, sufficiently awake now to remember the last time she let Joanna pick out her wardrobe, but she plodded obediently into the bathroom.

'Nothing I can do about that, darling,' Joanna said, wrinkling her nose as she began to rummage through Lydia's things.

Lydia held her breath as she followed Joanna into the dining room. She had rejected Joanna's first choice of outfit for her as it was all black and made her look like she was in mourning, and then flatly refused to put on the mini skirt and sexy basque that she had been privately planning to seduce Stephen with on Christmas morning. In the end she settled on a wine-red sweater dress over black tights and long boots, brushing her hair out and putting on a little mascara. Joanna said it was the perfect look to confront your snowbound ex with, but that didn't make Lydia feel any better.

As usual, Katy had dressed the table to within an inch of its life, and it was glittering with candles and festooned with holly that must have just been cut from the tree in the garden, as it still sparkled with rapidly melting snow. She must have negotiated at least a temporary truce with the electric oven, because she'd somehow produced a roast belly of pork stuffed with Parmesan and Italian herbs, with a dish of dauphinoise potatoes on the side.

Although the smells made Lydia's stomach grumble, the twist of nerves at seeing Stephen, sitting at the end of the table furthest from her, vanquished her hunger pangs almost immediately. Their eyes met and he smiled such a warm, sad smile that Lydia was not sure if she should run over there and hug him or run right back upstairs to her room. Choosing the middle ground she opted to return the smile and, knowing she didn't want to be anywhere near Jackson, she slid into the corner seat at the opposite end of the table, between Will and Tilly, who was feeding garlic roasted potatoes to Vincent even before her mother had carved the pork with the ostentatiously brandished electric carving knife.

'Can I play with that after?' Jake asked no one in particular, which was just as well as no one answered him, except for his mother after a fashion who flicked him lightly across the head with a pair of chicken-headed oven gloves.

'Still here?' Lydia asked Will. 'I thought you'd have clawed your way through icebergs in bare feet to escape us.'

Will shrugged, smiling quietly. 'I decided to stick around for a bit. The entertainment's a million times better here than at my place. And besides, for what's it's worth, I thought you could use someone to hide in the boathouse with. Look, I heard about the break-up . . .'

Caught off guard by the remark, Lydia turned to look at him. 'Why are you being nice to me?' she asked him suspiciously.

Will sighed and tapped the table for a moment or two while seeming to debate with himself whether or not to tell her. Finally he gave a quick nod. 'I seem to like you, even if you are southern and very moany and only drink wine.'

Lydia wanted to laugh but thought it might seem inappropriate.

'I'm not trying to hit on you, or anything,' Will added hastily. 'I just like you. I think what you did was brave, and it never hurts to have another person in your corner.'

'Oh.' Lydia smiled, disarmed by his spontaneous offer of friendship. 'Thanks, that's really, really nice.'

Will nodded in agreement as Katy put a plate of steaming food in front of him. 'Well, I am famous round these parts for being a good bloke,' he told her.

'Right,' Katy said, breathing a sigh of relief as she sat down at last. 'The turkey's in the fridge, the heating is on, we have enough booze to keep us drunk until next Christmas and all I have to do now is wrap presents.'

'Doesn't Father Christmas wrap the presents?' Jake asked, nonchalantly.

'Yes, obviously,' Katy said. 'He and the elves wrap the presents he brings. But Mummy and Daddy have got you presents too, so I have to wrap those.'

'So all the presents from Father Christmas will have totally different paper to all the ones from you and Dad, won't they?' Jake asked her, wide eyed. 'Because he wraps his in the North Pole and they haven't got a Tesco there, have they?'

Katy blinked at him. 'Obviously,' she said.

'Or a WH Smiths,' Jake added. 'Or a . . .'

'I expect Father Christmas's presents will be wrapped in some lovely homemade paper,' Katy said, cutting him off with just an edge of frustration. 'But part of the fun is waiting and seeing, isn't it?'

'Can I just say something?' Stephen stood up at the other end of the table and Lydia's heart sank, and a million dreadful scenarios about what he might say ran through her head in an instant. 'I know that the last thing Lydia and I want is for . . . for what's happened to cause any tension or upset for everyone else . . .'

'What has happened?' Tilly asked, eyes wide. 'Has Mad Molly done something?'

'Aunty Lydia's chucked that bloke,' Jake told her helpfully, nodding at Stephen.

'Oh,' Tilly said, immediately disinterested. 'Was she going out with him, then?'

'Children, hush,' Katy warned them.

'Anyway, I just want to say that there is nothing but good will and affection between Lydia and I, and that there is no need for anyone to feel awkward or embarrassed about what's happened. I love her; she doesn't love me. It's no one's fault. Okay, it's probably my fault, but anyway I understand. Well, I don't understand, actually. I think I'm a pretty good catch, as it goes, but still, each to their own. There are no hard feelings. Unless you count my broken heart.' Everyone at the table warily studied the plate in front of them, even the children. 'That's all, I just wanted to put you all at your ease.'

Stephen sat down, slightly askew so that his chair tipped back and would have toppled him onto the floor if Jackson hadn't stabilised him.

'Well, I know I'm thoroughly at ease now,' Joanna said brightly. 'More wine everyone?'

'Ah!' A sharp gasp from Alex drew everyone's attention as she clasped her hand to her belly and took a deep breath.

'Ambulance!' David shouted, standing up and knocking over a bottle of wine.

'Sit down, moron,' Alex snapped at him. 'It's nothing, just a bit of Braxton Hicks and a bit of indigestion and a bit of the baby wanting to leave before it gets any more embarrassing in here.'

'Are you sure?' David peered at her. 'Have your waters broken?'

'David, do you think if I had just evacuated several litres of amniotic fluid under the table I wouldn't mention it? Get a cloth and clear up the wine!' Obviously biting back his response, David picked up some spare paper napkins and began dabbing at the stain.

'Steady on, Al,' Jim said, clearly also rather the worse for wear after an afternoon of boozing. 'The bloke's just looking after you.'

'That's rich coming from you,' Alex muttered under her breath.

'Alex,' Katy whispered urgently.

'I beg your pardon?' Jim asked her, bullishly.

'Nothing.' Alex shrugged, tight-lipped.

'Go on, speak your mind,' Jim replied. Lydia looked at Joanna warily. Inviting Alex to speak her mind was never a good idea.

'Okay, I will.' Alex crossed her arms. 'You let Katy do everything, all the cooking, all the cleaning, all the childcare, all the worrying, while all you do is swan about like some bloody overgrown boy scout. Katy is doing her damnedest to make things work, and you are quite happy to sit back and watch her run herself into the ground. She's already got two kids, she doesn't need another one.'

'What? Bloody cheek! That's not how it is at all, is it, Katy?' Jim protested. 'It's just that Katy isn't a bloody henpecking shrew, like you. Honestly, the way you talk to Dave is shocking. Katy, grab another bottle of wine from the cellar, would you?'

'Jim, don't talk to my wife like that,' David said, quietly but firmly.

'Oh, grow a pair, mate, you've got to take a stance now otherwise you'll be out on your ear like fella-me-laddo over there, or under the bloody thumb all your life. Katy? Wine?'

'GET YOUR OWN MOTHER FUNNING

WINE!' Katy stood up, yelling at the top of her voice. 'Alex is right. I am your wife, Jim, your *wife*. Not your nanny. Not your skivvy, or your business manager, your chef or your bloody maidservant. And from now on, I am on strike. Sorry, everybody, Christmas is cancelled.'

Tilly's wail rose instantly above the general chaos as Katy stormed out with her distraught daughter in her arms, leaving Jim staring open mouthed after her.

'I hate you,' Jake told Jim, running at him and kicking him firmly in the shins.

'Fuck!' Jim gasped.

'And I don't even care if I don't get any presents, you deserve it.' Fighting to keep back the tears, Jake let Joanna pull him into a hug.

'Jake, come on, darling, let's go and find Mummy,' Joanna said as Lydia watched, dumbfounded. 'Don't worry, Mummy doesn't mean it about Christmas, she's just a bit over tired, that's all.'

'David, I want to go to bed too,' Alex said, wincing as David helped her up.

'What the fuck just happened?' Jim asked Jackson first and then Stephen. What happened?'

'Boathouse for an imaginary smoke?' Will asked her.

Lydia wanted nothing more at that moment to get out of the room and go and not smoke with Will, but she shook her head. 'I can't, Katy will need me.'

Will nodded. 'It's great being a lass, you've always got your mates.' He stood up. 'I'm just going for a smoke.'

'Jim,' Lydia said calmly. 'I think you're a bit drunk, I'll go and make you a coffee.' She looked at bleary-eyed Stephen and Jackson, who watched her quietly, as if he had a lot to say to her as soon as he got the chance. 'I'll make you all coffee and go and check on Katy.'

'I love that woman,' Jim was telling the other two vehemently as she left the room. 'I bloody love her more than anything on earth. I'd die for that woman. I'd die for her, that's what I'd do, I would, I'd . . .'

Lydia was very happy to let his voice recede into the distance as she hurried to the kitchen.

Katy was sitting at the kitchen table, with Tilly sobbing into her neck and Jake standing at her side patting Tilly's back ever so slightly more firmly than was necessary, while Vincent lay at her feet, gazing up at her with anxious brown eyes.

'I'm sorry, guys, I didn't mean it,' she was saying, reassuring her children. 'Of course Christmas isn't cancelled. As if I would do that. I was just cross, darlings, and thoughtless. I'm so, so sorry.'

'Here you go,' Joanna said. 'Irish coffee. Want one, Lyds?'

Lydia nodded. 'Would you like me to get the kids to bed?' she asked Katy, who shook her head.

'No, thanks, Lydia. I think that, before they go to bed, these guys need me and their dad to make up. I don't know what came over me.'

'I do,' Joanna said. 'It's Christmas, you see, people put all this pressure on themselves to be happy and . . .' Joanna caught sight of Lydia's pursed lips just in time. 'And you are tired and a bit drunk and it's been quite a day, what with Lydia chucking Stephen and having a hot sexy handyman already in her sights.'

'What does sexy mean?' Tilly asked, her red little face appearing from amongst Katy's curls.

'It means really lovely and cuddly,' Joanna told her.

'Like Vincent?' Tilly said.

'In many, many ways,' Joanna said.

'And anyway,' Lydia said, 'Will is really nice and I really like him, but there is no way I'm ready for another relationship. Not for months and months, and especially not him, he's not . . .'

'Your type?' Will said appearing in the door.

'Does everyone always have to come into a room like a bloody Ninja?' Lydia exclaimed. 'And he's not into me that way, I was about to say,' Lydia said.

Will nodded, as ever with that playful little smile threatening the corners of his very kissable mouth, Lydia thought, realising at the moment that she was very drunk and couldn't be trusted to say another word to anyone about anything, ever again.

'Look,' Will said. 'Do I have to go back in there with the men? They are dickheads, no offence.'

Katy giggled. 'Stay here and have an Irish coffee with us, Will.'

'I said I'd deliver coffee to those two,' Lydia said, looking down the long dark hallway to where the last two drunken men were standing, no doubt commiserating with each other.

'I'll take it,' Joanna said, winking at Lydia and blowing silent kisses to Will behind his back. 'Then I might actually get to see my boyfriend for a bit tonight and find out what's eating him.'

'Trouble in paradise?' Katy asked her, repeating the question Joanna had asked her earlier that day.

'I don't know, he's just been really quiet today, a touch distant. Do you think it was too soon to bring him home to meet the relatives? Do you think you lot have scared him away with your mentalism?'

Lydia bit her lip. She had barely seen let alone spoken to Jackson since that moment between them in his and Joanna's bedroom, and so much had happened since then. What if he thought that what happened between her and Stephen was something to do with him? What if he was planning to do the same with Joanna? She had to talk to him as soon as she could, to tell him nothing had changed.

'Listen, if a few whiney women scare him off, then he's no man worth keeping,' Will told Joanna, breaking into one of his rare, breathtaking, full smiles, so ravishing that for a moment all the women and the one dog in the room were quite overcome.

'What he said,' Katy chuckled, nodding at Will.

'Come on, guys, let's help Joanna take Daddy coffee and all have a big, big hug, okay?'

Left alone with Will, and remembering that she couldn't trust herself to be sensible, Lydia decided to wash up.

'So I'm not into you that way?' Will asked her casually.

'That's what you said.' Lydia glanced at him over her shoulder. 'It's cool, I don't expect every man I meet to fall down at my feet in love!'

'Makes a change from most women,' Will said. 'And I *am* your type, you say?'

'Now if anyone is acting like a girl, it's you, fishing for compliments!' Lydia laughed, turning round, her wet hands glittering with soap bubbles.

'You've caught me out.' He grinned and Lydia thought it best to turn her attention back to the roasting tin, trying to think of something witty and erudite to say.

'How did anyone ever survive without a dishwasher?' Not exactly what she'd be hoping for, but still.

'So what are you doing now?' Will asked her. 'I mean, I'm starving. It's very hard to get through a whole meal in this place without someone kicking off.'

'Cheese sandwich?' Lydia offered.

'I'll make it,' Will said. 'You finish the washing up.'

'And that, right there,' Lydia said happily, 'is equality of the sexes in action.'

* * *

The house was quiet when Lydia finally said goodnight to Will, choosing not to follow him upstairs to her big empty room but to return to the still cosy sitting room, where the last embers of the fire still glowed in the grate and Vincent was more than willing to share a corner of the sofa with her in return for a tickle behind the ear. Lulled almost to sleep by the animal's rhythmical breathing, Lydia felt her lids grow heavy, and she settled back into the sofa cushions, the room warm despite the snow drifting down outside the window.

'Are you okay, Lydia Grant?' Jackson's whispered voice in her ear startled Lydia awake. Sitting up, she blinked a few times and realised that Vincent's less than fragrant heat and warmth and been replaced by Jackson's thigh pressing along the length of hers.

'What are you doing up?' she asked him, still confused by sleep.

'I've been desperate to talk to you all day,' Jackson said, 'and all night, ever since I kissed you again. I know I shouldn't, but I can't stop thinking about you, Lydia.'

'Jackson, stop it.' Lydia was firm, edging away from him. 'We had our moment. Back then, I fell for you hook, line and sinker. If you'd asked me to go to the ends of the world for you, I would have. And I'd have done it economy class, too. But you didn't, you left. You didn't phone, or e-mail, or send a pigeon, you disappeared and now you are with my best friend. And even if I did still feel anything for you, that would rule you out completely. Do you understand?'

For a moment Lydia held his intense gaze, the visceral memory of the summer they'd spent together building on the heat the seemed to flow so freely between them. Feeling it was safer, she slid down off the sofa and onto the rug, where Vincent eyed his usurper resentfully.

'I'm not saying that I got it right, I didn't,' Jackson said. 'I messed up about as badly as I could have. But does that mean I don't get a second chance? Especially now when the reason I left you alone is gone.'

Lydia shook her head. 'And what about Joanna? What about her in all this? I'm pretty sure you've romanced and seduced her, just like you did me, and that you have given her every reason to believe that what is happening between you is real and has a future. You're even taking her home to New York to meet you mother!'

'What?' At Jackson's barked question, Lydia turned sharply to look at him. He seemed genuinely surprised by the information. 'Look, I like Joanna, I like her a lot, she's a great fun girl,' he said, 'but even before we got this far, taking her home to Mom was not on the table. I mean, I might have mentioned it in passing, perhaps as a joke, but we've only been together for two months. I didn't mean for her to take it seriously!'

Lydia studied his face. In the dim light of the dying

embers, it was impossible to tell if he were lying, but it didn't matter: whether he'd been serious or not, Joanna believed it was a sign of the importance of their fledgling relationship. 'Joanna thinks it's true,' she said firmly. 'And, anyway, you've come away with her for Christmas. Everyone knows that once you've spent Christmas together you might as well get married!'

Jackson shook his head, plumping back into the sofa cushions, exasperated. 'Like you and Stephen? Look, I had Christmas all planned out – dinner with Mom at our favourite Italian on East 55th street – until the snow came in down south, and there were all the severe weather warnings. Mom and I talked about whether I should risk spending Christmas in a departures lounge and we decided I'd go out to the States when the weather cleared, in the New Year. As soon as I told Joanna about it, she begged me to come up here. She said it would be fun, she didn't want me to be alone, couldn't wait to show me off. She threatened to stay with me, if I didn't come along.'

Lydia stared at him. None of what he said sounded like Joanna at all – she just wasn't needy or clingy. Why on earth would she make up the trip home to meet his mother, though, or anything else, for that matter? And yet he seemed very convincing. Then again, he was good at that, making her believe in him. He'd had her convinced from the moment they met.

'Anyway,' Jackson said softly, reaching out to touch

her face, even as Lydia backed away from him, 'even if any of that were true, it doesn't make these feelings that we have between us imaginary, does it?' He leaned forward a little. 'Are you really telling me that you don't feel it too? You don't feel your heart racing, the hairs standing up on the back of your neck, your skin on fire, longing to be touched, your lips aching to be kissed? You don't feel any of that, Lydia?'

'I . . . I think you are trying to have your cake and eat it. I think it's just some sick game you're playing. You're probably a sex addict. You should go to a clinic for that.'

'I am addicted to you, that's true,' Jackson said, inching closer to her. 'You're the one thing I find I can't give up.'

Tired, weak and confused, Lydia let Jackson pull her up to him without resistance, dragging her body between his knees and his arms encircling her torso. As he kissed her, just then she was lost, utterly lost in the oddly surreal moment, powerless to resist his persistent mouth devouring hers, succumbing to his searching hands as if in a dream as he pulled up her dress, the heat of that long ago summer burning between them.

'Christ almighty!'

Lydia and Jackson sprang apart as Alex stood in the doorway, her mouth open.

'Alex!' Lydia hurriedly pulled her dress back down over her hips, shock at the situation she found herself in sobering her up like an ice-cold bucket of water in the face.

'Look, it's not . . .' Jackson began, but Alex stopped him with the palm of her hand. 'Get out, go upstairs and see your girlfriend. And you,' she said, turning to Lydia, 'stay put.'

'I'm not going anywhere,' Jackson said, re-buttoning the shirt that Lydia didn't remember undoing.

'Jackson, go,' Lydia said, her cheeks burning. 'Please.'

'Fine, but if you need me—'

'You'll be in bed with Joanna,' Alex told him.

Lydia sat on the sofa, her hands folded in her lap.

'Explain,' Alex said. 'Because the Lydia I know is not the sort of person who would go after her friend's boyfriend, not unless there's been some sort of invasion of the bitch snatchers going on and I haven't noticed.'

'I knew him before,' Lydia said quite simply.

'What do you mean?' Alex asked her.

'I mean that the last person I expected Joanna to turn up here with was the man I had that summer affair with just before I met Stephen, the one I was seeing when you nearly sacked me from being your bridesmaid. The one you were helping me get over by forcing me to go on a fun run.'

'He's *Jack*?' Alex sat down with difficulty. 'I swear if I don't got into labour now, it will be a Christmas miracle.'

Alex listened while Lydia talked, the room growing chilly as the last remnants of heat died along with the cooling ashes, and even Vincent gave up his spot, choosing to nose his way out of the narrow gap in the door and go in search of some warm, friendly child's bed to sleep on. Lydia told her everything, how it had been between her and Jackson in London, how it had ended so suddenly. How she thought he'd just dumped her when in fact a family tragedy had kept them apart. She also told Alex how shocked she had been to see him arrive with Joanna, and how he claimed he still felt about her.

'And how do you feel about him?' Alex asked her, tartly.

'I don't know, Alex.' Lydia sighed. 'He left at the height of our honeymoon period. I didn't have time to find out if he had any irritating habits, if actually after looking at him for three months straight I'd find his Roman nose repulsive. So I don't know.'

'But you do know that he is with Joanna, and that she's crazy about him,' Alex stated. 'And you know that, despite apparently really being into her, he's getting off with you while she sleeps upstairs. He might have had a good reason for leaving you but that doesn't give him license to cheat on his girlfriend. I mean, that alone would be reason enough to leave him well alone, wouldn't it? He's obviously a pig.'

'It's always so clear cut with you, so black and white,' Lydia said. 'I do know that, of *course* I do. But I can't help thinking, what if . . . what if he's the one?'

'Well, don't,' Alex said. 'What ifs don't get you anywhere. What you have to concentrate on now are facts. And the facts are that you've just been making out with Joanna's man. You have to come clean, you have to tell Joanna everything.'

'Are you crazy?' Lydia asked her. 'I've already brought this whole event to the brink of disaster as it is by splitting up with Stephen so publicly, and now you want me to push it over the edge and maybe wreck our friendship for ever?'

'What if it had been Joanna who'd walked in on you just now? Then your friendship really would be over.' Alex took a sharp breath, pressing a palm into her side. 'Look, she will find out and I don't know what will hurt her the most, that fact that he's lied to her, or that you have. And if you don't come clean, then I'll be lying to her too. And I can't do that, Lydia. Not even for you.'

Lydia buried her head in her hands. 'Okay, tomorrow is Christmas Eve. We're only here a couple more days. *Please*, don't make me be the one who totally trashes this for Katy and the kids, *please*. I promise that as soon as we get back to London I'll come clean, I'll tell her everything.'

'And you'll stay away from Jackson in the meantime?' Alex asked. 'No more nonsense like that?'

'Definitely not. I'll stay as far away from him as I possibly can,' Lydia said.

'Then I suppose we'll just have to ride it out.' Alex sighed, leaning her head back on the sofa. 'Fuck me, I only came down for some Gaviscon. I left it in my handbag.'

'Here.' Lydia reached for Alex's bag and handed it to her, watching as Alex swigged the liquid directly from the bottle.

'Poor Lyds,' Alex said. 'Let's just hope they are wrong when they say that bad things always come in threes.'

Chapter Twelve

24 December
The Night Before Christmas

The first thing Lydia became aware of was the shooting pain running down her neck and into her left arm. Typical, she thought, I'm dying of a heart attack and I haven't even had a chance to wear my new red dress yet. The second thing was the awful racket the cherubs made; Lydia was sure heaven was meant to be a good deal more serene than this. Also, as far as she knew, it didn't smell of wet dog.

'*On the fifth day of Christmas my true love gave to me, five loo rolls, four stinky farts, three little poos, two pairs of pants and a bra that was meant to hold threeeeeeeeee!*'

Lydia prized open one eye to find Jake and Tilly serenading her, and concluded that she was not dead; she had woken up on the sofa. And just at that moment, the realisation seemed rather disappointing.

'Shhh!' Lydia pressed her finger to her lips, pushing aside large quantities of Vincent, who appeared to be on top of her, in order to sit up. As the blood began to flow back into her limbs, they tingled and popped. 'Guys, a bit less of the singing.'

'But it's Christmas Eve . . . Day,' Tilly said, excitedly, hoping from foot to foot.

'I know and it's lovely, but . . . do you know "Silent Night"?'

'*Silent Fart, Holy Fart,*' Jake immediately began singing at the top of his voice.

Lydia groaned, her head spinning as clunk after clunk, the memory of what had happened last night thudded into place in her poor sore head.

'Aunty Lydia I'm hungry and Mummy and Daddy have locked the bedroom door and are doing animal impressions,' Tilly said. 'Will you feed us?'

'If you stop singing,' Lydia said.

'Look what I found!' Jake held up Lydia's bra, which she dimly remembered unhooking and feeding through the arm of her dress last night, somewhere towards the bottom of a bottle of very passable Shiraz. '*And a bra that was mean to hold three!*'

'Hey! Come back!' Lydia called lamely, as Jake raced off into the depths of the house, holding her bra aloft, with a giggling Tilly in his wake. A quick check determined that Vincent had spent the night with his nose buried in her tights, so Lydia had no option but to venture out into the world wearing her wine-red knitted dress and panties, and nothing much else. Hopefully, Katy and Jim's locked door meant they were making up, and judging by the amount of drinking going on last night, she was hopeful that everyone else would be in bed long enough for her to throw some cereal at the kids and go and get a shower.

Vincent grumbled as she pushed his paws off her lap and stood up, taking a moment to steady herself. Braless, tightless, boyfriendless, and, if Joanna found out about what had happened with Jackson, soon to be friendless.

If anyone asked Lydia to name her worst ever Christmases, then the one when her father left would have been number one, closely followed by the year when her father was still with horrid Karen and had banned Lydia from visiting. Lydia had been bereft at being rejected by her father, her feelings not helped by the realisation that this also meant she didn't have to go to see the Wicked Witch of the Midlands that year. Her mother had been really excited about a new boyfriend, who she'd said had even got her a present. Lydia had never forgotten opening that box to see two little beady eyes staring back at her. Her Christmas present had been a badly stuffed dead hedgehog, courtesy of the boyfriend's taxidermy hobby.

Later – much later – she'd been able to laugh about it with her friends, and had even kept Mrs Twiggywinkle on her desk during all of her final exams. At the time, though, it had been horrendous, a symbol of all that had been wrong about her childhood. This year, however, was shaping up to achieve the impossible and be even worse than the year of the dead hedgehog.

The children were already in the kitchen when Lydia arrived to see Tilly attempting to open a packet of bacon with a very large bread knife.

'Whoa!' Lydia stepped in, removing the knife and bacon from Tilly just in time.

'How about this?' Jake said, revving up the carving knife that he'd plugged in next to the oven.

'Or,' Lydia suggested, dancing across the cold stone tiles in her bare feet to confiscate the deadly weapon, 'how about some Weetabix?'

'Weetabix isn't Christmas Eve breakfast,' Tilly complained. 'We have to have something special and Christmassy.'

Lydia looked around, her hand on her hips. 'Mince pies?'

'Aunty Lydia!' Tilly rolled her eyes. 'Bacon and eggs, please.'

'But you had bacon and eggs yesterday,' Lydia said. 'How is that Christmassy?'

'Because it's our favourite,' Tilly assured her, in a very patronising tone of voice.

'But how is it Christmassy?' Lydia protested.

'It just is!' Tilly said, rolling her eyes.

'Do you want to know where you bra is?' Jake said mildly, smiling sweetly.

Squinting at him as menacingly as she could, Lydia

turned on the grill, and Vincent sloped into the room with the prescient knowledge that there would soon be cooked pig.

Everything had been going to plan. Lydia had found her stiletto ankle boots to wear as slippers, she had coffee on the go, the children had hot chocolate topped with squirty cream from a can plus a sprinkling of ground cinnamon – which was her token gesture in honour of the season – she had sliced bread and garnished it with Ketchup ready for the bacon that was nearly done.

'Oooh, look.' Lydia found some croissants in the bread bin. 'I'll warm these up too.'

No sooner had she switched on the oven than there was a loud bang and the oven went dark.

'Oh,' Lydia said, going to the plug and switching it off and on again. 'Um.'

'What is it?' Tilly asked her.

'Run about and try all the lights and things,' Lydia, told the children, who scooted off obediently, for once. Anxiously, Lydia tried all of the kitchen lights and found nothing working. 'Oh fuck, I've broken the house and destroyed the cooker in the process. Katy is going to kill me. Everyone here is going to hate me and want to kill me too. Fuck.'

'Nothing's working,' Jake reported back. 'Shall I get Dad?'

'No, no . . . no, we don't want Mummy to worry just yet.' Lydia peered under the grill. 'Look, the bacon is done. You guys, stay here and eat your sandwiches and I'll go and ask Will if he can help.'

There was no answer the first time Lydia knocked on Will's door, nor the second. Perhaps he had taken his chances and absconded in the night, she thought, or maybe he'd gone out to the boathouse again. Trying the door handle, she found it unlocked, so she quietly pushed open the door, slowly advancing into the room.

His bed had been slept in but was now empty.

'Fuck, fuck, fuck!' Lydia whispered bitterly.

'Sorry?' Will appeared behind her, wearing nothing but a towel. Lydia yelped, swore again and then, remembering she was barely dressed herself at the exact same moment that she noticed Will's rather impressive torso, she pulled at the hem of her skirt.

'Shit, you scared the life out of me.'

'Sorry,' Will said. 'But you have sort of broken into my room.'

'I didn't break in; the door was open. Normal people lock their doors.'

'No, normal people knock,' Will informed her, his gaze slipping to her unbridled bosom before being hurriedly redirected to a spot on the wall just above her left shoulder. Looking down, Lydia realised that the early chill in the air meant it was especially easy to tell that she wasn't wearing a bra; her nipples were clearly visible beneath the fine knit of the dress. Mortified, she again pulled down the constantly riding-up hem of her dress over her naked thighs, and then crossed her arms over her chest. Will coughed, careful to look anywhere but at her as he grabbed a T-shirt and pulled it over his head, obviously as uncomfortable about her state of virtual undress as she was. He had very nice arms, Lydia thought, wistfully, and a very manly chest. Just the sort of chest she could imagine resting her head on as she drifted off to sleep.

'Look, why are you here?' Will asked her, snapping her out of the spell of his partial nudity.

'Oh right, yes. I've blown up the cooker and now no lights are working downstairs,' Lydia told him. 'And it's Christmas Eve and if I've really killed the cooker, Katy will kill *me* and I can't take any more, I can't. Everybody hates me as it is.'

'Er, excuse me?' Will gestured for Lydia to turn around.

Obediently, Lydia moved away to stare out of his bedroom window at the steep incline of the back garden, where somewhere, under feet of snow, poor Mad Molly was buried. She heard the soft thud of wet towel hitting carpet and then the jingle of loose change in pockets as Will pulled up his jeans, followed by the rasp of the zip and the clank of the belt buckle. Will was buttoning up his shirt as she turned around, forgetting, in her anxiety, to cover her chest or stop her dress from creeping up her thighs again. Will sighed, crossly.

'Look, I'm really sorry to ask you, but look at it this way – you are literally saving Christmas if you can fix the oven, which must be good karma. Do you think you can fix it?' Lydia bit her lip, wondering if Will, who was glaring out of the window himself now, was angry with her because she was southern, or because he wasn't a morning person, or maybe not so fond of strange half-dressed women invading his privacy.

'I'll take a look at it,' he agreed.

'Great, thanks.' Lydia took two or three steps towards him. 'I'll make you a luke-warm coffee. The kettle boiled just before everything went kaput.'

'Before you do . . .' Will still couldn't quite manage to look at her.

'What?' Lydia asked him.

'It's just, well . . . could you get dressed first?'

'Yes, fine, fine. God, sorry I didn't realise I was so offensive.' Lydia turned on her heel, leaving Will in his room looking at his feet. He stood there for a good moment or two longer before taking a breath and going downstairs, quietly swearing to himself under his breath as he went.

By the time a very irritable and embarrassed Lydia came back downstairs, properly attired so as not to offend the sensitive nature of the local handyman, Will was in the kitchen, lying on his side on the kitchen floor, unscrewing the back of the cooker, with Jake's chin practically resting on his shoulder as he watched, fascinated by the secret world of wiring.

Will looked up at Lydia, who'd found jeans and a jumper, not to mention all the appropriate underwear, as she came in. 'White and two sugars, please.'

'This decent enough for you?' she snapped at him.

'I just didn't want you to catch a chill,' Will said, returning his attention to the oven.

'We put aunty Lydia's bra on our snowman,' Jake told Will, conversationally. 'It took two massive snowballs to fill it!'

'Hmphf.' Lydia put the kettle on.

'The element's blown, which tripped the lights on this floor,' Will explained as she stepped over him to find a mug. 'Which at least means this place is wired properly. I just had to reset it to get the power back on. It's not quite so simple for the oven, I'm afraid. It's knackered. There is no way I can find a replacement part for something this old, in one day, not on Christmas Eve, maybe not ever.'

'Oh, God.' Lydia kneeled on the floor, absently taking a sip from Will's coffee before she handed it to him. 'No oven, no hob. Katy is going to kill me. You know what, I'm just going outside, I may be some time . . .'

'I'm going to tell Mum,' Jake said bouncing to his feet, Tilly and Vincent in his wake, and Lydia didn't stop him. Better for a six-year-old boy to break the news than her; she was fairly sure Katy wouldn't throw her own son into the lake.

'For what it's worth, this at least isn't your fault,' Will told her. 'Same thing would have happened to whoever it was switched the oven on next.'

'I'm too helpful,' Lydia complained. 'You never get Joanna accidentally blowing up ovens on Christmas Eve. Oh, no, she's still in bed . . . doing stuff. And Alex is busy being heavily pregnant, so she *never* gets into trouble.'

'How selfish of her,' Will said, able to look at her again now she was covered up. 'Look, it probably seems bad, being snowed in with your recent ex, a very dead turkey and an oven that doesn't work, but trust me, it's not the end of the world.' He pushed himself into a sitting position, leaning his back against the defunct cooker.

'No, not in the grand scheme of things, probably,' Lydia conceded. 'I mean, better that Stephen and I split up now, rather than after he proposed to me, and at least we've got a turkey, even if it is in bits. But the oven, not working, is going to be the end of Christmas. I swear, I am like a Christmas curse, wherever I go shit follows. Next year, I'm going to lock myself in my bedroom and never come out.'

Will nodded. 'I think we'd all sleep sounder in our beds if we knew that.'

'Hey!' Lydia caught his eye, and saw the smile hiding around his lips. 'Go on, tease me, if it makes you feel better. *You* must be mental. After all, you're still here. You could be at home by now, getting your girlfriend to bring you mince pies, with your feet up in front of a roaring fire and not a dysfunctional person from the wrong side of the Watford Gap in sight.'

'Aye, I could.' Will sighed and smiled simultaneously. 'Instead, I'm working for free, trapped with a load of lunatics, one who insists on breaking into my room, half naked, to get a look at me in a towel. Good job I haven't got a girlfriend when you think about it, or a wife, seeing as you're asking.'

Lydia couldn't help smiling, irrationally cheerful that Will didn't have a girlfriend or a wife, even though he was mocking her for trying to find out these things with about as much subtlety as a curious elephant.

'Seriously, though,' Lydia asked him, as they sat on the kitchen floor, their feet touching, 'why are you still here?'

Will's dark eyes met hers for a moment. 'Isn't it obvious?' he asked her, his voice low.

'What? Isn't what obvious?' Lydia squeaked.

'Someone's got to point out to you numpties that you don't need an ancient leccy oven when you've got a massive great Aga in your kitchen. Or did you think it was shoe storage?'

'It doesn't work!' Lydia said, her cheeks blazing,

furious that she'd let herself be drawn in by those dark eyes.

'Probably the burner just needs cleaning.' Will handed her his empty mug. 'Now, make me another warmish coffee, woman, while I do my third job for free.'

'It's working?' Katy stared at the Aga, her hands clasped together like a little girl who's just found a puppy in a shoe box.

Will patted the Aga, and checked his watch. 'Yep, it should be ready to use at around eight tomorrow morning. 'If you'd had a whole turkey, you'd have needed to brown it in the roasting oven first and then slow cook it for eight or ten hours in the simmering oven, which means you wouldn't be eating Christmas dinner until midnight. So it's lucky really that Lydia mutilated it beyond recognition. When you think about it, she did you a favour because now you can probably cook the whole thing in the roasting oven for four or five hours.'

'Oh my God, I love you!' Will froze as Katy threw her arms around him and kissed him on the lips for about ten more seconds than was seemly.

'Fuck, no one said we were swinging,' Joanna said as she appeared. 'If we're swinging, I want a turn on Will next.'

'Please say you'll stay and have Christmas lunch with

us,' Katy invited Will as she released him, looking more than a little shell shocked. 'That is, if you've got nothing else planned?'

'I normally have Christmas lunch in The Royal Oak with the whole village,' Will said, stuffing his hand in his pockets, as if he'd just noticed he was surrounded by unpredictable women. 'It's sort of a tradition. We all bring something, stick it all on a table and get horribly drunk. I've got a Yule log.'

'Oh, oh well, that sounds very nice,' Katy said, her enthusiasm slightly dimmed. 'First I've heard of it, but still . . . how nice. The whole village getting together for Christmas. Wouldn't it be lovely to be part of something like that?'

'No reason why you couldn't come down,' Will told her. 'Everyone's welcome.'

Tilly and Jake arrived, pushing their way between the legs of the grown-ups.

'Mummy, Aunty Lydia forgot to cook us eggs when she blew up the cooker,' Tilly complained. 'I'm still hungry.'

'Ah well.' Will crouched down to meet Tilly's eyes. 'Want me to show you two how to cook eggs in a coal shovel, on an open fire?'

'Yes, please!' Jake said enthusiastically.

'Won't it taste of coal?' Tilly asked.

'Best bit,' Will said, grabbing a box of eggs and plate from the side, as Tilly and the ever-hopeful Vincent followed him out. 'I was practically raised on coal, never did me any harm.'

'I think my ovaries just palpated,' Joanna said. 'I love that man.'

'Back of the queue,' said Katy firmly, '*I* love that man. He got my Aga working.'

'May I be the voice of reason.' Alex lumbered into the kitchen. 'Joanna, you allege that you are in love with that hunky American you've been giggling with all morning. And Katy, judging by your massive shag hair, you love your husband much more today than you did yesterday. Lydia can't possibly love him because she's on the rebound, from Stephen. So it's official. If he's cooking breakfast, I love him, and I'm going to name the baby after him, even if it's a girl.'

Chapter Thirteen

To her shame, Lydia had been so caught up in the drama of the morning that she almost forgot about Stephen until she found him sitting on her bed when she went back to her room to find an extra pair of socks for an unexpected expedition. After delighting everyone by cooking eggs on a coal shovel, Will suggested that he could go back to the village and fetch his Calor gas oven, as there was no other way of heating food until at least tomorrow.

'Seriously, mate, any chance you could be a bit less dashing?' Jim asked him. 'You're making the rest of us chaps feel most inadequate.'

'Just trying to help out,' Will said modestly. Lydia pressed her lips together to suppress a smile, as she watched all the women swoon, and Jim and David perk up as they realised another possible expedition to the pub was on the cards. But their hopes were dashed.

'Want to come with me?' Will asked Lydia, who checked over her shoulder to see if he was talking to someone else. He wasn't.

Lydia could see it was taking all of Joanna's willpower

not to say. 'Ooooh, get you,' so she answered quickly. 'Er, yeah. Yes, why not?'

'Seems a shame for you not to see the landscape properly, while you're here,' Will said, as if he needed to provide an explanation.

'There are windows.' Alex raised a brow.

'What about me? It's a shame I haven't seen the landscape either,' Joanna said, pouting.

'You'll need proper boots, and at least one more pair of socks,' Will instructed Lydia quite seriously, ignoring Joanna. 'And a proper coat, gloves and that. It's not far, but it's cold out there. Always best to be prepared.'

'Prepared, totally.' Lydia nodded. 'Like a boy scout.'

'Well, go on, then.' Will ushered her away with a flick of his hand, and, whirling about, Lydia found herself crashing into Jackson's chest.

'Oh, sorry,' she said, rubbing her nose.

'You okay?' he asked her in a tone just soft enough to make Alex glare at her and Joanna come and drape a proprietorial arm over his shoulder. Lydia had run all the way upstairs and was quite out of breath when she found Stephen in her room.

'You didn't sleep here last night,' he said, nodding at the perfectly plumped pillow.

'No,' Lydia said, guiltily. 'I crashed out on the sofa with the dog. Did you sleep?'

Stephen nodded. 'I was dead drunk. Look, I don't

remember much about last night, but I'm sorry if I showed you up.'

'You didn't.' Lydia sat down next to him. 'You've been brilliant. You could have made life hell for everyone, and no one would have blamed you. But you're not that sort of man, are you, Stephen?'

'I think,' Stephen said, 'the worst thing about breaking up with someone who doesn't love you any more is that they aren't sad.'

'I am,' Lydia insisted. 'I am sad, really sad.'

'No, you're not. I mean, you are sad that you've hurt me, because you care about me. But you're not sad that we aren't together any more and, well, that's okay. It sort of helps, actually. I feel like I've had the stuffing kicked out of me, but looking at you now, with your eyes all sparkling and some colour in your cheeks, makes me realise that it's pointless pining over you for too long.'

Lydia reached out and covered his hand with hers. 'Oh, Stephen, you just need the right woman. The woman who makes you stop long enough to realise how much you need her, the woman who is more important to you than work or a cause ever would be, one who you want to spend every spare minute with, even if you can't. You need to be with a woman who you miss even when she's in the next room. And if you're honest, I was never that woman. I could never get you to stop for more than about a minute.'

Stephen nodded. 'I know, and so I just wanted to say that I'm okay. Don't let this spoil your Christmas. I want you to have a happy one, although I'm now a bit short of a gift . . .'

'What about you? Will you be able to have a Happy Christmas?' Lydia asked.

'Yes.' Stephen nodded. 'I'm going to get very drunk and eat so much food that I'll have to drive home with my trousers unzipped. Now, if you'll excuse me I'm going to listen to 'Last Christmas' and all the other Christmas break-up songs I can think of on my iPod.' He paused in the doorway. 'Where are you going?'

'Into the village, with Will, to get a camping stove,' Lydia said, fidgeting with the hem of her sleeve as if she were somehow betraying Stephen.

Stephen nodded. 'All you girls seems rather taken with Will. Is he really that amazing?'

Lydia laughed. 'Amazing? No, not at all. Whatever gave you that idea?'

For some reason, Lydia had thought that Will inviting her to accompany him to fetch his camping stove and see the scenery meant that he might want to talk to her, but they had trudged through the thick drifts of snow for at least twenty minutes in total silence. For a good while, Lydia busied herself with looking around at the stunning scenery, breathing in the cool air, and trying to keep up with Will, which was difficult. She was well wrapped up, as ordered, in Jim's outsize coat, Katy's snow boots and a quite small, pink, glittery knitted bobble hat that sat on her head at a rather precarious angle, and which she suspected might belong to Tilly.

'It feels like there might be no one else alive in the whole world, docsn't it?' Lydia said, giving in to the urge to break the silence. 'It's so quiet, there are no planes in the sky, no cars on the road . . .'

'No people wittering on,' Will added.

'Sorry,' Lydia replied, wryly. 'I didn't realise I had to take a vow of silence when I agreed to come with you. You're normally quite chatty.'

'Chatty?' Will stopped and looked at her.

'Yes, chatty. So why have you gone all strong and silent now?'

Will frowned, marching on once more for several paces before replying. 'I thought I might be able to give you the stove to bring back by yourself, but you'd probably just break a nail, get lost and die in a ditch, and then I'd feel responsible.'

Lydia chuckled. 'I'm sure that if the idea of going back to Heron's Pike horrifies you so much, I could find my way back on my own. I mean, I just have to follow this road, right? I don't have to track tiny otter paw prints, or navigate by the stars?'

This time it was Will's turn to smile. 'You've got a lot to say for yourself,' he said, which in the absence of any expansion on the statement, Lydia decided to take as a compliment.

'It's my job. As a barrister, I sort of have to talk for a living. Argumentatively, usually.'

'Ah.' Will nodded. 'Makes sense.'

'Sense? Of what? That I don't just agree with everything you say like a proper girl should?'

'No.' Will smiled. 'Posh girl, posh job. Makes sense.'

'Posh!' Lydia gasped. 'I'm not posh. Just because I don't mispronounce vowels like the people round here, it doesn't make me posh, you know.'

'Whoa, touchy.' Will held up his gloved hands.

'I'm sorry,' Lydia said. 'It's just that I don't come from money, or anything like it. My parents never had any money when they were married, and even less after they split up. Until she remarried, my mum rented a house next door to funeral home, because it was cheap, and Dad lives in his latest wife's house. I wasn't supposed to do anything. I wasn't supposed to get A levels or go to uni, and I certainly wasn't supposed to spend so many years studying to become a barrister. I was supposed to get a job at the age of sixteen and pay my way, but I didn't. I was stubborn. I worked my way through law school, waitressing, bar work, temping – once I even dressed up as a Mexican cow girl and followed a giant Taco round Leicester Square. I did anything to earn money, well, nearly anything. It wasn't easy, but like I said, I'm stubborn. I wouldn't give up my dream.'

'So why a barrister?' Will asked her.

Lydia stopped walking and looked thoughtfully at Will, who'd carried on a couple of steps and then turned to wait for her. Over the years she'd been asked this question time and time again, and she always came out with a trite or flippant answer: I love the stylish outfit, she'd say, or the money, or the status or the challenge. But there was something about Will that made her want to tell him the real reason she'd struggled and scraped to get where she was today; something that made her think she could trust him.

'Do you promise not to laugh?' she asked him.

'Okay.' Will nodded.

'Or scoff?' Lydia added. 'Cynical scoffing is not permitted.'

'Go on.'

'For most of my childhood, I felt like was caught up in a whirlwind that I had absolutely no control over. Parents ripping each other to shreds, even after the divorce, shunted around from house to house, whether or not I wanted to go, whether or not I was even wanted. I didn't have a say about anything and, most importantly of all, I didn't have anyone on my side, to speak up for me or to defend me. No one to say this has got to stop, this isn't right. I felt, I *was*, helpless.

'Then, one Saturday afternoon when I was about fourteen, I found the film *To Kill a Mockingbird* on TV. You know, the one with Gregory Peck in it, as Atticus

Finch. He's noble, so strong and more importantly he won't let anything or anyone stand in the way of doing the best for his client. He had the guts to say this is not right and this has to stop. And I decided then and there that I wanted to be Gregory Peck, well, Atticus Finch. Or at least as close to it as a little English girl in a crummy seaside town can get. I wanted to be the person that would be there, just when life seemed to be at its very worst, the person who is on your side, no matter what.'

Lydia faltered into silence, suddenly feeling very self-conscious about pouring her heart out to a near stranger in the middle of the snow, wanting him to know what she had never told another soul, for reasons that she didn't fully understand.

'I suppose that sounds pretty ridiculous,' she added at last, half laughing.

Will took a step back towards her. 'No, far from it,' he said gently. 'It sounds pretty amazing, as it goes.'

'Oh, well.' Lydia felt herself blush. 'I can't pretend the money isn't good, and that I don't enjoy the drama of it, and the wigs are fabulous . . .'

'Hey, listen.' Will stopped her with a smile. 'You don't have to pretend with me. I know you're not as shallow and as flippant as you like to make out. I can see it in your eyes. You really care about what you do, it means to the world to you, and I really respect that. I've not known you long but you're different from most girls.'

'Different?' Lydia asked him, not sure if it was a compliment or not. 'How?' she asked him tentatively as his black eyes looked intently into hers.

'Don't ask me,' Will said, a deep furrow between his eyes. 'Right now, I don't know whether I'm coming or going. Yes I do, I'm going – we're going – to the village to get the gas stove. We'd better get a move on, else we'll get frozen to the spot.'

'So why *did* you ask me to come with you?' she asked him, a little confused. 'Why not one of the boys?'

'Because they are all idiots,' Will said. 'Nice blokes, and all. But idiots.'

'Oh, and I'm not an idiot?' Lydia brightened.

'I just thought you'd rather have a bit of time out of the house,' Will said. 'You've been stuck in there for days.'

'Nice of you to care,' Lydia said. 'You make me sound like a dog that needs walking.'

'I don't care, I . . .' Will stopped himself. 'I just know what it's like. Breaking up with someone. I was engaged for a bit.' Will marched on with even more determination, leaving Lydia standing for a moment in the snow.

'Wait!' she called after him breathlessly. 'Will, hold on. Look, you can't just drop a bombshell like that and then run off.'

'I wouldn't call it a bombshell,' Will said, stopping to wait for her until she caught up. 'I was engaged and then I wasn't. So I know that you probably could do with a bit of space to sort you head out. Which doesn't normally require chatting.'

'But, what happened? Who was she?' What did she look like? Lydia thought but didn't ask. 'Did she dump you?'

Will's brows knitted together in a deep frown. 'Why do women always need to know everything?'

'I don't know. I don't, I suppose. I've shared with you; I thought maybe you'd like to share with me. After all, you brought it up,' Lydia said. 'I'm sorry. It's just I don't know how I'm supposed to be feeling right now. I mean, this was the most serious relationship I've ever had, so I'm pretty sure I'm not supposed to be feeling the way I do.'

'Which is?' Will asked her.

'Relieved,' Lydia said. 'And right now . . . happy. Happy to be out here, in the snow, with these amazing surroundings. I feel exhilarated. Which makes me sound very callous, doesn't it?'

'Or it shows that you made the right decision.' Will shrugged. 'Her name was, is, Rachel,' Will said as he walked on, holding out a hand to help her through a particularly deep drift. 'She was pretty, nice. Read a lot of books but still, you know, funny.' Lydia reluctantly let go of his hand as she privately seethed about this beautiful, literate comedienne called Rachel. Boring name anyway, Lydia thought. 'We'd known each other a long while. She had a gift shop in the town. I'd see her on her bike, riding into work every morning. We'd stop and chat.'

Lydia wondered when they were going to get to the breaking up part.

'I'm not the sort of bloke who goes in all guns blazing. I suppose I don't give much away,' Will said. 'It's hard for me to let a lass know I like her. I was building up to asking her for a drink when one day she just asked me right out if I fancied her, just like that. I said yes. That was that, we were going out.'

'And then what happened?' Lydia asked him, almost sorry to see, some way ahead among the trees, the tip of the village church spire come into view.

'We went out,' Will said. 'For two years.'

'But you must have loved her if you asked her to marry you?' Lydia persisted.

'Not sure I actually asked her,' Will said, looking genuinely perplexed. 'We were out in the town, I'd just sold on this place I'd done up in Keswick, made quite a bit on it. Rachel said we should do something really mad, really spontaneous. We were standing outside this jewellery shop when she said it. So I bought her a ring, caught up in the moment, you know. And then we were engaged. I'm not sure I knew about it until afterwards, and then I sort of just went with it.'

'Wow,' Lydia said. 'This Rachel had moves even Joanna would be proud of. What happened?'

'I liked her a lot,' Will said. 'Like I said, she was

the prettiest girl around for miles, funny, smart. Had it all.'

'Obviously not all,' Lydia said, a touch snippily. 'Otherwise you would have married her.'

'You're right,' Will said simply, stopping at the crest of a hill that fell away to reveal the village, nestling in the crook of the hill, rooftops covered in snow, smoke rising from chimney stacks and snaking into the air.

'Oh,' Lydia breathed, as she took in the view. 'It's so beautiful, it's lovely.'

Will looked sideways at her. 'You think so? I've lived here all my life, and I never get tired of walking to the top of this hill and seeing that. It's home, you know? Whatever else is going on in the world, to know you've got a home to come back to, like that. It lifts the heart.'

Lydia looked at him. 'You can be quite poetic when you want to be,' she said.

Will smiled faintly, taking hold of her gloved hand and not letting go as he led her down the hill towards the village, even though this time there didn't appear to be any obstacles that she needed guiding over.

'I realised I didn't love her,' Will said as they walked on. 'She didn't make my heart race every time I looked at her, or even thought about her. I didn't miss being with her, even though I hardly knew her, and I didn't feel the instant urge to build her a house, exactly the way she liked it, even if I suspected it might have turrets, and live in it with her for ever. And I thought she deserved someone who did feel that way about her, so I broke it off. It was bad, she was very upset, but that was a year or so ago now. She's with someone new, she doesn't hold a grudge any more.'

'I think it's amazing,' Lydia said. 'Not that you broke up with her. I mean, that you have such a clear idea about love, about what it's supposed feels like. I broke it off with Stephen because I know that I don't love him. But I don't think I know what it really feels like to be in love.'

'Don't ask me,' Will said, noticing her hand was still in his and dropping it rather suddenly. 'Romantic stuff, not my strong point. I'm not the sort of bloke who does the wining and dining business. I haven't got all the chat. If I'm honest, most of the women I've been out with have chased me, and I've let them. But your gut, maybe I should say your heart, knows what it knows, right? I mean, you know inside how a person makes you feel; even if it doesn't make the most sense, you *know*.' Will seemed as perplexed by his own thought process as Lydia was.

'So are you in love now?' she asked, just as the snow began to fall again.

Will reached out, capturing a flake in the palm of his hand and watching it melt away. 'We should stop for a pint and a pie before we head back,' he said, which, by way of response, was frustrating. 'Come on, I'll introduce you around.'

* * *

The Royal Oak was full, of heat, light and above all people. It really did feel to Lydia as if the whole village was crammed into the tiny ancient building, which was packed from its flagstone floor to its ancient ceiling beams.

Children chased each other through the throng of legs, older people sat at the tables, laughing and reminiscing, families shared meals and raucous jokes, mothers swayed with babies of varying ages slung over their shoulders, or balanced on their hips as they compared sleepless nights, and teenagers buried their faces in their hair, their thumbs glued permanently to their phones. The old oak beams of the interior had been garlanded with mistletoe and holly, and strung with flashing coloured lights, and a roaring fire crackled in the grate. It didn't escape anyone's notice that Will had come in with a strange woman, and while the pub didn't exactly fall silent while the locals stared at her, Lydia could feel many sets of eyes give her the once over as Will led her to the bar.

'Now, then,' the bar man greeted Will with a nod. 'We thought you'd gone off somewhere, Will. Where you been?'

'Up at the Pike, helping the new folk settle in,' Will said.

'And where did you find this young lady?' Lydia smiled and waved, remembering her pink bobble hat a little too late.

'This is a friend of theirs, Lydia. She's from London but she seems okay. Lydia, this is Mal, the landlord. He's best mates with Jim.'

'Oh yeah, Jim from the Pike, he's a good bloke, he is, likes his ale.' Mal nodded. 'What'll it be?'

'Pint,' Will said, looking at Lydia. 'Lydia?'

'Um, do you have a wine list?' Lydia asked, finding herself inexplicably speaking exactly like Celia Johnson in *Brief Encounter*, her averagely middle-class south coast accent suddenly accelerating, against her will, through the roof to the height of poshness. 'Oh, no, I mean. I'll have a pint too. As long as it's wine.'

Mal laughed, producing a leather-bound and actually very comprehensive wine list from under the bar. 'But you should have a mug of my Kirstie's mulled wine, there's a double shot of brandy in every one, it'll warm you up, if you need it, that is.'

Mal winked at Will, who maintained a steady eye contact with his pint.

'So you're staying up at the Pike, are you?' Lydia turned to find herself being addressed by a woman probably a little younger than her, with a sleeping toddler nodding on her shoulder. 'What's it like up there now?'

'Really lovely,' Lydia said. 'You should go up and visit it in the New Year,' Lydia suggested, remembering how lonely Katy was. 'My friend's got two kids and she'd love some visitors. What's your name, I'll tell Katy to expect you.'

250 • *Scarlett Bailey*

'Alice, pleased to meet you,' the girl said, smiling pleasantly before lowering her voice. 'I think I've seen your friend on the school run, blonde curly hair? Keeps herself to herself, comes across a bit stuck up?'

'No! She's not stuck up at all,' Lydia exclaimed. 'She's just really shy. If you got to know her, you'd find she's lovely.'

'Well, the school mums do a coffee morning at each other's houses every other Tuesday. The next one is at my place after New Year. Here, take this lump a second and I'll write the address down. Tell her to come along and let us have a good look at her.'

Lydia's knees buckled briefly under the unexpected burden of the sleeping child she found in her arms as Alice scribbled her details on the edge of a beer mat.

'So, you and Will? How long has that been going on?' Alice asked as they exchanged beer mat and child again.

'Me and . . .? Oh no, we barely know each other. I only just met him. He just asked me along for the walk.'

'Will asked *you* out for a walk and then brought you in here?' Alice looked sceptical. 'That's marrying talk, around here, especially coming from Will.'

'Oh, I hardly think so,' Lydia said. 'He's just taken pity on me.'

'Fit, though, isn't he?' Alice said, eyeing Will's bottom as he leaned over the bar to look at a child's drawing that Mal was showing him. 'All the girls round here have tried to get him over the years, me included.' Alice sighed. 'Never asked *me* to go for a walk with him.'

'Hello, I'm Cathy.' Lydia turned to find a lady about her mum's age. 'You've come in with Will, so how long has that been on?'

And gradually, with her mug of mulled wine in one hand, Lydia found herself travelling around the pub, manoeuvred by the natural current of the throng from one set of people to another, asking her questions, mainly about how long she'd known Will, but also making her welcome, telling her jokes, gossiping about the last person she'd spoken to or the next, and in the case of one old gentleman, finding a great deal of excuses to pat her bottom. As she settled down next to a charming old lady called Gracie, who wanted to tell her all about the trips she used to make as a young woman to a Lyon's Corner House on Piccadilly Circus, Lydia looked across to the bar where Will was sipping his pint, watching her, that shadow of a smile edging up the corner of his mouth.

'Sorry,' she mouthed, thinking that intense, brooding look on his face might be something to do with her having been whisked away, but he simply raised his pint to her and turned back to Mal.

'What I liked best about being a Wren was the soldiers, all very handsome,' the old lady told her. 'Kissed more than my fair share during The Blitz, let me tell you. But I was glad to come back here after the war. I've never seen so many busses in my life, you know. Unhealthy great things.'

'Really?' Lydia said, anxiously, as she watched Will finish his pint and then head out of the door. He wouldn't leave her here, would he? Would he? Everyone kept telling her how Will liked his own company, wasn't often seen out with a girl, was a quiet, shy sort of man, which either made him incredibly sweet or a serial killer, Lydia couldn't decide which. Either way, it felt like a very real possibility that the prospect of making conversation with her during the mile trek back to the house might strike Will as a conversation too far.

'I'm really sorry, I've got to go . . .' Lydia said goodbye and made her way through the crowd, stopping to give a kiss under the mistletoe to the old gentleman who, along with the fondness for her bottom he'd already demonstrated, turned out to have a very opportunistic tongue.

As she opened the pub door, a cold blast of air instantly cooled her heated face, and she looked up and down the road. Will was nowhere to be seen, and annoyingly, having boasted about being able to find her way back easily enough, Lydia couldn't exactly remember which direction they'd arrived from, as the village seemed to be located at the foot of more than one hill.

She stomped out into the middle of the road. 'Bloody men. Bloody, bloody men. Drag you all the way out here for no apparent reason and then just sod off and . . .'

'And what?' Will appeared behind her, settling a sizable a rucksack on his shoulders.

'Oh, I thought you'd gone,' Lydia said. 'But you haven't. Here you are, creeping up on me again.'

'I just went to get my stove and some stuff,' Will said, gesturing vaguely towards a cluster of cottages. 'Can't wear the same clothes indefinitely, can I?'

'Clothes?' Lydia asked him. 'Does that mean you're staying another night? I thought you were coming here, to the pub, for Christmas lunch.'

'I was,' Will said, a study in nonchalance. 'But then I thought I couldn't really be arsed walking you back to the Pike and then hiking back here again. So I thought I might as well stay there as here. Makes no odds to me. And I packed my Yule log, so . . .'

Lydia found herself grinning, and, as she hooked her arm through his and they turned up the path back towards Heron's Pike, she couldn't help wondering if it was just the climb up the hill that was making her heart race.

The walk home was a good deal quieter than the walk there, but somehow Lydia didn't mind the silence at all this time. The winter sun was already beginning to set as they rounded the last corner that brought Heron's Pike into sight, casting a coppery pink light across the hills, making the snow-edged branches of the hedgerow glow and glisten. Without even realising it, the two of them came to a gradual halt as Lydia paused, taking in the beauty of her surroundings.

It took maybe as much as a minute before Lydia realised that Will wasn't looking at the view; his eyes were fixed on her.

'Lydia.' The sound of her name on Will's lips startled her and she looked up at him. He put down his rucksack, watching her face bathed in the glow of the molten sky. 'Lydia.'

As if in slow motion, Will reached out one ungloved hand and touched her face, his fingers tracing their way into her hair, and he gently guided her closer to him, bringing their lips together. Quite breathless, Lydia found she was trembling as he brushed her mouth with his. At first it was the lightest of kisses but it ignited a heat that raged through her like a wildfire.

'Lydia,' he said again, more urgently this time, his other arm encircling her waist and gathering her into him, his kisses becoming deeper, more passionate, covering her face, and what little of her neck was exposed. 'You are so . . .' Will broke away, his rare unbridled smile, as he gazed at her, utterly charming. '. . . dressed.'

Lydia giggled and Will laughed too.

'That was unexpected,' she said.

'Really?' Will asked her. 'I thought you could tell a mile off that I liked you.'

'I'd hate to see what you're like when you're playing it cool,' Lydia said, her mind racing to keep up with her furiously beating heart.

'Look.' Will paused, searching for words. 'I'm sorry I kissed you like that, I didn't plan to, it was just you looked so beautiful and I really wanted to. It's not like me at all.'

'I know.' Lydia smiled. 'Everyone in the pub told me all about you.'

Will shook his head. 'Trust me, I didn't expect to come up here to fix the boiler and meet *you*.' He said the last word very expressly, as if he were referring to a specific person.

'Me?' Lydia said.

'Yes, you, the girl I can talk to without thinking about it, the girl I *want* to talk to. The one whose smile makes me want to kiss her, the woman who looks so incredible wearing nothing much more than a jumper that it put me in a right awkward position . . .'

'Oh!' Lydia's eyes widened. '*Oh.*'

'Yeah, *you*. Bloody hell, Lydia I don't do this sort of thing. Talking to girls, kissing them, at least not until I've known them for about a decade. But there's something about you, Lydia, that makes me want to . . . to build a house for you.'

Lydia stared at him, unable to speak, her breath crystallising in the air around her.

'It's too soon.' Will looked stricken. 'I should have

known, you've only just finished with Stephen. I shouldn't have kissed you. I mean, just because I . . . doesn't mean that you . . . Fuck. I'm sorry. Listen, let's just forget it ever happened.'

Before Lydia could move, let alone speak, Will swung his rucksack onto his shoulders, and began marching down the drive towards the house, leaving her rooted to the spot, unable to quite fathom just exactly what had happened.

Chapter Fourteen

*'Twas the night before Christmas when all through
the house,
Not a creature was stirring, not even a mouse . . .'*

Lydia stopped outside the living room door, listening to the sound of Jim reading to the children.

'Are there mouses in our house?' Tilly asked him rather anxiously.

'No, sweetheart,' she heard Jim say. 'And not likely to be, either, and Vincent is a very rare breed of mouse-hunting hound, and they are all scared of him.'

'Good,' Tilly said.

'There are spiders, though,' Jake said. 'There's one at the bottom of your bed the size of my head.'

'Dad!'

Pushing the door open, Lydia found that Jim and the children were the only ones in the cosy room, with Vincent curled up at Jim's feet. She noticed two knitted red and white stockings hanging above the fireplace.

'Father Christmas is coming tonight,' Tilly told Lydia, clenching her fists with barely containable excitement.

'I'm getting an Xbox,' Jake said.

'Possibly, or possibly something even better,' Jim said carefully, winking at Lydia. 'So how was your walk?'

'Good. Did you see where Will went?'

'I sent him to find the girls; they are present wrapping in the kitchen. Katy's more or less refused to move from beside the Aga in case it goes into decline. I think she might sleep on it tonight. Stephen's been in his room most of the day, Alex's been putting her feet up and bossing David; and Joanna and Jackson went out for a walk. I think she was a little put out that foxy Will asked you out.'

'He didn't ask me out.' Lydia blushed as she remembered how expertly Will had kissed her, not with the panache and Hollywood style that Jackson employed, but with something more real. 'We just went for a walk, that's all. It was nice.'

'Well, I'm trying to get these two to settle down to something calmer than fever pitch so that when they go to bed they won't be bouncing off the walls. Because,' he said, looking from one child to the other, 'Father Christmas doesn't come if you're awake.'

'I'll leave you to it, then,' Lydia said, listening to Jim begin to read again as she walked up the hall.

'The stockings were hung with the greatest of care,
In the hope that St Nicholas would soon be there . . .'

'Who's St Nicholas? I don't want him, I want Father Christmas!'

Katy, Alex and the Calor gas stove were all in the kitchen, but Will was nowhere to be seen.

'Ah, the wanderer returns,' Katy said. 'How was your walk with Will?'

'What do you mean?' Lydia asked her, defensively.

'I mean, how was your walk. With Will?' Katy raised an eyebrow. 'Touchy!'

'We just went for a walk,' Lydia said. 'What is all the fuss about?'

'You tell me.' Katy grinned. 'All I know is that Will came in here, dumped that on the table and then went out to the boathouse for a smoke.'

'The boathouse?' Lydia knew she wanted to talk to Will, to see him again as soon as she possibly could, because if she could see him standing in front of her she might be able to make sense of some of what she was feeling. But there was no way she could run off to the boathouse now and ever live it down. 'Irish coffee, anyone?'

'Give her a break,' Alex said, curling ribbon ferociously with a pair of scissors. 'Let the corpse of her and Stephen's relationship cool a little bit before you start trying to fix her up with the help.'

'I'm just saying, it would be great if Lydia had a local love interest. She'd visit all the time, then, and I wouldn't be so lonely.'

'You know what you should do,' Lydia said, heaping coffee into a cafetière. 'Next time Jim goes to the pub, go with him and take the kids. I've met about twenty people today, and they wanted to know all about you. I even got you an invite to a local mums group.' She handed Katy the beer mat with Alice's number on it and explained about meeting her, omitting Alice's less than flattering first impression of Katy. 'Everyone seemed really friendly. You've got to get out there, Katy, make a bit of an effort. I bet you'd make loads of friends in no time.'

'Maybe,' Katy said cautiously, but she pinned the beer mat to the fridge with one of the assortment of magnets that lived there. 'I'm just worried they might all club together and burn me in a wicker man.'

'They only do that to virgins,' Alex said, her face suddenly contorting in pain.

'Braxton Hicks *again*?' Katy asked her. Alex nodded. 'They seem very strong, Alex. Should I call NHS Direct?'

'What are they going to do, deliver the baby down the phone line?' Alex asked her, her expression relaxing as the pain eased. 'Look, this one isn't due for weeks. And it says in my book that Braxton Hicks can be really strong. Besides, I don't feel like I'm in labour. I mean, I'd know, wouldn't I? If I was? There'd be screaming, and amniotic fluid everywhere.'

'I don't know, they sent me home four times with

Jake,' Katy said. 'I had to beg them to let me stay in the end.'

'Look, I'm fine now,' Alex said, getting up, spreading her arms and waggling her fingers to emphasise her point. 'So let's just get on with wrapping, shall we?'

'Don't forget, that pile has to be wrapped in the potato print paper, and that pile in the shop paper,' Katy said. 'I swear I've spent double on them this year, since the paper obsession started. I don't want them thinking Father Christmas doesn't bring them their dream present, and I don't want them thinking that Mummy and Daddy haven't got them anything.'

'In my day, we got an orange and a piece of coal and were grateful,' Alex said, so seriously and so untruthfully that everyone burst out laughing.

'*There* you are.' Joanna appeared in the doorway, dressed in a luxurious charcoal-coloured mohair sweater, her hair falling in glorious coppery curls.

'What do you mean: there we are? We've been here, prepping vegetables and rolling tiny sausages in bacon all day. It's you and Lyds who've been swanning around, out and about,' Alex said, a touch resentfully. 'Just because I'm the only one who couldn't run fast enough to escape the clutches of Martha Stewart over there.'

'Oh, yes.' Joanna tipped her head to one side and looked Lydia up and down. 'How was your walk? Was the scenery invigorating?'

'Bloody hell!' Lydia said. 'It was just a walk!'

'Are you sure?' Joanna teased her. 'I think he's got designs on you and, after all, you're single now, so why not?'

'Because her ex-boyfriend is still somewhere in this house and, contrary to popular belief, she is not a total slut?' Alex sighed heavily, as she dropped another present on the pile. 'Oh, hang on, I can't remember if I wrapped that in the right paper.'

'I'm not saying rub his nose in it, I'm just saying if he's interested don't let the grass grow.' Joanna grinned. 'Take Jack and me, since we've been together I've kept him busy, really, really busy, so he hasn't had a moment to have second thoughts.' Alex and Lydia exchanged brief glances.

'Lucky you,' Katy said. 'This morning was the first time I've had sex in weeks. If Jim's not snoring his head off on the sofa, he's flat out as soon as his head touches the pillow. It's not like I miss the sex, so much. It's the kissing. There really is nothing like a good kiss . . .'

'Must be something in the air,' Joanna said, peering at Lydia. 'Is that stubble rash, Lydia? You look suspiciously like you've been kissed by an unshaven northern man.'

'What? Where?' Lydia ran to peer at her reflection in the stainless steel breadbin. 'There's nothing.' Joanna and Katy dissolved into schoolgirl giggles, which billowed into gales of laughter as Will returned from the boathouse. He stood in the doorway for a second, glancing first at Lydia, then at the hysterical women and then at the Calor gas stove. And then he went back out of the door again.

'Poor man,' Alex said. 'Go and fetch him in, someone, before he freezes to death. And you two, stop laughing. Anyone would think this was Christmas.'

Lydia found Will leaning against the wall, staring up at the wonderfully clear sky, all the secrets of the universe laid out above them, so close that you almost felt you could take a single step and walk among the stars.

'I'm sorry,' Lydia said, approaching him cautiously. 'I didn't react very well, back then when we . . . It's not that I didn't react; it's just that I couldn't. I was so surprised . . . I thought you thought I was a bit silly.'

'I do think you're a bit silly,' Will said, without looking at her. 'Weird thing is, I like it.'

'That kiss was . . . I mean, wow,' Lydia said. 'I didn't think a person could get that turned on wearing fleece.' She watched Will's profile carefully for any sign of that elusive smile. 'It's just that everyone in the pub said you never make the first move . . .'

'I never do,' Will confirmed. 'Never felt like it before. It's doing my head in.'

Lydia took a moment to let the information sink in. 'The thing is, Will, I would like to kiss you again. A lot. But I've literally just broken up with Stephen, and we're all going to be sitting around the table eating beans on toast in a minute and . . . well, there has been some other stuff going on that's made me realise that the way you think you feel, isn't always the way you feel, and that sometimes you can get caught up in something so much, only the be disappointed later. I guess what I'm trying to say is that I can't kiss you again, not until I've sorted out the mess I'm in. But as soon as I've done that, then I'd be very open to a good deal more kissing at your convenience. Although the three hundred miles or so between our addresses might make it tricky.'

Will nodded, looking at her. 'Good.'

'Good?' Lydia was confused.

'Good, I'm glad you aren't the sort of person to jump from one man to the next, and I'm glad you care about Stephen's feelings and how hard it must be for him to lose you. And whatever mess you're in, I'm pleased you want to sort it out first, before you kiss me again.' He reached out, touching the tips of her fingers with his as he looked into her eyes. 'As long as you do kiss me again.'

'Oh,' Lydia breathed. 'Stop that, you're making it awfully hard not to kiss you now.'

'Can't have that, can we?' Will smiled. 'Let's go inside and fire up the stove.'

Surely, Lydia said to herself, as she took extra care over her appearance for her dinner of camping fare, surely it wasn't the done thing to fall for a man you barely knew when you'd only just split up with your almost-fiancé and had quite recently snogged your best friend's boyfriend? And yet there seemed to be a connection between her and Will stronger than any she had felt with Stephen, or even Jackson.

That briefest of kisses in the snow had made one thing abundantly clear to Lydia: if another man could make her feel the way Will had in a matter of seconds, then any residual feelings she had for Jackson, which had been stirred up by seeing him so unexpectedly, simply weren't real. Jackson had been her movie moment, a perfect romance that was only ever meant to last a few frames and then melt away into a cherished memory after the final credits rolled. Perhaps what he'd said last night, about missing her and wishing he'd got in touch sooner, even if it was all true, maybe they were things she was never supposed to know. Just because some twist of fate had brought them together again, it didn't inevitably mean they were *meant* to be. And now Lydia knew that, she wanted to make sure Jackson did too; and more importantly, that Joanna never found out what had happened last night on the sofa.

Standing back, Lydia studied her reflection in the mirror. Perhaps a scarlet velvet dress was a little over the top for beans on toast, but she had no idea how long Will would stay around, and now seemed as good a time as any to pull out a showstopper. Carefully, Lydia adjusted the straps so they sat just off the shoulder, flowing into the sweetheart neckline, than made the best of her generous cleavage. She smoothed her hands over her waist and hips, glad for the first time that she hadn't dieted her curves away, like she'd been promising to do for months now. For a moment, she saw herself how she hoped Will might see her – dark hair and eyes, smooth creamy skin – and Lydia felt beautiful. Slipping her feet into her favourite black Kurt Geiger heels, Lydia took a breath and prepared herself to be teased by her friends for over-dressing to impress a man. After all, she was guilty as charged.

As she reached the top of the stairs, everyone else was at the foot, standing around the tree, sipping mulled wine and rather self-consciously singing carols, led by Tilly and Jake, whose shining faces gazed up at the tree as if Father Christmas might appear from behind it at any moment. Lydia watched as Katy rested her head on Jim's shoulders, and David put his arms around Alex and their baby bump, holding them both so closely. And then she saw Joanna whispering into Jackson's ear, and giggling, and Stephen with one hand on top of Vincent's head as the dog leaned against his legs in commiseration. And finally, there was Will, who looked up at her as she walked down the stairs, the slow smile that Lydia had discovered she spent every moment away from him longing to see, spreading across his face.

Beautiful, that was how she felt.

*   *   *

For all its lack of Christmas pomp, dinner went well. Stephen came into his own, chopping onions and fresh tomato into the baked beans, joking quietly about his former career as a boy scout, while Will and Jim cooked sausages and toast over the fire, before carrying them into the dining room.

'Do you know,' Katy said as her husband put her plate of glorified beans on toast in front of her, 'I think this might be the nicest meal I've ever eaten.'

Lydia let the evening slip away quite happily, feeling herself relax for the first time, not only since she arrived, but in months. Stephen was quietly stoical, and more than slightly drunk, and it seemed odd to Lydia to think that the man she'd arrived with only a few days ago was now already becoming a stranger to her. Sitting across the room from her, laughing with Jim and David, making jokes with Jake, and yet it felt right, as if that was the way it was supposed to be. She and Stephen were meant to be fond acquaintances, never lovers.

Joanna was obviously a little put out by Lydia's decision to go with her best outfit tonight, and at the risk of being upstaged had managed to slip upstairs some time between carols and beans, and change into a stunning white and silver shift dress.

'I bet that dress cost more than my entire wedding,' Alex said as Joanna reappeared, framing herself in the doorway for a moment, for maximum effect.

'Start as you mean to go on, I always say,' Joanna

said, winking at Jackson, whose smile in return was a little reserved, a fact Lydia noticed didn't escape Joanna. 'Do you like?' she asked him coquettishly.

'You look lovely,' he told her. 'Like a Christmas angel.'

'Like the fairy on top of the tree, more like,' Alex grumbled, holding her side. 'What? You all look like models and I'm wearing a tent. A tent with sequins on, admittedly. I'm in hell, over here.'

Quite soon after the children had gone willingly to bed, a little later than usual in the hopes that sheer exhaustion would get them off to sleep, the wine ran out.

'There appears to be a distinct lack of alcohol down here,' Jim said, peering into his empty glass as if he'd merely mislaid its contents. And I'm certainly not drunk enough. It's fast becoming a family tradition that I should have a truly terrible hangover on Christmas Day so that the kids can make it a hundred times worse when they jump on top of me at dawn. I must have more booze, now!'

'Well, our heating might be dodgy and our cookery implements are rather lacking, but wine is one thing we have in abundance,' Katy said. 'I'll go down to the cellar and get some.'

'Let me,' Jackson said, waving down Katy's protest. 'Listen, I've spent my whole visit here letting you guys run around after me. I can fetch a bottle of wine.'

'Or five,' Jim instructed him.

Lydia caught his eye as he slipped out of the room, sensing that he wanted her to find a reason to follow him. Perhaps it was the wine she'd drunk already, or the heady exhilaration of knowing Will was just across the table from her, but she thought she saw the perfect moment to set things straight with Jackson for good, and to finally extricate herself from this whole complicated mess.

'Just off to powder my nose,' she said, a couple of minutes after Jackson had left. 'Back in a mo.'

'Are you sure?' Alex caught her hand as she edged behind her chair.

'What are you, the wee police?' Lydia rolled her eyes, and set off to find Jackson, unaware that Joanna's eyes were glued to her back.

Jackson was waiting at the foot of the cellar stairs, leaning against the wall, his hands in his pockets.

'What took you so long?' He smiled as she made her way down the uneven steps, holding out a hand to help her down the last couple. 'God, it seems like an age since last night. I haven't been able to stop thinking about you all day, and you weren't here.' Jackson kissed her hand. 'Joanna made me walk up a bloody hill with her, and I was mad with jealousy, missing you while you were with that Will guy. Look, I know it's complicated, but I've been thinking we should just tell her . . .'

'Jackson,' Lydia said, interrupting him. 'Jackson, listen, I think we should talk, that's all. Seeing you here took me off guard. It confused me. I didn't know how to feel when I saw you. The time we had together, it meant so much to me. And when you left so suddenly, I was badly hurt. I was so sure that you were out of my life, that I didn't have any choice. I had to get over losing you. And then suddenly here you are and it's like a dream, a lovely, confusing, scary dream.'

'I know, right. Just like a dream.' Jackson took a step closer to her, tugging Lydia a little closer. 'A dream come true.'

'But it's not real, you and me,' Lydia went on. 'We had this most amazing romance, and it was lovely. But it's over. It's been over for a really long time. I know now that I want it to stay that way.'

'You don't mean that,' Jackson breathed into her ear, insistent, persistent. 'You didn't come to dinner dressed like without wanting me to want you as much as I do, right now.'

'No, I mean yes, I did. This dress isn't for you; it's for me. I don't want you to want me. I want you to be with Joanna, and make her happy, and for us all to be friends.' She smiled at him, taking a step towards the stairs, but Jackson moved to block her way.

'Lydia, stop pretending.' He grinned confidently. 'You know you want to kiss me.'

'No, I . . .' Jackson's mouth collided against Lydia's

at exactly the same moment as Joanna walked down the stairs.

'What the hell?' Joanna shouted. Furiously, Lydia pushed Jackson away at the same moment Joanna dragged him off her.

'Joanna, I can explain . . .' Lydia began.

'Why?' Joanna asked, her eyes full of tears. 'Why would you do this to me?' Jackson gently touched Joanna's shoulder, but she whirled round, slapping him across the face with all of her might, snapping his head back sharply. 'I knew it,' she sobbed. 'I knew it.'

'Knew what?' Lydia was confused. 'Joanna, there is nothing to know!' Suddenly sober, Lydia's heart sank as Joanna stumbled back up the stairs. 'Please, wait!' she called out, scrambling after her friend, turning her ankle over on her heel at the top of the stairs and sprawling on the floor as Joanna disappeared towards the dining room. 'Joanna!'

But it was too late. Seconds later, when Lydia reached the others, Joanna was in Alex's arms with Katy at her side, sobbing about Jackson and Lydia. She stared around the uncomfortably silent room.

Unable to look at Lydia, Stephen barged his way past her, pausing only briefly. 'So everything you said, it was just guff, just hot air to cover up what was really going on?'

'No, Stephen no – I didn't want this . . .'

To her horror, Lydia watched as Will slowly got up,

walking past her too, without a word or a look. Stopping in the doorway behind her, she heard him address Katy.

'Look, thanks for everything, but I think maybe I'll get my stuff and go home. Give me a call in the New Year and I'll give you that quote you wanted.'

'Will, please . . .' But he was already walking away.

Lydia closed her eyes for a moment. Will had thought there was something special about her, something magical, and for a while she even believed it herself. Now he, and everybody else, had seen her at her very worst. It didn't matter that she had been trying to end any leftover connection between her and Jackson. What mattered was that she'd thought about being with him; despite Stephen, despite Joanna, she'd thought about it, and now she was probably going to get what she deserved.

'We'll be next door,' Jim said, making his escape with David. 'Let you girls fight it out between you.'

Lydia breathed deeply as she took in the sight of her three closest friends, in each other's arms, standing united against her.

'Joanna,' Lydia said. 'I'm so sorry.'

'You, of all people?' Joanna sobbed, raising her red, tear-streaked face to look at Lydia. 'I thought, I thought I could trust you. I thought you would see how much I cared about him, how much he meant to me, and that you'd let me have him.'

'Let you have him? This is crazy, as if I could take

anyone away from you!' Lydia said, as Joanna buried her face in Alex's neck.

'I just can't believe this,' Katy said. 'I can't believe you, Lydia. You barely know the man. I mean, I know things have been rocky between you and Stephen, but making a play for Joanna's boyfriend, in my house, it doesn't make any sense. It's just not you, what's happened to you?'

'Tell them,' Alex said, flatly. 'I told you to tell them, and said she'd find out. Tell them now.'

'What?' Katy looked appalled. 'What now?'

'She already knew Jack.' Joanna sniffed, breaking free of Katy's embrace. Lydia stared at her. 'He was the mystery man she had that fling with, the summer before last.'

'You knew?' Alex was aghast.

'I've known for ages,' Joanna said, cool as an icicle.

'When did you find out?' Lydia gasped. 'How long have you known?

'Since I went through his phone, quite soon after we met. I found a photo,' Joanna said. 'Of you. After all that time, he still had this photo of you.'

'And you didn't think to say anything?' Lydia said. 'To warn me that I was about to spend Christmas with him?'

'I really like him, I think I love him,' Joanna said miserably, sinking down further into her chair. 'You never really talked to me about what went on between you and him. It's always Alex you go to. But I knew that when it ended *you* were heartbroken. And here *he* was still carrying around your photo. I didn't want to lose him. I thought if I told everyone how much he meant to me, how he was the first person I really could see myself having a future with, then it would stop you from going after him again, or letting him make a pass at you. Because you're supposed to be my friend.'

'Jo-Jo, I would have been shocked, sure, and probably upset, and if you'd told me how you felt about him, I might even have tried to warn you off, given the way he left me. But I would never, ever have tried to take him from you,' Lydia told Joanna, who shook her head in disbelief.

'Sorry, wasn't that you kissing my boyfriend just now? Exactly how do you define taking a girl's boyfriend away?'

For once, Lydia could find no defence for her actions. She had let Jackson kiss her, more than once, of that she was certainly guilty, even if she had been confused and reluctant.

'Besides, I wanted to see how he reacted when he met you,' Joanna went on. 'And when he pretended he didn't know you, I thought everything would be okay. I thought he was trying to protect me, because he loved me. But I was wrong, nothing's been the same since we got here, and the more I've tried to get his attention, the less he wants to look at me. He doesn't want me, he wants you, and you want him.'

'No, that's not true at all. Jackson is the last man I want. You've got to listen to me, Jo . . .'

The heavy sound of trickling fluid spattering on the carpet stopped Lydia in her tracks. Bemused, Alex looked at her feet for a moment and then, clasping her hand to her side, bent over, a low moan of pain rising in her throat.

'Alex,' Katy said, staring at her carpet. 'I think you are in labour.'

'No shit,' Alex said, and then she screamed.

Chapter Fifteen

'Right, right,' David said. 'Well, what we need is, we need . . .'

'Stop talking and call me a bloody ambulance,' Alex told him, clinging on to Katy and Joanna. 'I need a drink, is there any reason I can't have a drink now?'

Jim arrived back in the dining room, his phone in his hand. 'I called an ambulance, there's no way they can get here by road and the winds are too high to get a chopper up right now, but they are on standby and as soon as the weather clears, they'll come.'

'This is your fault!' Alex glared at Lydia. 'This is all your fault! This baby isn't meant to come for five more weeks, but oh no, you've got to go and get off with anything that's got a pulse.'

'Hang on a minute,' Jim said, looking a little bewildered. 'I've got this nice lady, Maxine, on the phone. She says to get you into bed and make you comfortable.' Alex groaned again. 'Maxine wants to know how fast your contractions are coming.'

'Too fast,' Alex cried, reaching out for David. 'I'm frightened, David, the baby is not ready, it's too soon. We're in the middle of nowhere.'

'It will be fine.' David took her face in his hands, looking into her eyes. 'Trust me, okay? Right, Katy, help me get her to bed. Joanna, Lydia, I need fresh sheets, clean towels, boiled water and . . . some string.'

'String?' Alex wailed.

'Maxine says you don't need string,' Jim said, waving the phone indiscriminately. David took it from him and listened for a while, nodding.

'Okay, Maxine says that at thirty-five weeks the baby should be fine,' he told Alex. 'There's no reason why it won't be perfectly healthy.'

'Apart from the fact that our baby is being born in a bloody hovel, with a dog as a midwife!' Alex sobbed, as Vincent dropped a chew toy at her feet, perhaps hopeful that it might stop her howling.

'Hovel?' Katy looked at Lydia. 'That's a bit much.'

Appearing in the doorway, Will dropped his rucksack at the sight of Alex.

'What's going on?' he asked.

'What does it look like?' Alex snapped at him. 'Why do you live in the bloody middle of fuck all, why can't I have an ambulance? I want a hospital with drugs, and . . . drugs. *And I want my mum!*'

Alex sobbed, leaning heavily on David, who passed the phone to Katy so that he could put his arms around his wife.

'It's not a hovel,' Katy told an uninterested Maxine,

before listening to further instructions. 'Maxine says we need to get her comfortable.'

'Then get me drugs!' Alex begged.

'Right,' Will said. 'I know the GP. She'll be in the pub, probably, but she's a good man. Woman. You know what I'll mean. I'll go and fetch her. I might be able to get one of the lads to bring her up on a tractor . . .'

'I'm coming,' Jim said, clearly eager to be out of the way, spotting Stephen, who was loitering in the hallway. 'And you, Steve. Don't worry, Alex, it will be fine and when that little blighter's born, you can name him after the lads who saved the day.'

'FUCK OFF!' Alex yelled at him as another wave of pain hit her. For a second, Lydia's eyes met Will's across the room. He hesitated for a moment, then picked up his rucksack and hurried after Jim.

Not knowing, or at that moment caring, where Jackson was, and united in their concern, Lydia and Joanna anxiously followed Katy and David as they tried to help Alex up to bed. But Alex couldn't take more than a few steps without having to stop.

'I can't do this,' she wept, clinging on to David when they stopped for the fifth time as yet another wave of pain hit her. 'I'm so sorry; I've changed my mind. Can you tell someone, please?'

'It's okay,' David said, looking around as he listened to Maxine, his eyes falling on the chaise. 'We need a place for you to lie down. This sofa thing will do. Lydia, you need to get me some clean sheets and towels, to put over this, and something to wrap the baby in when it comes.'

'Oh, my chaise,' Katy muttered under her breath as she kneeled beside Alex, brushing her damp hair away from her forehead. 'This will take more than Vanish. Lydia, there's a waterproof undersheet in the linen cupboard. I had to use it for Tilly when we first moved up here. Bring that and we can put it under the sheets.'

Lydia hurried upstairs to find the cupboard on the first floor. As she reached the top of the stairs, she found Jackson, his bag packed, looking set to leave.

'Where are you going?' she asked him. 'You can't go now!'

'Why not?' Jackson asked her.

'Why not? Because Alex is in labour, there's ten feet of snow out there, and you've no hope of getting anywhere in your car, and because you need to talk to Joanna, explain to her what happened. Tell her that what she saw wasn't what she thought and that there's nothing between us now.'

'Alex is in labour?' Jackson put his bag down. 'Since when?'

'I don't know.' Lydia stepped past him, walking towards the vast linen cupboard. 'I think maybe she's been getting contractions all day. They seem to be coming really fast now, and her waters have broken. It could be really soon. I've been sent to get sheets.'

She began looking for Katy's plastic undersheet, pulling it from under a pile of dressing gowns.

'What can I do?' Jackson asked her.

'Here, hold this while I find what I need.' Lydia began to pile sheets and towels into his arms, deciding to take as many she could, to be on the safe side.

'I was going to walk down to the village, see if there was any B&B going,' Jackson told her as she loaded him up. 'I don't think anyone wants me around here now.'

Lydia looked at him as he received the pile of linen into his arms.

'You can't just disappear into the night, not again. It wasn't fair on me then, and it's not fair on Joanna now. Look, she knew about you and me. In her head, she thought that throwing us together like this, with neither of us knowing what was coming, would stop anything from happening, not start it. She cares about you a lot, maybe even loves you. And she is one of my best friends, so I'm not letting you leave until you've talked this through with her. For once, you need to face up to things, not run away. Be a man. I'll lock you in that cupboard if I have to.'

Jackson laughed. 'I don't suppose you'd be locked in there with me too, would you?'

'Jackson, please, just bloody give it up, will you?'

Jackson looked hurt, and Lydia felt sorry for being so blunt, but it seemed to be the only thing that worked.

'Do you think,' he said, 'that if I'd have come back in time, if I hadn't seen you with Stephen, do you think things might have been different for us?'

Lydia looked into his eyes, trying to picture for a moment the very different reunion they could have had if fate hadn't had other plans for them. Was Jackson the man she thought she'd fallen in love with? No. He wasn't a bad man, just a confused one, as weak and as fallible as she had been herself. Even if meeting him again hadn't jeopardised her friendship with Joanna, was he someone she could fall in love with now? In that moment, Lydia didn't think so. She and Jackson had met at a particular time in her life, when she had been a very different person. Maybe her relationship with Stephen hadn't worked out, but it had taught her what she did want and had helped her grow up a little.

Lydia only wanted to know where she stood, no games, no pretences, no half-baked broken promises. She wanted to be with someone she could love and rely on always to be there. Someone who she knew loved her back, without having to think about it any more, because it was simply a fact. She wanted a man with Jackson's passion and Stephen's stability. Did such a creature even exist outside of romance novels and the movies she adored? She didn't know for sure, but the fact remained that as beautiful and passionate and irresistible as Jackson was, he was half the man she needed him to be, and not the man for her. Loving a man like him would eventually drive her mad.

'Honestly, when I think about it, I'm glad things ended between us when they did,' Lydia told him. 'It was a beautiful summer and . . .' Lydia smiled, thinking of the number of times they'd watched *Casablanca* together. '. . . we'll always have Paris.'

Jackson nodded, sighing heavily, as he focused for a moment on the swirls and patterns in the carpet.

'Right, I'll talk to Joanna as soon as things calm down. I'll straighten this mess out, I swear. In the meantime, I must be able to do something now?'

Lydia nodded. 'Jim said they'd get the air ambulance up as soon as the winds drop enough. I don't know where it will land round here, somewhere flat, I guess. So if you could keep an eye out for it from up here, and when you see it, you can go out and meet it. Bring them back to the house, it might save some time.'

'Right.' Jackson grabbed her arm as she headed for the stairs. 'Lydia, I'm sorry. About before. I didn't mean for that to happen. I never wanted to hurt Joanna, or you.'

'Well, it has happened,' she said. 'And as soon as I get the chance, I have to make things right with Joanna, and so do you.'

Jackson nodded. 'I'll keep a look out for the air ambulance.'

* * *

When she arrived back in the sitting room, David was walking Alex up and down, with Katy following them anxiously.

'About time,' Joanna said, as Lydia hurriedly spread the sheets out on the chaise. 'Did you find a little distraction up there? Someone else's boyfriend to kiss, maybe?'

'I found Jackson on the verge of leaving,' Lydia said, unfurling towels. 'I told him he couldn't go until he'd talked to you.'

'Oh, well, thanks for that, Lydia, because you really are the right person to be giving me relationship advice.'

'Jo-Jo,' Katy said. 'Maybe now's not the time?'

'Perfect time.' Alex grimaced. 'Watching these two scrap it out is the next best thing to gas and air.' Alex leaned heavily against David, while Lydia and Katy did their best to make the chaise comfortable for her, and Joanna slipped a dressing gown that Lydia had retrieved around her shoulders, pulling her skirt and underwear off once she was covered.

David's face blanched as Joanna gathered up Alex's underwear and trousers to put in the wash.

'What is it?' Lydia asked him, whispering as he stared at the greenish stained clothes. She followed David into the foyer as he spoke in hushed tones into the phone.

'There's meconium,' David said into the phone. 'It means the baby is in distress, doesn't it? That it needs to be delivered soon. When will the ambulance get here? We're not enough; we can't cope with this! I can't help but panic, this is my wife and my baby! What can I do? I need to do something!'

David pressed his hand over his mouth, handing the phone to Lydia.

'Hello?' Lydia heard a woman's voice on the other end of the line.

'Hi, David's a little upset at the moment,' Lydia said. 'I'm Lydia, how worried do we need to be?'

'Hello, Lydia, I'm Maxine. Meconium isn't great news, but it's pretty common, plenty of babies are born at home when meconium is present, and they are perfectly healthy. All you can do at the moment is concentrate on keeping Alex calm. We've got the air ambulance on standby, and it will be in the air the minute it's safe. The hospital in Carlise is also ready and waiting. Once we're given the all clear, it will be a matter of minutes until we can get Alex the help she needs.' Lydia went to the window, peering out into the darkness, where the ferocious wind was flinging snow full pelt, smattering it against the glass. 'And in the meantime?'

'Give me back to David, let me talk him through what to do next.'

David listened to Maxine, and taking a deep breath went back to be with his wife.

'David, David, I'm sorry, so sorry, but I can't do this,'

Alex wept. 'I'm a rubbish wife, you should divorce me, I'd understand.'

'Don't be silly.' David kissed her damp forehead. 'You can do anything, Alex, anything at all. And I'm here, I won't let anything bad happen.'

'Promise not to go anywhere,' Alex begged him.

'You should probably watch him around Lydia, in any case,' Joanna said snippily before David could reply. 'Best not to leave your man alone with her.'

'Right, we need to get everything as clean as we can,' David told them, ignoring Joanna's barbed comment. 'Lydia, Joanna – boil water.'

'What for?' Joanna asked.

'Just do it, okay? For once, this isn't about you and your bloody little drama queen lives. This is about my wife and my child. So just get out of here and make yourself useful.'

In the kitchen, Lydia began to fill the kettle.

'How's that going to help?' Joanna snapped irritably, snatching the kettle off her. 'We're not making a cup of tea, are we? We need lots and lots of water . . . Here, help me fill this pan.' She picked up a huge, double-handled metal saucepan that Katy kept on the floor of the pantry, quite possibly to catch leaks, and carried it over to the sink.

'Well, that will take hours to boil,' Lydia said. 'And anyway, the oven's not working so how are we going to heat it? We'll have to keep boiling the kettle and fill that pan up.'

'Why are we even doing this?' Joanna asked her. 'It's not like we've got anything to sterilise. We should be googling home delivery, and not the kind that brings you shoes from the internet in the three to five working days.'

Lydia hazarded a smile, thinking that if Joanna was still prepared to joke with her then things couldn't be that bad.

'I think David's made it pretty clear that he's in charge and he doesn't want you or me hanging around, bickering.' Lydia said. 'I think we're boiling water to get us out of the room. No matter what she says, the last thing Alex needs right now is you and me at loggerheads.' Both women lifted their heads as Alex's cry echoed down the hallway, making Lydia's stomach clench in anxiety.

'I wonder how many babies have been born in this house,' Joanna said, more to herself than Lydia. 'If only walls could talk.'

'Joanna.' Lydia tipped the contents of the whistling kettle into the pan. 'Why didn't you didn't tell me about Jackson as soon as you found out that he and I had . . .' Lydia said, 'I'd have told you.'

'Oh, would you?' Joanna looked sceptical. 'You went through that whole affair with him, more or less disappeared off the face of the earth for weeks, and barely said a word to me about him. And we lived together. Why not?'

'I don't know why,' Lydia said thoughtfully. 'I suppose I wanted to keep it special, separate. I think I knew, even then, that it was never going to go somewhere, but I wanted to get lost in it, lost in my own love story. You know, like you do in a good book or a film. I wanted to lose myself in what Jackson and I had for as long as we had it. Which wasn't very long. Look, Joanna, it's not as if I've been running around trying to steal your boyfriend. He left me, don't forget, it was over. You're the one who brought him here, knowing it would put me, and him, in an impossible position. Why?'

Joanna's laugh was mirthless. 'Why? Don't you think I've asked myself that question? The minute I met Jack, I wanted him. He was so funny and charming and sexy. He was like a whirlwind of romance, it really did feel like I was in the middle of my own daydream, it was magical. And when I was with him, he made me feel so . . . special. As if he couldn't live without me.'

'Yes,' Lydia said, filling the kettle again. 'He is very good at that.'

Joanna sighed. 'He was not only perfect, but different from any other men I've known. I'm used to boys falling in love with me straightaway. Jackson held back, just a little, and I wanted to know why, was there someone else? Was it just that he wasn't that into me? Well, you know what I'm like, I couldn't let it lie, so I waited until he was in the shower one morning and I checked his phone for anything, anything he might have said about me, any contact with another girl.

'There were no texts, no voicemails, nothing at all that incriminating; although, as you can imagine, there were rather a lot of women in his contacts! I was really only looking at his photos for fun when suddenly there you were staring out at me. You were in bed, naked, I suppose, under his sheets, smiling at him. You looked beautiful.' Joanna shook her head. 'I couldn't believe what I was seeing. I was in shock. Perhaps I should have confronted him about it or called you then, but to me the fact that he kept that photo meant he still thought about you. I didn't want to lose him to you.'

'Joanna.' Lydia shook her head incredulously as she looked at her friend. 'As if I could ever beat you in a straight contest.'

'Oh, don't do that.' Joanna rolled her eyes.

'What?' That thing you do, all that false modesty, pretending that you're not beautiful and clever and funny and brilliant.'

'What?' Lydia stared at her. 'Don't be mad, Jo-Jo. Everyone knows that you're the beautiful one, the head turner. I'm just normal.'

Joanna studied her for a long moment. 'You really think that, don't you? You really don't see how amazing you are. I know I'm beautiful, and witty, and have a high-profile, well-paid, glamorous career as a model slash presenter slash actress, if selling fleeces embroidered with wolves can be called glamorous. But even if you do wear your heart permanently on your sleeve, you're so . . . genuine, Lydia. I'm all fakery and sham. I worried that I couldn't keep Jackson for long. I just wanted to keep him for as long as I could, and telling you about him, or him about you, didn't seem like a good way of doing that. '

'Even if that makes sense, which it doesn't, by the way . . . you brought him here? What were you thinking?' The kettle began to rumble and bubble, busily.

'I wanted Jackson and I to stay together, and short of never seeing you again, I knew if we were going to be together then he was going to meet you sooner or later,' Joanna said. 'I know it sounds insane, but perhaps I have gone a little mad. Being in love does that to a person, doesn't it?' Lydia raised her eyebrows; having recently kissed a man she barely knew, in the snow, she was in no position to judge. 'I thought if I brought him here, after making it clear to you how much he meant to me, and with Stephen about to propose to you . . .'

'Hang on, you didn't know about Stephen and the ring until after we got here.'

'I did,' Joanna said flatly, leaving Lydia utterly confused. She sighed. 'Fine, you might as well know the whole story. I ran into Stephen on Bond Street a few weeks ago. I was looking for a new bag and he was window shopping, looking in jewellers! Well, I put two and two together and congratulated him on doing the right thing and finally proposing to you. Couldn't be better, I thought; you settling down with Stephen meant I could relax about being with Jack. Thing is, Stephen was just looking for your Christmas present, he hadn't exactly decided definitely to propose, and I suppose I might have railroaded him a little, maybe suggested that perhaps, if he didn't pop the question soon, he might lose you for good . . .'

'You did *what*?' Lydia gasped. 'You told Stephen to propose to me?'

'No, I helped him along. I was doing it for you, Lyds. Anyway, when he thought about it a bit, he realised I was right, that he should seize the day, but he had no idea what sort of ring to get you. Well, obviously you and I have talked and talked about that for the last ten years at least, so I told him I knew just what you wanted. I took him to Tiffany.'

'You picked out my ring?' Lydia was aghast. All that time she'd wrangled with how much Stephen must have cared for her, going to so much trouble and expense to find exactly the right ring, and it had been Joanna all along.

'So when I told you that I'd found the ring and that I wasn't sure about marrying Stephen, you knew all the time? I bet you were furious that I was having second thoughts, especially as you planned to have me safely engaged and out of the way when you finally revealed who your boyfriend was.'

Joanna chewed her bottom lip for a moment, lifting the kettle off the base and pouring its contents into the pan.

'When you put it like that, it does seem a bit mad . . . I did feel terrible when you told me how you felt about Stephen. I never would have meddled if I thought you weren't happy. I thought that if you and Jackson were suddenly brought together, I'd be able to see if he still wanted you. It never occurred to me that you might want him back.'

'But I didn't! I don't want him back,' Lydia said, firmly. 'Maybe, perhaps for a moment or two, seeing him when I was so uncertain about how I felt for Stephen did make me wonder . . . But, in reality, I never would have done that to you, of all people. Honestly, Jo-Jo, if you'd just told me who he was, then all the crap I've gone through over the last few days, all the confusion and angst, could have been avoided.'

'Except that he wanted you, of course he did, he's made that perfectly clear.'

'Are you crazy?' Lydia asked her.

'You're the one everyone always falls in love with,' Joanna said quietly. 'You're the kind of woman men want to marry, I can't compete with you.'

'Me?' Lydia exclaimed. 'Which one of us has been engaged five times?'

'Exactly,' Joanna said. 'I can't keep a man interested in me long enough to marry.'

'That's ridiculous,' Lydia said. 'You chuck them almost as soon as you've got a ring on your finger.'

'Yes, before they get the chance to change their minds,' Joanna said, pitifully. 'Everyone has always left me, Joanna. Mum, Dad, everyone. I just wanted to keep Jack.'

'Oh, Jo-Jo, you are clinically insane, but don't you know by now that not everybody leaves you? Me, Katy and Alex. We will always be here.' Lydia held out her arms to her friend, just as the whistle on the kettle began to sing, seeming, as the two women hugged, to morph into one long high-pitched scream.

'Alex.' Joanna and Lydia looked at each other and ran to help their friend, a half-filled pan of boiled water left cooling on the table.

David was on his knees, mobile phone in one hand, about to peer between Alex's firmly clenched knees.

'Get away him from there!' Alex wailed. 'Katy, get him away from there! I've told him he's not to go down there. If he sees this we'll never have sex again.'

'Here.' Lydia put an arm on David's shoulder. 'I think she really needs you up that end. Let me take a look.'

Perhaps a little relieved, David shuffled away from the business end and took Alex's hand.

'Oh God,' Lydia said, her eyes widening, any fear or revulsion she thought she might feel disappearing in a moment. 'I can see the head. Oh I . . . whoa, I think this little fella is nearly here.'

David tried to look, but Alex dragged him back. 'Please, stay with me here. Lydia, push it back in. I'm not ready, I'm not ready to be a mum . . .'

Alex squeezed her eyes tightly shut, tears escaping down her cheeks as the next wave of pain hit her.

'Okay, don't think pushing him back in is an actual option, and I don't think waiting for the ambulance is either,' Lydia said, holding her hand out for the phone. 'Let me speak to Maxine, tell her what I see.' She deftly caught the handset that David threw.

'Hello? Lydia here, again.' Lydia tried to keep her voice down, so that Alex wouldn't hear the fear in her voice. But one look at her friend's face told her that Alex was lost in her own world, totally caught up in the process of bringing her child into the world. 'I think the moment is somewhat nigh.'

'Okay, Lydia, have a look and tell me what you can see.'

Bracing herself, Lydia looked again, 'Fuck, it's amazing. I can see the top of the baby's head, he's really hairy!'

'Okay, Lydia,' Maxine said, her voice even and calm in tone, and not remotely matching the panic rising in

Lydia's chest as she realised the burden of responsibility she was taking on. 'It's possible that on the next contraction the head and shoulders will appear, and then it will be very quick until baby's out.'

'Oh . . . kaaay,' Lydia said.

'As soon as you see them, support baby's head and shoulders, and when he comes out, if you can get him to his mother's breast as soon as possible. The sooner baby starts suckling the sooner the uterus will begin to contract and the less blood she'll lose. The good news is, I've just had word that the chopper's up. We'll be there in minutes.'

'Ambulance is on its way, Alex,' Lydia told her. 'So now all you have to do is concentrate on getting that baby here for its first helicopter ride, okay?'

Alex nodded, squeezing Katy's hand so tightly that the tips of her finger blanched white. 'I'm ready.'

'Good. David, help Alex get her bra off. Alex – next contraction, get ready to meet your baby, okay?'

'Yes,' Alex wept, 'let's do this!'

There was a short period of quiet, save for the ticking of the clock on the mantel, and then David yelped as Alex squeezed his hand

'I've got you,' David said, his arms around Alex.

'I can feel it coming!' Alex's scream roared through the room, echoing in the halls, stairways and all the rooms of Heron's Pike, and Lydia gasped as the baby emerged in a gush of fluid into her arms.

'Oh my God! Oh my God, it's a girl!' She stared at the tiny pink and red creature in her hands, the most beautiful thing she had ever seen. And then she realised the baby was perfectly still. 'Katy, quick, the phone!'

Dropping Alex's hand, Katy held the phone up to Lydia ear.

'What's happening?' Alex asked. 'Where's my baby?'

'She's here,' Lydia said into the phone. 'She not breathing.'

'Hold her with her head down,' Maxine said calmly. 'This helps drain any fluids that might be getting in the way, and rub her back, you can be quite firm.'

'Nothing!' Lydia's voice quivered as she held the tiny scrap of life in her arms.

'Just wait one moment.' Terrifyingly, Lydia thought she could hear fear in Maxine's voice for the first time.

And then the baby seemed to gasp, and cough, audibly sucking in a breath of air, which it held for a fraction of a moment before letting it out again in one long, wonderful wail.

'Thank God, it's worked.' Lydia let herself breathe along with the baby, aware of sudden tears streaming down her cheeks.

'Good work, Lydia,' Maxine said. 'Now get that baby to her mum. Keep her warm. Help will be there any minute.'

Still sobbing, Lydia placed the tiny girl against Alex's breast, and the friends watched in awe as, after a moment, her little rosebud mouth latched on to Alex's nipple and she began to suckle.'

'Oh my God, she's so beautiful,' Alex said, gazing fondly at her daughter. 'Isn't she beautiful, darling?'

'The most beautiful thing I've ever seen,' David said, breathless with wonder, as he stroked the baby's head with the back of one finger. 'You did it, darling, you did it,' he told Alex, tears in his eyes. 'I knew you would.'

'I couldn't have done it without you,' Alex told him fondly, before beaming at her friends. 'Or you lot! Especially you, Lydia!'

'You were nothing short of a bloody fucking hero!' David added.

A blast of cold air whipped through the room as the back door opened and suddenly the place was full of people, all the boys, including Will, along with a woman bundled up in a very thick coat and carrying a doctor's bag, plus two paramedics wearing high-visibility coats. Lydia stood back, discovering that she was still trembling, as she watched the doctor check over Alex and the baby before the paramedics transferred them onto a gurney, wrapped tightly in blankets and safely secured by belts.

As they wheeled her away, Alex held out her hand to Lydia. 'Thank you,' she said. 'I don't know what I would have done without you.'

'Well, it was really a team effort,' Lydia said, tears welling up in her eyes.

'I know, thank you, all of you. What would I – we – have done without you? Now bloody well make up and have a happy Christmas Day, for our sake, okay?'

Lydia nodded, looking at Joanna. 'We will.'

'One thing,' Alex said sleepily to David as they wheeled her out of the room. 'At least we get out of eating that mutilated turkey.'

Chapter Sixteen

25 December

The very distant sound of laughter and squealing prised open Lydia's exhausted eyes and tear-swollen eyelids. It was Christmas morning, Lydia realised, and it had to be quite late because pale, watery light was creeping in under her thick curtains. Reaching across the empty half of the bed, she picked up her watch and looked at it. It was almost nine on Christmas Day. The day that Lydia had always wanted to be perfect, magical and above all happy. The day that for as long as she could remember had been none of those things.

Still, just because she'd singled-handedly managed to upset and alienate the three men in her life in one fell swoop, and somehow end up single instead of engaged, it didn't mean she couldn't eat her own body weight in turkey and Christmas pudding, which was exactly what she planned to do. Fate, it seemed, had her destined always to be alone, so she might as well get really, really fat, and perhaps become an alcoholic, which was her first preference when it came to hobbies suitable for elderly spinsters.

Clambering reluctantly out of bed, Lydia shuddered as she went to the wardrobe and brought out the obligatory glittery top, a long fine-knit silk top, shot through with silver, which slid rather attractively off one shoulder, not that anybody would care, Lydia thought morosely, as she teamed it with her black velvet skinny jeans. Or that anybody was ever going to graze that poor shoulder with a stubbly kiss ever again. She picked out the sparkliest bling she could find in her travel jewellery box, a pair of chandelier diamante earrings that Joanna had brought home from work and given her for her birthday, and a huge fake red ruby ring, which she slipped onto the third finger of her left hand in pure defiance. Who wanted to be engaged, anyway? It made a girl sound like a public convenience.

In the wake of witnessing her very own Christmas miracle, Lydia had been filled with warmth and goodwill to all men, even Jackson. Even after Alex and David had at last been spirited away into the night sky, and despite the drama and the oddness of Joanna's strange confession, it felt as if they had made up and that somehow working together to deliver the baby had cancelled out everything that had gone on during the hours before the little girl made her dramatic entrance. Even the fact that Joanna had rigged Lydia's engagement, and that Lydia had made out with Joanna's boyfriend, seemed insignificant as the three remaining women toasted the baby, and congratulated themselves on their new midwifery skills. That was the magic of Christmas, Lydia had thought warmly, not even slightly cross with Stephen that he'd pretended proposing to her was all his idea and that he'd picked out that ring all on his own. If ever there was a time of year that was all about new beginnings, hope and faith, then this was it.

Suddenly seeing quite clearly exactly what she needed to do, Lydia went to find Will, her nerves fizzing with anticipation and her heart thundering in her chest, inspired to do exactly what every reasonable and rational bone in her body told her not to do: tell the man exactly how she felt about him. Lydia was prepared to lay all the cards on the table, and tell Will that the kiss they'd shared meant just as much to her as it had to him, and that even though the whole thing seemed crazy, it seemed crazier still not to act on something that felt so right.

Which was why it was rather an anticlimax when, to her dismay, she found Will in the lean-to getting ready to leave with the doctor.

'Hello, Miriam Day.' The woman, who was a little older than Lydia, held out her already gloved hand, smiling warmly. 'Well done you, Alex told me as I was settling her in the ambulance that you delivered baby and got her breathing. You must have nerves of steel!'

'Oh well, I . . . just did what had to be done,' Lydia said, watching Will as he zipped up his jacket and wound his scarf around his neck. 'Anyone would have done the same.'

'Nonsense, I've seen junior doctors run a mile from a dilated vagina!' Dr Day chuckled. 'Brightened up my Christmas, anyway. Nothing like a medical emergency to get you out of the house!'

'You're going?' Lydia asked Will as he picked up his rucksack.

'Doesn't seem much point in me sticking around here now.' Will was polite but cool. 'Baby's delivered, Aga is working, heating is on. You don't need me any more.'

'Oh, everyone always needs a man like Will!' Dr Day giggled. 'Don't you agree?'

Lydia smiled tightly, nodding, trying to think of some reason to ask Dr Day to wait outside in the freezing snow while she talked to Will. She hadn't envisioned an audience for her romantic declaration.

'Don't you think you're being a tiny bit over-dramatic, leaving now?' Lydia began. 'We kissed and it was lovely, really lovely, actually. But as far as I'm aware, we didn't get married or anything.'

'Ah,' Dr Day said. 'I might just see you in the tractor, Will.'

A chill blast of air swept across Lydia as Dr Day hurriedly made her exit, and Will looked sharply at her. 'Nobody said we did, it's just . . . I thought you were one sort of person, it turned out that you were another. My mistake. No big deal.'

'Will!' Lydia exclaimed, infuriated. 'What sort of person are you, to judge me on something you know nothing about? You turn up out the blue, smouldering away, and then without any encouragement at all from me, pretty much tell me I'm the best thing since sliced bread, get all stroppy because I'm so surprised that I don't immediately fall into your arms all overcome with gratitude, and *then*, without knowing any of the facts *whatsoever*, change your mind completely about me, based on another man trying to kiss me!'

Finally, Lydia paused for breath. She had to acknowledge that as romantic declarations go, this one wasn't quite panning out how she'd planned it.

'I take people as I find them,' Will said, unmoved by her outburst. 'I'll leave the stove, just in case. Would you ask Jim to drop it back, next time he's passing.'

'Hang on a minute.' Lydia softened her tone as she put her hand on the arm of his coat, stopping him in his tracks. 'You like straight talking, well, here is some. I really thought that we'd connected, you and I. And, yes, the fact that we met during quite possibly the most complicated week of my life did give me pause. But I put it to you that you knew that when you kissed me. You knew that I'd only just broken up with Stephen, and that any decent sort of person would be rather thrown off balance by something so . . . surprising. And as far as Jackson is concerned, I've been taught that the central principle of justice is that an individual is innocent until proven guilty. Talk to Joanna, and Jackson, and they'll tell you the real story about what happened in the cellar.'

Will did not respond, but neither did he leave, which Lydia took as a good sign. 'I am pretty blown away by you, Will. I didn't expect this, but it's happened and I don't want to fluff it over nothing. You seem like an honest sort of man to me, and I just don't believe that everything you said you felt has evaporated over night. Apart from anything else, you said there was something about me, something that made you want to build me a house. Well, there's something about you too, Will.' Lydia took a breath. 'Something that makes me think I might want to live in it. With you.'

Having made her declaration, Lydia pressed her lips together as Will looked into her eyes, and for one second she was absolutely certain he was going to kiss her. And then he shook his head and walked away.

'It must have been snow blindness,' Will said. 'You're a city girl, a southerner. I'm a country bloke. We are three hundred miles and worlds apart. I don't know what I was thinking, saying all that stuff to you out of the blue. It wasn't fair and I shouldn't have done it, I should have learned by now that nothing good ever comes of saying too much. I'm sorry, Lydia, but I'm heading home. Have a happy Christmas.'

Will looked past her. 'Ready?'

'Ready.' Jackson nodded, walking towards them.

'But . . .' Lydia turned to him. 'What about Joanna, what about this mess you're walking out on?'

'Joanna won't talk to me,' Jackson said. 'I figure I need to give her some space. Take care, Lydia, you know where I am if you change your mind.'

Lydia stood in the drafty lean-to, goose bumps punctuating her skin, as Will helped the doctor and then Jackson clamber onboard the tractor and they rumbled off, leaving Lydia, hugging herself against the cold, to look up at the sky and wonder how she'd managed to get everything so exactly wrong.

Arming herself with her best smile, Lydia brushed out her hair until it shone, slipped on her stiletto ankle boots, and went to the kitchen, where Katy and Joanna were peering at the Aga with the kind of hopeless, desolate expressions that should only be reserved for funerals.

'Happy Christmas?' Lydia offered the salutation uncertainly.

'Did you know you appear to have put on some Christmas tree decorations?' Joanna asked Lydia, smiling sweetly. 'And by the way, at some point in the night, the Aga passed away, peacefully and in its sleep. Time of death we think approximately three a.m. as it is stone cold now, and rigor mortis has already set in. Much like my love life, now I come to think of it.'

'I blame you for this,' Katy told Lydia, seemly surprisingly sanguine about the demise of the beast. 'If you'd secretly copped off with the right one of the Three Kings you've been road testing over the last few days, then Will would still be here and he'd know what to do about it.'

'Yes, Lydia, you really are a dreadful slut, kissing anyone who's passing,' Joanna said mildly. 'But then again, I suppose I'm the megalomaniac with control issues, so who am I to talk?'

'Joanna told me the whole story,' Katy said, with the same disapproving air she reserved for her children when they'd been doing something they shouldn't. 'Honestly, you two, you do know that you're grown women and not teenagers? When are you going to start acting like it, get married and settle down?'

'When they stop making men irrational and impossible to talk to,' Lydia said, thinking of the look on Will's face as he left.

'Not to mention dishonest and downright tricky,' Joanna said. 'Honestly, I thought it was women who were supposed to be the complicated ones. I'll never understand men as long as I live.'

'Well, this is turning out to be a great Christmas Day, you two in the Slough of Despond and no Christmas dinner.' Katy sighed. 'At least we're warm and the children are having a good time. Come on, there's no point in standing around here staring at that bastard thing. Let's go and see my wonderful, beautiful children, who gave me the best ever Christmas present by sleeping through the night for the first time in months.'

'I'm really sorry to be so down,' Lydia said, hanging her arms around her friends shoulders and kissing each of them as they made their way towards the sound of childish hysteria emanating from the living room. 'Quite soon, I'm planning to drink myself into a coma, and then I'll be much less bother. Any news of Alex?'

'Yes.' Joanna beamed. 'Mother and baby are doing well, father in mortal fear for his life, but happy. And they say little Joanna Katherine Lydia is adorable.'

'Really? They've named her after us? And I got bottom billing?'

'Don't be ridiculous.' Joanna rolled her eyes. 'She's called Carole, after Alex's mum. Born on Christmas Day and called Carole, the poor, poor child. I think I might open an account for her private therapy sessions now.'

'And Alex?' Lydia smiled. 'Apart from displaying appalling taste in names, how is she?'

'Good, great. On cloud nine, in actual fact. It must be all those drugs, either that or the discovery that she has a masterful husband after all!'

'Mummy!' Tilly ran to greet them, resplendent in a particularly garish tiara, courtesy of Joanna, with Vincent snapping at her heels, a huge red bow tied around his collar. 'Daddy's had the best idea!'

'Impossible.' Katy beamed at her little girl, swooping

her up into her arms and smiling at Jim, whose head was just visible above a mountain of wrapping paper, which Vincent seemed to making it his business to shred between his paws. 'Daddy never has good ideas.'

'Well, how's this,' Jim said. 'We take what food and drink we've got, pack it all up, whack it on the sleigh. Wrap up warm and head down to the pub for Christmas lunch. Everyone will be there, there'll be hot food and, more importantly, beer.'

'And they've got a picture of a lady in a bikini behind the nuts,' Jake said enthusiastically.

Katy looked uncertain. 'Christmas lunch in a pub with a load of strangers? It's not exactly how I planned our first Christmas here.'

'Well, you could look at it like that,' Jim said, standing up to reveal that he was wearing a light sabre on his belt. '*Or* you could look at it as a real traditional country Christmas with our new neighbours and friends. A proper community, rallying round in times of need, welcoming the poor Aga-less vagrants looking desperately for some warmth and shelter and booze. We've even got a Christmas baby story all of our own, although I expect Will may have trumped us with that already.'

'Will? He's going to be there?' Lydia asked, although she knew the answer to the question. 'And Stephen and Jackson, I suppose.'

'To be honest, I think for once in his miserable life Jim is right,' Joanna said, hooking her arm through

Lydia's. 'Listen, you and I are not the type of girls to hide ourselves away, all shame faced, are we? I look fabulous, you look over dressed, and if anyone deserves a decent Christmas Day, it's us. Who cares who's there? We can get drunk and pull a young farmer each. Show those pigs what they're missing.'

'Will already thinks I'm stupid and frivolous . . .'

'You are,' Katy said.

'I don't want him thinking I'm a stalker too.' Lydia shook her head. 'You go. I'll stay here and guard the Aga.'

'No,' Katy said, gesturing at her children. 'Either we all go or none of us do. Look at their tiny shining faces, Lydia. Do you really want to be the woman who disappoints them on Christmas Day, just because you feel like you've been humiliated enough?' Jake pouted, Tilly fluttered her lashes and even Vincent managed a pathetic whine.

Lydia sighed. 'Fine! Let's do it!'

Katy clapped her hands together and the children cheered.

'Can I bring my light sabre?' Jake asked her. 'I want to see if I can use the force on sheep.'

Chapter Seventeen

There was no one in the pub when Lydia and the motley crew of stragglers plus a one-eared dog made the final descent into the heart of the village. It seemed that everybody, including a small brass band consisting mainly of awkward and resentful-looking teenagers, was gathered around the village war memorial, singing carols that were being conducted very enthusiastically by the vicar, whose fur-collared black overcoat lent him quite a camp air, for such an elderly man.

A very blonde and tanned lady, decked out in full neon-pink ski gear and cradling a stack of hymn sheets, beamed at them, handing them each a sheet as they dragged the sleigh, now bearing Tilly and Jake too, to the edge of the gathering.

'*Once in Royal David's city*,' Jake climbed out of the sleigh and joined in loudly, brandishing his light sabre. '*Stood a lonely battleship* . . . Death star, probably,' he whispered to Tilly, who hopped from one red polka-dotted wellie to the other as she sang.

Setting down her carrier bag full of turkey limbs between her feet, Lydia unfolded her hymn sheet and joined in with the age-old English tradition of singing

along to the music, very quietly, and looking exceptionally embarrassed and apologetic about it. Still, she was
certain nobody minded, as Jake was belting out an
approximation of the words at the top of his voice and
Joanna was doing that ridiculous descant thing she did,
as if two weeks in the university choir, while she was
shagging the choirmaster, qualified her as the next
Katherine Jenkins.

As she sang, Lydia looked around the group for any
faces she might recognise, and sure enough, there, right
at the back of the gathering, on the other side of the
memorial, were Jackson and Stephen, best friends now,
apparently. Jackson was singing out loud and proud,
with that kind of misty-eyed optimism that Americans
did so well, and Stephen was mumbling into his scarf.
Lydia smiled fondly to herself; he really did have a
terrible voice, so terrible that his mother had actually
banned him from singing in the house as a child, which
Lydia had thought was very unkind until she'd heard
him singing in the shower and had been forced to go
out. Her two exes were already a little merry, judging
by their ruddy cheeks and Stephen's rhythmic sway, but
there was no sign of Will at all. Perhaps he wasn't here,
Lydia thought, stung by the disappointment she felt.
His absence should have been a relief, but it wasn't. At
that moment, even being moodily ignored by him
seemed a better prospect than never seeing him again.

'Pull yourself together, woman,' Lydia muttered, as

the congregation launched into 'The Twelve Days of Christmas', those of them who were standing within earshot of Tilly and Jake learning some new lyrics pretty quickly.

Lydia couldn't help but feel happy as she watched the children singing, and looked around her at the beautiful little village covered, quite literally, in Christmas. Pristine snow capped every roof and carpeted the surrounding sweep of the mountains, sparkling under the clear blue sky, punctuated with a ghostly half moon lying on its back. For a few days at least, the snow had made everything perfect, even the people, huddling together for warmth as they sung, half of them decked out in the brand new scarf sets they'd received that morning. Lydia's Christmas Day so far had been devoid of any actual present, unless you counted the papier-mâché egg cup that Tilly had made her, but this moment, in the shadow of the mountains and under this flawless sky, was as perfect a Christmas memory as any she could ever have hoped for, and it was impossible not to feel her spirits rise.

Maybe nothing she had hoped for had gone to plan, she told herself, and perhaps she really had royally messed up everything that she possibly could, but she was surrounded by good people, more than willing to take in strangers and make them feel welcome, and she still had her friends. Even Joanna, who by rights should be her mortal enemy, still loved her. Best and most impressively of all, last night she had, practically single-handedly, delivered baby Carole. Lydia had been the first person in the world to hold that tiny life in her hands and feel her little chest rise with her first breath, and it had been in that moment that Lydia realised Christmas wasn't about snow, fairy lights, presents and forced happiness. It wasn't about the Hollywood ideal she'd pursued so hopelessly since she was a little girl. It was just about a baby, being born surrounded by hope and expectation, and remembering to treasure the people that matter.

Men were okay, Lydia thought, as she straightened her shoulders and sang a little louder, but love, and all the crazy irrational things it made you do, was over-rated. Just look at her, making ridiculous declarations to a man she barely knew, and who probably farted in bed just like the rest of them. And look at Joanna, so desperate to hang on to her boyfriend that she'd lied, cheated and manipulated her way to being single once again. Joanna was worth more than that, and so was Lydia. And standing there in the snow, with slowly numbing toes and the smell of Christmas dinner beginning to wend its way out of the pub, Lydia decided that nothing was going to ruin the rest of Christmas Day for her, not even the fact that she had accidentally fallen for the world's most annoying man. With extra gusto, she flung aside her English reserve and belted out the very last line of the song.

'And a bra that was meant to hold threeeeeeee!'

Shame, really, that she was a line too late, and delivered Jake and Tilly's alternate ending to a silent crowd, preparing to be addressed by the vicar.

'Well.' The vicar repressed a smile. 'It wouldn't be Christmas if there wasn't always one who hit the sherry a little too early.'

It turned out that it was impossible for the sixteenth-century building that was the pub to fit the entire village within its walls, and so Mal had put up a large, and thankfully heated, marquee attached to the back of the building via the pub's French doors. Someone had taken great care in decorating it, adorned as it was with string after string of coloured, flashing, fairy lights. There was a fully decorated Christmas tree in each corner, looking like they'd been lifted out of four different living rooms, and a single spinning glitter ball hanging in the centre of the ceiling. The space had been filled with tables of various sizes, each one surrounded by an assortment of odd chairs that Lydia guessed had been borrowed from local homes, and dressed with a holly and mistletoe table decoration, crackers and a single red candle stuck unceremoniously into a clove-studded orange.

Along one side of the marquee, there were several trestle tables laid end to end, laden down with a buffet made up from the contributions that everyone had brought to the communal feast, including a selection of hams, a quantity of lovingly decorated Christmas cakes and stack upon stack of mince pies.

Relieving Lydia of her carrier bag, Katy and Joanna followed Alice, who had immediately gone to greet Katy and introduce herself, and some of the other women into the kitchen, where the main attraction was being prepared, letting the children and Vincent loose to run round and round in endless circles with the other village kids in the pub garden. Jim headed straight to the bar, embracing Jackson and Stephen as if he hadn't seen them for years rather than hours, leaving Lydia standing alone in the bustling marquee, at a loss what to do next. Deciding to take the bull by the horns, Lydia edged through the crowd to greet her two exes.

'Hello!' She smiled brightly, kissing them each on the cheek. 'Happy Christmas! Listen, I just want to clear the air. I'm sorry about everything that has happened. I didn't behave in the best possible way, I know, and I hope you'll forgive me, Stephen . . . even though you let Joanna talk you into proposing to me when you weren't sure if you wanted to. And Jackson, I'm sorry that I let you kiss me a little bit. I was confused and off balance, but I know it must have been confusing for you too. I'm prepared to let bygones be bygones, if you can?

'There are no hard feelings here.' Jackson smiled ruefully. 'And I figure, if Stephen here and I can be friends, then there's no reason why you and I can't too. Besides, I've been thinking about everything, and you're right. Joanna is an amazing woman. I don't want to let her slip through my fingers too. If she'll let me, I'd really like to give the two or us another chance.' As he talked, he caught sight of Joanna's flame-coloured hair at the back of the room. 'Excuse me a moment.'

Lydia took his place and stood next to Stephen; neither of them spoke for a while.

'Are you all right, really?' Lydia asked him finally, feeling a pang of what she had lost, the companionship of a decent man.

'Are you?' he asked her.

Lydia sighed and gave a little shrug. 'I will be. Stephen, I'm so sorry I dragged you up here for this. Honestly, we'd have been much better off at my mother's, or even yours, and that's saying something.'

'Maybe so, but then you wouldn't have had your epiphany about us, and quite probably, right at this moment you'd be engaged to the wrong man,' Stephen said with a small, sad smile.

'It would have been wrong for us to get married, though, wouldn't it?' Lydia asked him. 'Not just for me, but for you too. I'm not the girl for you, Stephen. I can't be, because if I was, then it wouldn't have taken Joanna to strong-arm you into buying me a ring.'

'I am awfully embarrassed that you found out about that,' Stephen admitted, adding, 'I promise you, I was a hundred per cent behind the idea, once I'd had a chance to warm up to it. But you're right, now everything that's happened has begun to sink in, I feel, well, don't take this the wrong way, but I feel relieved. All I want from life is a wife who adores me, three bedrooms in the suburbs and two kids, one of each. You're a career girl, a high flier, there's no way you'd ever settle for domestic bliss.' Lydia thought about Will, and the house he'd fleetingly planned to build for her, and wondered if that was strictly true.

'It's not that I wouldn't settle for it,' she said, thoughtfully. 'It's just that I'd want both. Knowing my luck, I'll probably end up with neither.'

Lydia looked up and across the room, and saw the back of Will's head, dipped to one side as he talked to a very pretty girl in her early twenties who made a point of laughing at everything he said, and tossing her long blonde hair over her shoulder into the bargain.

'That girl'll end up with whiplash, if she's not careful,' Lydia said, pursing her lips.

'He got to you, didn't he?' Stephen asked her. 'Will.'

Lydia shook her head. 'No, not at all. I hardly know the man.'

'And yet you can't take your eyes off him.' Stephen turned back to the bar. 'You never once looked at me like that, Lydia Grant.'

'Didn't I?' Lydia asked him. 'Really?'

'Not once,' Stephen said, picking up his drink. 'I'd have noticed.'

Constantly aware of wherever Will was in relation to her, and which pretty young thing, middle-aged wife or fetching older lady was flirting her head off with him at any given moment, Lydia still let herself relax as she settled into a plate of turkey with all the trimmings.

Seated around a table with Katy, Jim, the children, Joanna and a fishing boat hire operator called Craig, Lydia was also reunited with Gracie, the old lady she had met the day before. Her silver hair was worn in a girlish ponytail high on her head, and she was wearing a very smart, hot-pink two-piece. Gracie was thrilled to see Lydia again, insisting that she sit next to her, spending most of lunch whispering in lurid detail about every single sexual liaison she'd had during her years as a Wren in London, during the Blitz.

'And so I just grabbed it and gave it a good tug,' Gracie told her, with a wicked chortle. 'You should have seen the look on his face.'

'It's amazing you had any time to do any Wrening at all,' Lydia teased her gently, full of admiration for the lady who was pushing ninety but still had the sparkly violet eyes that must have once caused quite a stir in the heart of a young soldier.

'Well, we all thought we were going to die, you see?'

Gracie told her. 'It gave you a marvellous sort of freedom. Think about it, if you thought there was a good chance that you wouldn't still be here tomorrow, what would you do?'

'See what kind of big fish I could get on my hook, that's what I'd do,' Joanna said, pouting at a very bemused-looking Craig, shifting uncomfortably in his chair. Lydia looked over at Will, seated at a table on the other side of the marquee, and being all but smothered between the ample bosoms of a very statuesque lady who would have looked stern if she hadn't been reduced to a pool of girlish giggles by even the merest hint of Will's smile.

If she knew for a fact that she wasn't going to be here tomorrow, she'd walk over there right now and kiss him until he realised he couldn't live a moment longer without ripping her clothes off.

'Goodness, Lydia, what are you thinking about?' Katy asked her, 'Whatever it is, stop it – there are children present!'

'Sorry,' Lydia said, glancing back at Will again as she took her fourth or fifth mince pie and crammed it in one piece into her mouth. Not once had she caught him looking at her, not for the whole day. Why would a man go around kissing a girl and talking about house building, if within a few hours he was going to treat her like they'd never met? It wasn't on, it really wasn't.

'Oh, go on,' Gracie said, digging Lydia in the ribs with a bony elbow. 'Go over there and have him.'

'I beg your pardon?' Lydia looked at her.

'It's obvious you're smitten with him and I saw the way he looked at you when he brought you into the pub. I've known that lad since he was in nappies, and in all my years, I've never seen him look at a lass the way he looked at you. Proper old fashioned, it was. So what if he's been giving you the cold shoulder all day, a man's pride is always his biggest downfall. Go over there and tell you want him and I bet you my pension you'll get him. The direct approach never fails to work for me.' Gracie puffed herself up, proudly. 'I've had eighty-six lovers, you know.'

'Right,' Lydia spluttered through the remnants of her last mince pie. 'You know what, Gracie, you're right. Fuck it, I will, then!'

'Lyds!' Joanna gasped as Lydia got up, slightly unsteady on her feet after perhaps a little more warm Cava than was entirely sensible. 'Where are you going?'

Lydia pointed at Will's back as he headed out of the marquee and into the pub.

'To tell that man that he can't live without me.'

It seemed an impossible feat, particularly as she'd changed from wellies into her stilettos at the first opportunity, to catch up with Will as he headed inexorably towards the door. Nice, kind, friendly locals kept stopping her, some of whom she'd met before, some new folks, but all greeting her warmly. Always compulsively polite, Lydia found it impossible to ignore them, and she was only thankful that Will was in equally great demand for a chat and several kisses under the tired-looking sprigs of mistletoe. Finally, as she saw him head outside into the night, and spurred on by Gracie and two or three glasses of Cava, she left Mrs Grimsdale from the dairy mid-sentence, and barged through the crowd after him, yelling over her shoulder, 'Sorry, got a man to catch!'

'Will!' she called out after him as he disappeared out of the well of light coming from the pub, and into the darkness. Tottering forward with some difficulty in her heels, Lydia was just about able to make out his figure in the gloom.

'Will!' He stopped in his tracks and then, ever so slowly, turned around. He was waiting for her.

'Will.' Lydia repeated his name once more as she finally caught up with him, slightly out of breath, and stumbling like a newborn foal.

'Lydia.' He said her name, slowly, deliberately.

'I didn't want you to go.' Lydia gasped in a breath of cold air. 'What I mean is I didn't want things to end between us like this, not that they ever really started, I suppose . . . But, anyway, I didn't want you to walk out on me without you realising that . . . well, Gracie says I should just tell you I want you and drag you to bed, but I don't have the kind of balls that Gracie does, and anyway, I don't think you're the sort of man to be dragged anywhere. But what I'm really trying to say is, don't go, because you really do need to kiss me again.' Lydia banged her forehead with the heel of her hand. 'That sounded much better in my head.'

Will almost smiled, resting his hands on his hips as he looked up at the stars.

'Lydia, Lydia, Lydia,' he said, redirecting his gaze to her. 'Jackson told me the whole thing, about him and Joanna and you.'

'Did he?' Lydia said uncertainly. 'And how did I come out of that?'

'Maybe a little confused and impulsive,' Will said. 'He said that none of it was your fault, really. He said that you were one of the most remarkable women he'd ever met, actually. And he was a fool to let you go.'

'Really?' Lydia asked him. 'Remarkable? What does that even mean?'

'I don't know,' Will said, darkly. He started walking again, forcing Lydia to try and canter alongside him, to keep up with his long strides.

'Oh fine,' she said bitterly. 'Fine, fine, fine. I come out here and all but throw myself at you, and if all you can do is be moody and northern and mysterious, then I don't want to kiss you anyway. It can get old, you know, the whole Heathcliff-Bob-the-Builder fusion thing you've got going on.'

Will stopped dead outside a little double-fronted

cottage, which had a simple holly wreath tied with a red ribbon to its shiny brass knocker.

'Can it?' he said. 'Well, so can you, getting off on all the men that follow you around finding you bloody "remarkable". Bloody Americans.'

'Oh, oh well, as we're on the subject of delusions of grandeur, you might *think* you're the best-looking man around here, but quite frankly a sheep in a hat would give you a run for your money.'

'Would it?' Will took a step closer to her. 'Would it really? You come out here in your high heels and your off-the-shoulder top . . .'

'Yes, and another thing . . .' Lydia did not get to complete her sentence as Will took her unceremoniously in his arms and covered her mouth with his. No gentle kiss, this time, no shy politeness. Instead he crushed her body into his body, encircling her entirely with his arms, so that she couldn't move a muscle, not even to return his embrace. But Lydia didn't care, she was lost in the sensation of the heat of his lips against hers, the grate of his stubble on her neck, the whisper of his breath in her ear, so much so that when he finally broke off, she groaned. 'No, don't stop. More kissing.'

'But you're freezing,' Will whispered. 'You must have left your coat behind when you came running after me.'

Freeing one arm, with some difficulty, Lydia punched him lightly on the chest. 'I did not come running after you. It's impossible to run anywhere in these shoes.'

'Come on.' Will took her hand, leading her through the little wrought-iron gate that sat neatly between the slate-built walls and up the short path to the cottage door.

'Don't you think these people will mind us going into their house?' Lydia asked him. 'Although I must say, it's so quaint, this whole never having to lock a door business.'

'Quaint? Did you actually just say that?' Will raised a brow. 'This is *my* house. And I always lock it.'

'Your house?' Lydia looked at the smartly painted front door with new significance. Will had a proper, grown-up house, which surprised Lydia, although she didn't know why. Perhaps she had suspected that he lived in a cave he'd carved out of the rock face with his own bare hands. 'With your bedroom in it?'

'Most houses do contain at least one,' Will said. 'Even up here in the north. *And* I've got an indoor loo.'

Unlocking the door, he pushed it open and gestured for Lydia to walk in.

'What are you suggesting we do in this house?' she asked him, primly. 'Because I don't want you think I'm easy.'

Will's smile was unbridled. 'Lydia Grant, in the last thirty-six hours you've kissed three men, why on earth would I think you were easy?'

'Yes, but only because . . .' Lydia began to protest, but Will stopped her with a kiss.

'Don't be dim,' he said. 'Easy is the very last thing you are. I'd say that you are actually extremely difficult.'

Nervously, Lydia walked into the flagstone hallway, lined with what looked liked certificates of various building awards, and to her left an open door revealed a small sitting room, floorboards stripped bare, a distressed but comfortable-looking brown leather sofa and an old telly, on a stool in one corner. There were a few framed photographs on the wall that caught her attention. They looked old, like they might be of relatives long gone.

'Come here, you'll like this,' Will said, leading her into the sitting room and standing her before a sepia-toned photograph.

'Recognise that veranda?' he asked her.

Lydia found herself looking at a photograph of two Victorian women, sitting side by side. Struggling to see past their faces, unsmiling and of indeterminate age, but definitely well past the first flush of youth, she studied the architectural detail, the pattern in the wrought iron pillars and the lacy wood detailing.

'Oh, it's Heron's Pike!' she exclaimed.

'Yes, back when it was two houses, and that is Margaret, on the left, and her sister, before she ran away to get married, I suppose.'

Lydia studied Mad Molly's face; it didn't look mad at all, but even behind the composed mask of respectability that was fashionable in those early days of photography, Lydia thought she could see some expression in her pale eyes, one of sadness and loss. Or perhaps she was just imagining it.

'Where did you find this?' Lydia asked Will, fascinated.

'Flea market, this one,' Will said. 'I collect as many old photos as I can find. I think it's sad. All these peoples, all their lives and hopes and pride put on display for their future generations, and then in just a few years they end up nameless and lost with no one to look at their faces, wonder what they were like or even remember their names. And besides, it's great to document all that authentic detail for my renovation work.' Will caught Lydia gazing dreamily at him. 'What?'

'I've just never met anyone like you,' Lydia said.

Suddenly uncertain of what to do, or how to act, Will turned away, slipping off his jacket and hanging it on the door.

'So, what shall we do now?' Lydia asked him, her stomach spinning itself into knots.

'Hmmm,' Will said thoughtfully, looking her up and down with such intensity that his gaze swept a wave of shivers along the length of her body. 'Well, you look a little cold, so . . .' He took her by the hand and sat her on his sofa, next to the inglenook fire place, where the ashes of an earlier fire lay cold and grey. Filled with anticipation, Lydia watched as, with expert efficiency,

Will built up the fire again, and had it roaring away within a few minutes. Wiping ash from his hands on his jeans, he turned round and looked at her.

'You are on my sofa,' he said. 'That makes me feel nervous.'

'Does it?' Lydia said. 'I could move.'

'No, stay right there.' Lydia held her breath as Will kneeled down in front of her, leaning over to slowly kiss her, teasing and tickling her lips with his tongue, flicking it gently across her mouth. Catching his breath, he pulled back.

'This is surreal, having you here. I never thought this would happen,' he told her. 'I thought my stupid stubborn streak had blown it.'

'You are quite stubborn,' Lydia agreed, smiling sweetly.

'I know, but now I've got you here, I want to savour every moment. Can I take your clothes off, Lydia?'

'Oh, um . . . okay, then,' Lydia squeaked.

Taking her hands, Will sat Lydia up a little, pulling her Christmas sweater dress over her head and dropping it in a silk pool on the floor boards at her feet. With each of her wrists gently secure in his hands, Lydia forced herself to keep her eyes open as his gaze roamed freely over her. Releasing one hand, he traced the swell of her cleavage with his forefinger, slipping it under first one bra strap and then the other, sliding them down over her shoulders. And then, with both hands, he pulled away the cups, scooping out her heavy, full breasts. Lydia sighed as his thumbs caressed her nipples, his eyes drinking her in.

'You are very beautiful,' Will told her, his voice hoarse. 'I could look you for ever.'

'I'd rather you didn't.' Pulling him between her knees, Lydia wound her arms around his neck, and kissed him hard, thrilling at the touch of his rough shirt against her bare skin. Will pushed her back, his lips tracing a path down her neck and breasts, circling her nipples with his tongue. Urgently, Lydia pulled his shirt over his head, running her fingernails along his back, feeling the muscles of his shoulders rippling and shuddering under her touch.

His hands and mouth everywhere, Will guided her off the sofa and onto the floor, laying her out on the floorboards, pausing to admire her for a moment in the firelight, her dark hair spread out around her.

'Wait a second,' Will said, running out of the room.

'What? Where are you going?' Lydia laughed, propping herself up on her elbows. 'Have you lost your nerve?'

'No . . . I thought we'd better . . .' Will looked a little rueful as he produced a packet of condoms. 'Good news is, they're still in date. Just about.'

Lydia held her arms out to him as he joined her on the floor, kissing her deeply.

'Off,' he muttered, fumbling with the buttons of her jeans for too long, standing up to remove his own as Lydia lifted her hips and slid hers off, deliberately choosing to leave on the lace panties she was wearing. Looking up at Will, standing naked over her, Lydia caught her breath. He was a very impressive-looking man.

Kneeling down, Will ran his palms across her thighs, circling her breasts and groaning as he gripped the lace of her underwear and pulled it aside, sliding the weight of his hot, hard body into hers.

'Now,' Lydia whispered, looking into his eyes. Will groaned and in the next moment he was moving inside her, filling her up with the most exquisite sensation of pleasure. His eyes fixed on hers the whole time, Will cupped her cheek in his hand, kissing her as each thrust of his hips brought her closer to climax. And then, in one perfect moment, Lydia cried out with joy, feeling a rush of pure pleasure as Will collapsed, spent, onto her, tenderly kissing her face again and again.

'Lydia.' He whispered her name into her hair. 'I don't want ever to let you go.'

'Then don't,' Lydia whispered back, winding her arms around him. 'Don't ever let me go.'

Chapter Eighteen

26 December

Lydia woke up smiling, and happily exhausted. At some point during the night, they had made it to Will's bedroom, but had slept very little until perhaps an hour or so ago. Yet, as tired as she was, Lydia didn't want to sleep. Real life was so very much better than her dreams.

Rolling onto her side, she looked at Will, who was lying on his back, his black lashes sweeping the rise of his perfect cheekbones, dark stubble thickening in the dimple of his chin. He really had the most handsome nose she had ever seen, and, she decided, the kind of strong, manly jaw that would be at home on the cover of any romance novel. And as for his body . . . ever so lightly, Lydia traced the tip of her finger over his torso, biting her lip as it reached where the dishevelled sheet lay across his hips. Lifting it, she took a peak at what lay below, and quietly congratulated herself. She'd managed to cop off with the modern-day equivalent of a Greek god, and best of all, a Greek god who, it seemed, not only didn't mind her fleshy hips or rounded bottom, but actually rather loved them.

Withdrawing her hand and rolling onto her back, Lydia pressed her palm across her mouth, suppressing the gurgle of laughter that bubbled in her chest. This was ridiculous, she was acting like a love-sick sixteen-year-old, and part of her wanted to laugh out loud, text all her friends and write his name in Tipp-Ex on her pencil case.

Except that, if she did, she would wake him, and then she wouldn't be able to admire the dramatic sweep of his eyebrows or the perfectly proportioned pout of his full but manly lips. It was safer to get up, Lydia decided, not only for her but also for Will, who she thought probably couldn't take her pouncing on him again. After all, she had to give some time to recover, at least half an hour, she thought.

Carefully, Lydia climbed out of bed, and, as all of her clothes were still on the sitting room floor, including a very ripped pair of lace knickers, she slipped on one of Will's shirts that she found in his wardrobe, and a pair of socks neatly rolled into a ball in his top drawer. Make him breakfast in bed, that's what she'd do, Lydia thought happily; feed and hydrate him, and then ravish him. It sounded like a plan to her.

Quietly, she tiptoed down the creaky stairs, remembering as she ran her fingers down the oak banister what delights she had sampled last night on that very spot. It was all she could do not to skip across the flagstones to the kitchen, where she revelled being in a room that was so purely Will. Hand-built units, that seemed to be made from an assortment of reclaimed and recycled pine furniture, resulted in a harmonic patchwork of cupboard doors and drawer fronts, each finished off with a different style of brass, ceramic or glass handle, all topped off with the distinctive greenish Cumbrian slate that Will loved so much. The whole room made Lydia smile, loving that someone so forthright and mannish as Will would screw a cream ceramic door handle, delicately decorated with a pink rosebud, into his cupboard door.

Cheerfully, she opened and closed cupboards until she found a jar of instant coffee and two mugs, and some pretty stale bread to toast, humming to herself as she waited for the kettle to boil. Drawing the window blind up a little to peer outside, Lydia supposed that it must have started raining sometime in the night, not that she'd noticed, what with all the wild passionate love making, and it was still raining now. So heavily, in fact, that patches of green were already beginning to show through the snow, a cascade of water was running in a steady stream down the guttering and into the drain, and the icicles that hung from the roof edge, above the kitchen window, were dripping steadily onto the sill. The thaw was here at last, and chances were, Lydia thought to herself, the roads would be clear enough tomorrow for her to head back to London as planned.

And then it was as if the heavy rain cloud that crouched over the peak of the mountain outside the window settled in her heart, and Lydia realised that tomorrow she would have to leave, and go back to real life. Working all hours, never sleeping enough, eating and drinking too much, watching TV all night instead of sleeping and, most importantly, not kissing Will.

Don't be stupid, Lydia told herself. Don't let your silly romantic head break your heart for no reason again. Will is brilliant; he's amazing. But don't forget you thought that about Jackson too, and he still left and then you didn't want him anyway. Don't kid yourself this is yet another love affair that means more than it really does. Grow up, Lydia Grant, and remember who you are. Barrister, crusader for justice, that's you.

'How can you be awake?' Will's arms encircled her waist from behind, his stubble grazing her cheek. 'You've worn me out, woman, I need to sleep for a month and I would have, except I missed you.'

'The snow's thawing,' Lydia said, swivelling round in his arms. 'The roads will be clear soon.' Will smiled into her eyes as it took a moment for him to realise what that meant.

'We should have started this holiday romance a lot sooner,' he said, softly kissing the tip of her nose. 'Next time I meet an incredible but confusing woman, remind not to waste so much time.'

'I don't want you to meet any other women, ever,' Lydia said. 'Is that was this is, a holiday romance?'

The toast popped out of the toaster, making them both jump.

Will shook his head, thoughtful. 'Honestly, I don't know. At this moment, I want to say no, it's not. This is something more. But how can it be? Will you stay here, with me in this house, and not go back to London, and not be a barrister and not do the work you love?'

Lydia searched the depths of his dark eyes, unable to find an answer.

'What about you?' she said. 'Would you leave all this beauty, your home, your friends and family and follow me to London? Would you find your way around the tube, and come flat-hunting with me?'

Will said nothing, his finger stroking the nape of her neck.

'I don't want you to go,' he said.

'I don't want you to stay here,' she replied.

'We could see each other at weekends,' Will suggested. 'I could drive down south, it's only about six hours to London, maybe seven in traffic. Or you could come up? There are trains.'

'Yes, and there would be holidays and stuff,' Lydia said. 'We could see each other in the holidays. Not that I ever take any holidays . . .'

'Me either, no need when you live here,' Will said.

Lydia rested her forehead against his chest, sighing. 'It won't work, will it?'

'Probably not,' Will agreed sadly. 'I mean, yeah, maybe for a while. But not for ever. Even I would think you were mad to abandon your career for a man you've only just met.'

'And I know you'd hate to be in the city away from all this,' Lydia said, looking out of the window to where the steep incline of the hillside rushed upwards to meet the rain heavy sky.

'It doesn't mean I don't feel how I do about you, Lydia,' Will said.

'No, I know.' Lydia smiled at him. 'It's the same for me.'

'So,' Will said, on a ragged breath. 'What now?'

'Well.' Lydia made herself smile. 'We've got until tomorrow. That might as well be for ever. Let's go back to bed.'

The rain didn't stop, battering the cottage's tiny windows, until what little of the sun that made it through the clouds disappeared once more into the wet night, and Lydia and Will did not move out of bed, except to find something to eat in his kitchen or fetch a bottle of wine. Lydia didn't think she'd ever laughed so much, or felt such warmth flowing through every cell of her body just to be near Will. Inevitably, whether she liked it or not, she couldn't help but compare the out-of-the-blue romance with the intense summer she had spent with Jackson. Wasn't this just like that, she told herself, as the few hours they had together slipped away, minute by minute. Wasn't she simply doing what she always did, throwing herself in too soon, careless of the disappointment and pain that would follow?

Just remember, this time, not to let your heart go, Lydia told herself as she studied her reflection on the ornate gold-framed mirror with which Will had finished off his otherwise utilitarian bathroom. It wasn't only her shining eyes, tangled hair and rosy, stubble-scraped skin that told her how difficult it would be to do that. It was the fact that, in the space of just a few hours, it seemed impossible to imagine life without him.

The trouble was, Lydia knew she was drawn to a grand romance like a moth to a flame, even though all of her experience of worldly matters had taught her that life isn't like that. That's it's not all hearts and flowers, noble goodbyes in train stations and tearful reunions on skyscrapers. Look at what had happened with Jackson. She had thought she was hopelessly in love with him, but she wasn't, not really. Perhaps it was just that her normal life was often so dark and so difficult, seeing day by day how people's lives could fall apart and crumble away at the whim of fate. The thought of escaping into her own love story, just as she did with the films she loved, was difficult to resist. And yet now, when everything was so perfect, was exactly the time she had to be pragmatic and sensible. Because tomorrow, she had to say goodbye.

'Come back!' Will called to her from the bedroom. 'You've been gone way too long.'

It was soon after they realised they had nothing for dinner but half a bottle of Bailey's one of Will's clients had given him that someone banged on the front door of the cottage.

'Who's that?' Will said, his brow furrowing.

'Best way to find out is to open the door, usually,' Lydia teased him.

'Yes, but I'm only wearing boxers and all you've got on is that shirt,' Will said, smiling at her. 'And I was kind of hoping to get you out of it, again. Or maybe get you to keep it on, I haven't decided yet.'

The bell sounded again.

'Well, whoever it is, they aren't taking the hint,' Lydia said. 'Go on, I'll hide in here.'

But no sooner had Will opened the door than Joanna rushed in like the force of nature she was, shaking an umbrella all over Will's flagstones, and tossing it in the sink.

'So you're not dead, then!' Joanna exclaimed, kissing Lydia on the cheek and turning to admire a scantily clad Will, who was speedily clambering into the trousers he'd rescued from the sitting room floor. 'Far from it, by the looks of things, you slut. Honestly, Lydia, you could have texted or something, we've been worried sick.'

'Have you?' Lydia was touched.

'Well, not sick. That batty old nymphomaniac lady from the pub told us you'd gone off with Will, but still we didn't know for certain that he's not the district's foremost serial killer. You could have let us know what you were up to.'

'Sorry,' Lydia said, smiling at Will, who was sheltering in the doorway, buttoning up his shirt. 'Time sort of ran away with me.'

'So, the big news is I drove here, in Jim's Range Rover! The roads are clearing fast now. There are all sorts of chaps with ploughs and grit making themselves useful out there. Stephen took a punt and set off this afternoon. He said he hoped you didn't mind him not saying goodbye . . .'

Lydia winced; she had forgotten all about Stephen.

'Don't beat yourself up too much, darling,' Joanna said. 'After we got back last night, Stephen and I drowned our sorrows together; and you know what, he's going to be fine, really. He even asked me out on a date. I declined, of course; one of your cast-offs is quite enough. Anyway, Jackson, who is now staying at the pub, is going to take me home, so we can talk things through. It was his suggestion, which means something, don't you think? I don't know what, but . . . oh, fuck, I love him, Lyds, I've got to find out.'

'I think you should,' Lydia said. 'It's always better to know than to wonder, right?'

'Good, so the thing is, will you be okay getting the train back? I thought perhaps Will could take you to the station? Or if not, I'm sure Katy would. She's in a much brighter mood, you know, since yesterday. She's come home with loads of numbers and invites round to tea. I don't think she feels quite so isolated any more, although she is obviously still married to a prat. Still, one can't have it all, apparently.'

'Yes, that would be fine,' Lydia said, really wishing that Joanna would stop making her think about tomorrow.

'I was reading the tourist information pack that Katy left in the bedroom, now sex is off the table, and did you know they filmed that old movie you keep going on about in a station about an hour's drive away? Oh, you know, the one with the woman with her knickers in a twist and the train thrusting into a tunnel. You made me sit through it once and I almost had to kill myself.'

'*Brief Encounter*, really? The station's nearby?'

'Fifty miles or so, but you could persuade "someone" to take you there. You can catch a train to Lancaster and then go straight down to London.'

Lydia looked at Will, wondering what it would be like to kiss him goodbye on the same platform as Celia and Trevor had.

'Sounds like a bit of a trek. I reckon I'll get a cab to Carlisle, and catch the train from there. It'll be quicker and if there's time I can pop and see Alex and the baby.'

'Are you sure?' Will asked her. 'I don't mind. I'd like to take you to see something that's so special to you.'

'Yes.' Lydia steeled herself to rejoin the real world. 'Yes, I'm certain.'

'Really? That's not like you, Lydia, to pass up a chance to pretend you're on the silver screen! Anyway, look, it strikes me that you're going to need a place to stay, so here's the spare key to my place. Don't worry, if things do work out between me and Jack, then I'll make sure I stay at his place. If not, I'll be constantly available for vodka and Diazepam.' Joanna paused long enough to plant a kiss on each of Lydia's cheeks. Lydia looked at her in grateful astonishment. 'You'd let me move back in with you, after all that's happened?' she asked, albeit a tad warily.

'Water under the proverbial, darling. Besides, I wasn't exactly blameless. Not nearly as much to blame as you, mind you – but I did do a little bit of mildly psychotic meddling.'

'But I . . .' Lydia began, stopping when she saw Joanna's expression.

'Oh God! Do we really have to do all that tedious soul searching before normal service resumes in our friendship? You appear to have mistaken me for Oprah

Winfrey! All right, here goes: you made a mistake – who hasn't? Don't do it again. Let's cut to the next scene, camera's rolling, tra la la . . .' She paused to glare at Lydia some more. 'God, you are so naked under that shirt; it's revolting. Anyway, just in case I don't see you, don't forget to come to my New Year's Eve party! It's going to be the best one yet. Ciao, darling.'

And with a stolen kiss from Will, she was gone, letting a wet gust of wind blow in through the door as she walked out of it.

'Well, your mate seems to have forgiven you,' Will began, after the whirlwind of Joanna had worn off a little.

'Yes, without all the tedious business of talking about it.' Lydia smiled ruefully, before turning to Will. 'The road's are clearing.'

'Oh, well,' Will said. 'I suppose it couldn't snow for ever.'

'No.' Lydia smiled at him. 'Will you book me a taxi for the morning, via Heron's Pike, so I can pick up my stuff?'

'Let me drive you,' Will said, pulling her closer to him by the lapels of his shirt. 'I want to.'

'No.' Lydia shook her head. 'I want to say goodbye to you here. You have to be naked, though.'

'We should exchange numbers, e-mails,' Will said.

'No.' Lydia shook her head again before she'd even thought about what she was saying.

'No?' Will looked surprised and hurt.

'We've decided, we can't make this into a relationship based on twenty-four hours of perfect sex. And I'm a girl; e-mail and phone calls or texts won't help me get my head around it. They'll make me pine and write poems and phone you at three in the morning and play soppy songs to you. This has been special, I don't want to ruin it by sending you poems.' Lydia smiled. 'Trust me, making promises you can't keep never works out, and then one of you gets run over by a taxi and ends up in a wheelchair while the other one is on top of the Empire State building. It sucks.'

'I have no idea what you are talking about,' Will said. 'But you should know the fact that you are almost certainly mental doesn't make me fancy you any less.'

'It's a film, *An Affair to Remember*.' I'd tell you to watch it, but I suspect you might find a tiny bit girly.'

'Sounds like a horror film.' Will grinned. 'So, nothing. No contact after today at all? Are you sure?'

'I am,' Lydia lied. 'I need to sort my life out, Will. I need to grow up. And now is the time to do it. You don't want me like this, all over the place.'

'Actually, I sort of do want you all over the place,' Will said softly, popping open the top button of the shirt she was wearing.

Lydia thought for a moment. 'The chances are that I'll be back here again, some time. Perhaps we'll bump into each other. How about we agree that, if we both still think about each other, we'll meet at Heron's Pike, the night before next Christmas, in the boathouse?'

'In a year?' Will said. 'How have you gone from kissing anyone who's passing to being the hardest to get woman in history?'

'Because if we still feel then, the way we feel now, after all that time apart – then we'll know. That maybe this *is* something worth changing our lives for. Only on your way over, keep an eye out of taxis.'

'Mental.' Will kissed her, warming her from the tips of her toes to her rosy cheeks with his embrace. 'Okay, next Christmas Eve, at Heron's Pike. And as that's not for a year, I'd better make the most of you now.'

Lydia yelped as Will lifted her into his arms and carried her up the stairs, loving him utterly at that moment, because he did a very good impression of pretending that she weighed no more than a feather.

Chapter Nineteen

27 December

'And that was it, you just had a sex marathon and then said goodbye and thanks for all the orgasms? That doesn't sound like you at all!' Alex cooed in a singsong baby voice, cradling little Carole in her arm, gazing at her adoringly as they sat on the pink wipe-downable chairs in the day room. 'Oh, look at that little nose, have you ever seen such a darling, warling, ickle nosey? Have ooo? Have ooo? No you haven't, because there isn't one, that's why!'

Despite crediting herself with being the main reason that Carole was here today, and although she was undeniably sweet, Lydia did rather fail to see the endless adorable qualities and peerless beauty that her smitten friend had raved on about ceaselessly since she'd arrived at the hospital with a heavy heart and an hour to kill.

'Yes, her nose is very darling . . . um . . . warling.' Lydia coughed and after a moment decided not to mention her boathouse pact with Will; it did rather tarnish her announcement, and besides, it would probably never come to anything anyway. She preferred to keep her plans for the next night before Christmas locked away. 'Anyway, I know, but I've decided to be sensible. It's the new me. When it comes to my career, I'm a bulldog, ruthless, tough, logical . . . normal. So I've decided to apply the same approach to my love life. I'm giving up romance, in all its perfidious forms.'

'The same way you gave up drinking for lent that time, and then broke your wrist the next day in a vodka-and-trampoline-related incident?'

'Yes, I mean no. I'm serious. No more rushing into things without thinking them through, no more expecting my life to turn out like a film. Because what they never show you is what happens after the credits roll, do they? After the fun snow-fight montage, or the big violin swell and the tear-jerking kiss goodbye? They never show the bit where your ex-lover turns out to be dating your best friend and you end up finishing with your own boyfriend mid-proposal, more or less, and running away with the handyman. They never show you that bit, do they?'

'That's because you don't watch horror films.' Alex purred at her baby. 'Isn't it, poppet, isn't it? Slutty Aunty Lydia doesn't like stinky horror films, *no she doesn't!*'

'Wow, I thought it was only your placenta that got delivered along with the baby, not your brain too,' Lydia said. 'Anyway, you should be proud of me. I'm not doing what I did after Jackson. I'm not going into "I'll never love again" meltdown, and I'm not putting on the best part of a stone after ingesting more chocolate than any normal human can survive. I've enjoyed the moment, with Will. The passion and the sex, especially the sex . . .' Lydia paused, momentarily distracted, before having to literally shake herself free of an image of Will in a state of extreme undress as he kissed her goodbye that morning. 'I am preparing to face the future as a single, hardworking career woman.'

Alex didn't look the least bit surprised when Lydia burst into tears.

'I'll never love again!' she sobbed into her sleeve, attracting severe looks from a couple of other nursing mums.

'Don't cry, Lyds,' she said softly. 'Here, hold Carole, she'll cheer you up, and I've discovered you're much less likely to cry hysterically if you're worried about waking up a baby.'

Lydia took the baby, rather awkwardly at first, before she felt her warm little body settle into her arm, and she did have to admit that it was sort of soothing.

'I'm so stupid that I actually hate myself,' Lydia said. 'How can I care about Will when I've only just ended things with Stephen, and a few days ago I wasn't that sure I didn't want Jackson? I'm a train wreck. Have they got a psychiatric ward here? You should have me sectioned. I'm addicted to romance!'

'Hmm.' Alex looked at her. 'You are a bit, but I don't know . . .'

'What?' Lydia asked her, studying Carole's tiny, crumpled face.

'Well, I'm just saying.' Alex reached out and stroked her baby's cheek with the back of a finger, as if she couldn't bear not to touch her, even for a second. 'Love happens when it happens. It doesn't stick to a timetable. It doesn't say, well, I can't possibly bother this woman, she's married, or this man's no good, he's got a lot on at work. The trick is to spot when it's the real thing and make sure it doesn't pass you by. Look at me and David. Did I ever think the only man for me would be the one who was an inch shorter than I am and can't stop wittering on about bloody Saxons? No, I didn't, but he is and I adore him. Knowing I've got him and this little one, makes me the happiest woman alive.' Looking up at the ceiling, Alex blinked away a few tears. 'Honestly, fucking hormones, they make it really hard to keep up the heartless bitch thing.'

'We all know you are not a heartless bitch,' said Lydia, carefully handing the baby back to her mother. 'Well, you're not heartless, anyway.'

Alex treated her to an old-fashioned disapproving look.

'Just be careful that you don't decide to be all logical and practical at exactly the wrong time, that's all I'm saying. I know you and Will live far apart, and that you are all mental and impulsive and he's all handsome and rugged. I agree it seems unlikely that he'd fall for you, but you never know. And it's only three hours on the train into London from here. Every other weekend, you could swap who visits who,' Alex said.

'Stop it!' Lydia told her. 'Stop making it seem possible. We've decided, I've decided – this is how it's going to be. I feel down about it now, sure I do. But I'll be fine in a week or two, and I'll probably be obsessing fruitlessly over someone else.'

'If you're sure,' Alex said.

'Anyway, I've come to see you and all I've done is whinge about me – how are you, how's motherhood?'

'I'm extremely good, not a stitch in sight, and motherhood is the most amazingly wonderful thing that I have ever done.' Alex beamed. 'I don't think I could be happier if I tried.

'That's brilliant, Alex,' Lydia said, looking at her friend cradling her baby. 'You do seem to be a natural.'

'Please stay a bit longer,' Alex said, as Lydia began to pull on her coat. 'David will be back with my double cheeseburger and super-size fries in a minute. He so wants to thank you for what you did for Carole and for us.'

'I was pretty magnificent, it's true.' Lydia grinned. 'Although I suppose you had *something* to do with it. But I've really got to go, or I'll miss my train.'

'But you'll be at Joanna's party, won't you? New Year's Eve?'

'Will you?' Lydia looked sceptical.

'Yes, we're going home tomorrow, doctor says we're fighting fit, so I thought I'd pop Carole in a sling and we'll all be there, top of the Oxo Tower, brilliant!'

'Well, it's either that or sitting in watching TV, so yes, I might as well force myself into a party dress and fabulous heels and get drunk at Joanna's expense.' Lydia reached over and kissed her friend goodbye. 'I'll see you in a few days.'

Lydia took a few steps and then stopped. It was no good; she couldn't leave without saying what was really on her mind.

'It's not too late, you know,' she said.

'What isn't?' Alex asked her.

'To change your mind about calling the baby Carole.'

Joanna's flat was cold, empty and smelled faintly of bins, when a travel weary Lydia finally let herself in. Switching on the lights, and turning up the central heating, she paused at the answer phone, which was blinking insistently, and pressed play.

'Lyds, darling, thought I'd leave you a welcome home message. Sorry I'm not there, but put it this way, the trip back with Jack went better than imagined, and so we've checked into a Ramada for a . . . Well, anyway, we both agreed to just have fun, and enjoy ourselves, no strings, no secrets and no engagement rings. I hope that's okay with you, darling? Course it is, mwah!'

Lydia listened to the message, expecting to feel jealous,

cross, regretful or resentful, even. But there was nothing, not one single remnant of what she had thought she felt for Jackson. She was only glad that she hadn't completely managed to sabotage Joanna's relationship with him, and although she seriously doubted that Joanna would be able to keep engagement rings out of the picture for very long, she was glad that she sounded happy. As for Jackson, any secret feelings or hopes she had been harbouring for him were entirely gone.

'And that is what it will be like with Will too, probably,' Lydia said out loud, taking out her phone and deciding that their agreement not to swap phone numbers was a good idea, because if she had Will's phone number, she'd be calling him now, telling him she missed him. And later, after she'd drunk a bottle of claret that she found in Joanna's kitchen, she'd be phoning him, playing 'I've Had the Time of My Life' down the phone to him, while she sobbed pathetically in the background.

Right now, she might feel like she'd just left the love of her life in his birthday suit in Cumbria, but that's how she'd once felt about Jackson, and now her best friend was in bed with him and she didn't mind at all. And although the thought pained her, she had to admit that probably, some time between now and next Christmas, Will would stop thinking about her and start noticing one of the other of the many women who kept throwing themselves in his direction.

'Your trouble is you are a drama queen,' Lydia said, uncorking the bottle and pouring a third of it into a mug, which was the only thing she could find clean. 'You're not happy unless you're not happy . . . Well, not any more, now it's work, work, work. And perhaps a nunnery; you could be the world's first barrister nun.'

Switching on the TV, Lydia put her feet up on Joanna's sofa and supposed that she'd have to arrange a time to go round and pick up her stuff from Stephen's. But not today, today she was going to sit on Joanna's sofa, watch Joanna's TV, drink Joanna's wine and do her level best not to cyber stalk Will on the internet.

And as for tomorrow, well, Geoff, the head clerk, had a GBH case waiting for her at chambers. It was official, Lydia thought miserably, as Joanna's hideous, special offer, pink Christmas tree blinked at her. She was firmly back in the real world.

Chapter Twenty

New Year's Eve

It was cold on the terrace of the Oxo Tower bar, but that was where Lydia preferred to be, leaning on the railing, alternately taking the weight off the balls of each of her feet, as her very high-heeled, crystal-encrusted shoes were as painful as they were beautiful, rendering her more or less crippled within half an hour of going out. With her fourth or fifth glass of champagne in her hand, she braced herself against the sedate chill in the still city air, cold in such a different way than in Cumbria, and looked down the length of the Thames, across the city that sparkled and glowed before her.

Standing at the very top of the tower, Lydia saw the city she loved so passionately looking its very best, as if it had dressed itself up for a party along with all of its inhabitants. Glittering and glamorous, it flaunted its beauty, bristling with dark secrets, illicit adventures, filled to the brim with soul upon soul, destined that very night, the last night of the year, for romance, or intrigue or at the very least a shocking hangover. There were countless lives thriving out there, Lydia thought to herself as she gazed at the voluptuous horizon, already glittering with brazenly early fireworks, pinpointing a thousand other parties.

Each one of those people out there were expectant and hopeful of what the New Year would have in store for them, and normally so was Lydia. Never before had she gotten to eleven forty-five on New Year's Eve wishing that the next twelve months would evaporate in an instant and she would be sitting in the leaky-roofed boathouse at Heron's Pike, looking up through the broken skylight at the stars, with Will's arm around her, the heat of his body warming her, his rough cheek grazing hers.

Lydia's sigh materialised in the crystal air before her. It was extraordinarily tricky, this being sensible business.

Joanna's New Year's Eve party was lovely, full of beautiful people, and Lydia knew she'd be having a much better time if she threw herself into the melee, networking, making contacts in high places. Hiring out the entire bar, at goodness only knew what cost, Joanna had populated it with what seemed like every single person she'd ever met in her life, including four of her five ex fiancés. Even Stephen was in there, talking to some blonde PR girl that Joanna had hired for herself, declaring that this year was going to be the year she broke into to mainstream day-time television. And there was Jackson, of course, permanently attached to Joanna, who was keeping a very firm grip on his arm, like a child holding a balloon on a ribbon, afraid that he might float away should she let go of him.

Katy and Jim hadn't made it; they were opening up their doors to their first ever paying guests, and since hugging and kissing her friend goodbye on the steps of Heron's Pike, Lydia had decided not to phone Katy. She'd only end up asking her in a round about way where she'd been, what she'd done, who'd she'd seen and had any of them been Will? And how did he look and what was he doing and did he have the look of a broken-hearted man, maybe some shadows under his eyes and a slightly haunted, lovelorn look? And then, what if Katy said that no, actually he looked fine, and pretty happy as he was kissing that milkmaid, or whatever sort of country thing girls do in Cumbria? If he was, Lydia didn't want to know.

Alex and David weren't there either, declaring after all that they both hoped to be asleep by nine o'clock, and hoping that the New Year would bring them a baby that didn't like to stay awake twenty hours a day.

Patience, Lydia told herself, tracking the progress of an open-topped bus full of very drunk revellers over London Bridge. It had been less than a week since she'd left Will behind, although that was considerably longer than the time she had actually known him. What a stupid girl she was, Lydia thought, as she finished her glass of champagne and picked up another that had been abandoned on a table. No one falls in proper love after a few days. No one, ever, in real life.

Turning her back on her come-hither city, Lydia considered going back into the thick of the party. The trouble was, with two thirds of her friends absent, she didn't really have anyone she particularly wanted to talk to, and yet she didn't want to be in the back of a cab or on the tube when Big Ben chimed in the New Year. And most of all, she didn't want to go back to Joanna's empty flat on her own.

Earlier, Joanna had arrived back at the flat to get ready with her, with an armful of shopping bags and boxes tied with ribbons, that were sure to contain very tiny and very expensive items of underwear.

'Darling,' she'd said as she breezed in, 'I need to look amazing tonight, knock-out drop-dead gorgeous, and for that I need you and your unflappable false eyelash sticking on skills.'

And Lydia was happy to oblige, the fun of making up Joanna, as they cracked open the evening's first bottle of champagne, briefly taking her mind off everything else.

'I've missed this,' Lydia said, as she laced her friend into the Vivienne Westwood corset dress she had gone out and bought that afternoon. 'You and me; being girly together. Stephen was a nice flatmate. He always loaded the dishwasher and never left the seat up. But he never let me make him up, not once.'

'Darling, there's hardly a day goes by that I don't pop Jack in a pair of lacy undies, and give him a little coat of lip-gloss.' Lydia snorted, the red lipstick she'd been applying to Joanna shooting across her cheek like a firework.

'Ooops.'

'Never mind.' Joanna took a make-up wipe, and began again. 'Sorry, was that a little too much information?'

'No, it's just . . . he was never so adventurous with me. I don't suppose I knew him at all, really. Funny, isn't it, how you can spend such a lot of time utterly convinced that you are in love with virtual stranger?'

'Or, on the other hand, that you are not,' Joanna said, smiling sympathetically. 'Now, it's my turn to do you. Sit.'

Joanna had lent her a silver, satin-boned number, with a puffball skirt that sat above her knee. Lydia had been horrified when Joanna had produced it, but after realising she wasn't going to get any peace until she tried it on, she was surprisingly pleased with how it suited her, nipping in her waist and pushing up her bosom to boost her cleavage rather spectacularly.

'There, you look stunning,' Joanna had said, as Lydia twirled for her, putting her hand on her hips and tipping her head to one side. 'Too stunning, take it off, and put on something frumpy. I don't want Jackson lurching at you again.'

'He's not going to do that,' Lydia said. 'You two have

become inseparable, this is the first time you've been home in days!'

'It's true.' Joanna's smile faded, just a little. 'It's just, I sometimes worry that I'm the consolation prize, that he's turned to me to get over you. And that didn't work out so well for Stephen, did it?'

'Nonsense,' Lydia said, taking Joanna by the shoulders and standing her in front of her full-length mirror. 'You and Jackson are so different from me and Stephen. Besides, look at you, you will never be the consolation prize, and Jackson knows that. If there is anyone who can out-play him at his own game, then it's you, Jo-Jo, and maybe you are exactly the challenge he needs to realise a real relationship is more than just falling in love, time after time. Me and him, we were a blip, a puff of nothing, gone in one summer. But you, you've got the brains and the beauty to rein him in, if anyone has.' She knew she should stop there, but couldn't resist adding, 'Just as long as you remember who you're dealing with, and are careful not to get your fingers burnt again. You are playing it cool, though? Just don't let him know quite how much you love him yet.'

'I think it might be a little too late for that.' Joanna winced. 'Is it terrible, Lydia? It's like I don't care how much he loves me back, as long as he's there? I suppose that's what love is all about, though, isn't it? Taking a chance on a feeling and hoping it works out for the best. Don't you think?'

Lydia thought for a moment and gazed at her reflection. Joanna had tonged her hair so it fell in fifties film star waves over one shoulder, and she'd painted her lips a deep mulberry, highlighting her pale complexion. Tonight, Lydia felt about as beautiful as she ever had, and yet it didn't give her half as much pleasure as bird's nest sex hair and one of Will's shirts would have. Perhaps Joanna and Alex were right, perhaps she should take a chance again, find a way to contact Will. Except look at where rushing in had got her before, and Lydia wasn't sure if she could cope with Will, of all people, disappointing her.

'I think,' she'd said carefully, 'that you have to be ready to take that chance, ready to accept that it might go horribly wrong and that you might spend the rest of your life broken and alone, hopeless, bitter and full of regret. But if you are ready, which you obviously are, then you should go for it.'

'That's the thing about you, Lyds,' Joanna said, putting an arm around her as the two of them admired their reflection. 'You always know exactly what to say to make a girl feel better.'

The only conversation she'd had with Jackson all evening had been at the bar. He'd been acquiring two more glasses of champagne, attracting the barman's attention with one hand, the other still firmly gripped in Joanna's as she chatted to some media industry people Lydia didn't know.

'Happy New Year,' Jackson said to her, nodding. 'I'd kiss you on the cheek, but I think it might result in my certain death.'

Lydia smiled. 'You mean a lot her,' she said. 'Treat her carefully, Jackson. That woman is one of my dearest friends. Even after that whole debacle in Cumbria, she is still there for me. I won't let her get hurt. I will track you down and gouge out your eyes with a rusty nail if there is even a hint that you aren't making her one hundred per cent happy all of the time.'

'I believe you.' Jackson nodded. 'But, listen, you don't need to worry, you really don't. This whole thing's made me think hard about the kind of man I've let myself become. I've always loved women; I love being in love and the rush and the thrill of those first few weeks with someone new. I've chased that thrill for a long time now, playing the game for the fun of it. And I guess I was playing it still with you and Joanna. And then, when I saw what I almost did to you two, how I almost tore you apart . . . well, I realised I wasn't the kind of man that would make my dad proud. And that was pretty hard to take.'

Jackson took a deep breath, before taking a long draught of his drink. 'I have no idea if things will worth out with Joanna the way she wants them to, but it's quite an amazing thing to realise that someone as special as Joanna will give me a second chance after having so royally screwed up. I won't make the same mistake again. What sort of fool would that make me?'

'A very, very stupid one,' Lydia said, taking her own glass.

'And how about you? How are you doing?' Jackson asked, smiling fondly as he glanced over at Joanna, who was now fluttering her false lashes at a television producer with coquettish abandon.

Lydia sipped her champagne. 'Honestly? I actually don't know. A lot's changed recently. I just need some time to take a breath, take stock, develop my alcoholism.'

'Good luck with that.' Jackson gave a quick nod, not really listening, as Joanna dragged him away. 'I'd better go, it looks like my presence as Trophy Boyfriend is required!'

'Happy New Year!' Lydia called, watching him disappear into the crowd, smiling to see how Joanna loved parading him around, as if here was her very own prize bull. She was relieved to note that she just felt amusement rather than regret as he left her.

Alone again, Lydia had wandered about the room, for what seemed like hours, making polite conversation with people she barely knew, who invariably asked her if she'd ever defended anyone she knew was guilty or whether or not she might be able to give them some free advice. One man, more than a little the worse for wear, told her she had the finest cleavage in the room and asked to rest his head there, and another – nice enough and not bad looking – plucked up the courage to ask for her number, which she politely declined. Tiring of smiling in a room full of beautiful people, Lydia finally found her place on the terrace, leaning into the night as she admired the city she loved, intent on seeing in the New Year with herself.

'I've been in worse places, I suppose,' a voice said behind her. Lydia froze, frowning. Had someone spiked her last drink? They must have, because she was surely hallucinating. 'I mean, it's a bit smelly and there are a lot more people here than is natural, but from where I'm standing it looks pretty beautiful.'

Slowly, ever so slowly, Lydia turned around to find Will standing there. As mirages went, it was quite a doozy. He looked as gorgeous as ever, dressed casually in jeans and a white shirt, unbuttoned at the neck under his battered leather jacket, and carrying two glasses of champagne.

The world, time, everything seemed to stand still for an age as Lydia gazed at him, trying to make sense of what she was seeing. Will was *here*, in London? That couldn't be right.

'You're a sight for sore eyes,' Will said softly, taking a hesitant step closer to her. 'Although seeing you in that dress makes me think I should have worn a tie. I nearly didn't get in as it was. I had to get Joanna to come and tell the prat on the door that I was invited.'

Lydia opened her mouth, but there seemed to be a distinct lack of words to fill it.

'Say something,' Will said. 'Something that's going to make me feel like much less of an idiot for driving all the way down here to see you.'

'Joanna invited you? She never said!'

'I asked her not to,' Will said. 'And I sort of invited myself, as it goes.'

'W— Why?' Lydia asked him. 'I thought we'd agreed . . .'

'Yeah.' Will nodded emphatically. 'Yeah, I'd thought we'd agreed too, and then after you were gone for a day or two, and I got bored of drowning my sorrows, I suddenly realised that we hadn't agreed anything. You'd agreed it all on your own and I went along with you, because when you want to be, you're good at talking people into thinking they've agreed to stuff. It is your job, after all.'

Will drained one glass of champagne, and then after a moment's thought, finished off the other one too.

'The thing is, I don't agree, Lydia. I don't agree to us not seeing each other for a whole year. I don't agree to us being sensible, or practical, or putting our jobs first. I seem to have fallen in love with you. Strange, granted, as you are pretty tricky and complicated, not to mention very inconveniently located. But still, that's how I feel. And I was sitting in the pub, face like a smacked arse, when Gracie sat down next to me and said, don't be a twat, Will. That girl had the guts to go and get you. Now, be a man, and have the guts to go and get her.'

'She said that?' A tiny smile tugged at the corner of her mouth. 'Gracie called you a twat.'

'Yeah.' Will grinned. 'And she was right. I'm not the sort of man to let a girl tell me what to do. I don't know what I was thinking, letting you talk me into your plan of meeting in a bloody boathouse in a year. Well, I watched your film, *An Affair to Bloody Remember*, and if they'd both just gotten together when they fell in love, then she wouldn't have ended up in a wheelchair, and it would have been a lot shorter film. I mean, yeah, maybe you should wait and see if you're not sure, if things aren't quite right. But I *am* sure, and things *are* right, the rightest I've ever known them, in fact. So I've thought about it. I'm not prepared to leave the next time I see you to fate. I don't agree not to see you, or think about you, or want you, or long for you every second you are not there. I do not agree. What are you going to do about that?'

And in one fluid movement, Lydia closed the gap between them, flinging her arms around Will and kissing him, so enthusiastically that he stumbled back a couple of steps, finding his way into a seat, his hands on Lydia's waist as he drew her down into his lap, at what must have been the stroke of midnight as all at once he night sky lit up with an explosion of fireworks, heralding the New Year. Lydia's head resting on Will's shoulder, they sat curled up in each other, watching the spectacular display ignite the city into celebration.

Eventually, as the spectacle died down, Will took Lydia's hand in his, kissing her fingertips.

'So, just to be clear, are we now agreeing not to let the distance and our work and all the complicated crap get in the way, and to do as much as possible to see each other *as* much as possible? Because I need you Lydia, I need you here, next to me, as much as is humanly possible.'

'We are,' Lydia said happily, the tip of her nose touching his, as she stroked his hair from his face. 'I'm so stupid, I'd talked myself into thinking I was doing the right thing, making the right choice for once in my life. But the second I saw you standing there, I knew that I have to be with you. Maybe it will go horribly wrong and I will get my heart trampled on again, but I don't care. Because you are so worth taking the chance for, Will. I need you too.'

Will wrapped his arms around her, holding her so tightly that she could feel his heartbeat, thundering in time with hers.

'Happy New Year, Lydia Grant,' he whispered in her ear. 'I know it's going to be the best year of my life.'

Chapter Twenty-One

24 December
The (Next) Night Before Christmas

It truly was a silent night at Heron's Pike. Exhausted from a day of partying with the village children, Jake and Tilly had volunteered to go to bed even earlier than usual and, after tucking the turkey into the Aga, so that it would be ready just in time for them to take down to the pub in the morning, Katy and Jim had gratefully followed them not too long after. The couple had had a busy year, bookings picking up steadily until they were fully booked over the whole summer, and socially too now that Katy had made new friends in the village.

As Lydia felt the crunch of snow under her boots, she glanced back up at the house, seeing that there was still a light on in Jackson and Joanna's room, where no doubt Joanna was trying her new silk negligee out on her boyfriend. Twelve months in with no sign of a ring and Joanna had told Lydia she couldn't be happier, feeling something really special had gradually begun to develop between the two of them. 'And do you know what?' Joanna told Lydia earlier that day. 'Even if he did propose, I'd say no, for now, at least. I think I'm finally learning you don't need an expensive piece of metal and stone to make a person stay with you. All you need is love – whoever would have thought it!'

A night light still glowed in Alex and David's room, although Lydia was almost certain it was for very different reasons. Even on her first birthday, baby Lily Carole Amis was not particularly minded to do anything so boring as sleep. It was a good job that her parents adored the rosy-cheeked little scrap, Lydia thought, as she ruled the pair of them with a rod of iron. David had proved himself to be a brilliant father, and the moment that Lily had come into the world Alex had softened, almost as if now she had a child to care for she wasn't afraid to let the world see the real, sweet, vulnerable person she was. And the softer she became, the more self-assured David was, the three of the them forming a tight-knit, if utterly exhausted, little unit.

Lydia shuddered, wrapping her arms around herself as she continued the walk down to the boathouse, pausing as she saw the flickering light in the window, holding her breath in anticipation.

What a year it had been, what a hectic, crazy, wonderful year. Sometimes it had felt to Lydia that the only moments she was ever still were those blissful, all too short hours she spent in Will's arms. He had become her anchor, and she his, each of them gradually evolving and revolving their life around the other.

Early in February, Will had started to take restoration projects a little further south, until finally, during a wonderful dreamlike summer, he'd brought the most incredible seventeenth-century Cotswold manor house back from the brink of decay for a wealthy London couple who wanted a country pile and had heard that Will and his team were the best. Lydia had delighted in spending every weekend with him, lost in what seemed like a wonderland of cottage garden flowers, bumbling bees and heated kisses in the long grass. For the four months he'd worked on the project, Will chose to rent a cottage locally, and gradually the pair of them got to know, not only each other, but also the softer, more feminine landscape that ensconced them, and they gradually came to admire it, almost as much as Will did his own beloved lakeside mountains.

Then on the final day, as Will walked Lydia around the grounds of the beautiful old house, waiting for his clients to come and see the finished product, he'd remarked, 'You know what, I could almost live in this part of the world. Have a house here, at least. A base to branch the business out from.'

Kicking a patchwork of multi-coloured leaves into

the air with the toe of her boot, Lydia nodded in agreement.

'Me too. In fact, my chambers has offices in Oxford, so relocating would practically be a breeze . . .'

They both stopped stock still in the crisp afternoon, exchanging looks, but neither one of them wanted to say out loud that here in the swell of the Gloucestershire landscape, they might have inadvertently kicked up, along with the autumn leaves, a solution that meant a future together was possible.

Then autumn faded into winter and Lydia was entrusted with a career-enhancing murder case to defend, and Will headed back to Cumbria for a new job. Lydia had spent eight tortuous weeks without him, neither one of them able to find the time to close the aching gap between them. And yet, although she missed him so much that even her skin and her hair hurt, Lydia was not lonely, knowing that she'd speak to him every night before they went to bed.

'I hate being this far apart from you,' Will had said, last night, the last time they had spoken.

'Me too, but it's not long to wait now. You and me in the boathouse, the night before Christmas. Just like we planned.'

'I could come to the house, you know.' Will chuckled. 'I'll be back about nine?'

'Yes, you could, but that's not like a romantic movie

at all, is it, Will?' Lydia admonished him. 'I want the next time I see you to be in that shed, where we first got to know each other. And I insist on whiskey in a flask and an oil lamp.'

'It's a good job I love you,' Will pretended to grumble as he put down the phone.

Just then, as Lydia reached the boathouse door, she was hit with a terrible premonition. What if he wasn't here? What if something had happened between last night and now to change his mind; after all, he hadn't texted or called. She hadn't heard from him since he hung up. What if there had been an accident and she had lost him after all? The thought was so terrible that tears sprang into her eyes and she slammed open the boathouse door in a panic.

What Lydia found in the boathouse rendered her utterly silent.

Will was sitting in the boat, alive and well, and more than that he'd filled the shed with what had to be hundreds of candles, lined up along every surface, filling up one boat entirely, so many that the grimy shed was glowing with light and warmth.

'Oh, good,' Lydia breathed as she gazed around. 'You're not dead.'

'I'm not . . . *what*?' Will stood up in the boat, rocking it slightly, holding out his hand to her. Skipping, Lydia hurried to join him.

'For a second, just a second, I imagined what life

would be like without you, and I panicked. But you're here, and you've done this for me.' Lydia smiled. 'And it's so lovely.'

'*That's* the response I was looking for. It took me ages to light all these.' Will helped her into the boat, drawing her into his arms as they kissed.

'Christ, I've missed you,' he whispered into her hair.

'And I've missed you,' Lydia replied, smiling into his eyes. 'Did you bring whiskey?'

'Yes, but, listen . . . I've got something to say first.'

'What, is it bad? Do you want to split up?' Lydia asked him, anxiously.

Will frowned. 'Yeah, 'cos I always risk third degree burns on lighting a ton of candles when I want to dump a lass. Shush, woman, of course I don't want to split up.'

'What, then?' Lydia asked him, a little unsteady on her feet as Will checked both his jeans pockets and then found something, in the inner pocket of his jacket, which he brought out. Taking a deep breath, he opened a small box and showed the contents to Lydia. It was an antique ring, perhaps Victorian, a rich dark-red ruby set between two tiny diamonds, clasped in yellow gold.

'What I want to say,' Will said, 'is, have you got any plans on Tuesday, because, well . . . did you know that Gretna Green is only twenty miles away?'

'Are you asking me to marry you?' Lydia asked, tearing her eyes off the ring to look at him.

'Yes,' Will said anxiously. 'And I'm only joking about

Gretna Green, you can't actually go and get married there on the spur of the moment any more, I checked. Besides, I've got the feeling that you'd probably want something fancy, with a big dress and your friends and all that girly stuff. What I was trying to say was, if you'll have me, I would marry you on Tuesday, I would marry you now, tonight, if I could, because I can't marry you soon enough.'

Lydia said nothing.

'Is it the ring?' Will asked her anxiously. 'It was my grandmother's, and her mother's. I know it's not a great big Tiffany rock, but I never wanted to give it to anyone else, if that means anything.'

Still Lydia was silent.

'Say something, before the bloody building burns down!' Will exclaimed.

'Yes,' Lydia said. 'Yes, I will marry you, yes, it is the perfect ring, and yes I am going to want a fancy wedding with a big dress, and yes, I love you.'

'Brilliant.' Will's smile dazzled her. 'Oh, there is one other thing too.'

'Something else? Are you pregnant?' Lydia asked him, making him laugh.

He unfolded a dog-eared and grubby bit of paper that he produced from his back pocket, and handed it to her. Lydia looked at it. It was estate agent details for a derelict barn in four acres of land in the Cotswolds.

'I've bought you this barn as a Christmas present,' Will said. 'I know it doesn't look much, but I sort of thought I could make it into a house for you. I'll even put a turret on it, if you insist . . .'

The boat nearly capsized as Lydia lunged at Will, almost knocking him off his feet as she embraced him, and they collapsed into a giggling heap in the bottom of the boat.

'Happy Christmas, darling,' Will said as they gazed up at the stars through the broken skylight. 'Are you having a good one?'

'Best Christmas ever,' Lydia whispered, feeling the heat of his body warm her, and the graze of his cheek against hers. 'My perfect Christmas, at last.'

Ebury Press Fiction Footnotes

An exclusive interview with Scarlett Bailey:

What was your inspiration for THE NIGHT BEFORE CHRISTMAS?

Christmas is such a fabulous time of year to set a novel in. We are all under such pressure to be happy, and for everything to be perfect and of course to really like the people we are spending the day with. But in reality that doesn't always happen. I wanted to write a book that captures the fun and magic of Christmas but that also showed some of the things that can go wrong when we are trying to so hard to get it right (the turkey thing happened to me!) and to show that a perfect Christmas is less about how it's supposed to be and more about how it's meant to be. And also I really wanted to write about lots of kissing.

Have you ever been snowed in like Lydia?

Yes, up to my knees! But luckily I was with some very good friends, a lot of food and a great deal of wine. It turned out to be a very lovely Christmas.

What's the worst Christmas present you've ever been given? And the best?

The worst – a foot spa, from a now very ex-boyfriend. I've since learnt never to mention in passing anything you find vaguely interesting in the three months prior to Christmas! My best ever present was a dolls' house. My dad secretly made it in the garage for a whole year. I can remember to this day how thrilling it was to see it sitting under the tree waiting for me.

I love the glamorous setting for Joanna's New Year's Party – have you ever been to a party at the Oxo Tower?

Yes, and I remember how sophisticated I felt sipping champagne, looking at the views across London. I wanted to set Joanna's party somewhere just as fabulous as her and which had just a hint of the drama of the Empire State Building in *An Affair to Remember*.

Jack asks Lydia 'Book or movie?' about* Breakfast at Tiffany's, *which would you choose?

The book is so wonderful, but it's got to be the movie. Audrey Hepburn is such an icon, the young George Peppard is so handsome and I so want Holly to have the happy ending that the film gives her.

What's your favourite thing about Christmas? What's your least favourite thing?

Presents! I love choosing really special presents for

my friends and family, and put a lot of time into trying to find something particularly special for my favourite people. I love wrapping presents in lots of bows and glittery stuff and of course I love receiving them. Unless it's a foot spa! My least favourite thing about Christmas is having to take the decorations down, the whole world suddenly seems very dreary.

What's your favourite Christmas film?

Tricky one . . . I suppose I will have to go with *It's a Wonderful Life*, James Stewart is so brilliant in it and it truly sums up the spirit of Christmas.

What's your favourite romantic comedy?

I perhaps should say something featuring Doris Day and Rock Hudson, all of which I love. But truly it's *When Harry Met Sally*, which I don't think has been bettered yet in the rom com genre.

Which classic novel have you always meant to read and never got round to it?

I'm not sure I should admit it here, but I've never actually read *A Christmas Carol* by Charles Dickens. This year, for sure − I promise.

What are your top five books of all time?

Gone with the Wind by Margaret Mitchell − impossible to find a better epic tale of romance and adventure than this – I am a little biased; I was named after the lead character after all.

Jane Eyre by Charlotte Brontë – I have adored this book since I was a girl, and every time I read it I discover something new amongst the pages.

Pride and Prejudice – it would be very hard not to include the finest example of a romantic comedy ever written.

Great Expectations by Charles Dickens – no other writer has such a talent for complicated characterisation and plotting, which is really why I must get around to reading *A Christmas Carol* . . .

Breakfast at Tiffany's by Truman Capote. Like Lydia, a teacher did give me this book when I was a teenager, and like Lydia I carried around for years until it became so fragile it now sits on my bookshelf. It's impossible to get tired of Holly Golightly.

Do you have a favourite time of day to write? A favourite place?

I write 9 – 5 every week day at my burr walnut desk. It's very important to be disciplined, particularly for a person who is very easily distracted, like me.

Which fictional character would you most like to meet?

I would certainly like to have cocktails with Holly in sixties New York and perhaps a mint julep with

Scarlett at some plantation garden party, if she was in a friendly mood!

Who, in your opinion, is the greatest writer of all time?

In my opinion . . . Charlotte Brontë. She didn't write much, but everything she did write in her short life was nothing short of groundbreaking genius.

Other than your writing career, what other jobs or professions have you undertaken or considered?

I have been a bookseller, secretary, barmaid, waitress, dog groomer and cinema usherette!

What are you working on at the moment?

Why, my new novel of course . . . watch this space.

Turn the page for a few delicious recipes featured in
The Night Before Christmas:

Whole Salmon Baked in a Coarse Salt & Herb Crust, Stuffed with Black Olive Pesto

Preparation time: 20 mins
Cooking time: 50–60 mins
Serves: 6–8

Ingredients:
Approximately 2.5–3kg whole salmon, filleted,
1 orange, thinly sliced
1 lime, thinly sliced
1 bunch fresh dill
1 bunch lemon thyme
5 large eggs, whites only (save the yolks for making breakfast omelettes or Prairie Oysters – gross but effective hangover cure – as the need arises!)
2.5kg coarse salt

For the pesto (tip: can be made in advance and stored in the fridge):
Two cloves garlic, roughly chopped
Large bunch flat leaf parsley
Large bunch basil
1 sprig rosemary
4 sunblush tomatoes

150g pitted black olives
4 tbsp finely grated Parmesan
5 tbsp extra virgin olive oil

1. Place the garlic and herbs in a food processor and blend until finely chopped. If you don't have a food processor, it can be done in a pestle and mortar but is harder work! (Why not reward yourself with an extra mince pie!)
2. Add the tomatoes, olives and Parmesan and pulse until coarsely chopped.
3. Scoop the mixture into a bowl and stir in the olive oil to make a thick paste. (Alternatively, if you're strapped for time – and who isn't at this time of year – you can probably find olive pesto or olive tapenade in your local supermarket.)

Method:

1. Preheat an oven to 200°C. While the oven is heating, spread each fillet with the pesto, lay on the lime and orange slices and reassemble the fish.
2. Measure and combine the egg whites with the salt and finely chopped herbs. Mix until ingredients are thoroughly combined. Place one-third of the mixture on the bottom of a lined baking tray. Spread the mixture out to form a bed for

the salmon to rest on. Place the stuffed salmon on top of this mixture and gently press down.

3. Place the remaining two-thirds of the salt mixture over the salmon to completely cover the entire fish. Do not crush or smash the fish.

4. Place the entire pan into the oven and bake for approximately 50–60 minutes, or approximately 10–12 minutes per 500g of raw fish. Remove from the oven and carefully peel away the outer layer of salt. The crust will be a light golden brown and should peel away in sections.

5. Transfer onto to a serving platter, slice and serve immediately.

Don't worry; despite being cooked in a salt crust this isn't an overly salty dish, it's a great method for keeping fish moist – and a nicely dramatic way of serving the results of your labours!

Stuffed Pork Belly with Parmesan and Herbs

This recipe is very easy, but the results look impressive. It is perfect for a special dinner, or family lunch. The trickiest bit is probably the rolling and tying up of the belly but don't worry you don't have to have a brownie badge in knots to be able to keep your dish together!

Preparation time: 30 mins
Cooking time: 1.5–2hrs mins
Serves: 8

Ingredients:
3–4.5kg belly boneless pork, skin removed (but keep hold of it – this will be the crackling – the best bit!)
5 tbsp olive oil
Juice and zest of 2 lemons
2–4 cloves of garlic, chopped
Large bunch of flat leaf parsley, finely chopped
Handful of fresh sage leaves, finely chopped
4 tbsp of ground Parmesan

Method:

1. Mix together the parmesan, herbs, oil, garlic

and lemon juice and add salt and pepper to taste. Mix to a stiff paste and put into the fridge to solidify – this makes it easier to use.

2. Heat the oven to 220C/Gas 7

3. Dry the pork skin thoroughly and rub with salt. Cut into 5cm squares. Pop it in the oven on a baking sheet. (Keep an eye on it!)

4. Lay the belly out, with the fattier side down (this is probably the skin side). Tuck lengths of kitchen string underneath, so it can be pulled into a roll.

5. Spread the Parmesan and herb stuffing into the centre of the roll.

6. Roll up the belly, using the strings to secure the roll. Try to place the strings at about 3cm intervals as this will make serving easier.

7. Rub the outside of the pork with salt and pepper and pop on a baking sheet in the oven.

8. After 30 minutes turn the oven down to 180 C/Gas 4 and cook for another 40 minutes, or until the juices run clear when poked with a skewer.

9. The crackling is done when it is puffy, crispy and golden brown – don't let it burn! If your crackling is slow to crisp, you can 'cheat' by putting it in a frying pan.

10. Cut the pork roll into portions using the string as a guide. Top with a square of crackling.

Stephen's Boy Scout's Baked Beans

Serves: 8

Ingredients:
2 tins of baked beans
4 fresh tomatoes – chopped
2 onions – roughly chopped
1 tin of chopped tomatoes
A quantity of grated mature cheddar cheese

Method:

First, heat the beans over a medium heat, until they are simmering but not boiling. Then add the tinned tomatoes, fresh tomatoes and onions. Simmer for five minutes. Finally finish with a generous handful of grated cheese and serve on fresh crusty toast immediately.

Will's Shovel Fried Eggs

Serves: 8

Ingredients:
8 free range eggs
1 relatively clean coal shovel
A little oil or butter
A very hot fire (take care with your fingers!)

Method:

Lightly grease the shovel and allow it to get hot in the flames. Remove from the fire and, if you are very dextrous – like Will – use your free hand to crack an egg onto the shovel. If not, get a friend to do it. Being careful to hold the shovel level, hold it over (not in) the fire until the egg is cooked to taste. This method is fast, so you if you like a runny egg don't leave it on too long.

And finally, a local Cumbrian Christmas recipe for you. The ports on the Cumbrian coast were historically very active in the rum and spice trade, which has led to the popularity of these ingredients in traditional Cumbrian cooking.

Cumberland Rum Butter

Cumberland rum butter is traditionally served at Christmas, melted over Christmas pudding. It is also delicious on hot mince pies, baked apples, pancakes, or just spread on toast. Yum!

Soften and cream 170g low salt butter with 170g soft brown sugar. Beat in 6 tablespoons of dark rum. Put in a pot or glass bowl to chill in fridge. Use as required – put a generous knob of the butter on your hot Christmas pudding. It's delicious!

Cumberland Rum Nicky

Ingredients
170g shortcrust pastry
28g preserved ginger
14g caster sugar
54g chopped dates
28g butter
1 tbsp rum

Method:

1. Line a buttered pie dish with half the pastry and cover with the dates and ginger.

2. Beat the butter, sugar and rum and pour over the filling.
3. Cover with the remaining pastry and bake in a moderately hot oven for 10–15 minutes.
4. Then turn down the heat and bake for approximately 30 minutes.
5. Serve with crème fraiche.

You can combine rum, dried fruit and brown sugar with Cumbrian varieties of apple (such as Forty Shilling, Carlisle Codling and Keswick Codling) to make a different, but equally delicious, Rum Nicky.